"THE BOOK OF DISQUIET is one of life's great miracles. Pessoa invented numerous alter egos. Arguably, the four greatest poets in the Portuguese language were all Pe̲̲̲̲̲̲̲̲̲̲̲̲̲̲̲̲mes."

"Extraordinary—a s, autobiographical vi̲̲̲̲̲̲̲̲̲̲̲̲ary theory and cr̲̲̲̲̲̲̲̲̲̲̲̲
—George Steiner, THE OBSERVER

"As searing as Rilke or Mandelstam."
—THE NEW YORK TIMES BOOK REVIEW

"A meandering, melancholic series of reveries and meditations. Pessoa's amazing personality is as beguiling and mysterious as his unique poetic output."
—William Boyd

"To read and then contemplate him is to be lifted a little bit above the earth in a floating bubble. One becomes both of the world and not of it. There's no one like him, apart from all of us."
—Nicholas Lezard, THE GUARDIAN

"THE BOOK OF DISQUIET was left in a trunk which might never have been opened. The gods must be thanked that it was. I love this strange work of fiction and I love the inventive, hard-drinking, modest man who wrote it in obscurity."
—INDEPENDENT

"The saddest book in Portugal."
—Fernando Pessoa

The Book of Disquiet

The Book of Disquiet

Fernando Pessoa

Edited by Jerónimo Pizarro

Translated from the Portuguese by Margaret Jull Costa

 A NEW DIRECTIONS BOOK

First published in this arrangement in Portuguese by Tinta-da-china as *Livro do desassossego* in 2013.

 *Obra publicada com o apoio do Camões—Instituto da Cooperação e da Língua I.P.* (Published with the support of Camões—Instituto da Cooperação e da Língua I.P.)

Manufactured in the United States of America
First published by New Directions clothbound in 2017

Design by Erik Rieselbach

Library of Congress Cataloging-in-Publication Date to come
Names: Pessoa, Fernando, 1888–1935, author. | Pizarro, Jerónimo, editor. | Costa, Margaret Jull, translator.
Title: The book of disquiet : the complete edition / Fernando Pessoa ; edited by Jerónimo Pizarro ; translated from the Portuguese by Margaret Jull Costa.
Other titles: Livro do desassossego. English
Description: First edition. | New York : New Directions Publishing Corporation, 2017. | First published in Portuguese as Livro do desassossego.
Identifiers: LCCN 2017000589 | ISBN 9780811226936 (alk. paper)
Subjects: LCSH: Pessoa, Fernando, 1888–1935. | Poets, Portuguese—20th century—Biography.
Classification: LCC PQ9261.P417 Z46213 2017 | DDC 869.1/41 [B] —dc23
LC record available at https://lccn.loc.gov/2017000589

10 9

New Directions Books are published for James Laughlin
by New Directions Publishing Corporation
80 Eighth Avenue, New York 10011

Contents

Introduction

Fernando Pessoa's life divides neatly into three periods. In a letter to the *British Journal of Astrology* dated 8 February 1918, he wrote that there were only two dates he remembered with absolute precision: 13 July 1893, the date of his father's death from TB when Pessoa was only five; and 30 December 1895, the day his mother remarried, which meant that, shortly afterwards, the family moved to Durban, where his new stepfather had been appointed Portuguese Consul. In that same letter, he mentions a third date too: 20 August 1905, the day he left South Africa and returned to Lisbon for good.

That first brief period was marked by two losses: the deaths of his father and of a younger brother. And perhaps a third loss too, that of his beloved Lisbon. During the second period, despite knowing only Portuguese when he arrived in Durban, Pessoa rapidly became fluent in English and in French.

He was clearly not the average student. When asked years later, a fellow pupil described Pessoa as: "A little fellow with a big head. He was brilliantly clever but quite mad." In 1902, just six years after arriving in Durban, he won first prize for an essay on the British historian Thomas Babington Macaulay. Indeed, he appeared to spend all his spare time reading or writing, and had already begun creating the fictional alter egos, or as he later described them, heteronyms, for which he is now so famous, writing stories and poems under such names as Chevalier de Pas, David Merrick, Charles Robert Anon, Horace James Faber, Alexander Search, and more. In their recent book *Eu sou uma antologia* (*I am an anthology*), Jerónimo Pizarro and Patricio Ferrari list 136 heteronyms, giving biographies and examples of each heteronym's work. In 1928, Pessoa wrote of the heteronyms: "They are beings with a sort-of-life-of-their-own, with feelings I do not have, and opinions I do not accept. While their writings are not mine, they do also happen to be mine."

The third period of Pessoa's life began when, at the age of seventeen, he returned alone to Lisbon and never went back to South Africa. He returned ostensibly to go to university. For various reasons, though—among them, ill health and a student strike—he abandoned his studies in 1907 and became a regular visitor to the National Library, where he resumed his regime of voracious reading—philosophy, sociology, history and, in particular, Portuguese literature. He lived initially with his aunts and, later, from 1909 onwards, in rented rooms. In 1907, his grandmother left him a small inheritance and in 1909 he used that money to buy a printing press for the publishing house, Empreza Íbis, which he set up a few months later. Empreza Íbis closed in 1910, having published not a single book. From 1912 onwards, Pessoa began contributing essays to various journals; from 1915, with the creation of the literary magazine *Orpheu*, which he cofounded with a group of artists and poets including Almada Negreiros and Mário de Sá-Carneiro, he became part of Lisbon's literary avant-garde and was involved in various ephemeral literary movements such as Intersectionism and Sensationism. Alongside his day job as freelance commercial translator between English and French, he also wrote for numerous journals and newspapers, translated Nathaniel Hawthorne's *The Scarlet Letter*, short stories by O. Henry and poems by Edgar Allan Poe, as well as continuing to write voluminously in all genres. Very little of his own poetry or prose was published in his lifetime: just one slender volume of poems in Portuguese, *Mensagem* (*Message*), and four chapbooks of English poetry. When he died in 1935, at the age of forty-seven, he left behind the famous trunks (there are at least two) stuffed with writings—nearly thirty thousand pieces of paper—and only then, thanks to his friends and to the many scholars who have since spent years excavating that archive, did he come to be recognized as the prolific genius he was.

Pessoa lived to write, typing or scribbling on anything that came to hand—scraps of paper, envelopes, leaflets, advertising flyers, the backs of business letters, etc. He also wrote in almost every genre—poetry, prose, drama, philosophy, criticism, political theory—as well as developing a deep interest in occultism, theosophy, and astrology. He drew up horoscopes not only for himself and his friends, but also for many dead writers and historical figures, among them Shakespeare, Oscar Wilde, and Robespierre, as well as for his heteronyms, a term he chose over "pseudonym" because it more accurately described their stylistic and intellectual independence from him, their creator, and from each other—for he gave them all complex biographies and they all had their own distinctive styles and philosophies. They sometimes interacted, even criticizing or translating each other's work. Some of Pessoa's fictitious writers were mere sketches, some wrote in English and French, but his three main poetic heteronyms—Alberto Caeiro,* Ricardo Reis, Álvaro de Campos—wrote only in Portuguese and each produced a very solid body of work.

Yet even this "book" had more than one author and was never completed, never put into any order, remaining always fragmentary. Its first "author" was Vicente Guedes, who wrote semi-symbolist prose pieces for inclusion in something that, as early as 1913, Pessoa was already calling *The Book of Disquiet*. These texts often described particular states of mind or imaginary landscapes or offered advice to would-be dreamers or even unhappily married women (a subject about which the apparently celibate Pessoa knew nothing at all at first hand) or those who, like him, had

---

* Alberto Caeiro is Pessoa's main poetic heteronym, considered by his other two major heteronyms, Álvaro de Campos and Ricardo Reis, and by Pessoa himself, to be their Master.

lost their religious faith. Around 1920, however, the book seemed to lose its way, and Pessoa forgot about Guedes and the *Book of Disquiet*. Then, in 1929, the book took a different direction with a different "author," Bernardo Soares, a humble accounts clerk working in an office in downtown Lisbon and spending his leisure hours writing this "autobiography of someone who never existed." Soares was described by Pessoa as only a "semi-heteronym," because, "although his personality is not mine, it is not different from, but rather a simple mutilation of my personality. It's me minus reason and affectivity."

Pessoa clearly felt that Soares was a more suitable author and even drew up a plan of what to do with all those fragments:

> The organization of the book should be based on as rigorous a selection as possible of the various existing texts, adapting any older ones that are untrue to the psychology of Bernardo Soares ... Apart from that, there needs to be a general revision of style, without it losing the personal tone or the drifting, disconnected logic that characterizes it.

Pessoa never undertook this rigorous process of selection and adaptation. The "book" thus remained forever a work in progress. Indeed, although some fragments were published in magazines during Pessoa's lifetime, it did not appear in book form in Portuguese until 1982, forty-seven years after Pessoa's death. This was thanks to Maria Aliete Galhoz, Teresa Sobral Cunha and Jacinto do Prado Coelho, who deciphered Pessoa's near-illegible writing and put the texts (some dated, most not) into some coherent order. Every subsequent Portuguese edition and every translation has, inevitably, been different, including many of the same texts, but nearly always in a different order. This edition—meticulously put together by the Pessoa scholar Jerónimo Pizarro—proposes that we read *The Book of Disquiet* as it evolved, without mixing up texts from the Guedes phase with texts from the Soares phase. *The Book of Disquiet*, says Pizarro, is two very different books separated by about ten years, and it is only in the second book that Pessoa "discovered" Lisbon. The author of the first book inhabits a vague, almost spectral universe, whereas the second book embraces and celebrates Lisbon: "Oh Lisbon, my home!" [252]

What makes this such a rich and rewarding book? It is, after all, the "notebook" of a writer or writers filled with feelings of angst and alienation; the title *Livro do desassossego* can be translated variously as Book of Unease/Disquiet/Unrest/Turmoil/Anxiety, and yet most readers find these disparate texts a source of comfort, even exhilaration. This is, I think, in large part, because it is somehow consoling to find such moments, such states of mind, described so sympathetically and in the most extraordinary prose. What I love in this apparently cerebral book is the physical detail, like this street scene:

> The trams growl and clang around the edges of the square, like large, yellow, mobile matchboxes, into which a child has stuck a spent match at an angle to act as a mast; as they set off they emit a loud, iron-hard whistle. The pigeons wandering about around the central statue are like dark, ever-shifting crumbs at the mercy of a scattering wind. [240]

Or this meditation on waking up:

> With the coming of the dark light that fills with gray doubts the chinks of the shutters (so very far from being hermetic!), I begin to feel that I will be unable to remain much longer in my refuge, lying on my bed, not asleep but with a sense of the continuing possibility of sleep, of drifting off into dreams, not knowing if truth or reality exist, lying between the cool warmth of clean sheets unaware, apart from the sense of comfort, of the existence of my own body. I feel ebbing away from me the happy lack of consciousness with which I enjoy my consciousness, the lazy, animal way I watch, from between half-closed eyes, like a cat in the sun,

the logical movements of my unchained imagination. I feel slipping away from me the privileges of the penumbra, the slow rivers that flow beneath the trees of my half-glimpsed eyelashes, and the whisper of waterfalls lost among the sound of the slow blood pounding in my ears and the faint persistent rain. I slowly lose myself into life. I don't know if I'm asleep or if I just feel as if I were. [205]

The "second book" is very much a hymn to the Lisbon Pessoa loved and rarely left after his return from South Africa:

I love the Tejo because of the great city on its banks. I enjoy the sky because I see it from a fourth-floor window in a street in the Baixa. Nothing in the countryside or in nature can give me anything to equal the ragged majesty of the calm moonlit city seen from Graça or São Pedro de Alcântara. For me no flowers can match the endlessly varied colors of Lisbon in the sunlight. [358]

It is that sheer pleasure in language and pleasure in thinking and, indeed, pleasure in seeing, that makes *The Book of Disquiet* such a book of comfort, as it seems it was to the author(s):

I often write without even wanting to think, in an externalized daydream, letting the words caress me as if I were a little girl sitting on their lap. They're just meaningless sentences, flowing languidly with the fluidity of water that forgets itself as a stream does in the waves that mingle and fade, constantly reborn, following endlessly one on the other. That's how ideas and images, tremulous with expression, pass through me like a rustling procession of faded silks amongst which a sliver of an idea flickers, mottled and indistinct in the moonlight. [326]

When, in 1990, Pete Ayrton of Serpent's Tail asked me if I would (could?) translate Pessoa's *Livro do desassossego*, it was precisely that pleasure in language and thinking and seeing that made me say Yes.

The Serpent's Tail version followed the selection made by Maria José Lancastre and translated into Italian by Antonio Tabucchi. When, a year or so ago, I was asked if I would translate a more complete version following Jerónimo Pizarro's edition, I jumped at the chance.

Jeronimo Pizarro's edition contains many texts that were omitted from Maria José Lancastre's edition, and faced with those new texts, I was reminded of just how difficult it is for the translator to find meaning in those "meaningless" sentences—which can often be oblique or enigmatic—and, at the same time, reproduce that same languid fluidity in English, that seductive voice. Earlier in text 326, Pessoa writes: "I enjoy using words ... For me, words are tangible bodies, visible sirens, sensualities made flesh." And capturing that tangible sensuality is the third challenge for the translator. Here is the second sentence from text 264:

> As casas desigualam-se num aglomerado retido, e o luar, com manchas de incerteza, estagna de madrepérola os solavancos mortos da confusão.

> The houses, all different, stand together in a tightly packed crowd, and the equally uncertain moonlight puddles with mother-of-pearl this dumb, jostling confusion.

At a first reading, the sentence in Portuguese could be one of those "meaningless" sentences, and yet it is full of meaning. The difficulty for the translator lies (a) in understanding *what* the author means, (b) picturing the image he creates, and (c) transporting that meaning and that image into meaningful, tangible, sensuous English. Keeping close to the original simply won't work. Paradoxically, the translation has to take quite a bold step away from the original if meaning and imagery are to be preserved. The first verb "*desigualam-se*"—literally "become different or differentiated"—works far better, I felt, if turned into an adjective, "different." Needing another verb in that sentence, I chose "stand together" because, in my mind, those houses, seen at night from a distance, are like a packed, silent crowd, reluctantly rubbing shoulders. Their humanity is further emphasized by my use of "dumb" and "jostling" to describe that "*confusão*"; "dumb" is quite a long way from the usual sense of "*morto*," which is, of course, "dead," but which also has the sense of "dull," "lifeless," "weary," "extinguished," "muted." And "jostling" is quite a long way from "*solavancos*," which means "jolts" or "bumps." Then again, the words he uses in Portuguese are not necessarily words one would associate with houses. The addition of "equally" to "uncertain" is there because the word "uncertain" appears in the first paragraph too, and my addition is a way of explaining that repetition. And then there's "*estagna de madre-pérola*"—"stagnates with mother-of-pearl"—which makes no sense at all in English. Again, I had to picture what he was describing, the moonlight dappling—my interpretation of "*manchas*," "stains"—the houses with mother-of-pearl, but I wanted a verb that, like "*estagna*," had watery associations, and "puddles"—which is far from being a common verb in English—seemed to me to provide the necessary wateriness as well as furnishing that dappled effect. I am aware that I could be accused of straying too far from the original, but when faced by a sentence so complex as regards syntax and meaning, I felt I had no alternative but to reinvent the whole thing, while simultaneously—again that paradox—keeping as close as possible to connotation, nuance, rhythm, and, yes, oddity of phrasing or vocabulary. Pessoa's / Guedes's / Soares's prose, like all the best prose, forces the translator to stretch his or her own language to its limits and to mine his or her imaginative unconscious in order to find new ways to express meaning.

The Book of Disquiet has been translated into many languages, and each of those translated editions is different, with often different texts in a different order. In early 2017, Tim Hopkins of the London-based Half Pint Press produced yet another version, consisting of various fragments typeset by hand and printed by hand on a selection of ephemera—for example, a black-and-white photo, a book of raffle tickets, a napkin from a café, a visiting card, a matchbook—and housed unbound in a hand-printed box. It gives one a sense, in miniature, of what it must have been like to discover that trunk of papers after Pessoa's death, and to begin piecing together whole books of poetry and prose. In a way, though, its very incompleteness is enticing, encouraging the reader to make his or her own book out of those fragments. What awaits every reader of *The Book of Disquiet* is the sheer serendipitous pleasure of opening the book at random and reading whichever fragment you happen to alight on. And whenever I come across a photograph of Pessoa and his famously blank, not-wanting-to-be-seen face, I imagine his mind as being like that trunk, stuffed with all those other writers and endless never-completed projects, and, like *The Book of Disquiet*, stuffed with ideas and images and feelings.

MARGARET JULL COSTA

Editor's note

The Book of Disquiet, a portrait of Lisbon and of its portraitist, is now considered to be Fernando Pessoa's prose masterpiece and one of the twentieth century's greatest works of literature. This seems somewhat ironic when we think that Pessoa never completed *The Book of Disquiet*. What he did was accumulate hundreds of fragments in his trunks; he believed that completing it would be a form of cowardice, of impotence or a "March of Defeat" (a title he initially gave to the poem "The Tobacconist's Shop"). But this book, which successive editors have been striving to put together and finish, this happy cowardice, this fecund impotence, this triumphal defeat, is now a must-read book for anyone who wants to "begin" Pessoa. *The Book of Disquiet* started off as a kind of postsymbolist diary influenced by conventional nineteenth-century diaries and confessions, but it ended up as the diary of a fictitious person: first Vicente Guedes, and later Bernardo Soares, who worked in the downtown area of Lisbon. But more than this fictitious alter ego's diary, it was the portrait of an assistant bookkeeper in Lisbon, a portrait that is impossible to separate from the description of the city in which this latter-day Bartleby lives.

In a passage in which the fictitious author is trying to escape romantic influences, we find the following observation:

> Amiel said that a landscape is a state of mind, but the phrase
> is the feebly felicitous one of a feeble dreamer. A landscape

is a landscape and therefore cannot be a state of mind. To objectify is to create and no one says of a finished poem that it is a state of thinking about writing a poem. To see is perhaps to dream but if we use the word "see" rather than the word "dream," it's because we distinguish between seeing and dreaming. [...] It would be more accurate to say that a state of mind is a landscape; that would have the advantage of containing not the lie of a theory but the truth of a metaphor. [386]

As I see it, the landscape of *The Book of Disquiet* is not exactly the city of Lisbon, which so disquiets the protagonist; rather, it is Pessoa's own malaise or tedium that becomes the book's landscape. *The Book of Disquiet* both is and isn't an intimate diary like Amiel's *Journal Intime*. It is the diary of a writer and of someone who writes to while away the hours after dinner, but these modern-day *Confessions*—if we are thinking of St. Augustine and Rousseau—are only intimate or personal in the sense that all great fiction is universally personal. The portraits of Lisbon and of its portraitist, an office worker employed in various firms in downtown Lisbon (just like Pessoa), are the same. Pessoa's disquiet falls on the city like rain.

This edition proposes that *The Book of Disquiet* should be read as it emerged, rather than alternating the texts of the first phase with those from the second. There was a first and a second book—and several years passed between the two—and there is no need to make a thematic montage to unify what required no unification. There is an unnecessary violence about bringing together texts written many years apart, or creating longer texts out of smaller ones or minimizing the importance of Vicente Guedes as coauthor, imposing an authorial unity under the name of Fernando Pessoa, a name that always was and always will be both singular and plural.

In this edition, the texts mostly appear in the order in which they were arranged in my 2010 critical edition, *Livro do desassossego*, published by Imprensa Nacional-Casa da Moeda, and republished, without the same critical apparatus, by Tinta-da-china in

2013. In this last edition, I only changed the placement of certain texts intended as preliminaries and a few others that bore the initial indication "L. do D." followed by a question mark. I also, of course, consulted all the other editions of *The Book of Disquiet* available before June 2012 and made some further adjustments to my reading of some of the originals.

This book is, to use Pessoa's words, a "great symphonic certainty," which Margaret Jull Costa has succeeded in translating into English with—to quote one of Pessoa's aphorisms—"that re-inspiration without which translating is merely paraphrasing in another language." I would like to thank her for her excellent work and Nick Sheerin of Serpent's Tail for his unconditional support of this project.

JERÓNIMO PIZARRO

The Book of Disquiet

First Phase

Preface [1917?]

Installed on the upper floors of certain respectable taverns in Lisbon can be found a small number of restaurants or eating places, which have the stolid, homely look of those restaurants you see in towns that lack even a train station. Among the clientele of such places, which are rarely busy except on Sundays, one is as likely to encounter the eccentric as the nondescript, to find people who are but a series of marginal notes in the book of life.

There was a period in my life when a combination of economic necessity and a desire for peace and quiet led me to frequent just such a restaurant. I would dine at around seven each night and, as chance would have it, I was almost always there at the same time as one particular man. At first, I took little notice of him, but as time passed he came to interest me.

He was a man in his thirties, thin, fairly tall, very hunched when sitting though less so when standing, and dressed with a not entirely unself-conscious negligence. Not even the suffering apparent in his pale, unremarkable features lent them any interest, nor was it easy to pinpoint the origin of that suffering. It could have been any number of things: hardship, grief or simply the suffering born of the indifference that comes from having suffered too much.

He always ate sparingly and, afterwards, he would smoke a cigarette rolled from cheap tobacco. He would watch the other customers, not suspiciously, but as if genuinely interested in them. He did not scrutinize them as though wanting to fix in his memory their faces or any outward evidence of their personalities; rather he was simply intrigued by them. And it was this odd trait of his that first aroused my curiosity.

I began to observe him more closely. I noticed that his features were illuminated by a certain hesitant intelligence, but his face was so often clouded by exhaustion, by the inertia of cold fear, that it was usually hard to see beyond this.

I learned from a waiter at the restaurant that he worked as a clerk in a company that had its office near by.

One day, there was a scuffle in the street immediately outside the restaurant—a fight between two men. The customers all rushed to the windows, as did I and the man I've been describing. I made some banal comment to him, and he replied in kind. His voice was dull and tremulous, the voice of one who hopes for nothing, because all hope is vain. But perhaps it was foolish of me to attribute so much to my evening companion at the restaurant.

I don't quite know why but, after that, we always used to greet each other. And then, one day, prompted perhaps by the foolish coincidence of us both turning up for supper later than usual, at half past nine, we struck up a casual conversation. At one point, he asked whether I was a writer. I said I was. I mentioned the magazine *Orpheu*, which had recently come out.* To my surprise, he praised it, indeed praised it highly. When I voiced my surprise, saying that the art of those who wrote for *Orpheu* tended to appeal only to a small minority, he replied that he was one of that minority. Besides, he added, he was not entirely unfamiliar with that art, for, he remarked timidly, since he had nowhere to go and nothing to do, no friends to visit and no interest in reading books, he usually returned to his rented room after supper and spent the night writing.

So I met Vicente Guedes purely by chance. We often went to the same quiet, cheap restaurant. We knew each other by sight and

---

* The literary magazine *Orpheu* was started in 1915 by Fernando Pessoa, Mário de Sá-Carneiro and Luís de Montalvor. Although only two issues were produced, the magazine had a considerable impact on the evolution of modern Portuguese literature.

would, of course, always nod a silent greeting. Once, though, finding ourselves seated at the same table, what started as a brief exchange became a conversation. We began meeting there every day, at lunch and supper. Sometimes, once we had finished our supper, we would leave the restaurant together and go for a stroll, chatting as we went.

Vicente Guedes endured his empty life with masterly indifference, the foundations of his mental attitude being built on the stoicism of the weak.

He was constitutionally condemned to suffer all kinds of anxieties, but fated to abandon them all. I never met a more extraordinary man. He had abdicated everything to which he was by nature destined, but not out of any kind of asceticism. Though naturally ambitious, he savored the pleasure of having no ambitions at all.

The thin man gave me an awkward smile and eyed me distrustfully, but there was no malice in that look. Then he smiled again, sadly this time, before looking down at his plate and continuing his supper in silent absorption.

He furnished his two rooms—doubtless at the expense of a few basic necessities—with something akin to luxury. He took particular pains over the chairs—deep, soft armchairs—door curtains and carpets. He told me that this was his way of creating an interior that would "maintain the dignity of his tedium." In a modern-style room, tedium becomes a discomfort, a physical pain.

He had never been obliged to do anything. He had spent his childhood alone. He had never belonged to any group. He had never been to university. He had never been part of a crowd. As happens with many people or, possibly, who knows, with everyone, the chance circumstances of his life and the direction it had taken were dictated by his instincts, in his case inertia and detachment.

He had never had to deal with the demands of state or society. He even avoided the demands of his own instincts. He had never acquired friends or lovers. I was the only person who, in some way, became close to him. Along with the knowledge that I knew only that false personality of his—and the suspicion that he never really thought of me as a friend—came an awareness that he needed someone to whom he could bequeath his book. Even though, initially, I found this rather wounding, it now pleases me to think that, when I finally saw everything from the one point of view worthy of a psychologist, I did remain his friend, a friend devoted to the reason he had drawn me to him in the first place, that is, the publication of this his book.

It's odd, but even in this respect, he was fortunate, in that circumstances presented him with someone like me, who could be of service to him.

... this gentle book.

This is all that remains and will remain of one of the most subtly inert, the most dreamily debauched, of beings the world has seen. I doubt there has ever been an outwardly human creature who so completely embodied his image of his own self. A dandy in spirit, he paraded the art of dreaming through the pure happenstance of existence.

This book is the autobiography of someone who never existed.

No one knows who Vicente Guedes was or what he did, nor ...

This book is not *by* him, it *is* him. However, we should always remember that behind everything written here lies a shadow, a mystery ...

For Vicente Guedes, being self-aware was an art and a morality; dreaming was a religion.

He created an inner aristocracy, an attitude of soul that most closely resembles the attitude of body of the consummate aristocrat.

1   [1913?]

My soul is a hidden orchestra; I do not know what instruments, what violins and harps, drums and tambours, sound and clash inside me. I know myself only as a symphony.

All effort is a crime because every gesture is but a dead dream.

Your hands are like caged doves. Your lips are silent turtle doves (which my eyes can see cooing).
      All your gestures are birds. You are a swallow when you stoop down, a condor when you look at me, an eagle in your ecstasies as a proud, indifferent woman. You are merely a fluttering of wings, like those of the [...], you are the lake of my seeing.
      You are all winged, winged [...]

It's raining, raining, raining ...
      It's raining constantly, plaintively ...
      My body sets my soul shivering with cold, not the cold that exists in space, but the cold of me being that space ...

All pleasure is a vice because seeking pleasure is what everyone does in life, and the worst vice of all is to do what everyone else does.

2   [1913?]

I do not dream of possessing you. What would be the point? It would be tantamount to translating my dream for the benefit of a plebeian. To possess a body is to be banal in the extreme. To dream of possessing a body is perhaps, were such a thing possible, even worse; it would mean dreaming oneself banal—the supreme horror.

And since we choose to be sterile, let us also be chaste, because there can be nothing baser and more ignoble than to renounce in Nature all things fertile, and yet vilely keep back anything that takes our fancy among those things renounced. There are no partial nobilities.

Let us be as chaste as dead lips, as pure as dreamed bodies, as resigned to being both these things as mad little nuns ...

Let our love be a prayer ... Anoint me with seeing you, and out of the moments when I dream you I will make a rosary on which all my tediums will be Our Fathers and all my anxieties Hail Marys ...

Thus we will remain forever like the figure of a man in a stained-glass window opposite the figure of a woman in another stained-glass window ... Between us, shadows whose footsteps echo coldly—humanity passing by ... Between us will pass murmured prayers, secrets ... Occasionally, the air will fill with incense. At other times, to left or right, a figure like a statue will sprinkle us with prayers ... And there we will stay, always in the same windows, all color when the sun shines through and all dark lines when night falls ... The centuries will not touch our glassy silence. Outside, civilizations will come and go, revolutions will break out, parties will whirl past, meek, everyday people will rush by ... And we, my unreal love, will be frozen in the same pointless pose, the same false existence, and the same [...], until one day, after centuries of empires, the Church will, at last, crumble and everything will end ...

But we, knowing nothing of this, will still be here, quite how or where or when I don't know, like eternal stained-glass windows, hours of innocent art painted by some artist who has long been sleeping in a Gothic tomb where two angels, hands clasped in prayer, have set the idea of death in cold marble.

3

Glorification of the Barren

If, one day, I were to choose a wife from among the women of this Earth, may your prayer for me be this—let her be barren. But ask too, if you pray for me, that I never win that imagined wife.

Only barrenness and sterility are noble and dignified. Only killing what never was is rare, sublime, absurd.

4

Our Lady of Silence

Sometimes, when, feeling exhausted and humble, even the effort of dreaming unleaves and withers me, and the only dream I'm capable of having is thinking about my dreams, then I leaf through them, like a book that one leafs through once, then leafs through again, finding only the inevitable words. Then I wonder who you are, you, this figure strolling through all my lingering visions of slow landscapes, ancient interiors and lavish ceremonies of silence. In all my dreams you either appear as a dream or else accompany me like a false reality. With you I visit regions that are perhaps dreams of yours, lands that are perhaps embodiments of absence and cruelty, your essential body fashioned into a quiet plain or a mountain with a chilling profile in the garden of some hidden palace. Perhaps my only dream *is* you, perhaps when I press my face to yours I will read in your eyes those impossible landscapes, those false tediums, those feelings that inhabit the gloom of my wearinesses and the grottoes of my disquiets. Who knows, perhaps the landscapes of my dreams are simply my way of not dreaming you? I don't know who you are, but do I know precisely who I am? Do I know what it means to dream in a way that merits calling you my dream? How do I know that you are not a part, possibly a real, essential part, of me? And how do I know that I am not the dream and you the reality, or that I am your dream rather than you being a dream I am dreaming?

What kind of life do you have? What way of seeing is this way I have of seeing you? Your profile? It is never the same and yet never changes. And I say this because I know it, even though I do not know that I know it. Your body? Seeing it naked is the same to me as seeing it clothed, seeing it seated is the same as seeing it lying down or standing. What does this mean, simply that it means nothing?

5 [1913?]

[Our Lady of Silence?]
You belong to the sex of dream shapes, the nonsex of figures [...]

A mere profile sometimes, a mere pose at others, at still others barely a slow gesture—you are moments and poses made spirit in mine.

There is no implied sexual attraction in my dreaming of you, beneath your vague Madonna robe of inner silences. Your breasts are not the sort one would think of kissing. Your body is entirely flesh-and-soul, but never body-and-soul. Your flesh is not spirit, but spiritual. You are the woman from before the Fall, formed out of the first mud of paradise.

My horror of real women, sexual women, I mean, is the path I took to find you. Those earthly women, who in order to be [...] must bear the agitated weight of a man—who can love them? who does not feel love dissolving at the mere thought of sexual pleasure? Who can respect his Wife and not think of her simply as a woman in another sexual position? Who does not feel disgusted to have had a mother, to have been so vulval in his origins, so vilely expelled into the world? Who is not revolted by the idea of our soul's carnal origin, of the corporeal turbulence out of which our flesh is born, and which, however beautiful, is soiled by its origin, its birth?

The false idealists of Real Life gild the Wife with poetry, kneel before the idea of the Mother ... Their way of dreaming is a garment that conceals, not a dream that creates.

Only you are pure, Lady of Dreams, whom I can imagine as an immaculate lover because you don't exist. I can imagine you a mother and adore you because you were never soiled by the horrors of being impregnated or of having given birth. How could I not adore you, when you alone are worthy of adoration? How could I not love you, when you alone are worthy of love?

Perhaps by dreaming you, I am creating a real you, but in another reality; perhaps you will be mine there, in that other purer world, where we will love each other but never touch, with a different kind of embrace and other more essential ways of possessing one another? Perhaps you existed already, and I did not create you, but merely saw you with a different way of seeing, interior and pure, in another, more perfect world? Perhaps my dreaming you was simply finding you, perhaps my loving you was simply seeing you, perhaps my scorn for the flesh and my feelings of revulsion were only the obscure desire with which, before I knew you, I was waiting for you, and the vague hope that, even without knowing you, I loved you?

I really don't know if I loved you already, in a vacuum for which perhaps my perennial tedium is a kind of nostalgia. Perhaps you are another sort of nostalgia, a physical absence, a distant presence, female perhaps for reasons other than your being female.

I can imagine you both a virgin and a mother because you are not of this world. The child you hold in your arms was always a tiny infant and so you never had to soil it by carrying it in your womb. Since you were never other than you are now, how could you be anything but a virgin? I can love you and adore you because my love does not possess you and my adoration does not drive you away.

Be the Eternal Day and let my sunsets be the rays from your sun, possessing itself in you!

Be the Invisible Twilight and let my desires and disquiets take on the colors of your indecision and the shadows of your uncertainty.

Be Total Night, become the Only Night, and let my whole self be lost and forgotten in you, and may my dreams shine like stars in your body full of distance and denial ...

Let me be the folds of your cloak, the jewels in your crown and the starry gold of the rings on your fingers.

I could be ashes in your hearth, what does it matter if I am mere dust? Or a window in your room, what does it matter if I am mere empty space? Or an hour in your hourglass, what does it matter if I pass, if, because I am yours, I will endure; what does it matter if I die if, because I am yours, I will not die, or if I lose you, if losing you means finding you?

Creator of absurdities, disciple of sexless sentences. Let your silence rock me to sleep, let your merely-being caress and soothe and comfort me, O Herald from the Beyond, O Empress of Absence, Virgin Mother of all Silences, Hearth and Home of shivering souls, Guardian Angel of the abandoned, Human landscape—unbelievably sad—eternal Perfection.

6 [1913]

[Our Lady of Silence?]

My life is so sad, and yet I do not even consider weeping over it; my hours are so false, and I do not even dream the gesture that might end them.

How could I not dream you? How could I not?

Our Lady of the Hours that Pass, Madonna of stagnant waters and dead algae, Tutelary Goddess of vast deserts and dark landscapes of barren rocks, free me from my youth.

Consoler of the inconsolable, Tears of those who never cry, Hour that never sounds—free me from joy and happiness.

Opium of all silences, Lyre never to be plucked, Stained-glass Window of distance and abandon—may I be hated by men and scorned by women.

Dulcimer of Extreme Unction, touchless Caress, Dove lying dead in the shadows, Balm of hours spent sleeping—free me from religion because it is gentle and from unbelief because it is strong.

Lyre fading at evening, Coffer of withered roses, Silence between prayer and prayer—fill me with loathing for life, hatred for health, scorn for youth.

Make me useless and sterile, O Reaper of all empty dreams; make me pure for no reason and deceitful with no lover to deceive, O Rushing Stream of Sadnesses Endured; let my mouth be a landscape of ice, my eyes two dead lakes, my gestures a slow unleaving of old trees—O Litany of Disquiets, O Purple-Mass of Weariness, O Corolla, O Fluid, O Ascension!

How it grieves me to have to pray to you as if to a woman and not love you as I would a man, and not to be able to hold you up to the eyes of my dream like the Topsy-Turvy-Dawn of the unreal sex of those angels who never got into heaven!

7   [1913?]

Our Lady of Silence

You are not a woman. You do not even evoke within me something I might experience as feminine. It is only when I speak of you that the words I use name you as female, and my expressions give you female shape. And because I must speak to you as if in a tender, loving dream, the words only find a voice for this by addressing you in the feminine.

But you, in your vague essence, are nothing. You have no reality, not even your own. I do not, properly speaking, see or even feel you. It is like a feeling that is its own object and belongs entirely to its innermost self. You are always the landscape I was just about to glimpse, the hem of a dress I did not quite see, lost in an eternal Now that lies just around the corner. Your profile relies on you not being anything and the shape of your unreal body unstrings and scatters the pearls of the very idea that you even have a shape. You have already passed, you have already been, I have already loved you—that is how I feel your presence.

You occupy the intervals of my thoughts and the interstices of my feelings. That is why I neither think you nor feel you, or, rather, when I feel your presence, my thoughts are ogival and when I evoke you, my feelings are gothic.

Moon of lost memories shining down on the dark landscape, bright in the stillness of my imperfect understanding. My being feels you vaguely, as if it were an invisible belt encircling you. I bend over your white face reflected in the nocturnal waters of my disquiet, but I will never know if you hang in my sky in order to cause that disquiet or are instead a strange submarine moon merely feigning disquiet.

If only I could create a New Way of Looking with which to see you, as well as New Thoughts and New Feelings with which to think and feel you!

When I attempt to touch your mantle, my words drain of all energy the very effort of reaching out, and a stiff, painful weariness turns my words to ice. Like the flight of a bird that seems to be approaching but never arrives, that same weariness hovers above what I would like to say about you, but the matter of my sentences is incapable of imitating the substance or the sound of your footsteps or the trace left behind by your glances, or the sad, empty color of the gestures you never made.

8 [1913?]

Apotheosis of the Absurd

I am speaking seriously and sadly; this matter is not a joyful one, because dream joys are sad and contradictory and, for that reason, pleasurable in a particularly mysterious way.

Sometimes inside me, I cast an impartial eye over those absurd, delicious things that I cannot see because they are apparently illogical—bridges that begin nowhere and go nowhere, streets with no beginning and no end, upside-down landscapes—the absurd, the illogical, the contradictory, everything that detaches and distances us from the real and from its misshapen retinue of practical thoughts and human feelings and desires for useful, effective action. The absurd saves us, despite the tedium, from that state of soul that begins with the sweet fury of dreaming.

And somehow I find a strange, mysterious way of envisioning those absurdities—I don't know how else to explain it, but I see things of which visibility cannot even conceive.

9 [1913?]

Apotheosis of the Absurd
Let us absurdify life from east to west.

10 [1913?]

Out of my abstention from collaborating in the existence of the outside world comes, among other things, a curious psychic phenomenon.

By abstaining internally from action, taking no interest in Things, I can see the outside world, when I look at it, with perfect objectivity. Since there is no point, no reason to change it, I do not.

[And thus I ...]

11 [1913?]

My dreams: since I create friends in my dreams, I walk with them. Their alien imperfection ...

Be pure, not in order to be noble or strong, but to be yourself. To give love is to lose love.

Abdicate from life in order not to abdicate from yourself.

Woman is a good source of dreams. Never touch her.

Learn to separate out ideas of voluptuousness and pleasure. Learn to enjoy everything, not for what those things are, but for the ideas and dreams they provoke. Because nothing is what it is, and yet dreams are always dreams. That is why you must not touch anything. If you do, your dream will die, and the touched object will take over your feelings.

Seeing and hearing are the only noble things that life contains.

The other senses are plebeian and carnal. The only aristocracy lies in not touching. Do not get too close—that is true nobility.

12 [1913?]

It is noble to be timid, illustrious not to know what to do, great to have no talent for living.

Only Tedium, which is a form of aloofness, and Art, which is a form of scorn, gild our [life] with a semblance of contentment.

The will-o'-the-wisps given off by our own putrefying selves do at least provide light in our darkness.

Only unhappiness raises us up—and the tedium we draw from that unhappiness is as heraldic as being the descendant of distant heroes.

I am a well of gestures never made, of words never thought or spoken, of dreams I forgot to dream until the end.

I am the ruins of buildings that were never more than ruins that someone, in the midst of building them, grew tired of even wanting to build.

Let us not forget to hate those who take pleasure in things because they take pleasure in them, to despise those who are happy because we ourselves do not know how to be happy. That false scorn, that feeble hatred, are merely the rough, grubby pedestal on which we raise up, haughty and unique, the statue to our Tedium, a dark shape on whose face glows an impenetrable, darkly secret smile.

Blessed are those who do not entrust their lives to anyone.

13 [1913?]

Interval

This dreadful hour that either shrinks into possibility or grows into mortality.

May the dawn never break, and may I and this whole room and the atmosphere to which I belong be distilled into Night, into absolute Darkness, and let nothing remain of me, not even a shadow that defiles with my memory whatever is left behind.

14

Anything that involves action, be it war or reasoning, is false; and anything that involves abdication is false too. If only I knew how not to act and how not to abdicate from action either! That would be the dream crown of my glory, the silent scepter of my greatness.

I do not even suffer. My scorn for everything is so great that I despise myself; for since I despise other people's suffering, I also despise my own, and thus I crush my own suffering beneath the weight of my disdain. Ah, but then I only suffer more, because giving value to one's own suffering gilds it with the golden sun of pride. Great suffering can give us the illusion of being Pain's Chosen One.

15 [1913?]

Money is beautiful, because it is a liberation ...

Wanting to go and die in Peking and not being able to is something that weighs on me like the idea of some imminent cataclysm.

The buyers of useless things are always wiser than they think: they are buying small dreams. They are children when it comes to buying. They are drawn to small, useless objects, which beckon to them when they realize there is money to be spent, and the buyers take possession of them as gleefully as a child picking up shells from the beach! For a child, no two shells are ever alike. He falls asleep with the two prettiest ones clasped in his hand, and when they are lost or thrown away—a near-crime, as if bits of his soul had been stolen or fragments torn from his dreams!—he weeps like a God who has been robbed of his newly created universe.

16 [1913?]

Painful Interlude

Everything wearies me, even those things that don't. My joy is as painful as my grief.

I wish I could be a child sailing paper boats on a pond in the garden, with the sky above crisscrossed by the vine trellis, casting checkerboards of light and green shade on the somber reflections in the shallow water.

A tenuous pane of glass stands between me and life. However clearly I see and understand life, I cannot touch it.

Should we reason our way out of sadness? But why, when reasoning requires effort? And the sad man lacks the necessary energy to make any effort at all.

I do not even abdicate from the banal gestures of life from which I so wish I could abdicate. Abdication takes effort, and I do not have enough soul to make that effort.

How often it pains me not to be the captain of that ship, the driver of that train! To be some other banal individual whose life, because not mine, fills me with delicious longing and a poetic sense of otherness!

I would not then be horrified of life as a Thing. The notion of life as a Whole would not weigh down the shoulders of my thoughts.

My dreams are a foolish refuge, about as reliable as an umbrella in a thunderstorm.

I am so inert, such a poor wretch, so entirely lacking in gestures and actions.

However deep I plunge into myself, all the paths of my dreams lead into clearings of anxiety.

Even though I am a prolific dreamer, there are times when dreams escape me. Then things appear clearer. The mist I surround myself with dissipates. And all the now visibly rough edges wound the flesh of my soul. All the hard surfaces bruise the part of me that knows them to be hard. All the visibly heavy objects weigh on my soul.

It's as if someone were using my life to beat me with.

17 [1913?]

Peristyle

During those hours when the landscape forms a halo around Life, and dream is simply a matter of dreaming oneself, I created, O my love, in the silence of my disquiet, this strange book like a series of arches opening up at the end of some abandoned avenue.

In order to write this, I plucked the souls from all the flowers, and out of the ephemeral moments of all the songs of all the birds I wove eternity and stagnation. Sitting at the window of my life and forgetting that I was alive, that I existed, I began to weave shrouds in which to shroud my tedium, chaste linen cloths for the altars of my silence.

And I am offering you this book because I know it to be both beautiful and useless. It teaches nothing, preaches nothing, arouses no emotion. It is a stream that runs into an abyss of ashes that the wind scatters and which neither fertilize nor harm—I put my whole soul into its making, but I wasn't thinking of that at the time, only of my own sad self and of you, who are no one.

And because this book is absurd, I love it; because it is useless I want to give it to you, and because there is no point in wanting to give it to you, I give it anyway ...

Pray for me when you read it, bless me by loving it and forget it as I forget those women, mere dreams I never knew how to dream.

Silent Tower of my desires, may this book be the transforming moonlight in the night of the Ancient Mystery!

River of Painful Imperfection, may this book be the boat set adrift on your waters and washed down to an undreamed-of sea.

Landscape of Alienation and Abandonment, may this book be as much yours as your Hour, and transcend you as it does the fateful purple Hour.

An eternal river flows beneath the window of my silence. I can always see the other shore, and I don't know why I do not dream of being there, different and happy. Perhaps because only you console, only you sing me to sleep and only you anoint and officiate.

What White Mass do you interrupt in order to send me the blessing of showing me that you exist? At which point in this meandering dance do you stop, and with you Time, in order to make of your stopping a bridge to my soul and of your smile the purple of my robe?

Swan of rhythmic disquiet, lyre of immortal hours, hesitant harp of mythical griefs—you are the Expected One and the Lost One, who both caresses and wounds, and who gilds our joy with pain and crowns with roses our sadness.

What God created you, what God hated by the God who made the world?

You do not know or even know you do not know, you do not want to know or not know. You stripped your life of purpose, haloed your appearance with unreality, clothed yourself in perfection and intangibility, so that not even the Hours could kiss you, or the Days smile at you, or the Nights see you hold the moon in your hands so that it resembled a lily.

My love, scatter me with the petals from your finest roses, your most perfect lilies, chrysanthemum petals that smell of the melody of your name.

And I will let my life die in you, O Virgin who expects no embrace, seeks no kiss, no intention.

II

I will make myself a poet out of the act of dreaming you, and my prose, when it describes your Beauty, will contain the rhythms of poetry, the curves of strophes, the sudden splendors to be found in immortal verses.

Book of Disquiet—End

I

You do not exist, I know that, but can I be sure that I exist? Does the I who allows you to exist in me necessarily have more real life than you, than the dead life that lives you?

Halo-thin flame, absent presence, rhythmic, female silence, twilight of vague flesh, glass left over at the banquet, stained-glass window painted by a painter-*cum*-dream in the middle ages of another Earth.

Chaste chalice and host, the abandoned altar of some still-living saint, the dreamed corolla of a lily in a garden no one ever entered...

You are the only form that does not radiate tedium, because you change with our feelings, because, in kissing our joy, you cradle our grief and our tedium, you are the opium that comforts and the sleep that brings rest, and the death that gently folds our hands on our breast.

Angel, what substance are your wings made of? What life keeps you earthbound, you who have never taken flight, never risen into the skies, you who are all distracted delight and rest?

[(last section)]

II

Let us create, O Only-Mine, you because you exist and me because I see that you exist, an art quite different from any other art.

May I find a way of drawing from your futile amphora body the forgotten glow of new verses and in your slow wavelike rhythms— a wave that has no beginning—may my tremulous fingers find a way of seeking out the perfidious lines of a virgin prose never before heard.

May your vague, vanishing smile be, for me, the visible symbol and emblem of the fate of the numberless world on finding itself a mere mistake, an uncertainty.

May your harpist's hands close my eyes when I die of having built my life for you. And you, who are no one, will be eternally, O Supreme One, the beloved art of the gods who never existed, and the barren, virgin mother of the gods who never will exist.

19 [1913?]

From the terrace of this café I look tremulously out at life. I can't see much of it, just the bustle of people concentrated in this small bright square of mine. A weakness like the beginnings of drunkenness illuminates for me the souls of things. In the footsteps of passersby and in the measured fury of movement, life, obvious and unanimous, flows past me. In this moment when my feelings all stagnate and everything seems other than it is—my feelings a confused yet lucid mistake—like an imaginary condor, I spread my wings but do not fly.

As a man of ideals, perhaps my greatest aspiration really does not go beyond occupying this chair at this table in this café.

Everything is as vain as stirring up cold ashes, as vague as the moment just before dawn.

And the light falls so serenely and perfectly on things, gilds them with such a sad, smiling reality. The whole mystery of the world appears before my eyes carved out of this banality, this street.

Ah, how mysteriously the everyday things of life brush by us! On the surface, touched by light, of this complex human life, Time, like a hesitant smile, blooms on the lips of the Mystery! How modern all this sounds, yet deep down it is so ancient, so hidden, so different from the meaning that shines out from all of this!

20 [1913?]

Let us not touch life even with our fingertips.

Let us not love even in our thoughts. Let us not experience a woman's kiss, even in dreams, as a real sensation.

Artificers of languor, let us concentrate on teaching disillusion. Those of us who are curious about life, let us peer out of every door and window, in the weary foreknowledge that we will see nothing new or beautiful.

Weavers of despair, let us weave only shrouds—white shrouds for the dreams we never dreamed, black shrouds for the days when we die, gray shrouds for the gestures we only dreamed of, imperial purple shrouds for our futile feelings.

In the hills, valleys and on the shores of lakes, hunters hunt for wolves and deer and wild duck. Let us hate them not because they kill, but because they enjoy themselves (and we do not).

Let the expression on our face be a wan smile, like that of someone about to burst into tears, a distracted gaze, like that of someone who does not wish to see, a faint look of disdain in every feature, like that of someone who despises life and only lives in order to have something to despise.

And let us despise those who work and struggle and let us hate those who trustingly wait.

(END)

21   [1913?]

Painful Interlude

I find no consolation even in pride. What reason have I to be proud if I am not the creator of myself? And even if there were something in me I could feel vain about, how many more things are there not to?

I lie recumbent in my life. And I do not even know how to dream the gesture of getting up, so empty of soul am I that I do not even know how to make the effort.

The makers of metaphysical systems, of psychological explanations, are still new to suffering. Systematizing, explaining ... building? And all this—arranging, ordering, organizing—is nothing but energy expended and all too desolatingly like life!

I am no pessimist. Happy are those who can make of their suffering something universal. I don't know if the world is sad or bad, nor do I care, because I feel bored and indifferent in the face of other people's suffering. As long as they don't cry or moan—which I find irritating and embarrassing—I greet their suffering with a shrug of the shoulders, so deep is my disdain for them.

I like to believe that life is half-light, half-shade. No, I am not a pessimist. I don't complain about the horrors of life. I complain only about the horrors of my life. The only important fact for me is the fact that I exist and that I suffer and cannot entirely dream myself out of feeling that suffering.

Pessimists are happy dreamers. They make the world in their own image and so always manage to feel at home. What hurts me most is the difference between the bustle and joy of the world and my own sadness, my own bored silence.

Life, despite all its griefs and fears and jolts, should be good and happy, like a journey in a rickety old carriage in the company of others (and with a window to look out of).

I cannot even experience my suffering as a sign of greatness. I don't think it is. But I suffer over such base things, I'm wounded by such banalities, and I dare not insult with that hypothesis the hypothesis that I might be a genius.

The glory of a beautiful sunset never fills me with joy. I always think: how contented someone who is happy must feel to see this!

This book is one long cry of pain. Once I have written it, António Nobre's *Só* will no longer be the saddest book in Portugal.*

Beside my pain, all other pains seem false or insignificant. They are the pains of happy people or of people who are alive enough to complain. Mine is the pain of someone imprisoned in life, cut off…

Between me and life, I see only things that cause anxiety and feel

---

* António Nobre (1867–1900) was a Portuguese poet who published only one volume of poetry in his lifetime, *Só* (*Alone*), which he himself described as the saddest book in Portugal.

none of those things that bring joy. I've noticed that unhappiness is something you see rather than feel, and joy is something you feel rather than see, because by not thinking and not seeing, you do acquire a certain contentment, like that of mystics and bohemians and utter scoundrels. All unhappiness enters through the window of observation and the door of thought.

22 [1913?]

Otherwise, I don't dream, I don't live. I dream real life. All ships are dream ships as long as we are capable of dreaming them. What kills the dreamer is not living while he dreams; what wounds the man of action is not dreaming while he lives. I blended into one happy color the beauty of the world and the reality of life. You can possess a dream, but you can never possess it in the way you possess the handkerchief in your pocket, or, if you like, your own flesh. Even if you live your life engaged in full, frenetic, rumbustious activity, you cannot avoid coming into contact with others or stumbling over obstacles, however small, or feeling time passing.

To kill our dream is to kill ourselves. It is like mutilating our soul. The dream is what is most truly, impenetrably, ineradicably ours.

The Universe, Life—whether real or illusory—belongs to everyone, everyone can see what I see and possess what I possess or can, at least, imagine seeing or possessing it ...

But only I can see what I dream, only I can possess it. And if my way of seeing the external world is different from the way others see it, that is because I cannot help but see it through whatever my dream has filled my eyes and ears with.

23 [1913?]

Lake of Possession

For me, possession is an absurd lake—very large, very dark and rather shallow. It only seems deep because it's full of filth and lies.

Death? But death is part and parcel of life. Do I die completely? I can't tell. Do I survive myself? I continue to live.

Dreaming? But dreaming is part and parcel of life. Do we live the dream? We live. Do we only dream it? We die. And death is part and parcel of life.

Life pursues me like a shadow. And a shadow only ceases to exist when there is no shade. Life only ceases to pursue us when we surrender to it.

The most painful aspect of dreaming is not existing. We cannot really dream.

What does possession mean? We do not know. How then can we want to possess anything? You will say that we don't know what life is, and yet we live. But do we really live? Is living without knowing what life is really living?

24 [1913?]

Futile landscapes like the ones that adorn porcelain cups, beginning at one side of the handle only to come to an abrupt halt at the other side. The cups are always so small. Where would it end up, that landscape that went no farther than the handle of the cup?

It's possible that certain souls feel profoundly sad because the landscape painted on a Chinese fan lacks three dimensions.

25 [1913?]

Interval

I failed life even before I had lived it, because even as I dreamed it, I failed to see its appeal. All I felt was the weariness of dreams, and then I was filled with a final, false sensation, as if I had reached the end of an infinite road. I overflowed the bounds of myself although quite where I don't know, and there I lay stagnant and useless. I am some thing that I once was. I cannot find myself when I feel and if I go looking for myself, I don't know who it is looking for me. A sense of utter tedium saps my energy. I feel like an exile from my own soul.

I watch myself. I am a witness to myself. My feelings parade past some unrecognizable gaze of mine like things external. Everything about me bores me. Everything, right down to its mysterious roots, has taken on the color of my tedium.

The flowers the Hours gave me were already past their best. All I can do now is slowly pick off the petals, a process grown more complex with the years.

I find the slightest action impossible, as if it were some heroic deed. The mere thought of making the smallest gesture weighs on me as if it were something I was actually considering doing.

I aspire to nothing. Life wounds me. I feel uncomfortable where I am and uncomfortable where I think I could be.

The ideal would be to undertake no more action than the false action of a fountain—rising only to fall in the same place, glittering pointlessly in the sunlight and making a noise in the silence of the night that would set any dreamer dreaming of rivers, an absent smile on his lips.

26 [1913?]

The journey never made

It was one vague autumn evening, as darkness was coming on, that I set off on the journey I never made.

The sky—which I, impossibly, can recall—was nothing but a remnant of purple and dull gold, and above the lucid, dying line of the mountains hung a kind of halo, whose deathly tones gently penetrated those elusive contours. On the other side of the ship (where, beneath the awning, it was colder and darker), the ocean lay trembling as far as the sad eastern horizon, where a breath of darkness hovered like a heat haze, casting night shadows on the dark, liquid line on the farthest edge of the sea.

The sea, I remember, had shadowy overtones mingled with faint, flickering lights—and it was all as mysterious as a sad thought in a moment of joy, prophesying what I do not know.

I did not leave from any known port. Even today I could not say which port it was because I have never yet been there. Besides, the ritual purpose of my journey was to go in search of nonexistent ports—ports that were merely entry points; forgotten estuaries, straits between irreprehensibly unreal cities. On reading this, you will doubtless judge my words to be absurd, but then you have never traveled as I have.

Did I set off? I could not swear to you that I did. I found myself elsewhere, I saw other ports, passed through cities other than that one, although neither one nor the other were cities at all. Nor can I swear that it was I who set off rather than the landscape, that I visited other lands rather than them visiting me. Not knowing what life is, I do not even know whether I am the one living it or if my life is living me (if we allow that empty word "live" to mean whatever it wants to), and I should not really swear to anything at all.

I traveled. It seems pointless to explain that I did not travel for months or days or for any quantity or any other measure of time. I did travel in time, that much is true, but not on this side of time, where we count in hours and days and months; I traveled on the other side of time, where time is not counted or measured. It passes, but one cannot measure it. It passes both more quickly than our time and not as quickly, nor as quickly as if counted in years. You may well ask me what these words mean, but there you are wrong. Do not make the infantile mistake of asking the meaning of things and words. Nothing has any meaning.

In what ship did I make this journey? In the steamship *Anyship*. You laugh. So do I, possibly at you. Who is to say that I am not writing symbols for the gods to understand?

Not that it matters. I left at twilight. I still have in my ears the rusty sound of the anchor being weighed. Out of the corner of my memory I can still see slowly moving, before finally returning to their usual inertia, the arms of the ship's hoist, which, hours before, had bruised my vision with endless trunks and barrels. Bound by a chain, these burst suddenly over the side of the ship, where they paused, scraping the rail, then, swaying, allowed themselves to be pushed and pushed until they were just above the hold, into which, suddenly, they descended and, with a dull, wooden thud, crashed down into some hidden part of the hold. Then from below came the noise of them being unchained, and, immediately afterwards, the chain came clanking up into the air, and everything began again, *as if in vain*.

But why am I telling you this? Because it's absurd to be telling you, given that I said I would speak to you of my journeys.

I visited New Europes, and other Constantinoples welcomed my arrival by sailing ship in false Bosphoruses. A sailing ship, you ask? Yes, it's true. The steamship on which I left arrived in the better port of [...] as a sailing ship. But that's impossible, you say. And that's why it happened.

News reached us, on other steamships, of wars dreamed in impossible Indias. And when we heard talk of those lands we suddenly felt nostalgic for our own, merely, of course, because our land was no land at all.

27 [1913?]

To organize our life so that it is a mystery to others, so that those who know us best only unknow us from closer to. That is how I shaped my life, almost unintentionally, but I put so much instinctive art into it that I became, even for myself, a not entirely clear-cut individual.

28 [1913?]

An Aesthetics of Indifference

What the dreamer should try to feel for any object is the utter indifference that it, as object, provokes in him.

To know, immediately and instinctively, how to abstract from every object and event only what makes for suitable dream material and to leave for dead in the External World any reality it contains, that is what the wise man should aim to achieve in himself.

Never to feel one's feelings wholeheartedly and then to elevate that wan victory to the point of being able to regard one's own ambitions, longings and desires with indifference; to pass by one's joys and griefs as one would a person in whom one feels no interest.

The greatest self-discipline one can achieve is indifference towards oneself, believing one's self, body and soul, to be merely the house and garden in which Destiny has ordained one should spend one's life.

One should treat one's own dreams and intimate desires with the haughty indifference of a great lord, showing the highest degree of delicacy in not even noticing them. One should have a sense of modesty regarding oneself and understand that in the presence of ourselves we are never alone, we are witness to ourselves, and it is therefore important to act always as we would before a stranger, adopting a studied and serene exterior, indifferent because aristocratic and cold because indifferent.

In order not to demean ourselves in our own eyes, it is enough that we should become accustomed to harboring no ambitions, passions, desires, hopes, impulses or feelings of disquiet. To achieve this, we must remember that we are always in the presence of ourselves, that we are never alone, can never be at ease. Thus will we master all passions or ambitions because passions and ambitions render us defenceless; equally we must nurture neither desires nor hopes because they are merely brusque, inelegant gestures; nor must we be prone to sudden impulses or to disquiet because, in the eyes of others, precipitate behaviour is rude and impatience is always vulgar.

An aristocrat is someone who is always conscious of the fact that he is never alone; that's why custom and protocol come naturally to the aristocracy. We must internalize the aristocrat. We must drag him away from his drawing rooms and gardens to enter instead our thoughts and our consciousness of our existence. Let us always treat ourselves with due custom and protocol and with careful gestures deployed for the benefit of others.

Each one of us is a whole society, an entire God's people; it is as well then at least to bring a certain elegance and distinction to life in our part of town, to make sure that the celebrations held by our senses show good taste and reserve, and sober pomp and courtesy in the banquets of our thoughts. Let other souls build their poor, shabby dwellings around us, but let us clearly mark where ours begin and end, and make sure that from the façades of our houses to the inner sanctums of our timidities, everything is noble and serene, elegantly and discreetly sculpted.

We must find for every feeling the most serene mode of expression; reduce love to a mere shadow of a dream of love, a pale, tremulous interval between the crests of two small waves gleaming in the moonlight; make of desire something vain and inoffensive, the delicate, private smile of a soul to itself; make of it something that never even considers announcing its presence, let alone realizing itself. We must lull hatred to sleep like a captive snake and order fear to preserve the agony only in its eyes and in the eyes of our soul, the only fitting attitude for an aesthete.

29   [1913?]

An Aesthetics of Artifice

Life gets in the way of being able to express life. If I were to experience a great love, I would never be able to describe it.

I myself don't know if the "I" I am setting before you in these serpentine pages really exists or is merely a false, self-created aesthetic concept of who I am. Yes, I live aesthetically in another being. I have sculpted my life like a statue made of a material alien to myself. Sometimes, I don't even recognize me, so external to myself have I become, and so entirely artistically have I deployed my consciousness of myself. Who am I behind this unreality? I don't know. I must be someone. And if I do not seek to live, to act or to feel, it is—believe me—so as not to disturb the already laid-down lines of my false persona. I want to be exactly what I want to be and am not. If I were to live I would destroy myself. I wanted to be a work of art, at least as regards my soul, since physically that's impossible. That is why I sculpted myself calmly and indifferently and placed myself in a hothouse, far from draughts and direct light—where the exotic flower of my artificiality can bloom in secluded beauty.

I sometimes think how lovely it would be if I could unify my dreams and create a continuous life, with one day succeeding another, with imaginary banquets attended by imaginary guests and to live and suffer and enjoy that false life. Misfortunes would befall me there; I would experience great joys. And none of it would be real. But it would have a superb logic all its own; it would follow a rhythm of voluptuous falseness and take place in a city made of my soul, stretching as far as the quay beside a calm bay, far away inside myself, far, far away ... And it would all be very clear and inevitable, as in the less aesthetic external life lived far from the Sun.

30   [after 10 May 1913]

Put your hands together, place them between mine and listen to me, my love.

In the soft, consoling voice of a confessor offering advice, I want to tell you how the desire to achieve something far outstrips what we actually achieve.

I want to recite to you the litany of despair while you listen intently.

There is no work of art that could not have been more perfect. Read line by line, no poem, however great, has no single line that could not be improved upon, no episode that could not be more intense, and the whole is never so perfect that it could not be even more perfect.

Woe betide the artist who notices this, who one day thinks this. His work can never again be a joy, he will never again sleep peacefully. He'll become a young man bereft of youth and grow old discontentedly.

And why bother to express oneself? What little one has to say would be best left unsaid.

If I could only convince myself of the beauty of renunciation, how painfully, eternally happy I would be!

Because you do not love what I say with the ears with which I hear myself saying it. If I hear myself speaking out loud, the ears with which I hear myself speaking out loud do not listen to me in the same way as the inner ear with which I dare to think those words. And if, when listening to myself, I frequently have to ask myself what I mean, how little others will understand me!

Other people's understanding of us is made up of so many complex misunderstandings.

Anyone who wants to be understood will never know the delight of being understood, because this happens only to the complex and misunderstood; simple souls, the ones whom other people can understand, never feel a desire to be understood.

31   [after 10 May 1913]

[Litany of Despair?]

Have you ever thought, O Other, how invisible we are to each other? Have you already pondered how little we know each other? We see each other and do not see each other. We hear each other, and we each hear only a voice inside us.

The words of others are errors in our hearing, shipwrecks in our understanding. How confidently we believe in our interpretation of other people's words. The sensual pleasures that others put into words taste to us of death. We read sensuality and life into the words others say with no intention of saying anything profound ...

The voice of streams that you interpret, O pure explainer, the voice of trees on whose murmurings we impose meaning—ah, my unknown love, how much of this is simply us and mere ashen fantasies that slip through the bars of our cell!

[Epiphany of the Absurd (or of Lies)?]

Given that possibly not everything is false, that nothing, my love, cures us of the almost pleasurable spasm of lying.

Such refinement! Utter perversion! The absurd lie has all the charm of the perverse with the added and still greater charm of being innocent. The perversion of innocent intent, who could improve on such refinement? The perversion that does not even aspire to giving us pleasure, that lacks the furious desire to cause us pain, that falls to the floor half-pain, half-pleasure, as useless and absurd as a crudely made toy with which an adult sought to amuse himself!

Do you not know, O Delicious One, the pleasure of buying unnecessary things? Do you know the savor of roads which, if taken while one's thoughts were elsewhere, would be taken in error? What human actions are as beautiful in color as spurious ones, which give the lie to their true nature and lie about their true intention?

The sublime pleasure of wasting a life that could have been useful, of never carrying out a work that was sure to be beautiful, of abandoning halfway the certain road to victory!

Ah, my love, the glory of works lost and never to be found, of treatises of which only the titles survive, of libraries that went up in flames, of broken statues.

Blessed with absurdity are the artists who burned a very beautiful work, or those who, although they could have made something beautiful, deliberately made it imperfect, or those great poets of Silence who, realizing that they could create something utterly perfect, chose never to dare. (Although if it had been imperfect, that would have been another matter.)

How much more beautiful La Gioconda would be if we could not see her! And if someone stole her and burned her, what a great artist he would be, far greater than the man who painted her!

Why is art beautiful? Because it is useless. Why is life ugly? Because it is all aims and purposes and intentions. All its roads are intended to go from A to B. If only we could be given a road built between a place that no one ever leaves and another that no one ever goes to! If only someone were to dedicate their life to building a road beginning in the middle of a field and ending in the middle of another, and which, if extended, would be useful, but which remained sublimely, simply, the middle of a road.

The beauty of ruins? The fact that they were no longer of any use.

The sweetness of the past? Being able to remember it, because to remember the past is to make it the present again, and the past is not and cannot be the present—the absurd, my love, the absurd.

So why am I writing this book? Because I recognize that it is imperfect. Were I to dream it, it would be perfection; the mere fact of writing makes it imperfect, which is why I am writing it.

And, above all, because I defend uselessness and the absurd—I am writing this book in order to give the lie to myself, to betray my own theory.

And the glory of all this, my love, is the thought that perhaps this isn't true and that perhaps even I don't believe it to be true.

And when the lie begins to give us pleasure, let us speak the truth in order to lie to the lie. And when it causes us anxiety, let us stop, so that suffering neither dignifies us nor brings us some kind of perverse pleasure …

33 [1913?]

Pedro's Eclogue

I don't know where I saw you or when. I don't know if it was in a painting or in an actual field, among trees and plants contemporary with your body; it was perhaps in a painting, so idyllic and legible is the memory I have of you. I don't even know when it happened or if it really did—because it could be that I didn't even see you in a painting—but I know with every feeling in my intelligence that it was the most serene moment of my life.

You, the little oxherd, and a huge, gentle ox were both walking calmly along the broad stripe of the road. I saw you from afar, or so it seems to me, and you came towards me and walked straight past me. You seemed not to notice me there. You were the slow, distracted keeper of that large ox. Your gaze had forgotten to remember, and there was a great clearing in your soul; you had abandoned all consciousness of yourself. At that moment, you were nothing more than a ...

Seeing you, I remembered that cities change, but that fields are eternal. We call the stones and the hills biblical, because they are always the same, just as the stones and hills in biblical times must have been.

It is in that brief glimpse of your anonymous figure that I place all the evocative power of the fields, and when I think of you, all the calm I've never felt fills my soul. Your gait had a slight sway to it, a hesitant roll, your every gesture was like a bird alighting; invisible creepers wound around your body. Your silence—the sun was going down and a weariness of sheep came bleating, bells clacking, down the pale slopes of the hour—your silence was the song of the very last herder who, having been left out of an eclogue that Virgil forgot to write, remained eternally unsung, eternally silhouetted against the fields. It's possible that you were smiling; to yourself, to your soul, picturing yourself in your own mind and smiling. But your lips were as calm as the shape of the hills; and the gesture of your rustic hands, which I forget, was garlanded with flowers of the field.

Yes, I must have seen you in a painting, but where did I get the idea that I saw you walking towards me, then passing by, while I walked on, not turning round so as to be able to see you now and always? Time stops to allow you to pass, and I misplace you by trying to place you in life—or in a semblance of life.

34   [1913?]

I don't get indignant, because indignation is for the strong; I don't resign myself, because resignation is for the noble; I don't keep silent, because silence is for the great. And I am neither strong nor noble nor great. I suffer and I dream. I complain because I am weak and, because I am an artist, I amuse myself by weaving music around my complaints and arranging my dreams as best befits my idea of beautiful dreams.

My only regret is that I am not a child, for that would allow me to believe in my dreams and believe that I am not mad, which would allow me to distance my soul from all those who surround me ...

Taking dreams for reality, living too much in dreams, has left me with the thorn of this false rose, my dreamed life: for not even my dreams please me, because I find fault with them.

Not even by painting this pane of glass with colored dreams can I conceal from myself the murmur of other lives beyond.

Happy the makers of pessimistic systems! Not only do they take comfort in having made something, they take pleasure in things explicable and feel part of universal suffering.

I do not complain about the world. I do not protest in the name of the universe. I am not a pessimist. I suffer and I complain, but I don't know if suffering is the general rule or if it is human to suffer. Why should I care if this is true or not?

I suffer, possibly deservedly. (A doe pursued.)

I am not a pessimist, I am merely sad.

35   [1913?]

Let us live on dreams and for dreams, undoing the Universe and remaking it, distractedly, as best suits our moment to dream. Let us do this conscious of its utter futility. Let us ignore life with all our body, disconnect from reality with all our senses, abdicate from love with all our soul. Let us fill with useless sand the pitchers we take to the well, then empty them out, only to refill them and empty them out again; the more futile the better.

Let us weave garlands and, once they're finished, carefully, meticulously unpick them.

Let us choose paints and mix them on the palette with no canvas before us to paint. Let us send for stone to chisel when we have no chisel and we are not sculptors. Let us render everything absurd and adorn our sterile hours with more futilities. Let us play hide-and-seek with our consciousness of being alive.

Let us, with an amused, incredulous smile on our lips, listen to God telling us that we exist. Let us watch Time painting the world and finding the resulting picture not only false but hollow.

Let us think in contradictions and speak in sounds that are not sounds and colors that are not colors. Let us say—and understand, which is, of course, impossible—that we are conscious of having no consciousness, that we are not what we are. Let us explain all this in an obscure, paradoxical way, saying that things have a divine, othersidedness to them, and let us not believe too much in that explanation so that we do not have to discard it.

Let us carve out of empty silence all our dreams of speaking. Let us allow all our thoughts of action to slide into stagant torpor.

Yet dreamed landscapes are merely the smoke from known landscapes and the tedium of dreaming them is almost as great as the tedium of looking at the world.

And hovering distractedly above all this, like a vast blue sky, the horror of living.

36   [August 1913]

In the Forest of Alienation

I know that I woke and that I am still asleep. My old body, worn down by life, tells me that it is still very early ... I feel distantly feverish. For some reason, I weigh heavy on myself ...

In a state of lucid torpor, heavily incorporeal, I stagnate between sleep and wakefulness, in a dream that is a shadow of dreaming. My attention floats between two worlds and I peer blindly into the depths of a sea and into the depths of a sky, and those two depths interpenetrate and mingle, and I do not know where I am nor what I am dreaming.

A shadowy wind blows the ashes of dead intentions over the person I am when awake. The warm dew of tedium falls from an unknown sky. A great inert anxiety fumbles at my soul and tentatively ruffles me, like the breeze ruffling the treetops.

In my warm, languid bedroom, the dawn outside is merely a dark breath. I am all quiet confusion ... Why does the day have to dawn? Knowing that it will dawn wearies me, as if it required some enormous effort on my part.

Vaguely, slowly, I grow calmer. I sink back into torpor. I float in the air, half-waking, half-sleeping, and another kind of reality emerges from who knows where, with me in the middle of it ...

It emerges, but without erasing the reality of this warm clammy bedroom or that strange forest. They coexist in my mind, handcuffed to those two realities, like two columns of smoke mingling.

This tremulous, transparent landscape so clearly belongs both to this reality and another.

And who is this woman who, like me, clothes the alien forest with her gaze? Why do I even have this moment to ask myself that question? I don't even know if I want to know ...

My empty bedroom is a dark glass through which I knowingly look out at that landscape ... a landscape I have known for a long time and, for a long time too and with this same unknown woman, I, a different reality, have wandered through her unreality. I sense in myself a centuries-old knowledge of those trees and those flowers and those pathless paths and of the I who strolls them, ancient and visible to my gaze, and which the knowledge of my being here in this room clothes in shadowy sight ...

Now and then, in that forest where I can see and feel myself from afar, a slow wind sweeps away the smoke, and that smoke becomes the clear, dark vision of the bedroom in which I am present, of these vague bits of furniture and curtains and their nocturnal torpor. Then the wind passes and everything becomes nothing but the landscape of that other world ...

At other times, this narrow room is an ash-gray mist on the

horizon of that alternative land ... And there are moments when the ground we tread is this same visible room ...

I dream and drift, a double self, me and that woman ... A great weariness becomes a black fire that consumes me ... A great, passive yearning becomes the false life embracing me ...

Such a dull happiness! Being eternally at a point where two paths fork! I dream and behind me someone else is dreaming with me ... Perhaps I am only the dream of that nonexistent Someone ...

Outside, the ever-distant dawn! The forest so intensely present to those other eyes of mine!

When I'm far from that landscape, I almost forget it, and only when I have it here before me do I miss it, and only when I walk through it do I weep and long for it ...

The trees, the flowers, the secret, tree-thick paths!

We would sometimes walk together, arm in arm, beneath the cedars and the Judas trees, and neither of us even gave a thought to living. Our flesh was a vague perfume and our life the echo of a bubbling spring. We would hold hands, and our eyes would wonder what it would be like to be a sensual being and to want to make flesh the illusion of love ...

In our garden there were flowers of every beautiful kind—roses with curled petals, white lilies tinged with yellow, poppies that would have been hidden had their red blush not betrayed their presence, a few violets on the crowded edges of the flower beds, tiny forget-me-nots, camellias barren of scent ... And, erect above the tall grasses, the wide eyes of lone sunflowers would watch us.

Our all-seeing souls were caressed by the visible coolness of the mosses and, as we walked past the palm trees, we felt an intimation of other lands ... And our eyes then filled with tears because not even here, where we were happy, were we happy ...

We stumbled over the dead tentacles of ancient, knotty oak trees ... Tall plane trees stood stock-still ... And in the distance, glimpsed through the trees, ripening bunches of dark grapes hung on silent trellises ...

Our dream of living flew ahead of us, and we smiled at it with the same detached smile, our souls in agreement, with no need for any exchange of glances, aware of each other only as an arm resting on the willing weight of the other person's feeling arm.

Our life had no inside. We were entirely outside and other. We did not know ourselves, as if we had simply appeared to our souls after a journey through dreams ...

We had forgotten about time, and, when we looked up at it, even the immensity of space seemed small to us. Apart from those nearby trees and those distant vineyards, and those mountains on the far horizon, was there anything that was real and that merited the scrutiny one gives to things that exist?

The clepsydra of our imperfection marked the passing of the unreal hours with slow, regular drops of dreaming ... Nothing is worthwhile, my distant love, except knowing how sweet it is to know that nothing is worthwhile ...

The static motion of trees; the restless stillness of fountains; the indefinable exhalation given off by the secret rhythms of the sap; the slow sunset of things, which seems to come from within and reach out a sympathetic spiritual hand to the growing sadness, so distant and so near to the soul, and which comes from the lofty silence of the sky; the falling of leaves, measured and futile, like drops of alienation, in which the landscape becomes something for the ears alone, like a nostalgia for a remembered homeland—all this bound us uncertainly together, like a constantly unbuckling belt.

There we lived for a time, a time incapable of passing, in a space one could not even think of measuring. A passing of time outside of Time, a space that knew nothing of the usual habits of real space ... O futile companion of my tedium, what hours of happy disquiet appeared to be ours! Hours of ashen wit, days of spatial longing, inner centuries of outer landscapes ... And we did not ask ourselves what it was for, because we took pleasure in knowing that it wasn't for anything.

By a sixth sense we did not have, we knew somehow that the

painful world where we would be two, if indeed such a world existed, lay beyond the farthest horizon where the mountains are merely breathed shapes, and beyond which there is nothing. And it was because of the contradiction of knowing this that our time there was as dark as a cave in the land of the superstitious, and the fact that we could feel this was as strange as the sight of a Moorish city silhouetted against an autumnal evening sky ...

On the audible horizon, the waves of unknown oceans broke on beaches we would never see, and it was a joy to us to hear this, to the point where we could see inside ourselves that ocean on which caravels doubtless sailed with aims quite different from the practical ones demanded by the Earth.

We would suddenly notice, like someone suddenly noticing they are alive, that the air was full of birdsong and that, like the ancient perfumes of rich satins, the wavelike lapping of leaf on leaf was more deeply embedded within us than our awareness that we could hear it.

And thus the murmurings of the birds, the whispering of the trees and the monotonous, forgotten background noise of the eternal sea placed around our abandoned life an aura of not-knowing. For days we slept wakefully, content to be nothing, to have no desires or hopes, to have forgotten the color of love or the taste of hatred. We thought ourselves immortal ...

There we lived hours full of an entirely different way of experiencing those hours, hours of an empty imperfection, perfect in their imperfection, diagonal to the rectangular certainty of life ... Imperial hours from an ousted empire, hours clothed in faded purple, hours fallen into this world from another world far prouder of its many demolished anxieties ...

On the bedroom curtains, the morning is a shadow of light. My lips, which I know to be pale, taste of a desire not to live.

The air in our neutral room weighs as heavy as a door curtain. Our somnolent attention to the mystery of all this is as limp as the train of a dress dragging over the ground in some twilight ceremony.

There is no reason for any of our desires to exist. Our attention is an absurdity allowed by our winged inertia.

I do not know what shadowy oils anoint our idea of our body. Our weariness is the mere shadow of a weariness. It comes to us from far away, like our idea of having a life …

Neither of us has a name or a plausible existence. If we could ever be noisy enough to imagine ourselves laughing, we would doubtless laugh at the thought of thinking we were alive. The warm coolness of the sheet caresses our feet (both yours and mine), feet that feel quite naked to each other.

Let us not be deceived, my love, about life and its ways. Let us flee from being us … Let us not remove from our finger the magic ring which, when rubbed, summons the fairies of silence and the elves of the shadows and the gnomes of forgetting …

And when we dream of speaking about the forest, it once more rises up before us, even more perturbed now than our perturbation and sadder than our sadness. Like a thinning mist, our idea of the real world flees before it, and I again possess myself in my errant dream, a dream framed by that mysterious forest …

Ah, the flowers that I saw there! Flowers that sight translated into names, when I knew them, and whose perfume my soul picked, not from the flowers themselves, but from the melody of their names … Flowers whose names were, when repeated in sequence, whole orchestras of sonorous perfumes … Trees whose voluptuous green cast shade and cool over their names … Fruits whose name was a biting into the very soul of their flesh … Shadows that were relics of happy once-upon-a-times … Clearings, clear clearings, that were the most candid of smiles from the landscape that lay yawning near by … O multicolored hours! Flower-instants, tree-minutes, O time stagnating in space, time lying dead in space and covered in flowers and the perfume of flowers and the perfume of the names of flowers! …

A mad dream in that alien silence!

Our life was all of life … Our love was the perfume of love … We lived impossible hours, full of being us ... And that is because we knew, with all the flesh of our flesh, that we were not a reality ...

We were impersonal, empty of ourselves, something else entirely ... We were that landscape vanished from its own consciousness ... And just as the landscape was two—the real and the illusory—so we were obscurely two as well, neither of us quite knowing if the other was or was not him or herself, or if the uncertain other was alive ...

When we suddenly found ourselves before the stagnating lakes, we felt a desire to weep ... There, the landscape had its eyes filled with tears, unmoving eyes, full of the innumerable tedium of being ... Yes, full of the tedium of being, of having to be something, real or illusory—and that tedium had its homeland and its voice in the silence and exile of those lakes ... And even though, all unknowing, we were still walking, it seemed that we were lingering by the shores of those lakes, because so much of us lingered and lived there, symbolized and absorbed ...

And what a fresh and happy horror it was that no one else was there! Not even us, who were walking there, being there ... Because we were no one. We were nothing at all ... We had no life that Death might have to kill. We were so tenuous, so insignificant that the passing wind left us helpless and the passing hour caressed us like a breeze in the top of a palm tree.

We had no age and no objective. We had left the purpose of all things and all beings at the door of that paradise of absence. In order for us to feel ourselves feeling, nothing moved, neither the rough souls of tree trunks, nor the proffered souls of leaves, nor the nubile souls of flowers, nor the heavy-laden souls of fruits ...

And so we died to our own life, so intent on dying our respective lives that we did not notice that we were one and the same, that each of us was an illusion of the other, and inside each of us was the merest echo of our own self ...

A fly buzzes, uncertain and minimal ...

A vague, bright scattering of sounds flashes upon my mind, filling with daylight my consciousness of our room ... Our room? Ours in what sense, if I am alone? I don't know. Everything melts away and all that remains, fleetingly, is a reality-*cum*-fog in which my uncertainty sinks and my self-understanding, lulled by opiates, falls asleep.

Day has broken, fallen from the pale peak of the Hour ...

The kindling of our dreams has just gone up in flames, my love, in the fireplace of our life ...

Let us not be deceived by hope, because it betrays, or by love, because it grows weary, or by life, because it satiates but does not sate, or even by death, because it brings more than you want and less than you expect.

Let us not be deceived, O Veiled One, by our own tedium, because tedium itself grows old and does not fully dare to be the anxiety that it is.

Let us not weep, let us not hate, let us not desire ...

Let us, O Silent One, cover the stiff, dead profile of our Imperfection with a fine linen sheet ...

37 [1913?]

If only our life were one long standing at the window, if only we could just stay there, like an unmoving curl of smoke, frozen at the one moment in the evening that paints the curve of the hills with pain. If only we could stay there beyond forever! If, at the very least, on this side of the impossible, we could stay like that, without undertaking a single action, without our pale lips committing the sin of uttering more words!

Look, it grows dark! The positive peace of everything fills me with rage, with something that is the bitter aftertaste of the air I breathe. My soul aches ... In the distance a slow ribbon of smoke rises and disperses ... A restless tedium blocks all further thoughts of you ...

How unnecessary it all is! Us and the world and the mystery of both.

It's raining hard, ever harder and harder ... It's as if something were about to be unleashed in the blackness outside ...

The irregular, hilly heap of the city seems to me today more like a plain, a rain-filled plain. Wherever I look, everything is the color of rain, pale black.

I'm filled with strange sensations, all of them cold. Now it seems to me that the landscape is nothing but mist, and that the houses are the mist that veils it.

A kind of pre-neurosis of what I will be when I no longer am chills body and soul. Something like a memory of my future death makes me shiver inside. In a fog of intuition I feel I am dead matter, fallen in the rain, bemoaned by the wind.

And the cold of what I will not then feel gnaws at my present heart.

39   [1913]

How to dream well

Postpone everything. Never do today what you can put off until tomorrow. You don't have to do anything, tomorrow or today.

Never think about what you're going to do. Simply don't do it.

Live your life. Do not be lived by it. In truth and in error, in sickness and health, be your own self. You can only achieve this by dreaming, because your real life, your human life, does not belong to you, but to others. Therefore, replace life with dreaming and take care to dream perfectly. In all your real-life actions, from the day you are born until the day you die, it is not you performing those actions; you do not live, you are merely lived.

Become an absurd sphinx in the eyes of others. Shut yourself up in your ivory tower, but without slamming the door, for your ivory tower is you.

And if anyone tells you this is false and absurd, don't believe him.

But don't believe what I'm telling you either, because you shouldn't believe anything.

Despise everything, but in such a way that despising feels quite normal. Do not think you're superior when you despise others. Therein lies the noble art of despising.

40 [1913?]

Lake of Possession

Nothing penetrates, neither atoms nor souls. That is why nothing can possess anything else. From the truth to a handkerchief, nothing is possessable. (Property is not theft: it is nothing.)

41 [1913?]

How to dream well

First, take care to respect nothing and to believe in nothing. When faced by those things you do not respect, your attitude must be that of someone willing to respect something; your feelings of distaste when confronted by what you do not love should resemble a painful desire to love; of your scorn for life retain only the idea that it should be good to live and to love life. Thus you will be laying the foundations for your dreams.

Make sure that the building you propose to build is the tallest of all. To dream is to find yourself. You will be the Columbus of your soul. You are going in search of its landscapes. Make sure, then, that you are heading in the right direction and that your instruments are accurate.

The art of dreaming is difficult because it is a passive art, where any effort made is intended to create a total absence of effort. Doubtless the art of sleeping, if there is one, in some way resembles this.

Remember, the art of dreaming is not the art of directing your dreams. To direct is to act. The true dreamer surrenders himself to himself, allows himself to be possessed by himself.

Flee from all material provocations. There is, to begin with, a temptation to masturbate. Then there is the temptation of alcohol and opium ... All these things involve effort of some kind. To be a good dreamer, you must be only a dreamer. Opium and morphine can be bought in a pharmacy; how, therefore, can you use them to dream? Masturbation is a physical act; how, therefore, do you think ...

You might dream you are masturbating, fine; you might dream you are smoking opium, taking morphine, and grow intoxicated with the idea of that dream-opium and dream-morphine, and that is all very praiseworthy: you are in your golden role as the perfect dreamer.

Always judge yourself to be sadder and unhappier than you are. That's no bad thing. Since it is an illusion, it is one of the steps towards dreaming.

42 [after 12 Sep 1913]

Shipwrecks? No, never. And yet I have the impression that all my voyages ended in shipwreck, my salvation hidden away in intermittent states of unconsciousness ...

Vague dreams, confusing lights, perplexing landscapes—that is what remains in my soul after all my journeying.

I have the impression that I've known hours of every hue, loves of every flavor, desires of every shape and size. I've committed boundless excesses, and yet I was never enough for myself even in my dreams.

I should explain that I really did travel, but everything smacks to me of merely telling myself that I traveled, although I didn't. I carried back and forth, from north to south and east to west, the weariness of having had a past, the disquiet of living a present, and the tedium of having to have a future. And yet I struggle so hard to remain entirely in the present, killing inside me the past and the future.

I walked along the banks of rivers whose names I found I did not know. Sitting at the tables of cafés in the cities I visited, I found myself thinking that everything tasted to me of dreams, of emptiness.

I sometimes found myself wondering if I was still sitting at the table of our old house, motionless and dazzled by dreams! I cannot promise you that this is not what is happening, that I am not still there now, that all this, including this conversation with you, is false and imaginary. Who are you, by the way? The absurd thing is that you don't know either ...

43 [1913?]

Journey never made

I hide behind the door, so that when Reality comes in, it won't see me. I hide under the table and suddenly spring out to startle Possibility. I withdraw from myself, as if from the arms of an embrace, the two great tediums that encircle me—the tedium of being able to live only the Real, and the tedium of being able to imagine only the Possible.

Thus I triumph over reality. Are these sandcastles my triumphs? Of what divine substance are castles that are not sandcastles made?

How do you know that, by traveling in this way, I am not obscurely rejuvenating myself?

Childishly absurd, I relive my boyhood and play with the ideas of things as I once played with my toy soldiers, with which, as a boy, I did things that went totally against the very idea of soldiers.

Drunk on errors, I momentarily find myself erroneously alive.

44 [1913?]

Cascade

A child knows that the doll is not real, and yet he or she treats it as real, even weeping disconsolately when it breaks. The art of the child is that of making things unreal. Blessèd is that mischievous stage in life, when love is negated by the absence of sex, when reality is negated by play, treating as real things that are not.

Let me return to childhood and stay there forever, caring

nothing for the values that grown men give to things or for the relationships that grown men establish between them. When I was small, I would often stand my toy soldiers on their heads, legs in the air ... And is there any reason, with logical arguments to back it up, why real soldiers should not march about on their heads?

A child gives no more value to gold than to glass. And is gold really worth so much more? The child finds the passions, rages and fears that he sees on adult faces vaguely absurd. And is it not true that all our fears, loathings and loves are entirely absurd and vain?

O divine, absurd childish intuition! There is the true vision of the things we dress up in conventions whenever we see them stripped naked, the things we wrap up in the fog of our own ideas rather than seeing them directly!

Is God merely perhaps a big child? Does not the entire universe seem like a game, a prank played by a naughty child? So unreal ...

I tossed this idea up into the air for you, but seeing it from afar, I suddenly see how horrifying it is! (What if it's true?)

It falls at my feet and shatters into horrific dust and mysterious splinters ...

I wake in order to know that I exist ...

In my ear a great hesitant tedium burbles with an erroneous coolness that comes from the cascade, beyond the beehives, in the stupid depths of the garden.

45 [1913?]

Rainy landscape

All night, for hours and hours, the whisper of rain falling. All night, as I lay half-awake, the cold, liquid monotony of rain on the window nagged at me. Now, from higher up, a gust of wind made the waters whirl painfully and beat rapid wings against the glass; now, a dull sound lulled to sleep the dead world outside. My soul was the same as ever, whether between sheets or among people, agonizingly conscious of the world. Like happiness, the day was taking a long time to arrive, and at that hour, it felt as if it never would.

If only the day and happiness would never come! If only hopes could at least not suffer the disappointment of coming true!

From the far end of the street came the chance sound of a late-night cart jolting roughly over the cobblestones, crunching past beneath the window, before disappearing off down the street, into the depths of the vague sleep to which I could not quite succumb. Now and then, a door on the stairs slammed. Sometimes, there was the squelch of footsteps, the rustle of damp clothes. Occasionally, when there were more footsteps, these seemed louder, more intrusive. Then, as the footsteps faded, silence returned, and the rain continued immeasurably to fall.

Whenever I opened my eyes from that false sleep, I saw flickering on the darkly visible walls of my room fragments of dreams yet undreamed, faint lights, black lines, small nothings that rose and fell. The furniture loomed larger than it did during the day, blurred shapes in the absurd darkness. The presence of the door was indicated only by something neither paler nor darker than the night, but different. As for the window, I could only hear it.

New, fluid and uncertain, the rain continued to sound. The moments slowed to keep pace. The solitude of my soul grew, spread, enveloped what I was feeling, what I wanted, what I was about to dream. The vague objects, participants in the darkness of my insomnia, came to share both place and pain in my desolation.

46 [1913?]

I never let my sensations know what I'm going to make them feel … I play with them much as a bored princess plays with her large, quick, cruel cats …

I slam shut my inner doors, through which certain sensations were about to pass in order to be felt. I brusquely remove from their path any mental objects that might endow them with certain gestures.

Brief meaningless phrases slipped into the conversations we imagine we are having; absurd statements made out of the ashes of other statements that no longer mean anything.

—Your gaze has about it a suggestion of music played on board a ship, in the mysterious middle of a river with forests on the opposite shore ...

—Don't tell me it's because tonight is a moonlit night. I loathe moonlit nights ... And yet some people really are in the habit of playing music on moonlit nights ...

—That, too, is possible. And it is, of course, most regrettable ... But your gaze really does seem to express a yearning for something, but lacks the necessary sentiment to express it ... I find in the falsity of your expression a number of illusions that I myself have had ...

—Believe me when I say that I do sometimes feel what I say and, even, despite being a woman, what I say with my eyes too ...

—Aren't you being rather hard on yourself? Do we really feel what we think we are feeling? This conversation, for example, does it show any signs of reality? No, it doesn't. It would never be allowed in a novel.

—Yes, you're quite right ... I'm not even absolutely sure that I'm speaking to you ... Despite being a woman, I've made it my duty to be a picture out of the sketchbook of some mad designer ... I contain within me some extraordinarily clear details ... This does, I know, rather give the impression of an excessive and somewhat forced reality ... I believe that the only ambition worthy of a modern woman is that of being a picture. When I was a child, I wanted to be the queen on one of the old playing cards we had at home ... I thought this was a truly compassionate heraldic vocation ... But when one is a child, one does have such moral aspirations ... It's only later, at an age when our aspirations are all immoral, that we think about this seriously.

—Since I never pay much attention to children, I do believe in their artistic instincts ... You know, even while I'm talking to you right now, I'm trying to penetrate the deeper meaning of what you've been saying ... Will you forgive me?

—Not entirely ... We should never invade the feelings others pretend they are feeling. Such feelings are always far too personal

… Believe me, it really hurts me to be sharing these personal confidences with you, for, while they are all false, they do represent genuine scraps of my poor soul … Deep down, you know, the saddest part of us is the least real part, and our greatest tragedies occur in our own idea of ourselves.

—That is very true … But why say it? You've wounded me now. Why remove our conversation from its constant unreality? If we do that, it becomes almost a real possible conversation over a cup of tea, between a pretty woman and an imaginer of sensations.

—Yes, yes, you're quite right. Now it's my turn to apologize. I was distracted and didn't even notice that I'd said something true … Let's change the subject. How late it always is! Now don't get angry again. What I just said meant absolutely nothing …

—Don't apologize, don't even notice that we're talking … All good conversations should be a monologue *à deux* … We shouldn't really know for sure if we really are talking to someone or if we're imagining the whole thing … The most delicious and the most intimate conversations and, above all, the most morally instructive, are those that novelists write between two characters in a book. For example …

—Oh please! Surely you're not going to give me an example. That only happens in grammar books, not that we ever read them.

—Have you ever read a grammar book?

—Never. I always felt a deep aversion for knowing how one should say things. The only thing I liked in grammar books were the exceptions and the pleonasms. The truly modern view is to avoid rules and speak only nonsense. Isn't that what they say?

—Indeed. The worst thing about grammar books (have you noticed the delicious impossibility of us talking about this?), the very worst thing, is the verbs. They are the words that give meaning to sentences … An honest sentence should always have several meanings. Verbs! A friend of mine, who committed suicide—every time I have a longer than usual conversation, a friend commits suicide— had decided to spend his entire life destroying verbs …

—(Why did he commit suicide?)

—Wait, I don't know yet ... He was trying to discover and establish a way of completing sentences without appearing to do so. He used to tell me he was looking for the microbe of signification ... And, of course, he committed suicide because one day he understood the huge responsibility he'd taken on. The importance of the problem drove him mad ... A revolver ...

—Oh no, not that. Don't you see, it couldn't have been a revolver? A man like that would never shoot himself in the head ... You have very little understanding of these friends you never had ... That's a major defect, you know. My best friend—a delightful girl whom I invented ...

—Do you get on well?

—As well as we can ... But that girl, you just can't imagine ...

The two creatures sitting at the table drinking tea certainly never had this conversation, but they were so impeccably turned out, so well dressed, that it seemed a shame that they didn't. That's why I wrote this so that they'd be able to have had such a conversation ... Their attitudes, their slightest gesture, their childish looks and smiles, at those points in any conversation that open up spaces in one's sense of existence, clearly said what I am faithfully pretending they said ... When they each doubtless got married and went their separate ways—for they were far too similar to marry each other—were they ever to read these pages, I'm sure they would recognize what they never said and would be grateful to me for having interpreted so accurately not just what they really are, but what they never wanted to be and never knew they were ...

If they read this, let them believe that this really was what they said. There were so many things missing in the apparent words they heard each other saying—the perfume of the hour, the aroma of the tea, the significance of the flowers she wore pinned to her breast ... They forgot to mention any of those things, which also formed part of the conversation ... But it was all there, and my task is less that of writer and more that of a historian. I am reconstructing, completing … and that will be my excuse to them, that I was intently listening to what they could not have failed to have said.

47 [1914?]

Painful Interlude

Like someone who, looking up after long immersion in a book, experiences ordinary natural sunlight as a violent blow to the eyes, if I suddenly look up at myself, it wounds and burns me to see the clarity and independence-from-me of external life, the existence of others, the position and correlation of movements in space. I stumble over the real feelings of others, the clash of their psyches with mine hobbles and trammels my steps, I slip and slither between and over the sounds of their words, so strange to my ears, their firm, confident steps on real ground, their gestures that actually exist, their harsh, complex ways of being other and not merely variants of me.

I find myself then in one of those chasms into which I occasionally hurl myself, helpless and hollow, feeling as if I had died, and yet I live, a pale, grieving shadow that will be flattened by the first breeze that comes along and which, at the slightest touch, will crumble into dust.

I ask myself then if it was worth all the effort I put into isolating and elevating myself, if the slow calvary I made of myself to achieve my Crucified Glory was worth it, was religiously worth the trouble. And even if I know that it was, at that moment, I am weighed down by the feeling that it wasn't worth the effort and never will be.

48 [1914?]

Triangular Dream

In my dream on the deck, I shuddered—and through my Distant Prince's soul ran a shiver of foreboding.

A noisy, threatening silence invaded the visible atmophere of the room like a pale breeze.

All this lent a glaring, disquieting glow to the moonlight on the ocean that no longer rocked, but trembled; it became clear—even before I heard them—that there were cypresses growing near the Prince's palace.

The blade of the first lightning bolt flickered vaguely around my soul ... The moon on the high sea is the color of lightning, and the palace for the Prince I never was lies in ruins and in the distant past ...

Like a menacing, fast-approaching sound, the ship cuts through the waters, the room grows vividly dark, and he, the Prince, hasn't died, hasn't been captured, ah, what has become of him, what unknown, icy thing is now his destiny?

49   [1914?]

Living life falsely and in dreams is still living life. To abdicate is to act. To dream is to confess to the necessity of living, replacing real life with unreal life, and thus it is a compensation for the inalienability of the will-to-live.

What is all this ultimately but the search for happiness? And does anyone seek anything else?

Has my continual daydreaming, my uninterrupted analysis, given me anything essentially different from what life would give me?

In cutting myself off from people, I did not find myself, nor ...

This book is a single state of soul, analyzed from every angle, traversed in every possible direction.

Did this attitude at least bring me something new? No, I do not even have that as consolation. It was already there in Heraclitus and Ecclesiastes. *Life is a child's toy in the sand ... vanity ...* And in poor Job, in a single sentence: *My soul is weary of my life.*

In Pascal: ...

In Vigny: In you ...

In Amiel, so completely in Amiel: ...

In Verlaine, and the symbolists ...

All of them as sick as me ... I do not even have the privilege of even a hint of originality in my sickness ... I do what so many others before me did ... My suffering is already so trite and hackneyed ... Why even think these things when so many others have already thought and suffered them?

And yet, I did bring something that was new, although I am not responsible for that. It came from the Night and shines in me like a star ... None of my own efforts produced it or snuffed it out ... I am a bridge between two mysteries, with no idea how I was built ...

I listen to myself dreaming. I rock myself to sleep with the sound of my images ... They fade from me into recondite melodies.

The sound of an image-filled phrase is worth a hundred gestures! A metaphor can console one for so many things!

I listen to myself ... I hear ceremonies taking place inside me. Cortèges ... Sequins in my tedium ... Masked balls ... I watch my soul and am dazzled ...

Kaleidoscope of fragmented sequences ...

The pomp of sensations grown stale with living ... Royal beds in deserted castles, the jewels of dead princesses, a small cove glimpsed through the arrow-slit of a castle; the ships will surely return and, for the more fortunate, there might be cortèges in exile ... Sleeping orchestras, threads for making nets ...

50   [1914?]
And just as I dream, I also reason if I choose to, because that is merely another kind of dream.

Prince of better hours, once I was your princess, and we loved each other with a different kind of love, whose memory wounds me.

51   [1914?]
To wind the world about our fingers, like a thread or a ribbon a woman plays with as she sits dreaming at the window.

It all comes down to trying to experience tedium in a way that does not hurt.

It would be interesting to be two kings simultaneously: to be not one of their souls, but two.

52 [1914?]

I would like to set down a code of inertia for the leaders of modern societies.

Society would govern itself spontaneously if it did not contain people of sensitivity and intelligence. That, believe me, is the only obstacle. Primitive societies existed happily enough on more or less that basis.

The trouble is that the expulsion of a society's leaders would result in their deaths, because they do not know how to work. Or they might die of tedium, because there was not enough room for stupidity among them. But what I am talking about is a cure for human happiness.

Every leader who emerged in society would be exiled to the City of Leaders. There they would be fed, like animals in a cage, by normal society.

Believe me, if there were no intelligent people pointing out all our various human ills, humanity would not even notice them. Sensitive people make others suffer out of sympathy.

However, given that we exist in society, the sole duty of our leaders is to reduce to the minimum their participation in the life of the tribe. No newspapers should be read, except to find out about something trivial or odd that is happening; you cannot imagine the voluptuous pleasure I get from reading the news from the provinces. For me, the names alone open up doors onto the uncertain.

The supreme, most honorable state for a superior man is not even to know the name of his country's head of state, or whether he lives in a monarchy or a republic.

His whole attitude should be to arrange his soul so that he is untroubled either by things or events. If he fails to do this, he will be obliged, out of self-interest, to take an interest in other people.

53   [1914?]

I hold the most contradictory opinions, the most diverse beliefs. This is because I never think or speak or act ... Some dream of mine, in which I momentarily embody myself, thinks, speaks and acts for me. I begin to speak and I-Other speaks instead. As regards Me, I feel only an enormous incapacity, an immense vacuum, an incompetence in the face of everything that is life. I don't know the appropriate gestures for any actual act ...

I have never learned to exist.

I achieve everything I want, as long as it remains inside me.

If you were to ask me if I was happy, I would say that I am not ...

I want your reading of this book to leave you with the sense of having lived through some voluptuous nightmare.

What once was moral is now, for us, aesthetic ... What was social is now individual ...

Why watch the twilight coming on if I have inside me a thousand different twilights—including some that are not twilights—and if, as well as seeing them inside me, I myself am those twilights, inside and out?

54   [1914?]
How to dream metaphysics
Reason [...]—and everything will be easy and [...], because the dream, for me, is everything. I tell myself to dream something and I dream it. I sometimes create inside myself a philosopher who carefully sets out his philosophies for me, while, at the window of

his house, I, a pageboy, flirt with his daughter, whose soul I love.

I am, of course, limited by my own knowledge. I cannot create a mathematician ... However, I am contented with what I have, which allows for infinite combinations and innumerable dreams. Who knows, by dint of dreaming, I might achieve much more, but it's not worth the effort. I'm fine as I am.

The pulverization of the personality: I don't know what my ideas are or my feelings or my character ... If I do feel something, I feel it in the visualized person of some creature who appears inside me. *I have replaced myself with my dreams.* Each person is merely his dream of himself. I am not even that.

Never read a book to the end, and never read it straight through, without jumping ahead.

I never knew what I felt. When people spoke to me of this or that emotion and described it, I always felt they were describing some part of my soul, but when I thought about it later, I was unsure. I never know if the person I feel myself to be really is me, or if I merely think I am. I am bits of characters from my own dramas.

All effort is pointless, but it passes the time. Reasoning is sterile, but amusing. Loving is tedious, but possibly preferable to not loving. (The dream, however, replaces everything.) In dreams, you can enjoy the idea of effort without actually having to make any effort. In my dream, I can go into battle without ever feeling afraid or getting wounded. I can reason, without expecting to reach a truth, and without being upset when I never do; and without thinking I will solve a problem, knowing that I never will ... I can love without being rejected or betrayed or hated. I can change my lover without her ever changing. And if I want her to betray me or desert me, I can make that happen in precisely the way I want and in the way that gives me most pleasure. In dreams I can experience the greatest anxieties, the greatest torments, the greatest victories. I can experience all those things as if they were really happening; it depends solely on my ability to make the dream clear, vivid, real. This requires application and inner patience.

There are various ways of dreaming. One way is to abandon yourself to your dreams, without trying to make them clear, leaving them in the vague twilight of your feelings. This is an inferior approach and tiring too, because it's monotonous, always the same. Then there is the clear, directed dream, but the effort required to direct the dream highlights the artifice. The supreme artist, a dreamer like myself, needs only to want the dream to be a certain way, to take certain whimsical turns … and it will evolve before him precisely as he would have wished, but could never have imagined had he taken the trouble to do so. Say I suddenly wanted to dream myself a king … And there I am, the king of some country or other. The dream will tell me which country or what kind of country … because I have such control now over what I dream that my dreams always unexpectedly bring me what I want. Often they are so clear that they make perfect the rather vague order they received. I am completely incapable of consciously imagining the Middle Ages of the different epochs and different Earths I have seen in dreams. I am dazzled by the excess of imagination I did not even know I had and that my dreams reveal to me. I let my dreams go their own way … They always exceed my expectations. They are always more beautiful than I hoped, but this is something only the experienced dreamer can achieve. I spent years dreamily searching for that expertise. Now I achieve it effortlessly …

The best way of beginning to dream is through books. Novels are very useful for beginners. The first step: learn to surrender totally to your reading and live alongside the characters in a novel. It is a sign of progress to feel that your own family and its griefs are insignificant and repellent compared with those fictional characters.

Best avoid literary novels where your attention is distracted by the form of the novel. I am not ashamed to admit that I myself began like that. And yet oddly enough, I was instinctively drawn to detective novels.

I could never really concentrate on romantic novels. But that is a matter of personal taste, because I am not the romantic type, not even in my dreams. We should each, therefore, cultivate our own particular bent. Always remember that to dream is to look for ourselves. The sensual person should choose books that are the very opposite of those I would choose.

When the dreamer experiences an actual physical sensation, then you might say that he has gone beyond the first stage of dreaming. That is, when a novel about fights, flights and battles leaves your body actually bruised and your legs tired, then you will have reached the first stage. In the case of the sensualist, he should—resorting only to mental masturbation—experience an ejaculation when such a moment occurs in the novel.

Then he must try to transfer all of this onto the mental plane. The ejaculation, in the case of the sensualist (and I choose this example because it is the most violent and extreme), should be *felt without it actually happening*. The subsequent tiredness will be much greater, but the pleasure will be far more intense.

At the third stage, all sensations will be mental. The pleasure and the tiredness will increase, but the body no longer feels anything, and instead of your limbs feeling weak, it is your intellect, ideas and emotions that feel limp and flaccid … At this point, it is time to move on to the highest stage of dreaming.

The fourth stage is to construct your own novels. You should only attempt this when, as I said before, you have succeeded in completely mentalizing the dream. Otherwise, any initial effort to create novels will get in the way of the perfect mentalization of pleasure.

(Certain difficulties.)

Once you have trained your imagination, you only have to want to dream something, and your imagination will do the work for you. At this stage, there is almost no physical or mental tiredness. There is a total dissolution of the personality. We are merely ashes endowed with a soul, lacking any shape, not even that of water, which takes its shape from the glass containing it. Once all this is in place, whole dramas can appear inside us, line by line, evolving independently and perfectly. There may not even be any need for us to write them down. We will be able to create at second hand—we will imagine in ourselves a poet writing, and he will write in one style, while another poet might write in another. By dint of refining this ability to the nth degree, I can now write in all kinds of different styles, all of them original.

The highest stage of dreaming is reached when, having created a cast of characters, we live them all, all at the same time—*we are all those souls jointly and interactively.*

It's incredible how this depersonalizes the spirit, how it reduces it to ashes, and, I admit, it's difficult then not to succumb to the general lassitude that afflicts one's whole being. But what a triumph!

This is the only possible asceticism. It involves no faith, nor even a God.

I am God.

55 [1914?]

Landscape in the rain

With each drop of rain my failed life weeps with nature. There is something of my own disquiet in the steady drip and patter by which the day vainly empties out its sadness upon the earth.

It rains and rains. My soul grows damp just listening to it. So much rain ... My flesh turns liquid and watery around my consciousness of it.

An uneasy cold closes icy hands about my poor heart. The hours, gray and [...], stretch out, flatten out in time; the moments drag. How it rains!

The gutters spout tiny torrents of sudden water. Into my mind percolates the troubling sound of water rushing down pipes. The rain beats indolently, mournfully, against the windowpanes; in the [...]

A cold hand grips my throat and will not let me breathe in life.

Everything is dying in me, even the knowledge that I can dream! I do not feel well, not in any physical sense. My soul finds hard edges to all the soft comforts on which I lean for support. Every gaze I look on has grown dark, defeated by the impoverished light of this day now set to die a painless death.

56

Maxims

The possession of definite, firm opinions, instincts, passions and a fixed, recognizable character, all this contributes to the horror of making of our soul a fact, of making it material and external. Living in a sweet, fluid state of ignorance about all things and about oneself is the only way of life guaranteed to suit and bring comfort to the sage.

The ability constantly to interpose oneself between self and other things shows the highest degree of knowledge and prudence.

Our personality should be impenetrable even to ourselves: that's why our duty should be always to dream ourselves and to include ourselves in our dreams so that it is impossible for us to hold any opinions about ourselves.

And we should especially avoid the invasion of our personality by others. Any interest others take in us is a grave indelicacy. The only thing that prevents the everyday greeting of "How are you?" from being an unforgivable insult is the fact that in general it is utterly empty and insincere.

To love is merely to grow tired of being alone: it is therefore both cowardly and a betrayal of ourselves. (It is vitally important that we should not love.)

To give someone good advice is to show a complete lack of respect for that person's God-given ability to make mistakes. Furthermore, other people's actions should retain the advantage of not being ours. The only possible reason for asking other people's advice is to know—when we subsequently do exactly the contrary of what they told us to do—that we really are ourselves, acting in complete disaccord with all that is other.

The only advantage of studying is to take pleasure in how much other people did not say.

Art is an act of isolation. Every artist should seek to isolate other people, to fill their souls with the desire to be alone. The supreme triumph of a writer is for a reader, rather than read his books, to choose simply to own them and not read them. Not because this is what happens to the great writers, but because it is the greatest possible accolade…

To be lucid is to be indisposed towards oneself. The only legitimate state of mind when looking inside oneself is that of someone who sees only nerves and indecisions.

The only intellectual attitude worthy of a superior creature is a feeling of calm, cool compassion for everything that is not himself. Not that this attitude necessarily bears the stamp of what is just and true, but it is such an enviable one that he must have it.

57 [1914?]

Triangular dream

The light had turned an exaggeratedly slow yellow, a yellow grimed with gray. The intervals between things had grown longer, and sounds, more broadly spaced than usual, rang out disconnectedly, then suddenly stopped, as if cut short. The heat, which seemed to have increased, was both hot and cold. Through a chink in the shutters I could see in the one visible tree an exaggerated air of expectancy. Its green was a different green, filled as much with silence as with color. In the atmosphere, petals had closed. And the planes in the actual composition of space had shifted and disrupted the interrelationship of sounds, lights and colors.

58 [1914?]

Sometimes I think with ambivalent pleasure of the possibility of creating in the future a geography of our consciousness of ourselves. As I see it, the future historian of feelings will perhaps be able to reduce to an exact science his own attitude towards his consciousness of his own soul. Meanwhile, we are very much beginners in this difficult art, for it is still only an art, a chemistry of the feelings that has not yet gone much beyond alchemy. This scientist of tomorrow's world will have a special sensitivity to his own inner life. He will create out of himself the precision instrument necessary for its analysis. I see no great difficulty in making an instrument for self-analysis out of the steels and bronzes of thought alone. I mean by that, real steels and bronzes, but ones forged in the spirit. Perhaps that's how it really should be made. It may be necessary to come up with the idea of a precision instrument and physically see that idea before being able to proceed with any rigorous analysis of oneself. And naturally it will also be necessary to reduce the spirit to some sort of physical matter surrounded by a space in which it can exist. All this depends on a great refinement of our inner feelings which, taken to its limit, will no doubt reveal or create in us a genuine space like the space in which physical things exist but which, in fact, does not itself exist as a thing.

I don't quite know if this inner space will be just another dimension of the other space. Perhaps future scientific research will discover that everything, whether physical or spiritual, is just a dimension of the same space. In one dimension we live as body, in the other as soul. And perhaps there are other dimensions in which we experience other equally real aspects of ourselves. Sometimes

I enjoy letting myself be carried away by this futile meditation on just how far this research might lead.

Perhaps they'll discover that what we call God, and which clearly exists on another level from that of logic and spatial and temporal reality, is just one of our ways of being, one of the ways we experience ourselves in another dimension of existence. This doesn't strike me as impossible. Dreams may also be another dimension in which we live or even an overlapping of two dimensions. Just as a body exists in height, width and length, who knows but that our dreams may exist simultaneously in space, in the ideal world and in the ego: their physical representation in space; their nonphysical representation in the ideal world; their role as an intimate aspect of ourselves in the ego. Even each person's "I" may perhaps be another divine dimension. All this is very complex, but doubtless in time it will be resolved. Today's dreamers are perhaps the great precursors of the ultimate science of the future, not that I believe in any such ultimate science. But that has nothing to do with the case in hand.

Sometimes I invent a metaphysics like this with all the respectful, scrupulous attention of someone engaged in genuine scientific work. As I've said before, it reaches the point where I may really be doing just that. The important thing is not to pride myself too much on all this for pride is prejudicial to the precise impartiality of scientific exactitude.

59 [1914?]

Millimeters (the observation of infinitesimal things)

I believe that the present is very ancient simply because everything, when it did exist, existed in the present, and accordingly, because all things belong to the present, I feel for them all both the fondness of the antiquarian and the fury of the thwarted collector to whom the former dismisses my errors about things with well-founded, plausible, possibly even true, scientific explanations.

To my astonished eyes, the various, successive poses of a butterfly as it flies through the air seem like separate moments made visible in space. My recollections are so vivid that [...]

But I experience intensely only the tiny feelings of the tiniest things. This must come from my love of the futile or perhaps my passion for detail. But I think—I don't know because these are things I never analyze—that it's probably because what is tiny has absolutely no social or practical value and is, for that very reason, absolutely free of any sordid associations with reality. To me all tiny things taste of unreality. The useless is beautiful because it is less real than the useful, which enjoys a continuing and lasting existence; while the marvelously useless, the gloriously infinitesimal, remains where it is, never goes beyond being what it is, and lives free and independent. The useless and the futile create intervals of humble aesthetic in our real lives. The mere insignificant existence of a pin stuck in a piece of ribbon provokes in my soul all manner of dreams and wondrous delights! I pity those who do not recognize the importance of such things!

One of the most complex and widespread of those feelings that hurt one almost to the point of being pleasurable is the disquiet aroused by the mystery of life. That mystery is never so easy to spot as in the contemplation of tiny things which, because they do not move, are perfectly translucent, they stop to let it pass. It is more difficult to experience any sense of mystery when contemplating a battle—and yet pondering the absurdity of there being people and societies and battles between them is what can most easily prompt us to unfurl the flag of victory and celebrate the conquest of the mystery—than when contemplating one small stone on the road, which, because it does not evoke any idea in us beyond the fact of its existence, cannot, if we pursue our thought, fail to evoke in us the thought that immediately follows on from there, that is: the mystery of its existence.

Blessèd be moments, millimeters and, even humbler than these, the shadows of all tiny things! Moments [...]

Millimeters—their existence side by side, so close together on the ruler, provokes in me such an impression of wonder and daring. Sometimes such things cause me both pain and joy. I feel a kind of rough pride in this.

I am an endlessly sensitive photographic plate. In me every tiny detail is recorded and magnified in order to form part of a whole. I concern myself only with myself. For me the external world is pure sensation. I never forget that I can feel.

60 [1914?]

To create within myself a state with its own politics, its own political parties and revolutions, to be all those things myself, to be God in the royal pantheism of that I-the-people, the essence and action of their bodies, their souls, the ground they walk on and the things they do. To be everything, to be both them and not them. Ah, that is one dream I have not yet achieved. If I did, I might perhaps die, I don't know why, but one shouldn't be able to live after committing such a sacrilege, such a usurpation of the divine power to be everything.

What pleasure I would take in creating a jesuitism of the senses!

Some metaphors are more real than the people you see walking down the street. Some images one finds in books are more vividly alive than many men and women. Some literary phrases have an absolutely human individuality. Parts of certain paragraphs of mine send a shudder of fear through me, because they feel so like people, clearly silhouetted against the walls of my room, the night, the darkness … I have written sentences whose sound, whether read loudly or softly—for it's impossible to conceal the sound from them—is without a doubt that of something that has gained absolute exteriority and its own entire soul.

Why do I sometimes set down contradictory, irreconcilable methods of dreaming and learning to dream? Probably because I have grown so accustomed to experiencing the false as true, the dreamed as something actually seen, that I have lost the human ability—false, I believe—to distinguish between truth and lies.

I only have to see something clearly, with my eyes or ears or some other sense, for me to experience something as real. It may well be that I feel two entirely unconnected things at once, but that doesn't matter.

There are creatures capable of suffering during long hours simply because they cannot be a figure in a painting or on a pack of cards. There are souls on whom the impossibility of being someone from the Middle Ages weighs like a curse. I once felt this myself, but no longer. I have gone far beyond that. However, it does pain me, for example, not to be able to dream two kings from two different kingdoms, belonging, for example, to universes with different kinds of space and time. Not being able to do that really does hurt. To me it smacks of hunger.

Being able to dream the inconceivable and make it visible is one of the major triumphs that even I, great dreamer though I am, only rarely achieve. Dreaming, for example, that I am simultaneously, separately, unconfusedly, the man and the woman on a walk that a man and woman are taking by the river. Being able to see myself, simultaneously and with equal clarity, fully integrated and yet quite separate, as both a conscious ship on the South Seas and a printed page in an ancient book. How absurd this seems! But then everything is absurd, and dreams are among the least absurd of things.

61 [1914?]
Divine Envy

Whenever I feel pleasure in the company of others, I envy them their part of that feeling. It seems to me a kind of impudence that they should feel the same as me, that they should invade my soul via their soul by feeling in unison with mine.

The great difficulty with the pride I feel when contemplating landscapes is the painful fact that someone else will doubtless have contemplated them before with precisely the same feeling of pride.

At different times, it's true, and on different days, but to think thus would be to caress and soothe myself with a pedantry that is beneath me. I know that the difference is of little importance, and that others will have looked at the same landscape in the same spirit and in a way that was not like, but similar to, mine.

This is why I force myself to keep changing what I see so as to make it irrefutably mine—for example, changing the shape of the mountains against the sky while keeping it equally beautiful and the same; replacing certain trees and flowers with others, vastly and very differently the same; seeing other colors in the sunset but with identical effect—and thus I create, thanks to my experience and my customarily spontaneous way of looking, an inner way of looking at the outside world.

This, however, is the very lowest level of replacing the visible. In my better, freer moments of dreaming, I am the architect of far more ambitious things.

I make the landscape produce musical effects, evoke visual images—a curious and very complicated triumph of the ecstatic state, difficult because the evocative agent is of the same order as those feelings to be evoked. My greatest triumph was when contemplating the Cais do Sodré—at a certain strangely ambiguous hour as regards aspect and light—I clearly saw a Chinese pagoda with peculiar bells, like absurd hats, on the corners of the eaves—a curious pagoda *painted* in space, on that space-made-satin, I have no idea how, on the space that endures in some ghastly third dimension. And the hours actually smelled to me of a scrap of fabric being dragged along somewhere off in the distance and with a great desire to be real…

62   [1914?]

The truly wise man is the man who lets external events trouble him as little as possible. To do this, he needs to armor himself by surrounding himself with realities that are closer to him than those events, and through which the events reach him, changed so as to accord with those realities.

63 [c. 29 Oct 1914]

To think, yes, even to think, is to act. Only in absolute daydreams, where no activity intervenes, where all consciousness of ourselves gets terminally stuck in the mud—only there in that warm, damp state of nonbeing can one truly abandon all action.

Not wanting to understand, not analyzing ... To observe oneself as one observes nature; to gaze on one's impressions as one would on a field—that is true wisdom.

64 [after 31 Oct 1914]

The Milky Way

... with sinuous phrases of a venomous spirituality ...

... rituals of ragged purples, mysterious ceremonies contemporary with no one ...

... sequestered sensations experienced in another nonphysical body that is both body and physical in its own way, interleaving subtleties, some complex, some simple ...

... lakes above which hovers, with pellucid clarity, a hint of dull gold, and tenuously free of ever having once been made real, doubtless by certain serpentine refinements, a lily clasped by very white hands ...

... pacts made between torpor and anxiety, dark green, tepid to the eye, lodged wearily between sentinels of tedium ...

... mother-of-pearl of futile consequences, alabaster of frequent macerations—gold- and purple-edged sunsets as diversions, but no ships setting sail for better shores, no bridges leading to longer twilights ...

... not even the idea of ponds, many ponds, glimpsed from afar through poplars or perhaps cypresses, depending on the deeply felt syllables with which the hour spoke their name ...

... which is why there are windows that look out onto harbors, the continuous pounding of waves against docks, a confused, crazy, self-absorbed retinue like opals among which amaranths and terebinths write insomnias of understanding on the obscure walls of hearing ...

... threads of rare silver, bonds of unraveling purple, beneath the lime trees futile feelings, and along paths edged with box, silent, ancient couples, sudden fans, vague gestures, and doubtless superior gardens awaiting the placid weariness of nothing but more avenues and paths ...

... quincunx patterns of trees, arbours, grottoes, flower beds, fountains, the art left behind by dead masters, who, in between inner duels between dissatisfaction and the obvious, designed whole processions of dream-matter down the narrow streets of the ancient villages of feelings ...

... marble melodies in distant palaces, reminiscences joining hands with us, casual, indecisive glances, sunsets in fateful skies, growing dark among stars hanging over the silences of decaying empires ...

To reduce sensation to a science, to make psychological analysis a microscopically precise method—an aim that occupies, like a steadfast thirst, the center of my will ...

It is between sensation and my awareness of it that all the great tragedies of my life occur. In that shadowy, indeterminate region of forests and burbling water, indifferent even to the noise of our wars, flows the self I struggle in vain to find ...

I lie recumbent in my life. (My sensations are an epitaph, a long Gongoristic poem covering my dead life.) Death and sunset befall me. The most I can sculpt is my tomb for inner beauty.

The great doors of my detachment from life open onto infinite parks, but no one walks through them, not even in my dream—they stand eternally open to the futile and eternally closed to the false.

I pick the petals off lost glories in the gardens of inner pomp and, past dreamed box hedges, I clatter down dreamed paths leading to the Obscure.

I built whole Empires in the Obscure, on the shores of silences, in the tawny war in which the Exact will meet with defeat.

The man of science recognizes that he himself is his sole reality, and the only real world is the world given him by his sensations. That is why, instead of following the false path of trying to adjust his sensations to those of other people and thus make science objective, he strives, rather, after a perfect knowledge of his world and his personality. Nothing is more objective than his dreams. Nothing is more his than his consciousness of himself. He hones his science on those two realities. It is very different from the science of the scientists of ancient times, who, far from seeking the laws of their own personalities and the organization of their dreams, sought the laws of the "outside world" and the organization of what they called "Nature."

65 [after 31 Oct 1914]

[Milky Way?]
Second part
In me the habit of dreaming and the ability to dream are primordial. Ever since I was a quiet, solitary child, the circumstances of my life, along perhaps with other obscure hereditary forces that have molded me from afar and tailored me to their own sinister pattern, have made of my spirit a constant flow of daydreams. Everything that I am is bound up in this and even the part of me that seems farthest removed from the dreamer belongs without a doubt to the soul of one who only dreams, a soul raised to its highest level.

As best I can, and purely for the pleasure afforded by self-analysis, I would like to put into words all the mental processes that in me are but one thing: a life devoted to dreaming, a soul brought up only to dream.

When, as I almost always do, I view myself from the outside, I recognize that I am entirely unsuited to action, easily perturbed by the need to take steps or make gestures, uncomfortable when talking to others, lacking sufficient insight to entertain myself by grappling with spiritual matters and lacking, too, the necessary physical coordination to apply myself to any merely physical work.

It's only natural that I should be like this. Any dreamer understands that this is how it is. Any reality troubles me. Other people's conversations throw me into a state of terrible anguish. The reality of other people's souls is a constant surprise to me. The vast unconscious network that lies behind all actions seems an absurd illusion, with no plausible coherence, nothing.

But if you think that I must therefore be ignorant of other people's complex psychological processes, that I must lack a clear understanding of other people's intimate thoughts and motives, you're mistaken.

For I am not merely a dreamer, I am exclusively a dreamer. The singlemindedness with which I cultivate the habit of dreaming has given me an extraordinary clarity of inner vision. Not only do I see in frightening and, at times, disturbing relief the figures and backdrops of my dreams but, just as clearly, I see my abstract ideas, my human feelings—what's left of them—my secret impulses, my psychological attitudes towards myself. I mean that I see my own abstract ideas in me, I see them with real internal vision inhabiting a genuine inner space. And thus the smallest detail of their meanderings is visible to me.

That's how I have come to know myself so completely and, knowing myself completely, I know humanity just as completely. There is no base impulse, no noble instinct that has not flashed upon my soul; I know the gestures that accompany each one. I know evil ideas for what they are, whatever masks of goodness or indifference they put on. I know what it is in ourselves that struggles to delude us. And so I know most of the people I see around me better than they do themselves. I often apply myself to studying them in depth, because that way I can make them mine. I conquer the psyche I analyze, because for me to dream is to possess. And so you see it is only natural that a dreamer like myself should also possess these powers of analysis.

That's why plays are one of the few things I enjoy reading. Every day I put on plays inside myself and I know all there is to know about drawing up a Mercator projection of the soul. But the truth is I derive little entertainment from this; dramatists constantly make the same gross, vulgar mistakes. I've never yet found a play that satisfied me. Having seen human psychology with the clarity of a lightning flash illuminating every corner at a glance, I find most dramatists' clumsy construction and character analysis painful, and the little I've read in the genre is as displeasing to me as an ink blot on a page in one of my account books.

Things form the very stuff of my dreams; that's why I pay such distracted attention to certain details of the external world.

To give vividness to my dreams I need to know how it is that real landscapes and real-life characters appear so vivid to us. Because the vision of the dreamer is not like that of someone who sees things. In dreams one does not rest one's gaze equally on the important and unimportant aspects of a real object. The dreamer sees only the important part. The true reality of an object lies only in a part of it; the rest is the heavy tribute it pays to the material world in exchange for its existence in space. Similarly, certain phenomena that have a palpable reality in dreams have no reality in space. A real sunset is imponderable and transitory. A dream sunset is fixed and eternal. The person who can write knows how to see his dreams clearly (for that is what it means), to see life as if in dreams, to see life immaterially, taking photographs of it with the camera of his daydreams, on which the rays of anything boring, utilitarian and circumscribed have no effect, registering only as black on the photographic plate of the spirit.

This attitude, which all my excessive dreaming has only made worse, means that I see only the dream part of reality. My vision of things suppresses in them anything that is of no use to my dream. And thus I live always in dreams, even when I'm living in the real world. To me, looking at a sunset within myself or a sunset in the real world are one and the same thing, because I always see in the same way, because my vision is cut to the same pattern.

That's why the idea I have of myself is an idea that to many will seem mistaken. In a way it is. But I dream myself and I select out what is dreamable in me, composing and recomposing myself in every possible way until I fit my own requirements for what I should or should not be. Sometimes the best way to see an object is to destroy it, for it survives—although quite how I can't explain—in its own negation and destruction; that's what I do to large areas of my own being, which, once painted out from my portrait of myself, lead to a transfiguration of myself within my own reality.

How can I be so sure that I'm not deceiving myself about these inner processes of illusion? Because the process that draws one aspect of the world or a figure from a dream into a heightened reality draws with it an emotion or a thought; it therefore divests it of all claims to nobility and purity which, as is almost always the case, it has no right to anyway. You will notice that my objectivity is of the most absolute. I create the absolute object and give absolute qualities to its physical reality. I did not flee from life exactly, in the sense of seeking a softer bed for my soul, I simply swapped lives and found in my dreams the same objectivity I found in life. My dreams—which I will deal with elsewhere—exist independently of my will and often shock and wound me. Often what I find inside myself distresses, shames (some persistent shred of humanity in me perhaps—what is shame after all?) and frightens me.

Attentiveness has been replaced in me by uninterrupted daydreaming. I now superimpose on things I have seen, even things seen in dreams, other dreams I carry with me. Once I became sufficiently inattentive to perform well what I referred to as "seeing as if in dreams"—for that inattentiveness was motivated by perpetual daydreaming and by an (again rather inattentive) preoccupation with the course taken by my dreams—I could superimpose what I dream on the dream I see, and interweave the reality now stripped of its material reality with the absolutely immaterial.

From this comes my ability to pursue several ideas at once, to observe something and at the same time dream a great diversity of other things; to dream a real sunset over a real River Tejo at the same time as I dream a dreamed morning on some inner Pacific Ocean. The two dreamed things mingle without mixing, without really confusing the different emotional state each one gives rise to. Thus I am like someone watching a lot of people passing by in the street and being simultaneously in each person's soul (which presupposes a complete unity of feeling) and at the same time seeing their bodies (which must of necessity be perceived separately) passing one another in a street full of walking legs.

66   [1914?]

Making something and then recognizing that it is no good is one of the soul's tragedies. Especially when you also have to acknowledge that it's the best you can do. However, when you're about to write something, knowing beforehand that it's sure to be imperfect, a failure, that is the most spiritually tormenting and humiliating of feelings. I not only feel that the lines I write are unsatisfactory, I know that I will find any lines I write in the future equally unsatisfactory. I know this both philosophically and carnally, thanks to some obscure, razor-sharp insight.

Why do I write, then? Because, as a preacher of renunciation, I have not yet learned to practice what I preach. I have not yet learned to give up this leaning towards prose and poetry. I have to write as if I were doing a penance. And the worst penance is knowing that what I write is completely futile, failed and feeble.

As a child I wrote poetry. It was very bad poetry, but I thought it perfect. I will never again know the false pleasure of producing something perfect. What I write today is much better. It's better, in fact, than what the very best writers could produce. However, it's infinitely inferior to what I, for some reason, feel that I could—or perhaps should—write. I grieve over those bad poems from my childhood as if over a dead child, a dead son, a lost hope.

67 [1914?]

When I examine my own pain, I do so with that uncertain and almost imponderable malice that enlivens any human heart when confronted by other people's pain or discomfort; I take this to such lengths that I even enjoy those occasions when I'm made to feel ridiculous or mean-spirited, as if they were happening to someone else. By some strange and fantastic transformation of my feelings I do not feel any spiteful and all-too-human joy at other people's pain and absurdity. Confronted by other people's misfortunes, I do not experience pain but a feeling of aesthetic discomfort and a furtive irritation. This has nothing to do with kindness, it is simply because when someone is made to feel ridiculous, they appear ridiculous not only to me but to others too, and that is what irritates me; it hurts me that any animal of the human species should laugh at someone else's expense when they have no right to do so. I don't care if others laugh at me, because I'm protected by an efficient armor of scorn.

To mark the boundaries of the garden of my being I put up high railings, more daunting than any wall, so that while I can see others quite clearly, at the same time I exclude them and keep them other.

All my life I have concentrated all my attention and every moral scruple on finding ways of avoiding action.

I submit myself neither to the state nor to men; I put up an inert resistance. The only thing the state would want me for is to perform some action. If I refuse to act, the state can get nothing out of me. Since there's no capital punishment these days, all the state can do is make life difficult for me. Were this to happen I would simply renew the armor about my spirit and entrench myself still further in my dreams. But this has never happened. The state has never bothered me. I think good fortune must have protected me.

If I had written *King Lear*, I would be filled with remorse for the rest of my life. Because as a play it is so great that its defects, its monstrous defects, loom horribly large, as do the tiny things in certain scenes that keep them from achieving true perfection. Everything that has ever been made is full of mistakes, errors of perspective or of ignorance, moments of bad taste, weakness, sloppiness. No one has the necessary divinity to write a work of art large enough to be great, and precise and perfect enough to be sublime, and no one has the good fortune to have achieved this. What does not flow freely from us is the result of the uneven ground of our own imperfect self.

When I think this, my imagination feels a terrible grief, a painful certainty that I will never be able to do anything good or useful for the cause of Beauty. The only way of achieving Perfection is to be God. Any major effort takes time, and the time it takes travels through various states of our soul, and each of those states impresses its own particular personality on the individuality of the work. We can be certain of only one thing, that when we write, we write badly; the only great and perfect work is the one we never dream of creating.

Listen and pity yourself. Hear me out and then tell me if dreams are not worth more than life. Work never results in anything. Effort never gets us anywhere. Only abstention is noble and lofty, because it is an acknowledgement that any work we might produce is inevitably inferior, the physical article is always the grotesque shadow of the dreamed work.

If only I could write, in words on paper, if only the dialogues of the people in my imagined dramas could be read out loud and heard! Those dramas have perfect, flawless plots, faultless dialogues, but the plots are only sketches in my head and cannot be made real, nor is the substance of those intimate dialogues made of words exactly, words that could, if listened to attentively, be translated into writing.

I love certain lyric poets because they were not epic or dramatic poets, because they sensed, quite rightly, that they should never aim to fix in writing more than a moment of feeling or of dreaming. The more one writes unconsciously the closer one comes to possible perfection. No play by Shakespeare is as satisfying as a lyric poem by Heine. Heine's lyric poetry is perfect, and all dramas—whether by Shakespeare or someone else—are inevitably imperfect. To be able to build, to erect a Whole, to compose something like a human body, with a perfect correspondence between all its parts, with a unified, congruent life, unifying the diversity of each part!

You, who hear me and barely listen, you don't understand what a tragedy this is! To lose father and mother, to achieve neither glory nor happiness, to have neither a friend nor a lover—all those things are bearable. What cannot be borne is to dream a thing of beauty, but lack the skill to endow it with actions or words. The awareness that a work is perfect, the satisfaction of a work achieved—sweet is it to sleep beneath the shade of that tree, on a quiet summer's day ...

69 [1914?]

Kaleidoscope

I can find no meaning for myself ... Life weighs heavy ... Any emotion is too much for me ... Only God can know my heart ... Was I once so accustomed to stately processions that a kind of weariness with certain mysterious lost splendors now cradles any yearnings I may have for the past?

And what canopies? What sequences of stars? What lilies? What pennants? What stained-glass windows?

In what tree-shaded mystery did our finest fantasies occur, fantasies which, in the real world, are so reminiscent of streams and cypresses and box hedges, but find no canopies for their cortèges except by dint of abstaining?

Don't speak ... You are too real ... I regret being able to see you ... When will you be merely a nostalgia of mine? Until then how many you's will you be! And my thinking that I can see you is an old bridge that no one crosses ... That is what life is like. The others lay down their oars ... There is no discipline now among the troops. The knights left with the dawn and the sound of lances ... Your castles stood waiting to be deserted ... No wind abandoned the lines of trees on the hilltop ... Useless porticos, cutlery put away, predictions of prophesies—all that belongs to vanquished evenings in temples and not to our meeting now, because the only reason for the lime trees to give shade is your fingers and their belated gesture ...

More than enough reason for remote territories to exist ... Treaties signed by stained-glass kings ... Lilies from religious paintings ... For whom is the cortège waiting? ... Where did the lost eagle go?

70   [1914?]
I recognize today that I failed; the only thing that astonishes me sometimes is that I did not foresee that I would fail. Was there anything in me that promised victory? I lacked the blind strength of victors or the absolute vision of madmen ... I was as lucid and sad as a cold day.

Things that are very clear are comforting, as are the things illuminated by the sun. Watching life pass me by on a bright sunny day makes up for a lot. I forget endlessly, I forget more than I could remember. My translucent, airy heart is pierced by the sheer sufficiency of things, and it is enough for me to gaze on them fondly. I was never anything more than an incorporeal vision, with no soul apart from a vague breeze that came and then was gone.

I contain certain spiritual qualities appropriate in a bohemian, the kind of bohemian who allows life to pass by like something which, at some point, slips from his fingers or in whom even the merest gesture of reaching out to grasp life simply drops asleep at the mere thought of trying. However, I did not have the external compensation of the bohemian spirit—the easy idleness of instantly abandoned emotions. I was never more than an isolated bohemian, which is absurd, or a mystical bohemian, which is impossible.

Certain hours-*cum*-intervals I have lived through, hours spent contemplating Nature, sculpted out of the sweetness of isolation, will remain with me like medals. At such moments, I forgot any plans I might have for my life, any directions I might take. I enjoyed being nothing with all the plenitude of a spiritual calm that fell into the blue lap of my aspirations. Yet I have probably never experienced an indelible hour free from any spiritual undertow of failure and despair. In all my free hours, an ache always slumbered, almost blossomed, but the perfume and the actual color of those sad blossoms intuitively passed through the wall to the other side, and in the confused mystery of my being, that other-side, where the roses were blooming, was always the subdued this-side of my somnolent life.

The river of my life flowed into an inner sea. Around my dreamed estate all the trees wore autumn colors. That circular landscape is my soul's crown of thorns. The happiest moments of my life have been dreams, dreams of sadness, where I would gaze at myself in their lakes like a blind Narcissus enjoying the close coolness of the water, conscious that he was leaning over it, thanks to some earlier, nocturnal vision, whispered to his abstract emotions and stored away with an almost maternal care in the secret corners of his imagination ...

Your necklaces of fake pearls shared with me my finest hours and loved them too. Our favorite flowers were carnations, perhaps because they were more ordinary. Your lips soberly celebrated the irony of their own smile. Did you fully understand your destiny? It was because you knew it without understanding it that the mystery written in the sadness of your eyes cast such a shadow over your vanquished lips. Our homeland was too far away for roses. In the cascades of our gardens the water was pellucid with silences. In the small crevices between the stones, where the water chose to flow, lay childhood secrets, dreams the size of our tin soldiers, that could be placed on the stones of the waterfall, in static execution of some major military action, and our dreams lacked for nothing and nothing stopped the flow of our imaginings.

I know that I failed. I enjoy the indeterminate pleasure of failure like someone offering up exhausted thanks for a fever that keeps him cloistered in his room.

I had a certain talent for friendship, but I never had any friends, either because they never appeared, or because the friendship I had imagined was a mistake made by my dreams. I always lived an isolated life, which became more and more isolated the more I came to know myself.

71   [1914?]
Every gesture, however simple, represents a violation of a spiritual secret. Every gesture is a revolutionary act; an exile perhaps from the true […] of our aims.

   Action is a disease of thought, a cancer of the imagination. To act is to exile oneself. Every action is incomplete and imperfect. The poem that I dream is faultless until I try to write it down. This is written in the myth of Jesus, for God, when he becomes man, can end only in martyrdom. The supreme dreamer has as his son the supreme sacrifice.

The broken shadows of leaves, the tremulous song of birds, the outstretched arms of rivers, their cool light trembling in the sun, the greenness, the poppies, and the simplicity of sensation—when I feel all this, I experience a nostalgia for it as if I were not at that moment really feeling it.

Like a cart passing by in the evening, the hours return creaking home through the shadows of my thoughts. If I look up from those thoughts, the spectacle of the world burns my eyes.

To realize a dream it is necessary to forget it, to distract one's attention from it. That's why to realize something is not to realize it. Life is as full of paradoxes as roses are of thorns.

What I would like to create is the apotheosis of a new incoherence that could become the negative constitution of the new anarchy of souls. I have always thought it would be useful to humanity for me to compile a digest of my dreams. That's why I have constantly striven to do so. However, the idea that something I did could prove useful bruised me, silenced me.

I own country estates on the outskirts of Life. I spend my absences from the city of my Actions among the trees and flowers of my daydreams. Not even the faintest echo of the life led by my gestures reaches those green and pleasant retreats. My memory lulls me to sleep as if it were an endless procession marching past. From the chalices of my meditation I drink only the smile of the palest wine; I drink it with my eyes only, then close them, and life passes me by like a distant candle.

To me, sunny days savor of all I do not have. The blue sky and the white clouds, the trees, the flute that does not play there—eclogues interrupted by the trembling of branches ... All this and the silent harp whose strings I lightly brush.

The vegetal academy of silences ... your name ringing out like the poppies ... the pools ... my return ... the crazy priest who went mad during mass. These memories come from my dreams ... I do not close my eyes, but I can see nothing ... The things I can see are not here ... The algae ...

In a tangled way, the green of the trees is part of my blood. Inside me life beats in some distant heart ... I was not meant for reality, it was life that sought me out.

The torment of destiny! I might die tomorrow! Something terrible might befall my soul today! Sometimes, when I think about these things, I feel a kind of horror at the superior tyranny that obliges us to keep walking even though we have no idea what it is that our uncertainty is going to meet.

72 [1914?]

Practical life always seemed to me to be the least comfortable of suicides. As far as I was concerned, to act was always tantamount to condemning an unjustly condemned dream. To have influence in the outside world, to change things, to transform other beings, to influence people, always seemed to me even more nebulous than my daydreams. Seeing the immanent futility of all forms of action was, from childhood on, one of my favorite means of detaching myself even from myself.

To act is to react against yourself. To influence others is to leave home. I always considered how absurd it was that, since actual reality is a mere series of sensations, there should exist such complicatedly simple things as commerce, industry, social and family relationships, so desolatingly incomprehensible when faced by the inner attitude of the soul to the idea of truth.

73 [1914?]

One day
(Zigzag)

I so regret never having been the Madame of a harem!

At the end of this day there remains what was left behind of yesterday and what will be left behind of tomorrow: the insatiable, innumerable longing to be always the same and always other.

Descend the steps of my dreams and my tedium, descend from your unreality, descend and take the place of the world.

74 [1914?]
Absurd

Let us make ourselves into sphinxes, albeit pretend ones, until we reach the point where we no longer know what we are, because the truth is that we *are* pretend sphinxes and we really do not know what we are. The only way we can be in accord with life is to be in disaccord with ourselves. The absurd is the divine.

Let us create theories and think them through patiently and honestly, only to contradict them by our actions, and to justify those actions with theories that condemn our earlier theories … Let us carve out a path in life and then immediately take another contrary path. Let us adopt all the gestures and all the attitudes of something that we neither are nor want to be, nor even want to be thought to be.

Let us buy books in order not to read them, let us go to concerts neither to hear music nor to see who else is there; let us go for long walks because we hate walking and spend days in the countryside only because we loathe the countryside.

75 [1914]
Imperial Legend

My Imagination is a city in the Orient. Its composition in real space has the voluptuous feel of a soft, lavish rug. The crowds that multicolor its streets stand out against some kind of backdrop which is not somehow theirs, as if they were embroidered in yellow or red on the palest of blue satins. All the previous history of this city flutters around the lamp of my dream like a moth barely heard in the penumbra of the soul listening to it. My fantasy once lived among great splendor and magnificence and, from the hands of queens, received jewels veiled in antiquity. The sands of my nonexistence were carpeted in intimate softnesses, and clouds of algae floated in my rivers like shadowy exhalations. Thus was I porticos in lost civilizations, febrile arabesques on dead friezes, ancient black stains on the curves of broken columns, solitary masts on remote shipwrecks, the steps up to vanished thrones, veils veiling nothing, only shadows, ghosts rising up like smoke from censers dashed to the ground. My kingdom was a grim and bitter one full of wars on the frontiers far from the imperial peace of my palace. Always near, though, was the hesitant noise of distant celebrations, endless processions passing beneath my windows; but no dark goldfish swam in my ponds, no fruit grew among the still greenness of my orchards; not even the smoke from the chimneys of poor shacks where others live happily could lull to sleep with simple ballads the troubled mystery of my soul.

76 [1914?]

Every day the material world mistreats me. My sensibility is like a flame in the wind.

I walk down a road and I see in the faces of the passersby not their real expressions, but the expressions they would wear if they knew about my life and how I am, if the ridiculous, timid abnormality of my soul were made transparent in my gestures and in my face. In the eyes that avoid mine I suspect a mockery I find only natural, aimed at the inelegant exception I represent in a world that takes pleasure in things and in activity, and, in the supposed depths of these passing physiognomies, I imagine and interpose an awareness of the timid nature of my life that prompts guffaws of laughter. After thinking this, I try in vain to convince myself that I alone am the source of this idea of other people's mockery and mild opprobrium. But once objectified in others, I can no longer reclaim the image of myself as a figure of fun. I feel myself grow suddenly vague and hesitant in a hothouse rife with ridicule and animosity. From the depths of their soul, everyone points a finger at me. Everyone who passes stones me with merry, scornful insolence. I walk among enemy ghosts that my sick imagination has conjured up and planted inside real people. Everything jabs and jeers at me.

And sometimes, in the middle of the road—unobserved, after all—I stop and hesitate, seeking a sudden new dimension, a door onto the interior of space, onto the other side of space, where without delay I might flee my awareness of other people, my too-objective intuition of the reality of other people's living souls.

Is it that my habit of placing myself in the souls of other people makes me see myself as others see or would see me if they noticed my presence there? It is. And once I've perceived what they would feel about me if they knew me, it is as if they were feeling and expressing it at that very moment. It is a torture to me to live with other people. Then there are those who live inside me. Even when removed from life, I'm forced to live with them. Alone, I am hemmed in by multitudes. I have nowhere to flee to, unless I were to flee myself.

Ah, tall, twilight mountains, almost-narrow moonlit streets, if only I enjoyed your lack of awareness of the […] your spiritual vision of the material world, with no inner life, devoid of sensibility, with no room for feelings or thoughts or disquiet! Trees, never anything more than trees, with your green leaves so pleasant to the eyes, you are so indifferent to my cares and griefs, so consoling to my anguish because you lack eyes to see it or a soul to look through those eyes, to misunderstand and mock! Stones on the road, decapitated trees, the mere anonymous soil of the earth, your insensitivity to my soul is like a sisterly caress, a balm … Beneath the sun or beneath the moon of the Earth, my mother, so tenderly maternal, because you cannot criticize me, as my own human mother can, because you do not have a soul with which unwittingly to analyze me, nor can you shoot me rapid glances that provoke thoughts about me you would not confess even to yourself. Vast sea, my clamorous childhood companion, you bring me peace and cradle me because you have no human voice and will not one day whisper into other human ears of my weaknesses and imperfections. Vast sky, blue sky, so close to the mystery of the angels […] you do not look at me with envious eyes, and when you pin the sun on your breast, you do not do so to attract me nor [...] nor don a mask of stars in order to make fun of me ... Immense peace of nature, so maternal in your utter ignorance of me; distant quiet of atoms and systems, so fraternal in your utter inability ever to know me ... I would like to pray to your vastness and your calm, as an expression of my gratitude for having you and being able to love without suspicion or doubt; I would Iike to give ears to your not-hearing, eyes to your sublime blindness, and to be seen and heard by you through those imagined eyes and ears, glad to be present at your Nothingness, attentive to what is distant, as if to a definitive death, clinging to no hopes of any other life beyond a God, beyond the possibility of growing into a voluptuous nothing and taking on the spiritual color of all matter.

77 [1914?]

Where is God, even if he doesn't exist? I want to pray and weep, to repent of crimes I did not commit, to enjoy being forgiven as if it were a not-quite-maternal caress.

A lap in which to weep, but a vast, formless lap, capacious as a summer night, and yet close, warm and feminine, next to a hearth somewhere ... To weep over unthinkable faults whose precise nature I do not even know, tender feelings for things nonexistent, and terrifying doubts about some unknown future ...

A new childhood, an old nursemaid, and a small bed where I could fall asleep to stories barely heard, but listened to with rapt attention, dangers that penetrated my young hair, golden as corn ... And to have all this on a grand, eternal scale, definitive, the size of God, there in the sad, somnolent depths of the ultimate reality of Things ...

A lap or a cradle or a warm arm about my neck ... A voice singing softly as if to move me to tears ... The fire crackling in the hearth ... Warmth in winter ... My gently drifting consciousness ... And then, soundlessly, a gentle sleep in an enormous space, like the moon rolling past the stars ...

When I set aside my artifices and carefully, fondly—wishing I could cover them in kisses—tidy my toys away in one corner, my words, my images and phrases—I feel so small and inoffensive, so alone in that huge, sad room, so profoundly sad! …

After all, who am I when I'm not playing? A poor orphan abandoned in the Street of Sensations, shivering with cold on the windy corners of Reality, having to sleep on the steps of Sadness and eat the bread provided by Fantasy. I know my father's name; I was told he was called God, but the name means nothing to me. Sometimes, at night, when I'm feeling very alone, I call to him and weep, and I imagine him as someone I could love … But then I think to myself that I don't even know him, that perhaps he isn't like that at all, that he will perhaps never be the father of my soul …

When will all this end, these streets along which I trail my misery, and these steps where I sit huddled against the cold, feeling through my ragged clothes the touch of the night's icy hands? … If only one day God would come and find me and take me to his house and provide me with warmth and affection … When I think this, I weep with joy just to think that I can think it … But the wind whips along the street and the leaves fall on the pavement … I look up and see the stars in all their meaninglessness … And all that remains is me, a poor abandoned child, whom no Love wanted as an adopted son, and no Friendship chose as a playmate.

I am so cold. I am so weary of my abandoned state. Wind, go and find my Mother, carry me off in the Night to the house I never knew … O vast Silence, restore to me nursemaid and cradle and lullaby …

78   [1914?]
Letter
If only you could accept the idea that your duty is to be merely the dream of a dreamer. To be a censer in the cathedral of your daydreams. To shape your gestures as if they were dreams, so that they were windows opening onto new landscapes in your soul. To

design a kind of dream-body, so that anyone seeing you would be unable to think of anything else, so that you would remind them of anyone or anything but you, so that seeing you would be like hearing music and sleepwalking through vast landscapes of dead lakes, vague, silent forests lost in the depths of other ages, where diverse invisible people experience feelings we do not have.

I would want you only so as not to have you. Were I dreaming, and were you to appear, I would want to be able to imagine that I was still dreaming, perhaps not even seeing you, perhaps not even noticing that the dead lakes were filled with moonlight and that the echoes of songs were suddenly wafting through that vast, inexplicit forest, lost in impossible epochs.

The vision of you would be the bed on which my soul could fall asleep, like a sick child, in order to dream again of another sky. And what if you were to speak? Then hearing you would be not to hear you, but to see in the moonlight huge bridges linking the two dark banks of the river that flows down to the ancient sea, where the caravels are eternally new.

79 [1914?]

Letter? Conclusion

And if I chance to speak to someone far away, and if you, who are today a cloud of the possible, should tomorrow fall as real rain on the earth, never forget your divine origins as a dream of mine. Always be something that could be the dream of someone lonely and never a refuge for a beloved. Make of your duty an empty vessel. Fulfilll your calling as a superfluous amphora. Let no one say of you what the soul of the river might say to its banks, which exist only to constrain it. Better not to flow through life at all, better to let your dreaming dry up completely.

Let your genius lie in being superfluous, and let your life be the art of looking at life, of being the look, the never-the-same. Never ever be anything more than that.

Today you are merely the profile created out of this book, an hour made flesh and quite separate from the other hours. If I were certain this was what you were, I would build a religion around the dream of loving you.

You are what everything lacks. You are what everything requires for us to be able to love it always. The lost key to the gates of the Temple, the secret path to the Palace, the distant Island always swathed in mist and never seen …

80 [1914?]
A Letter

For an unknown number of many months you have seen me looking at you, looking at you constantly, always in the same hesitant, solicitous way. I know you have noticed. And since you have, you must have found it odd that my gaze, which is not exactly timid, never carries any meaning. Always attentive, vague and the same, as if contented to be merely the sadness of that meaninglessness … Nothing more … And inside your thoughts about this—whatever feeling you might have felt when you thought of me—you must have pondered my possible intentions. You must have thought to yourself, without feeling entirely satisfied with your explanation, that I must be either a very shy man of a most unusual and original type or something that came very close to madness.

As regards my looking at you, Madam, I am, strictly speaking, neither a shy man, nor totally mad. I am something else quite different as I am about to explain, without much hope of you actually believing me.

How often have I whispered to your dreamed self: Make of your duty a useless amphora, fufil your calling of being a mere empty vessel.

How nostalgic I felt for the false idea I wanted to have of you when, one day, I realized you were married! The day I found this out was a tragedy in my life. I wasn't jealous of your husband. It didn't occur to me that you had one. I simply missed my idea of you. My pain would be just as great if, one day, I were to discover the absurd fact that a woman in a painting—yes, in a painting—were married. Did I want to possess you? I don't even know how to set about possessing someone. And even if I bore the human stain of knowing this, what a disgrace I would be to myself, what a rank insult to my own greatness, even to think of putting myself on the same level as your husband!

Possess you? One day when you are walking alone down a dark street, an assailant might overpower you and possess you, might impregnate you and even leave behind him some uterine trace. But if possessing you means possessing your body, what is the value of that?

He would not have possessed your soul, you say? But how can anyone possess a soul? And if some skilful lover—your husband, say—should succeed in possessing that "soul," would I want to descend to his level?

How many hours have I spent in secret communion with my idea of you? How we have loved each other in my dreams! But even there, I swear, I never dreamed of possessing you. I am delicate and chaste even in my dreams. I am even respectful of the dream of a beautiful woman.

81 [1914?]

[Advice to unhappily married women?]

My dear disciples, in accordance with my own advice, I wish you infinite, redoubled pleasures not with, but through, the male animal to which the Church or the State has bound you by the womb or by your last name.

It is by pressing its feet hard against the earth that a bird takes flight. Let that image, my daughters, be a perpetual reminder of the only spiritual commandment that matters.

Be a cocotte, revelling in every kind of vice, without betraying your husband with so much as a look—think how pleasurable that would be if you could achieve it.

Be a cocotte *inside*, betray your husband from *inside*, betray him when you embrace him, in the kisses you give him while thinking of someone else—O superior women, O my mysterious Cerebral followers—therein lies true pleasure. Why do I not give the same advice to men? Because Man is a different kind of being. If he is of the inferior sort, I advise him to have as many women as he can: do this and enjoy my scorn when [...] The superior man has no need of any woman. He does not need to possess someone sexually in order to experience pleasure. Now women, even superior women, cannot accept this, for woman is a fundamentally sexual creature.

82 [1915?]

I look for myself but find no one. I belong to the chrysanthemum hour of bright flowers placed in tall vases. God made of my soul an ornament.

I do not know which particular magnificent details I would choose to define the essence of my spirit. Doubtless I love the decorative because I sense in it something identical to the substance of my own soul.

83* [1915?]

All I've ever done is dream. That, and only that, has been the meaning of my existence. The only thing I've ever really cared about is my inner scenario. My greatest griefs fade to nothing the moment I open the window onto my daydreams and lose myself in watching.

I never tried to be anything other than a dreamer. I never paid any attention to people who told me to go out and live. I belonged always to whatever was far from me and to whatever I could never be. To me, anything that was not mine, however base, always seemed full of poetry. The only thing I ever loved was pure nothingness. I

---

* This passage bears a note in English: "(our childhood's playing with cotton reels, etc.)."

only ever desired what was beyond my imaginings. All I ever asked of life was that it should pass me by without my even noticing it. Of love I demanded only that it never be anything more than a distant dream. In my own inner landscapes, all of them unreal, it was always the faraway that attracted me, and the blurred outlines of aqueducts, almost lost in the distance of my dream landscapes, imposed a dreamy sweetness on other parts of the landscapes, a sweetness that enabled me to love them.

My mania for creating a false world is still with me and will leave me only when I die. I no longer line up in my desk drawers cotton reels and pawns—with the occasional bishop and knight thrown in—but I regret not doing so ... and instead, like someone in winter, cozily warming himself by the fire, I line up in my imagination the ranks of constant, living characters who inhabit my inner world. For I have a whole world of friends inside me, each with his or her own real, definite, imperfect life.

Some go through hard times, others lead bohemian lives, picturesque and humble. Others are traveling salesmen (dreaming of being a traveling salesman was always one of my greatest ambitions—unfortunately never realized!). Others live in villages and towns near the frontier of a Portugal that I carry within me; they come to the city where I chance to meet and recognize them, warmly embracing them ... And when I'm dreaming all this, pacing up and down in my room, talking out loud, gesticulating ... when I dream this and imagine myself meeting them, I'm filled with happiness, I feel complete, I leap for joy, my eyes shine, I open my arms to them and feel an immense, inexpressible happiness.

Ah, there is no more painful longing than the longing for things that never were! What I feel when I think of the past I lived in real time, when I weep over the corpse of my lost childhood ... even this does not compare with the painful, tremulous fervor with which I weep for the unreality of the humble figures who people my dreams, even certain minor characters I can recall having glimpsed only once, by chance, in my false life, as they turned a corner in my imaginary scenario, entering a door on a street I had walked along during that dream.

The anger I feel knowing that pure longing is incapable of reviving and resurrecting the past is never more tearfully vented against the God who created these impossibilities than when I consider that my dream friends, with whom I have shared so many details of my imagined life, with whom I have enjoyed so many brilliant conversations in imagined cafés, have never had a space of their own where they could be truly independent of my consciousness of them! Ah, the dead past that I carry with me and that never existed except in me! The flowers in the garden of the small country house that existed only inside me! The vegetable gardens, the orchards and the pine forest of the estate that was merely one of my dreams! The imaginary summer resorts, my walks through a countryside that never was! The trees by the side of the road, the country paths, the stones, the peasants passing by ... all this, which was never more than a dream, is shut away in my memory where it lies aching, and I, who spent hours dreaming it all, spend as many hours afterwards remembering having dreamed it, and then I feel a genuine nostalgia, I weep for a real past, a real life that is dead and that I stare at solemnly as it lies in its coffin.

Then there are the landscapes and the lives that were not purely interior. For example, after spending many hours in the company of certain pictures or lithographs (none of any great artistic merit) that hung on the walls of certain rooms, those pictures became part of my inner reality. The pain I felt then was different, sharper and sadder, regardless of whether the scene was real or not. I suffered not to be included in the small engraving in a room I never in fact slept in when I was younger, I suffered not to be, at the very least, an additional figure sketched in at the edge of the moonlit wood. It pained me not to be able to imagine myself hidden there, in the wood by the river, in that eternal (albeit ill-drawn) moonlight, watching the man pass by in a boat beneath the drooping branches of a willow. I felt hurt by my inability to dream it all. My nostalgia took on other characteristics. My despairing gestures were different. The impossibility that tortured me produced quite a different order of anguish. If only this could find some meaning in God, some realization suited to the spirit of our desires, quite where I don't know, perhaps in some sort of vertical time, consubstantiate with the aims of all my longings and daydreams. If only I could have my own personal paradise tailormade for this purpose. If only I could meet the friends I dreamed, or walk along the streets I created, or wake up to the sounds of cockerels and chickens and the morning noises of the house, the country house I imagined myself in … and have all of this even more perfectly arranged by God and placed by him in perfect order to exist purely for my benefit in that precise form, unattainable even in my dreams, lacking only the dimension of inner space occupied by those poor realities.

I look up from the paper I'm writing on … It's still early, just gone midday, and it's Sunday. The sickness of life, the affliction of consciousness, enter my body and trouble me. Why are there not islands for those who feel uncomfortable here, ancient avenues for the lonely to dream in and that others cannot find? Having to live and, however feebly, to act; being bruised by the fact that in life there are other people, who are themselves real. Having to be here writing this, because my soul demands it, and being unable simply to dream it, to express it without words, even without consciousness, through some self I could construct out of music and evanescence, and for my eyes to fill with tears just to feel that expression of myself, and to feel myself flow, like an enchanted river, past the slow banks of my own self, ever closer to the unconscious and the Distant, with no meaning or direction except God.

84   [c. 7 Jan 1915]
When I was a child I used to play with trams … I loved them with a painful love—how well I remember it!—and was filled with compassion for them because they were not real …

And my joy when, one day, I got my hands on the remnants of a chess set! I immediately gave each piece a name and they became part of my dream world.

They all became distinctive figures, each with its individual life. One—to whom I had given an impetuous, sporty character—lived in a box on top of my chest of drawers, where, in the afternoon when I, and thus he, came back from school, he would travel in a tram made out of matchboxes, somehow tied together with wire. He always jumped out while the tram was moving. Ah, my dead childhood! A corpse ever alive in my breast! When I remember the toys I played with as an already full-grown child, my eyes fill with hot tears, and I am pierced by an intense, futile longing, rather like remorse. That is all gone now and remains in my past, dead and stiff, visible or visualizable, in my perpetual idea of my bedroom at the time, around my unvisualizable self as a child, seen from inside, who went from the chest of drawers to the dressing table and from the dressing table to the bed, driving that rudimentary tram through the air, imagining it to be part of the real tram company, bearing my ridiculous wooden pupils home.

To some I attributed certain vices—smoking or thieving—but since I am not myself a sexual being, I did not attribute any actions to them, apart perhaps from a predilection, which I thought merely playful, for kissing girls and trying to catch a glimpse of their legs. I would have my pupils hide behind a big box on top of a trunk where they would "smoke" a bit of rolled-up paper. Sometimes a teacher would come along. And feeling every bit as alarmed as they, for I felt obliged to feel what they felt, I would immediately hide the fake cigarette and place the smoker on the corner, looking suspiciously idle, waiting for the teacher and then greeting him, I don't remember exactly how, when he inevitably walked past … Sometimes the two figures were too far apart, and I could not, one-handed, manoeuvre them both. I would then have to move each in turn, which hurt me just as today it hurts me not to be able to give expression to a life … But why am I remembering all this? Why did I not remain for ever a child? Why did I not die there and then, caught up in my pupils' tricks and in the as-if-unexpected arrival of my teachers? I can't do that now … Today I have only reality, and I cannot play with that … Poor child exiled in his manhood! Why did I have to grow up?

Today, when I remember this, I'm filled with a nostalgia for other things too. More things have died in me than just my past.

85   [1915?]

The only way to experience new sensations is to build yourself a new soul. All your efforts will be in vain if you want to feel other things without yourself feeling in a different way, and to do so without a change of soul. Because things are as we feel them—how long have you thought you knew this without actually knowing it?—and the only way to have new things, to feel new things, is to find a new way of feeling them.

Change your soul. But how? That is for you to work out.

From the day we are born until the day we die, we are slowly changing souls, and it's the same with our body. Find a way to make that change more rapid, as rapid as the change in our body when we are ill or convalescing.

86   [1915?]

Advice to unhappily married women

I propose teaching you how to deceive your husband, but purely in your imagination.

Believe me, only vulgar creatures actually do deceive their husbands. Modesty is an essential condition of sexual pleasure. Giving yourself to more than one man is the death of modesty.

I concede that a woman's inferiority means that she does require a man. However, I believe that she should limit herself to just one, but make of him, if she needs to, the center of an expanding circle of imaginary men.

The best time to do this is in the days preceding menstruation.

So:

Imagine your husband's body as being whiter than usual. If you imagine successfully, you will experience the body lying on top of you as actually being whiter.

Refrain from being overly sensual. Kiss the husband lying on top of you and exchange him in your imagination for the handsome man lying on top of your soul.

The essence of pleasure lies in splitting yourself into more than one person. Open the window to the Feline in you.

How to annoy your husband.

It's important that your husband should, on occasion, get angry.

First, begin to feel attracted by things that repel you, without losing any of your outer discipline.

Great inner indiscipline combined with great outer discipline results in the perfect degree of sensuality. Any gesture that realizes a dream or a desire actually de-realizes it.

Substitution is not as difficult as you might think. By substitution, I mean the practice of imagining yourself being pleasured by man A while copulating with man B.

87 [1915?]

Letter

I would never know how to cajole my soul into persuading my body to possess yours. Even the thought of it makes me stumble over invisible obstacles inside me, to become entangled in unrecognizable webs. What else might happen to me if I really wanted to possess you?

I repeat that I would be incapable of trying. I cannot even make myself dream of doing it.

These, Madam, are the words I have to write in the margin of the meaning of your involuntarily interrogative glance. It is in this book that you will first read this letter to you. If you fail to understand that it is addressed to you, I will resign myself to that fact. I write more to amuse myself than to tell you anything. Only business letters are *addressed* to someone. All other letters should, at least in the case of the superior man, be written only for himself.

I have nothing more to say to you. Believe me when I say that I admire you as much as I am capable of admiring anyone. It would please me if you were to think of me occasionally.

88 [1915?]

My self-imposed exclusion from the aims and directions of life, my self-imposed rupture with any contact with things, led me precisely to what I was trying to flee. I did not want to feel life or touch things, knowing from previous occasions on which my temperament had come into contact with the world that the sensation of living was always painful to me. However, in avoiding that contact, I isolated myself and, in isolating myself, I exacerbated my already excessive sensibility, for which the best thing, were it possible, would be to end all contact with anything. Such total isolation, though, is impossible. However little I do, I still breathe; however little there is to do, I still move. And thus, with my sensibility heightened by isolation, I find that the tiniest things, which before would have had no effect even on me, buffet and bruise me like the worst of catastrophes. I chose the wrong means of escape. I took an awkward short cut that led me right back to where I was, compounding the horror of living there with the exhaustion of the journey.

I never considered suicide a solution, because I only hate life out of love for it. It took me a long time to be convinced of the lamentable error in which I live with myself. Once convinced, I felt displeased, as always happens when I convince myself of something, because it means the loss of another of my illusions.

By analyzing my will, I killed it. What I would give to go back to my childhood before I learned how to analyze, even to the time before I had a will!

A heavy sleep fills my gardens, pools lie somnolent beneath the noonday sun, the noise of insects throngs the hour and life weighs on me, not like a grief, but like an unending physical ache.

Distant palaces, dreaming parks, the narrow lines of avenues far off, the graveyard grace of the stone benches built for those who once were—dead splendors, ruined elegance, lost baubles. Sweet longing sliding slowly into forgetting, if only I could recover the pain with which I dreamed you.

89 [1915?]

The label that best defines my spirit today is that of creator of indifferences. More than anything else I would like my role in the world to be to educate others to feel more and more for themselves and less and less according to the dynamic law of the collectivity. To educate others in that spiritual asceticism, which would preclude the contagion of vulgarity, seems to me the highest destiny of the teacher of the inner life that I would like to be. That all those who read me should learn—little by little, as the subject demands—to feel utter indifference before the critical gaze and opinions of others, such a destiny would be reward enough for the scholastic stagnation of my life.

In me, the inability to act was always an affliction that had its origins in metaphysics. According to my way of experiencing things, any gesture always implied a perturbation, a fragmentation, of the external world; I always feared that any movement on my part would dislodge the stars or alter the skies. That's why the metaphysical importance of even the smallest gesture rapidly took on an extraordinary importance for me. I acquired, with regard to action, a transcendental honesty which, ever since I became aware of it, has inhibited me from having any strong links with the tangible world.

90

Wasting time has its own aesthetic. For those subtle connoisseurs of sensations, there is a kind of handbook on inertia, which includes recipes for every kind of lucidity. The strategy with which one battles with the notion of social proprieties, with the impulses of the instincts, with the demands of sentiment, calls for a study that not all aesthetes would be prepared to take on. A painstaking aetiology of scruples would have to be followed by an ironic diagnosis of our subservience to normality. We would also need to cultivate a certain nimbleness in the face of life's intrusions; a degree of caution should armor us against other people's opinions; a mild indifference should protect our soul from the dull blows inflicted by our unavoidable coexistence with other people.

91

The Sensationist

In this twilight age of all the disciplines, in which beliefs are dying and religions are gradually gathering dust, our sensations are the only reality left to us. The only scruple that need concern us, the only satisfactory science, is that of sensations.

I am more and more convinced that an inner decorativism is the superior, enlightened way of giving our lives a destiny. If I could live my life swathed in spiritual lace, I would have no gaping chasms of despair to complain about.

I belong to a generation—or, rather, to part of a generation—that has lost all respect for the past and all belief or hope in the future. This is why we live in the present with the desperate hunger of someone who has no other home. And since it is in our sensations—futile, frivolous sensations—especially in our dreams, that we find a present that reminds us neither of the past nor the future, we smile at our inner life and, with a haughty somnolence, detach ourselves from the quantitative reality of things.

We are not so very different perhaps from those who, throughout their lives, think only of having fun. However, the sun of our self-serving egotism is about to set, and our hedonism, bathed in contradictory, twilight colors, is growing cold.

We are convalescing. We are, in general, creatures who have never learned an art or a skill, not even that of enjoying life. Strangers to any long-term relationships, we tend to grow bored with our closest friends after having been with them for half an hour; we only long to see them when we think about seeing them, and the best times we spend with them are those when we are only dreaming we are with them. I don't know if this is evidence of little friendship on my part. Perhaps not. The truth is, though, that the things we love most, or think we love, only have their full value when we merely dream them.

We dislike shows or spectacles. We despise actors and dancers. Any such spectacle is nothing but a debased imitation of what we could dream.

Indifferent to other people's opinions—not right from the start, but through an education of the feelings imposed on us by various painful experiences—always polite to others, even genuinely liking them, through a form of self-interested indifference, because everyone is potentially interesting and convertible into dream material, into other people ...

Lacking the ability to love, we grow weary, even before they are spoken, of the words we would have to say in order to be loved. Besides, which of us wants to be loved? Chateaubriand's words "*on le fatiguait en l'aimant*" are not appropriate for us. The very idea of being loved wearies us to the point of alarm.

My life is a continual fever, a never-quenched thirst. I find real life as oppressive as a very hot day. There's something rather humiliating about that.

92 [1915?]

Man should not be able to see his own face. Nothing is more terrible than that. Nature gave him the gift of being unable either to see his face or to look into his own eyes.

He could only see his own face in the waters of rivers and lakes. Even the posture he had to adopt to do so was symbolic. He had to bend down, to lower himself, in order to commit the ignominy of seeing his own face.

The creator of the mirror poisoned the human soul.

93 [1915?]

In Amiel's diary, I always read with displeasure any references to the books he published. There the idol shattered. If it were not for that, what a great man!

Amiel's diary has always wounded me personally.

When I reached the point where he says that Scherer described the fruit of the mind as being "the consciousness of consciousness," I felt he was alluding directly to my own soul.

94 [1915?]

It will seem to many people that this diary of mine, written solely for myself, is too artificial. But it is in my nature to be artificial. How else should I amuse myself if not by carefully writing down these spiritual notes? Not that I do take much care over them. Indeed, I put them together with a polished lack of care. This refined language is the natural way in which I think.

I am a man for whom the external world is an internal reality. I do not feel this metaphysically, but with the usual senses with which I grasp reality.

Yesterday's frivolity is today a (constant) yearning gnawing at my life. .

This moment has its own cloisters. The sun has set on all our petty evasions. In the blue eyes of the ponds a final despair reflects the death of the sun. We were so much a part of the old gardens, so voluptuously incorporated into the presence of the statues lining the neat English avenues of trees. The dresses, the swords, the wigs, the bowings and scrapings were so bound up with the substance of which our spirit is made! Who is that "we"? Only the deserted garden and the fountain, its winged water flying lower now in its sad attempts at flight.

95 [1915?]

I experience time as a terrible ache. I get ridiculously upset whenever I have to leave anything: the miserable little rented room where I spent a few months, the table in the provincial hotel at which I dined on each of my six days there, even the waiting room at the railway station where I wasted two hours waiting for the train. But the good things of life hurt me metaphysically when I have to leave them, knowing, with all the sensitivity my nerves can muster, that I will never see or have them again, at least not as they are in that exact, precise moment. An abyss yawns open in my soul and a cold blast from the hour of God brushes my pale face.

Time! The past! There, something, a voice, a song, a sudden scent on the air, lifts the veil from my memories ... What I was and will never be again! What I had and will never have again! The dead! The dead who loved me when I was a child. When I remember them, my whole soul grows cold and I feel myself to be an exile from every heart, alone in the night of my own self, crying like a beggar at the closed silence of every door.

96 [1915?]

Two or three days of feeling something like the beginnings of love ...

All these things are useful to the aesthete because of the sensations they arouse in him. To go any farther would be to enter that domain where jealousy, suffering and arousal begin. In this antechamber of emotion, there is all the gentleness of love without its depths—there is, though, a shiver of pleasure, the vague aroma of desire, and while one loses the grandeur inherent in the tragedy of love, note that, for the aesthete, tragedies are interesting to observe, but uncomfortable to experience. The cultivation of the imagination is hindered by the cultivation of life. It is the uncommon man who rules.

Now I would be perfectly contented with this if I could persuade myself that this theory is not what it is, a complicated din I make in the ears of my own intelligence so that it will not notice that, deep down, when it comes to living, there is only my timidity and my incompetence.

97 [1915?]

An aesthetics of despair

Since we cannot extract beauty from life, let us at least extract beauty from our inability to extract beauty from life. Let us make of our failure a victory, something proud and positive, complete with pillars, majesty and spiritual acquiescence.

If life has given us only a prison cell, let us at least adorn it with the shadows of our dreams, with brightly colored drawings to leave a record of our oblivion on the stony stillness of its walls.

Like all dreamers, I always felt my calling was to create. Since I was never capable of actually making an effort or carrying out an intention, creating has always been the same thing to me as dreaming, wanting or desiring, and making in dreams the gestures I would like to have made.

98 [1915?]

Ethics of Despair

To be published = the socialization of the self. What a base necessity! And yet it is still quite removed from being an action, since it is the publisher who profits, and the typographer who produces the book ... At least it has the merit of incoherence.

One of man's greatest preoccupations, once he has reached the age of reason, is to make himself, as a thinking, acting being, in the image of his ideal. Since inertia is the ideal that best embodies the logic of our aristocratic soul's response to the hustle and bustle of modern life, the Inert, the Inactive, should, therefore, be our Ideal. A futile project? Possibly. But that will only worry those who are drawn to futility.

99 [1915?]

An aesthetics of abdication

To conform is to submit and to win is to conform, to be beaten. That is why all victories are essentially vulgar. Winners lose the feeling of despair with the present that originally led them into the battle that gave them victory. They feel satisfied, and satisfaction is felt only by someone who conforms, and who does not have the mentality of a winner. The true winner never wins anything. The truly strong are those who live in a permanent state of dismay. The finest and noblest thing is to abdicate. The supreme empire belongs to the Emperor who abdicates from all normal life, from other men, and on whom the cares of state do not weigh like a sack of jewels.

100 [1915?]

I cultivate a loathing for action as carefully as if it were a hothouse flower. I boast to myself about my dissidence from life.

101 [1915?]

"Feeling is such a bore." Those chance words spoken by someone during a brief conversation have always lain gleaming on the floor of my memory. The plebeian nature of the phrase lends it savor.

102 [1915?]

Even my dreams punish me. I have achieved such a degree of lucidity in them that I perceive as real everything I dream, and so everything I dream thereby loses all value.

If I dream of being famous I experience all the nakedness that comes with glory, the loss of privacy and anonymity that makes fame so painful to us.

103 [1915?]

Faith is the instinct for action.

104 [1915?]

Enthusiasm is sheer vulgarity.

The expression of enthusiasm is, more than anything, a violation of the rights of our insincerity.

We never know when we are being sincere. Perhaps we never are. And even if we are sincere today, tomorrow we might be sincere about something else entirely different.

I have never had convictions. I have always had impressions. I could never hate any place where I had seen a scandalous sunset.

To externalize impressions is more a way of persuading ourselves that we have them rather than actually having them.

105 [1915?]

Believing that each step of my life would mean contact with the horror of the New and that each new person I met was a new and living fragment of the unknown to be placed before me on the table for my daily horrified contemplation, I decided to abstain from everything, to go nowhere, to reduce action to the minimum, to avoid as far as possible meeting either men or events, to perfect abstinence and take abdication to new heights. That's how much living frightens and torments me.

Coming to a decision, ending something, finally leaving the doubt and the darkness behind, are things that seem catastrophic to me, like universal cataclysms.

That is how I experience life, as apocalypse and cataclysm. Each day brings an increasing inability in myself to make the smallest gesture, even to imagine myself confronting clear, real situations. The presence of others—always such an unexpected event for the soul—grows daily more painful and distressing. Talking to others makes me shudder. If they show any interest in me, I flee. If they look at me, I tremble. If [...]

I am constantly on the defensive. Life and other people bruise me. I can't look reality in the eye. The sun itself leaves me feeling discouraged and desolate. Only at night, by myself, alone, forgotten and lost—with no links with reality, no need to participate in anything useful—only then can I find and comfort myself.

Life chills me. My existence is all damp caves and dark catacombs. I am the great defeat of the final army that sustained the final empire. I taste of the fall of some ancient master civilization. I am alone and abandoned, I who was accustomed to give orders to others. I am without a friend, without a guide, I whose path was always smoothed by others.

Something in me pleads eternally for compassion and weeps over itself as over a dead god stripped of all his altars, when the pale coming of the barbarians dawned at the frontiers and life came to call the empire to account, to ask what it had done with happiness.

I'm always afraid people will talk about me. I've failed in everything. I've never even dared think of making something of myself; I've never even dreamed of thinking of desiring something because, in my own dreams, even in my visionary state of mere dreamer, I recognized that I was unsuited for life.

Not one feeling could make me raise my head from the pillow in which I bury it because I can't cope with my body nor with the idea that I'm alive, nor even with the absolute idea of life itself.

I don't speak the language of reality. I totter about among the things of life like a long-bedridden patient getting up for the first time. I only feel part of normal life when I'm in bed. I feel pleased when I succumb to a fever because it seems appropriate and natural [...] to my recumbent state. Like a flame in the wind I stutter and grow faint. Only in the dead air of closed rooms do I breathe the normality of my life.

Nothing remains of the shells I found by the shores of seas, not even a faint nostalgia. I resigned myself to having made of my soul a monastery and to being no more to myself than an autumn over a dry, deserted field where the only spark of life is a bright reflection like a light dying in the canopied dark of pools, with no more effort or color than the violet splendor, the spent exile, of the sunset on the mountains.

At bottom there is no greater pleasure than that of analyzing one's own pain, no more sensual pleasure than the liquid, sickly meanderings of feelings as they crumble and rot—light footsteps in the uncertain shadows, so gentle on the ear we do not even turn to find out whose they are; vague, distant songs, whose words we do not try to catch, but which lull us all the more because we do not know what they say or whence they come; the tenuous secrets of pale waters, filling the night with fragile distances; and, inaudible from here, somnolent in the warm torpor of the afternoon where summer slides into autumn, the rattle of far-off carts, returning from where and carrying what joys inside them? The flowers in the garden died and, withered, they became different flowers, older, nobler, their dead yellows more in keeping with mystery, silence and abandon. The bubbles that surface in the pools have their reasons for their dreams. Is that the distant croaking of frogs? Ah, the dead fields of my own self! The rustic peace known only in dreams! My futile life like that of a peasant who does not work but sleeps by the roadside with the smell of the fields seeping like mist into his soul, in a cool, translucent sleep, as deep and full of eternity as is everything that connects nothing with nothing, nocturnal, unknown, weary and nomadic beneath the cold compassion of the stars.

I follow the path of my dreams, making of their images steps into other images; opening out like a fan the chance metaphors to be found in the great paintings of my inner visions; I divest myself of life and lay it to one side like a suit that's grown too tight. I hide among trees far from the roads. I lose myself. For light, fleeting moments I manage to forget the taste of life, to let go of the idea of light and noise and die, feelings first, consciously, absurdly, like an empire of anguished ruins, a grand entrance amidst flags and victorious drums into a vast final city where I will weep for nothing, want nothing and not even ask to be myself.

The sickly surfaces of the pools I created in dreams wound me. The paleness of the moon I envision shining on forest landscapes is mine alone. The autumn of stagnant skies that I recall without ever having seen them is nothing but my own weariness. My whole dead life weighs on me, all my failed dreams, everything I had that was never mine, the blue of my inner skies, the visible murmur of the rivers of my soul, the vast, troubled peace of wheat fields on plains that I see and yet do not see.

A cup of coffee, a cigarette, the penetrating aroma of its smoke, myself sitting in a shadowy room with eyes half closed—I want no more from life than my dreams and this … It doesn't seem much? I don't know. What do I know about what is a little and what is a lot?

Summer evening out there, how I would love to be someone else … I open the window. Everything outside is so gentle, yet it pierces me with an indefinable pain, a vague feeling of discontent.

And one last thing pierces me, tears at me, leaves my soul in tatters, which is the fact that I, at this moment, at this window, looking out at these sad, gentle things, ought to present an aesthetic figure, beautiful, like someone in a picture—and I don't, I don't even do that …

May this hour pass and be forgotten … May the night approach, grow, descend on all things and never end. May this soul be my eternal tomb, and … may the Darkness be absolute and may I never more live or feel or want …

106 [1915?]

and the chrysanthemums waste away their weary lives in gardens made gloomy by their presence.

… the Japanese luxury of clearly having only two dimensions.

… the colorful existence overlaying the dull transparency of the Japanese figures on the cups.

… a table laid for a discreet cup of tea—a mere pretext for entirely sterile conversations—always seemed to me to possess something like its own existence, its own soulful individuality. It forms a synthetic whole, like any other organism, and is not just the pure sum of the parts (it comprises).

107 [1915?]

Being a retired major seems to me an ideal state. What a shame not to have always been merely a retired major.

The thirst to be complete left me in this state of pointless pain.

The tragic futility of life.

My curiosity, the sister of the skylarks.

The perfidious anxiety of sunsets, the shy shrouds of dawns.

Let us sit down here, where we can see more sky. The vast expanse of those starry heights is so consoling. Life hurts less when we see it; it caresses our cheek hot with life like the cool breeze from a light fan.

108 [1915?]

I have a sense that, for creatures like me, there are no propitious material circumstances, no situations that will turn out well. This sense is already enough to make me distance myself from life; indeed, it only makes me distance myself still more. The list of achievements which, for ordinary men, makes success inevitable, has, when applied to me, a quite different, unexpected and adverse result.

I sometimes have the painful impression that I am the victim of some divine enmity. It seems to me that the only explanation for the series of disasters that defines my life is that someone is consciously manipulating things in order to turn any such achievements into something malevolent.

The result of all this is that I never try too hard. Fortune, if it so wishes, may come and find me. I know all too well that my greatest efforts will never meet with the success others enjoy. That is why I abandon myself to Fortune and expect nothing from her. Why would I?

My stoicism is an organic necessity. I need to armor myself against life. Since all stoicism is really just a harsher form of epicureanism, I want as far as possible to enjoy my misfortune. I'm not sure to what extent I achieve this. I'm not sure to what extent I achieve anything. I don't know to what extent one can achieve anything . . .

Whereas one person triumphs, not by virtue of his own efforts, but because his triumph is inevitable, I never triumph and never would, however inevitable or however much effort I made.

I was perhaps born, spiritually speaking, on a very short winter's day. Night descended early on my existence. The only way I can live my life is in frustration and solitude.

Deep down, none of this is very stoical at all. My suffering is only noble when I put it into words. Otherwise, I whine and whimper like a sick child. I fret and worry like a housewife. My life is entirely futile and entirely sad.

109 [1915?]

Sentimental education

For someone who makes his dreams his life and makes of the hothouse plants of his feelings a religion and a politics, the first step—which tells him in his soul that he really has taken that first step—occurs when he begins to respond to tiny things in an extraordinary and exaggerated fashion. That is the first step, and nothing more. Knowing how to drink a cup of tea with the extreme voluptuousness that an ordinary man could find only in the great joys that come with an ambition suddenly achieved or a great longing abruptly assuaged, or in the final carnal act of love; being able to find in the contemplation of a sunset or some decorative detail the kind of intense stimulation generally only to be found, not in what one sees or hears, but in what one smells or tastes, the proximity of the sensory object that only the more carnal senses—touch, taste, smell—can imprint on the consciousness; being able to make one's inner eye or the ear of one's dream—in short, all the imagined senses or the senses of the imagination—as receptive and tangible as the senses that are normally turned outwards: from among all the astonishing sensations that can be achieved by the expert sensorial cultivator, I choose the latter—and there are obviously other analogous senses—simply in order to give an approximate, concrete idea of what I am trying to say.

Reaching this degree of expertise, however, imposes on the lover of sensations the corresponding physical weight or burden of the internal and external griefs that inevitably, and with the same mental intensity, impinge on his concentration. What prompts the dreamer to take the second step in his ascension into himself is the realization that while feeling to excess can provoke an excess of pleasure, it can also initiate a prolonged period of pain. I put to one side the step that he might or might not be able to take, and which, depending on whether he can or cannot take it, will determine his attitude, his gait if you like, in the steps he then goes on to take, depending on whether he can or cannot isolate himself completely from real life (and, of course, whether or not he is rich). It is obvious, I suppose, reading between the lines of what I am saying, that, depending on the degree to which the dreamer can isolate himself and turn in upon himself, he must focus entirely and obsessively on honing and awakening his sensitivity to things and to dreams.

Anyone who has to live among men, actively meeting them every day—and it really is possible to reduce to a minimum one's intimacy with them (for it is intimacy and not merely contact with people that is so prejudicial)—must turn to ice his social façade so that any fraternal or friendly gesture slides off him and does not penetrate or imprint itself on him. This seems a lot to ask, but it really isn't. It's easy enough to keep other people at a distance, it's simply a matter of keeping yourself at a distance. Anyway, I will pass over this now and return to what I was saying.

While giving an immediate intensity and complexity to the simplest and most inevitable of sensations does bring about a dramatic increase in the pleasure of feeling, it can also cause an inordinate increase in the suffering that comes from feeling. This is why the dreamer's second step should be to avoid suffering. He should not avoid it as a stoic or an epicurean might do, by unsettling himself as a way of hardening himself against pleasure and pain. He should, on the contrary, try to find pleasure in pain, whatever that pleasure might be. There are various ways he can achieve this. One is to make a detailed analysis of pain, the dreamer having first trained himself, as regards pleasure, to only feel and not to analyze; this is easier—for the more experienced dreamer, that is—than it might seem. Analyzing pain and getting used to surrendering to it whenever it appears, until he reaches the point where this happens instinctively and unthinkingly, means adding to pain the pleasure of analysis. By exaggerating and perfecting the dreamer's analytical abilities and instincts, this exercise will become all-absorbing, and all that will be left of pain will be a vague, indefinite substance for analysis.

Another subtler and more difficult method is to accustom oneself to projecting one's pain onto some imaginary figure, to create another "I" who takes on the burden of our suffering, who suffers what we suffer. The next stage is to create an inner sadism so entirely masochistic that it takes pleasure in your suffering as if it were someone else's. This method, which at first glance seems impossible, is not easy, but should not prove difficult for those who have labored to become expert at creating the inner lie. It is, in fact, eminently achievable and, once achieved, pain and suffering take on a taste of blood and disease, a strange tang of distant, decadent pleasure! Pain has all the disquieting, crushing power of a convulsion. Suffering—the long, slow variety—takes on the intimate, yellow hue of the vague contentment that follows a longed-for convalescence. And a threadbare touch of disquiet and grief comes close to resembling the complex unease brought on by the thought of the fleeting nature of all pleasures, and the pre-weariness born of the thought of the weariness that all future pleasures will inevitably bring.

There is a third method for subtilizing pains into pleasures and making of doubts and disquiets a soft bed, namely, by applying to anxieties and sufferings an almost irritating degree of attention, an intensity that, by its own excess, brings with it the pleasure of excess; just as in someone who, by habit and training, is devoted and dedicated to pleasure, the sheer violence of pleasure sometimes hurts because it is pleasurable to the point that it tastes of blood. And when, as in my case—as a refiner of false refinements, an architect who constructs himself out of sensations sieved fine by dint of intelligence, abdication, analysis and pain itself—all three methods are used in conjunction, whereby a sudden grief that leaves no time to create some inner strategy is instantly analyzed to death, ruthlessly thrust into an external "I" and buried up to the very hilt of grief, then I truly do feel myself to be the victor, the hero. That is when life stops, and art throws itself at my feet.

This is only the second step that the dreamer must take to create his dream.

However, who but I has taken the third step, which leads straight to the sumptuous threshold of the Temple? That is the most difficult step, because it demands an inner effort far greater than any physical effort one might make, but which rewards the soul in a way that life never could. When all things come perfectly and totally together, with all three subtle methods used until they are spent, this step passes sensation directly through pure intelligence, sifts it by means of superior analysis, giving it literary form and providing it with its own bulk and shape. Thus I gave sensation a permanent existence. Thus I made the unreal real and provided the unattainable with an eternal pedestal. Then, inside myself, I was crowned Emperor.

Please don't think I write in order to publish, or simply for the sake of writing or making art. I write as an end in itself, the ultimate refinement, the temperamentally illogical refinement, of my cultivation of states-of-soul. If I choose one of my sensations and test it to the point where I can weave from it an inner reality, which I call either the Forest of Alienation or the Journey Never Made, believe me, I do this not so that my prose sounds lucid and tremulous, or even because the prose gives me pleasure—even if I wanted this as the ultimate refinement, like a beautiful curtain coming down over my dreamed scenarios—but so that it gives total exteriority to what is interior, so that I thus realize the unrealizable, bringing together contradictions and, by making the dream external, giving it maximum potency as pure dream, in my role as stagnator of life, chiseler of inexactitudes, ailing pageboy to my Queen Soul, reading to her in the twilight hours not the poems that are in this book, open on the lap of my Life, but the poems I am constructing and pretending to read, and that she is pretending to hear, while the Evening, somehow, somewhere—in this metaphor erected inside Absolute Reality—eases the fading, tenuous light of a mysterious spiritual day.

110 [1915?]

The sweetness of having neither family nor companions, the gentle pleasure akin to that of exile, in which we feel the pride of distance shade into a hesitant voluptuousness, into the vague disquiet that comes with being far from home—yes, in my own indifferent way I enjoy all that. For one of the characteristics of my mental outlook is the belief that you should not over-cultivate your attention; even a dream should be treated with condescension, with an aristocratic awareness that the dream owes its existence to you. Giving too much importance to a dream would, after all, be giving too much importance to something that has merely broken away from us and, as best it could, made a place for itself in reality, thereby losing its absolute right to be treated by us with any delicacy.

Imaginary figures have more substance and truth than real ones.

My imaginary world has always been the only true world for me. I never knew loves so real, so full of blood and passion and life, as I did with the characters I myself created. What a shame! I miss them because, like all loves, they, too, pass ...

111 [1915?]

Sometimes, on elegant evenings of the Imagination, in my dialogues with myself, in weary twilight colloquies in imagined salons, during those intervals in the conversation when I am left alone with an interlocutor more me than the others, I wonder why our scientific age has not extended its urge to understand to the artificial. And one of the questions over which I linger most languorously is why, along with the usual psychology of human and subhuman beings, there is not also a psychology—as there should be—of those artificial figures and creatures who exist only in rugs or paintings. Anyone who limits himself to the organic, and does not accept the idea of statues and tapestries having a soul, must have a very dim notion of reality. Where there is form there is a soul.

These are not mere idle thoughts, but a scientific lucubration like any other. That is why—before coming up with an answer, which I haven't—I imagine what is possible and give myself over, in inner analyzes, to the imagined vision of possible aspects of that desideratum if made real. No sooner have I thought this than, inside the vision in my mind, I see scientists bent over paintings, conscious that they are poring over lives; microscopists studying the rough tessitura of rugs; physicists analyzing their broad, swirling friezes;

chemists attributing ideas to the shapes and colors of paintings; geologists studying the strata of cameos; psychologists—and this is the most important part—noting and collating one by one the sensations a statue must feel, the ideas that must pass through the colorful psyche of a figure in a painting or a stained-glass window, the mad impulses, the unbridled passions, the occasional sympathies and loathings, and the curious fixity and death in the eternal gestures of bas-reliefs and the invisible movements of figures on canvases.

Literature and music are more open than the other arts to the probing subtleties of a psychologist. The characters in a novel are—as everyone knows—as real as any of us. Certain sounds have a quick, wingèd soul, more susceptible to psychology and sociology. Because—as the ignorant should be told—whole societies exist inside colors, sounds, phrases, and there are regimes and revolutions, kingdoms, policies and [...]—literally and unmetaphorically—in the mathematical whole of symphonies, in the organized Whole of novels, in the square meters of a complex painting, in which pleasure and pain mingle in the colorful poses of warriors, lovers or symbolic figures.

When one of the cups in my Japanese collection gets broken, I dream that this was due not to the clumsy hands of a maid, but to the wishes of the figures who inhabit the curved flank of the cup; the grim, suicidal resolve that gripped them does not alarm me in the least. They used the maid, where we might use a revolver. Knowing this (as I do) is to go beyond today's science.

112 [1915?]

I envy in everyone the fact that they are not me. Of all impossibilities, and this always seemed to me the greatest, this was the one that made up the greater part of my daily dose of anguish, the despair that filled every sad hour.

A dull, terrifying ray of sun seared the physical sensation of seeing. A yellow heat stagnated in the dark green of the trees. Torpor [...]

113 [1915?]
Rainy day
The air is a concealed yellow, like a pale yellow seen through a grubby white. There is hardly any yellow, though, in the gray air. That pale gray, however, contains a tinge of imagined yellow.

114 [1915?]
The slight intoxication from a slight fever, when our bones are filled by both a mild discomfort and a penetrating cold and our eyes burn and our temples pound—I love that discomfort much as a slave loves a beloved tyrant. Give me that state of tremulous, broken passivity in which I glimpse visions, turn the corners of ideas and, among colliding feelings, feel myself being torn apart.

Thinking, feeling and wanting become a single confused thing. Beliefs, feelings, the real and the imagined are all mixed up, like the jumbled contents of various drawers emptied out onto the floor.

115 [1915?]
Advice to unhappily married women
The unhappily married includes all married women and some spinsters.

Free yourselves, above all, from cultivating any humanitarian feelings. Humanitarianism is vulgar.

I write coldly, rationally, thinking only of your well-being, poor unhappily married women.

All art, all freedom, lies in submitting your mind as little as possible, meanwhile leaving the body to submit as much as it chooses.

There is no point in being immoral, because it merely diminishes and trivializes your personality in the eyes of others. Be immoral within yourself, while surrounded by total respect. Be a corporeally virginal and devoted wife and mother, while having committed inexplicable acts of debauchery with all the men in the neighborhood, from the grocers to the [...]—that is the true aim of anyone who really wants to enjoy and expand her individuality, without descending to the methods of a maidservant, which, coming as they do from a maid, are necessarily base, nor falling into the rigorous honesty of the profoundly stupid woman, doubtless merely the fruit of self-interest.

Given your superiority, you feminine souls reading this will understand what I am saying. All pleasure comes from the brain; all crimes, as they say, are committed in our dreams. I remember a beautiful crime. It never occurred. Only the ones we can't remember are beautiful. Did Borgia commit beautiful crimes? He did not. It was our dream of Borgia, the idea we have of Borgia, that committed exquisite, royal, splendid crimes. I am sure that the real Cesare Borgia was a banal, stupid man; he must have been because to exist is always stupid and banal.*

I give you this advice disinterestedly, applying my method to a case that is of no interest to me. Personally, my dreams are all Empire and glory, and not in the least sensual. But I would like to be useful, even if it goes no farther than that, simply in order to annoy myself, because I detest the useful. I am, in my fashion, an altruist.

116   [1915?]

There are creatures who suffer deeply because they never met Mr. Pickwick in real life, never shook hands with Mr. Wardle. I am one of them. I have wept real tears over that novel, because I never knew or met those people, those real people.

Disasters in novels are always beautiful because no real blood is shed in them, nor do the dead rot; in novels, not even rottenness is rotten.

---

* Cesare Borgia (1475/6–1507) was an Italian nobleman, said to have been one of the inspirations behind Machiavelli's *The Prince*.

When Mr. Pickwick is ridiculous, he isn't ridiculous because he is being ridiculous in a novel. Perhaps the novel is a more perfect reality, a more perfect life than the one God creates through us, and that we perhaps—who knows?—exist only to create. Civilizations appear only to exist in order to produce art and literature, for what speaks of them, what remains of them, are words. Why shouldn't those extra-human figures be truly real? I am tormented by the thought that this might be true.

117 [1915?]

Often, in order to amuse myself—because nothing is as amusing as the sciences or pseudo-sciences when put to pointless use—I make a scrupulous study of my psyche as seen by others. The pleasure this futile stratagem provides is sometimes sad, sometimes painful.

I try to study the general impression I make on others, and to draw conclusions. I am, on the whole, someone whom people like and who even provokes a vague, curious respect. However, I tend not to arouse any strong emotions. No one will ever be my heartfelt friend. That is why so many can respect me.

118 [1915?]

Given the metallic, barbarous age we live in, only by methodically, obsessively cultivating our abilities to dream, analyze and attract can we prevent our personality from dissolving into nothing or into something identical to all the others.

The reality, if any, of our sensations resides precisely in its otherness. Reality is made up of what is common and shared. That's why we as individuals only exist in the spurious part of our sensations. How happy I would be to discover one day that the Sun was scarlet. That Sun would be mine, mine alone!

119 [1915?]

... and a profound, dull disdain for all those who work for humanity, for all those who fight for their country and give their lives so that civilization can continue ...

... a disdain filled with distaste for those who do not know that the only reality for each of us is our own soul, and everything else—the outside world and other people—is an unaesthetic nightmare, like the result in dreams of a bout of mental indigestion.

My aversion for any kind of effort becomes an almost hysterical horror in the face of violent effort. And war, productive, energetic work, helping others ... all that seems to me nothing more than the product of sheer impudence, [...]

And compared with the supreme reality of my soul, with the pure, sovereign grandeur of my most original and frequent dreams, everything that is useful and external seems frivolous and trivial. As far as I am concerned, my dreams are far more real.

120 [1915?]

In order to feel the delight and terror of great speed, I have no need of fast cars or express trains. I need only a tram, and the ability to cultivate my own extraordinary talent for abstraction.

In a tram, I am capable, by adopting a mathematical, instantaneously analytical attitude, of separating out the idea of the tram from the idea of speed, so that they are two different real-things. Then I can feel myself traveling not in the tram, but in its Speed. And going a stage farther, if I want to enjoy the delirium of high speed, I can transport that idea to the Pure Concept of Speed, and, at a whim, increase or decrease it, taking it way beyond all the possible speeds ever achieved by mechanical vehicles.

Quite apart from terrifying me—fear has nothing to do with my ability to feel to excess—running real risks disrupts the perfect attention of my sensations, discomfiting and depersonalizing me.

I avoid all risk. I feel both afraid of and bored by danger.

A sunset is an intellectual phenomenon.

121 [1916?]

My life: a tragedy booed off the stage by the gods after only the first act.

Friends: none. Just a few acquaintances who think they get on with me and would perhaps be sorry if I got knocked down by a train or if it rained on the day of the funeral.

The natural reward for my withdrawal from life has been their inability, which I created, to sympathize with me. There's an aura of coldness around me, a halo of ice that repels others. I still haven't managed not to feel the pain of my solitude. It is so difficult to achieve the necessary distinction of spirit to make isolation seem a haven of peace free from all anguish.

I never believed in the friendship shown me, just as I would not have believed in their love, which was, anyway, impossible. So complex and subtle is my manner of suffering that, although I never had any illusions about the people who called themselves my friends, I still managed to feel disillusioned by them.

I never doubted for a moment that they would all betray me and yet I was always shocked when they did. Even when what I was expecting to happen did happen, for me it was always unexpected.

As I never found in myself qualities that might be attractive to another person, I could never believe that anyone could feel attracted to me. That could be dismissed as the considered opinion of a foolish modesty if fact after fact—those unexpected facts I confidently expected—had not always proved it to be correct.

I can't even imagine them feeling compassion for me since, though I'm physically awkward and unacceptable, I lack the necessary degree of deformity to make me a likely candidate for other people's compassion, nor the sympathetic qualities that attract compassion even when not obviously deserved; and there can be no compassion for the quality in me that might merit pity, because there is no pity for spiritual cripples. So I was drawn instead into the gravitational field of other people's scorn where I am unlikely to attract anyone's sympathy.

I've spent my whole life trying to adapt to this without feeling too deeply the cruelty and vileness of it all.

One needs a certain intellectual courage to recognize

unflinchingly that one is no more than a scrap of humanity, a living abortion, a madman not yet crazy enough to be locked up; but having recognized that, one needs even more spiritual courage to adapt oneself perfectly to one's destiny, to accept without rebellion, without resignation, without a single gesture or attempt at a gesture of protest, the elemental curse Nature has laid upon one. Wanting to feel no pain at all is to want too much, because it is not in human nature to accept evil, recognize it for what it is and call it good; and if you accept it as an evil then you cannot but suffer.

My misfortune—a misfortune for my own happiness—lay in my imagining myself from outside. I saw myself as others saw me and I began to despise myself, not because I recognized in myself qualities deserving of scorn, but because I saw myself as others saw me and felt the kind of scorn they would feel for me. I suffered the humiliation of knowing myself. Since this was a calvary lacking in all nobility and not to be followed some days later by a resurrection, all I could do was suffer with the ignobility of it all.

I understood then that only someone lacking all aesthetic sense could possibly love me and, if they did, I would despise them for it. Even liking me could be no more than the caprice born of another's indifference.

To see clearly into ourselves and into how others see us! To see this truth face to face! Thence comes the final cry of Christ on the cross when he saw his truth face to face: My God, my God, why hast thou forsaken me?

122 [1916?]

*Declaration of Difference**

The things of the state and the city have no hold on us. What do we care if ministers and courtiers mishandle national affairs? That happens outside us, like the mud on rainy days. We have nothing to do with it, even though it has to do with us.

---

* A note follows this title: "(to be inserted in the *Book of Disquiet*)."

Similarly, we're not interested in any major upheavals like war and economic crises. As long as they don't visit our house, we don't care whose door they knock on. This may seem to show a great disregard for other people, but really it is merely the basis of our own sceptical view of ourselves.

We are neither kind nor charitable—not because we are the contrary of that, but because we are neither one thing nor the other. Kindness is the tact of the vulgar. To us, it is interesting only as something that happens in other people's souls, and in other ways of thinking. We observe and we neither approve nor disapprove. Our vocation is to be nothing.

We would be anarchists had we been born into the classes that describe themselves as underprivileged, or into any of the other classes from which one can fall or rise. The truth is that we are, in general, creatures born in the interstices of classes and social divisions—nearly always in that decadent space between the aristocracy and the (haute) bourgeoisie, the social arena for the geniuses and madmen with whom one can sympathize.

Action disorients us, partly because of a certain physical incompetence on our part, but far more because of a moral distaste. It seems to us immoral to act. We feel that all thoughts are degraded by being put into words, thus handing them over to other people, making them comprehensible to those capable of comprehending.

We have a great sympathy for occultism and the secret arts. We are not, however, occultists. We lack both the innate will and the patience to educate our will in such a way as to make of it the perfect instrument for maguses and hypnotists. And yet we do, nonetheless, have a sympathy for occultism, especially since it has a way of expressing itself that is incomprehensible to many who read it, and even to many who think they do comprehend it. Such elusiveness shows an exquisite superiority. It is also a copious source of mysterious and terrifying sensations: the astral spirits and strange beings with even stranger bodies conjured up in their temples by magical rites, the disembodied presences from that higher plane, which hover above our oblivious senses in the physical silence of inner noise—all these things touch us with a ghastly, viscous hand in our moments of darkness and distress.

In another respect, however, we do not sympathize with occultists, and that is because they are also apostles and lovers of humanity, a view that strips them of all mystery. The only reason for an occultist to operate on the astral plane is for the sake of some lofty aesthetic, not with the sinister aim of helping someone.

Almost unwittingly, we have a sneaking ancestral sympathy for black magic, for the forbidden forms of transcendentalism, for the Lords of Power who sold themselves to Damnation and to a degraded form of Reincarnation. Our weak, uncertain eyes are drawn, like a bitch in heat, to the theory of inverse degrees, inverted rituals, to the sinister curve of the descending hierarchy.

Whether we like it or not, Satan holds for us an attraction like that between dog and bitch. The serpent of Material Intelligence coiled itself around our heart, as it did around Hermes' staff, the Caduceus, symbolic of the God who communicates—Mercury, Lord of Understanding.

Those of us who are not pederasts wish we had the courage to be so. A distaste for action inevitably has a feminizing effect. We missed our true vocation as housewives and idle chatelaines because of a sexual mismatch in our present incarnation. While we do not totally believe this, to pretend we do savors of the blood of irony.

None of this is born of evil, but of weakness. In our solitude, we worship evil, not because it is evil, but because it is stronger and more intense than Good, and nerves that should have been a woman's are attracted to anything intense and strong. We cannot take Luther's *Pecca fortiter* as our motto, for we lack sufficient strength, we do not even have the strength of intelligence, which is the only strength we could possibly claim we had. *Think* of sinning greatly, that is the most such a dictum can mean for us. But sometimes even that is impossible: our inner life has a reality which, at times, wounds us because it is still a reality. The existence of laws for the association of ideas, as for all intellectual operations, insults our native indiscipline.

123* [1916?]

Any soul worthy of the name wants to live life to the Extreme. To be content with what one is given shows an attitude fit for slaves; only children ask for more; only madmen want to conquer more, for every conquest is [...]

To live life to the Extreme means to live it to the limit, but there are three ways of doing this and it falls to every superior soul to choose one of these ways. Life lived to the Extreme means taking full possession of it, making a Ulyssean journey through every human feeling, through every manifestation of externalized energy. However, at any time in the history of the world, there have never been more than a few who can close their eyes with a weariness that is the sum of all weariness, who have possessed everything in every possible way.

Only a few can make such demands on life and by so doing force her to surrender herself to them body and soul, knowing that they need feel no jealousy because they know they have all her love, and this should doubtless be the desire of every strong and lofty soul. When that soul, however, realizes that what he wants is impossible, that he does not have the strength to conquer every part of Everything, there are two other routes to follow. The first is that of total renunciation, formal and complete abstention, relegating to the sphere of sensibility what cannot be possessed fully in the arena of activity and energy. It is far better not to act at all than to act in vain, fragmentarily, inadequately, like the countless, superfluous, inane majority of men. The second is the path of perfect

---

* Written in English above this passage are the words "Chapter on Indifference or something like that."

balance, the search for the Limits of Absolute Proportion, in which the longing for the Extreme passes from the will and the emotions to the Intelligence, one's whole ambition becoming not to live life to the full, not to feel life to the full, but to impose order on life, to live it in Harmony and intelligent Coordination.

The longing to understand, which, in so many noble souls, takes the place of action, belongs to the sphere of sensibility. Replacing energy with intelligence, breaking the link between will and emotion, stripping of self-interest every manifestation of material life, that, if one can achieve it, is worth more than life, so difficult to possess completely and so sad if possessed only partially.

The argonauts said it was the journey that mattered, not life. We, the argonauts of an ailing sensibility, say it is not living that matters, but feeling.

124 [1916?]

Anteros—The Visual Lover

I have a superficial, decorative concept of deep love and its useful employment. I am subject to visual passions. I keep intact a heart given over to unreal destinies.

I cannot recall ever having loved in someone anything more than the "image" of them, not what portrait painters depict, but the purely exterior, into which the soul enters only to lend animation and life.

This is how I love: I fix on the image of a woman or a man—where desire is absent, gender is irrelevant—because they are beautiful, attractive or lovable, and that image obsesses, binds, grips me. However, all I want is to see it, for nothing horrifies me more than the possibility of getting to know and to speak to the real person of whom that image is the outward manifestation.

I love with my eyes and not with my fantasy. I don't fantasize about the image that obsesses me. I don't imagine myself connected to it in any other way because my decorative love has nothing psychological about it. I have no interest in finding out what this creature—who presents to me only their external aspect—is or does or thinks.

The endless procession of people and things that make up the world is for me an interminable gallery of pictures whose inner life bores me. It doesn't interest me because the soul is a monotonous thing and is always the same in everyone; it differs only in its personal manifestations and the best part of it is that which overflows into the face, into mannerisms and gestures, and thus becomes part of the image that so captures my interest, and keeps me diversely but constantly enamored.

As far as I am concerned, that creature has no soul. The soul is entirely his or her own business.

This is how I experience the animate exteriors of things and beings, in pure vision, as indifferent to their spiritual content as a god from another world. I only go deep into the surface of other people; if I want profundity I look for it in myself and in my concept of things.

What would I gain from having some personal knowledge of the creature I love as a decorative object? Not disappointment, because her possible stupidity or mediocrity is irrelevant, since what I love in her is only her appearance, from which I expected nothing anyway, and that outward appearance is still there. Moreover, personal knowledge of someone is harmful because useless, and what is useless in the material world is always harmful. What good would it do me to know the creature's name? And yet that is the first thing I find out on being introduced to her.

Personal knowledge ought to mean freedom to contemplate, which is precisely what my idea of love also desires. We cannot freely regard or contemplate someone we know personally.

Superfluous knowledge is useless to the artist because, by disturbing him, it lessens the effect he seeks.

My natural destiny is to be an unconstrained and passionate

observer of the appearances and manifestations of things, the objective observer of dreams, the visual lover of every form and aspect of nature.

This is not a case of what psychiatrists call psychic onanism, nor even erotomania. I don't, as is the case with psychic onanism, indulge in fantasies; I don't dream of making a lover or even a friend of the creature I contemplate and remember: I have no fantasies about him or her. Nor, like the erotomane, do I idealize and transport the object of desire beyond the sphere of pure aesthetics: to fulfill my desires and my thoughts, I want nothing more than what is offered to my eyes and to the pure direct memory of what my eyes saw.

125 [1916?]

It is not my custom to weave any kind of fantastic plot about the figures I amuse myself in contemplating. I just see them, and their value lies purely in the fact that I *can* see them. Anything I might add would diminish them, because it would diminish what I term their "visibility."

Whatever I fantasized about them would, from the start, inevitably ring false to me; and, whilst I like dreams, I find any kind of falseness repugnant. The pure dream delights me, the dream that has no connection, no point of contact, with reality. The imperfect dream, with its roots in reality, displeases me or, rather, it would if I ever bothered with it.

For me, humanity is one vast decorative motif, existing through one's eyes and ears and through psychological emotion. I demand nothing more from life than to be a spectator of it. I demand nothing more from myself than to be a spectator of life.

I'm like a being from another existence who passes, endlessly curious, through this existence to which I am in every way alien. A sheet of glass stands between it and me. I always try to keep that glass as clean as possible so that I can examine this other existence without smudges or smears distorting my view; but I choose to keep that glass between us.

For any mind of a scientific bent, seeing more in something than is actually there is, in fact, to see less. What you add in substance, you take away in spirit.

I attribute to this state of mind my distaste for art museums. For me, the museum is the whole of life, in which the painting is always exact and the only possible inexactitude lies in the imperfect eye of the beholder. I either try to diminish any imperfection or, if I can't, then I simply accept it the way it is since, as with everything, it cannot be other than it is.

126 [after July 1916]

So soft and airy was the hour, it was like an altar at which to pray. The horoscope for our meeting was clearly ruled by beneficent conjunctions, so silken and subtle was the uncertain matter of the dream slipping almost unnoticed into our consciousness of our feelings. Our sour notion that life wasn't worth living ceased like a summer, and the spring—which we might, erroneously, imagine we had enjoyed—was reborn. The pools, all too wretchedly like us, were also singing songs of lamentation among the trees and among the roses in the bare beds, accompanied—quite irresponsibly—by the vague melody of life.

There's no point in *thinking* you know or that you even actually *do* know what will happen. The future is a mist that surrounds us, and when you catch a glimpse of tomorrow, it seems very like today. My destinies are the clowns left behind by the circus, with the moon no brighter than the moonlight on the roads, the leaves rustled by nothing but the breeze and the uncertainty of the hour, and our conviction that we can indeed hear rustling. Distant purples, fleeting shadows, the never completed dream we do not believe even death will complete, dull rays of sunshine, the light in the house on the hillside, the agonizing night, the smell of death among the books, with life going on outside, the trees smelling green in the vast night, far starrier on the other side of the hill. Thus your sadnesses had their benign encounter; your few words gave a royal blessing to the voyage, no ships ever returned, not even the real ones, and the smoke of living wrapped about everything, leaving only shadows and emptiness, the bruised waters of fateful lakes framed by box-edged paths, seen from a distance through gates, like a Watteau painting, the anguish, and then nothing more. Millennia spent waiting for you to come, but there's no bend in the road, and so you never will come. Goblets set aside for the inevitable hemlock—not yours, but everyone's, and even the lanterns, the hidden places, the vague fluttering of wings—heard, and then only in the mind—in the hot, restless night, which, minute by minute, rises up and cuts through its own anxiety. Yellow, dark-green, love-blue—all dead, my mistress, all dead, and all the ships are that one ship that never will set sail! Pray for me, and perhaps God will exist because you are praying for me. Quietly, the distant fountain, uncertain life, the smoke fading above the village where night is falling, the obscure memory, the river far off ... Let me sleep, let me forget myself, Our Lady of Uncertain Intentions, Mother of Caresses and Blessings incompatible with my existence ...

127 [1916?]

Funeral March for King Ludwig II of Bavaria

Today, lingering even longer than usual, Death came to my door to sell her wares. Lingering even longer than usual, she laid out before me the rugs, silks and damasks of her oblivion and her consolation. She smiled with satisfaction at her goods, and didn't care that I could see her smile. However, when I tried to buy something, she told me it wasn't for sale. She hadn't come because she wanted me to buy, but so that I would want her because of what she had brought me. And she told me that her rugs were the rugs from her distant palace; that her silks were the only ones worn in her dark domain; and that even finer damasks covered the altars in her home beyond the world.

She gently released me from the bonds that had long kept me tethered to my austere home. "There is no fire in your hearth," she said, "so why have a hearth?" "There is no bread on your table," she said, "so why have a table?" "You have no companion," she said, "so why cling to life?"

"I," she said, "am the fire in cold hearths, the bread on empty tables, the solicitous companion of the lonely and ignored. In my great domain you will find the worldly glory that eluded you here. In my empire, love never wearies because it does not long to possess; nor does it suffer because it failed to possess. I place my hand gently on the heads of those who think, and they forget; those who waited in vain rest their head on my bosom and are filled with a sense of confidence and trust."

"The love they feel for me," she said, "is devoid of consuming passion or mad jealousy, nor is it tainted by neglect. Loving me is like a summer's night, when the beggars sleep out in the open and resemble shadows lying by the roadside. From my silent lips you will hear no siren songs, no melodiously rustling trees or burbling fountains; my silence is as welcoming as an inaudible music, my peace as caressing as the merest thought of a breeze."

"What binds you to life?" she said. "Love does not seek you out, nor does glory, and power has never found you. The house you inherited is a house in ruins. The crops in the fields you were given were scorched by frost, the promised harvest seared by the sun. The well on your estate has long since run dry. The lilies in your pond rotted before you even saw them. Weeds filled the paths and avenues that your feet never trod.

"But in my domain, where eternal night reigns, you will find consolation, because there you will have no hope, only forgetting, you will yearn for nothing, but will find rest, because you will have no life."

And she showed me how futile it was to hope for better days, when one was not born with a soul capable of finding better days. She showed me how dreams do not console because life only hurts all the more when one wakes. She showed how sleep brings no rest because it is haunted by ghosts, by the shadows of things, by the traces left in the air by gestures, by the dead embryos of desires, by flotsam from the shipwreck of living.

And speaking thus, she slowly, even more slowly than usual, rolled up the rugs I had found so tempting, the silks so coveted by my soul, the damasks from the altars on which my tears were falling.

Why try to be like other people, if you are condemned to being you? Why laugh, if, when you laugh, your own genuine joy is false, because it is born out of your forgetting who you are? Why weep if you feel it will not help, when you weep more because your tears fail to console you than because they do?

If you are happy when you laugh, then I have won; if you are happy because you have forgotten who you are, how much happier you will be with me, where you will remember nothing at all. If you achieve perfect rest, if you perhaps sleep a dreamless sleep, how deeply you will rest on my bed, where all sleep is dreamless? If you momentarily rise up because you have seen something beautiful, and you forget about yourself and about Life, how much higher will you rise in my palace, whose nocturnal beauty knows no discord, no age, no corruption; in my rooms where no wind disturbs the curtains, no dust covers the chairbacks, no light fades the velvets and the upholstery, and no time yellows the blank whiteness of the white walls?

Come, enjoy my affection, which never changes, and my love, which has no end! Drink from my inexhaustible cup the supreme nectar, which neither wearies nor embitters, which neither nauseates nor inebriates. Contemplate from my castle window not the moonlight and the sea, which are beautiful and therefore imperfect, but the vast, maternal night, the consummate splendor of the deep abyss!

In my arms you will forget the painful path that brought you to them. In my embrace you will no longer feel the love that made you seek it out! Sit beside me on my throne, and you will forever be the undethronable emperor of the Mystery and the Grail, you will coexist with the gods and with the fates, in being nothing, in having neither a here nor a hereafter, in having no need even of those things of which you have excess or that you lack or of which you have sufficient.

I will be your maternal wife, your long-lost twin sister found at last. And once I am married to all your anxieties, once everything you were looking for and did not find has returned to me, then you will become lost in my mystical substance, in my nonexistence, in my breast where all things founder, in my breast where all souls are extinguished, in my breast where even the gods vanish.

128 [1916?]

Sovereign Lord of Detachment and Renunciation, Emperor of Death and Shipwreck, living dream that wanders, in splendor, among the ruins and the exiles of the world!

Sovereign Lord of Despair and empty pomp, grieving master of palaces that bring no satisfaction, master of all the processions and the ceremonies that fail to blank out life!

Sovereign Lord risen from the tombs, who came by moonlight to tell your life to the living; royal pageboy bearing lilies that have lost all their petals; imperial herald of cold ivory!

Sovereign Lord and Shepherd of Sleepless Nights, knight errant of Anxieties, with no glory and no damsel to escort along moonlit roads; lord of hillside forests, in silent profile, visor down, riding through the valleys, misunderstood in villages, mocked in towns, scorned in cities.

Sovereign Lord whom Death consecrated as her own, pale and absurd, forgotten and unrecognized, reigning among tarnished jewels and faded velvets, on your throne at the far end of the Possible, surrounded by an unreal court of shadows and guarded by a fantastical militia, mysterious and vacant.

Pageboys, virgins, servants and maids, bring on the chalices, the salvers and the garlands for the feast to which Death invites us! Yes, bring them all and come dressed in black, your heads crowned with myrtles.

Fill the chalices with mandrake, fill the salvers with […], and weave garlands out of violets […], out of sad flowers redolent of sadness.

The King is going to dine with Death tonight in his ancient palace beside the lake, among the mountains, far from life, far from the world.

May the orchestra rehearsing for the feast be composed of strange instruments, whose very sound makes us weep. The servants should wear somber liveries in outlandish colors, as lavish and simple as the catafalques of suicides.

And before the feast begins, have the grand medieval cortège process down the avenues of broad gardens in a great, moving, silent ceremonial, like beauty in a nightmare.

Death is Life's triumph!

We live in death, because we exist today only because we are dead to yesterday. We wait for death, because we can only believe in tomorrow in the knowledge that today will die. We live in Death when we dream, because to dream is to deny life. We die in death even while we live, because to live is to deny eternity! Death guides us, death seeks us out, death accompanies us. All we have is Death, all we want is Death, Death is all we want to want.

A warning breeze ruffles wings.

He comes, like the death no one sees and the […] that never arrives.

Heralds! Sound your trumpets! Attend him!

Your love for dreamed things was your scorn for living things.

Virgin-King who scorned love,
    Shadow-King who disdained light,
    Dream-King who rejected life!

Among the muffled clamor of cymbals and drums, the Darkness acclaims you emperor!

129 [1916?]

And for you, Death, our soul and our belief, our hope and our respect!

Our Lady of Last Things, Carnal Name of the Mystery and the Abyss—reassure and comfort those who seek you without actually daring to do so!

Our Lady of Consolation [...]

Virgin Mother of the absurd World, a kind of incomprehensible Chaos, sow and scatter your kingdom over everything—over the flowers that sense they are fading, over the wild animals grown too old to walk, over the souls born to languish between error and the illusion of life!

Lake among the rocks in the serene moonlight, far from the mud and pollution of Life!

Life spiraling into Nothingness, infinitely yearning for what it cannot have.

130 [1916?]

Symphony of the unquiet night

Evenings in ancient cities, with unknown traditions written on the black stones of vast buildings; the tremulous hours before dawn in flooded, swampy fields, as damp as the air before the sun rises; the narrow lanes where everything is possible; the heavy trunks kept in old, old halls; the well at the bottom of the garden in the moonlight; the first love letters written to the grandmother we never knew; the musty smell of rooms where the past is stored away; the rifle no one knows how to use anymore; the fever of hot afternoons spent gazing out of the window; the deserted street; a disturbed night's sleep; the blight spreading through the vineyards; bells; the monastic pain of living ... Hour of blessings, your subtle hands

… The caress never comes, the stone in your ring bleeds in the near-darkness … Church celebrations with no belief in the soul: the physical beauty of the rough, ugly saints; romantic passions felt only in the mind; the salt tang of the sea as night falls on the harbors of the city grown damp in the cooling air …

Your thin hands winged and hovering over someone whom life is stealing away. Long corridors and narrow windows that stand open even when closed, the ground cold as the grave, a longing for love like a journey yet to be made to unfinished lands … The names of ancient queens … Stained-glass windows portraying staunch and sturdy counts … The morning light scattered like cold incense in the air of the church, distilled in the darkness of the impenetrable ground … Dry hands pressed together in prayer.

The scruples of the monk who finds occult teachings in the absurd symbols of an ancient book and the steps of an Initiation in the colored plates.

A beach in the sun and in me a fever … The sea glittering in the anxious knot in my throat … The distant candles, how they flicker in my fever … In my fever, the steps down to the beach … Warmth in the cool ocean breeze, *mare vorax, minax, mare tenebrosum*—the dark night of the argonauts somewhere far away, and my head burning [setting fire to?] those primitive caravels …

Everything belongs to someone else, except the pain of not having it.

Hand me that needle, will you? Today there is something missing in the heart of the house, her small footsteps and not knowing where she is, what she'll be working at, with pleats and colors and pins … Today, her needlework is shut up forever in the chest of drawers—superfluous—and gone is the warmth of a pair of dreamed arms around my mother's neck.

131   18 July 1916

No problem is soluble. None of us unties the Gordian knot; we either give up or cut the knot. We brusquely resolve with our feelings problems of the intellect and do so because we are tired of thinking or too timid to draw conclusions, because of our absurd need to seek help or because of our gregarious impulse to rejoin the others and rejoin life.

Since we can never know all the factors involved in an issue, we can never resolve it.

To reach the truth we lack both the necessary facts and the intellectual processes that could exhaust all possible interpretations of those facts.

132 [1916?]
For those not disembarking there are no quays at which to disembark. Never to arrive is never to arrive.

133 [1916?]
Having seen with what lucidity and logical coherence certain madmen (with method in their madness) justify their crazed ideas to themselves and to others, I have lost for ever any real confidence in the lucidity of my own lucidity.

134 [1917?]
I belong to a generation that inherited a disbelief in the Christian faith and that created within itself a disbelief in all other faiths. Our forefathers still felt an impulse to believe, which they transferred from Christianity to other forms of illusion. Some were enthusiasts for social equality, others were simply in love with beauty, others put their faith in science and its benefits, whilst others, even more Christian than ever, went off to East and West in search of other religions with which they could fill their consciousness of merely living, which seemed hollow otherwise.

We lost all this and were orphaned at birth of all these consolations. Every civilization cleaves to the intimate contours of the religion that represents it: to go after other religions is to lose that first religion and ultimately to lose them all.

We lost both our religion and the others too.

Each of us was left abandoned to ourselves, amidst the desolation of merely knowing we were alive. A boat would seem to be an object whose one purpose is to travel, but its real purpose is not to travel but to reach harbor. We found ourselves on the high seas, with no idea which port we should be aiming for. Thus we represent a painful version of the argonauts' bold motto: the journey is what matters, not life.

Bereft of illusions, we live on dreams, which are the illusions of those who cannot have illusions. Living off ourselves alone, we diminish ourselves, because the complete man is one who is unaware of himself. Without faith, we have no hope and without hope we do not really have a life. With no idea of the future, we can have no real idea of today, because, for the man of action, today is only a prologue to the future. The fighting spirit was stillborn in us, because we were born with no enthusiasm for the fight.

Some of us stagnated in the foolish conquest of the everyday, contemptible, vulgar beings scrabbling for our daily bread and wanting to get it without working for it, without feeling the effort involved, without the nobility of achievement.

Others, of better stock, abstained from public life, wanting and desiring nothing, and trying to carry to the calvary of oblivion the cross of simply existing. A vain endeavor in men whose consciousness, unlike that of the original carrier of the Cross, lacks any spark of the divine.

Others, busily engaged outside their soul, gave themselves over to the cult of confusion and noise, thinking they were alive because they could be heard, thinking they loved when they merely stumbled against love's outer walls. Life hurt us because we knew we were alive; death held no terror for us because we had lost all normal notion of death.

But others, the People of the End, the spiritual boundary of the Dead Hour, did not even have the courage to give it all up and seek asylum in themselves. They lived in negation, discontent and desolation. But we lived it all inside ourselves, making not even a single gesture, shut up for as long as we lived within the four walls of our room and within the four walls of our inability to act.

135 [1917]

The more I contemplate the spectacle of the world and the ebb and flow of change in things, the more deeply am I convinced of the innately fictitious nature of it all, of the false prestige given to the pomp of reality. And in this contemplation, which any reflective person will have experienced at some time or other, the motley parade of costumes and fashions, the complex path of progress and civilizations, the magnificent tangle of empires and cultures, all seem to me like a myth and a fiction, dreamed up amidst shadows and oblivion. But I do not know if the supreme summation of all these aims, vain even when achieved, lies in the joyful renunciation of the Buddha, who, on comprehending the emptiness of it all, woke from his ecstasy saying: "Now I know everything," or in the world-weary indifference of the Emperor Severus: *omnia fui, nihil expedit*—I was all things; all was worthless.

136* [1917]

The generation to which I belong was born into a world devoid of certainty for anyone possessed of both an intellect and a heart. The destructive work of previous generations meant that the world into which we were born had no security to offer us as regards religion, no anchor as regards morality, no stability as regards politics. We were born into a state of anguish, both metaphysical and moral, and of political disquiet. Drunk on external formulae, on the mere processes of reason and science, the preceding generations

---

* This passage is headed by a note in English: "1st article." It is likely that texts 134 and 136 were intended as preliminary texts. Around 1917, Pessoa sketched out not one but several attempts at a preface to the *Book*.

destroyed the foundations of the Christian faith because their biblical exegesis, which shifted from the textual to the mythological, reduced the gospels and the earlier hierography of the Jews to a collection of hypothetical myths and legends, to mere literature. Their scientific criticism gradually found out all the mistakes and wild ingenuities of the primitive "science" of the gospels and, at the same time, the freedom of debate threw open all metaphysical problems including religious questions. Under the influence of a vague theory they called "positivism," these generations criticized all morality and scrutinized all rules for living. All that remained from this clash of doctrines was uncertainty and the pain of that uncertainty. Naturally, a society so undisciplined in its cultural foundations could not but be a victim, politically, of that lack of discipline; and thus we woke to a world avid for social change that joyfully moved forward to conquer a freedom whose meaning we did not understand and an idea of progress we had never clearly defined.

Our forefathers' crude criticism bequeathed to us the impossibility of being Christians, but left us bereft of all possibility of contentment. They bequeathed to us a dissatisfaction with the established moral formulae, but did not bequeath to us an indifference to morality and to rules for living. Whilst they left political problems in a state of uncertainty, they did not leave our spirits indifferent to how these problems might be resolved. Our forefathers destroyed all this with a good conscience because they lived in an era that could still count on fragments of a past solidity. What they destroyed was the very thing that gave society its strength and allowed them to destroy it without even noticing the cracks in the walls. We inherited the destruction and its consequences.

In modern life the world belongs to the stupid, the insensitive and the disturbed. The right to live and triumph is today earned with the same qualifications one requires to be interned in a madhouse: amorality, hypomania and an incapacity for thought.

137 [1917?]

The human soul is inevitably the victim of the pain of the painful surprise provoked even by the most unsurprising of events. Thus the man who has always spoken of woman's inconstancy and mutability as being natural and typical will feel all the anguish of sad surprise when he finds he has been betrayed in love—just as he would had his dogma been woman's eternal faithfulness and loyalty. Just as another man who believes everything to be hollow and empty will experience as a bolt from the blue the sudden discovery that his writings are scorned by others, that all his efforts to teach have proved futile, and that he has failed utterly to communicate his feelings.

This is not because the men to whom these and other disasters happen were all insincere in what they said or wrote, and in whose words those disasters were foreseeable and certain. The sincerity of an intelligent statement has nothing to do with the naturalness of spontaneous emotion. It seems that the reason why the soul experiences these surprises is so that it will never lack for pain or opprobrium, so that it will always receive its fair share of suffering in life. We are all equal in our capacity for making mistakes and for suffering. Only those who feel nothing are exempt; and the loftiest, the noblest, the most far-sighted will suffer and experience precisely what they foresaw and what they disdained. That is what we call Life.

138* [1917?]

I have to choose what I detest—either the dream, which my intelligence loathes, or action, which is repugnant to my sensibility; either action, for which I was not born, or the dream, for which no one was born.

Since I detest both, I choose neither, but since, on some occasions, I must either dream or take action, I mix one thing with the other.

---

* This passage is headed by a note in Portuguese: "(Prefácio?)."

Wherever I've been in my life, in whatever situation, wherever I've lived and worked alongside other people, I've always been considered an intruder or, at the very least, a stranger. Among my relatives as among my acquaintances, I've always been thought of as an outsider. Not that even once have I been treated like that consciously, but other people's spontaneous response to me ensured that I was.

Everyone everywhere has always treated me kindly. Very few people, I think, have had so few raise their voice against them, or been so little frowned at, so infrequently the object of someone else's arrogance or irritability. But the kindness with which I was treated was always devoid of affection. For those who would naturally be closest to me, I was always a guest who, as such, was well treated, but only with the attentiveness due to a stranger and the lack of affection which is the lot of the intruder.

I'm sure that the source of all this—I mean other people's attitudes towards me—lies principally in some obscure intrinsic flaw in my own temperament. Perhaps I communicate a coldness that unwittingly obliges others to reflect back my own lack of feeling.

I get to know people quickly. It doesn't take long for them to grow to like me. But I never really gain their affection. I've never experienced devotion. To be loved has always seemed to me an impossibility, as unlikely as a complete stranger suddenly addressing me familiarly by my first name.

I don't know if this makes me suffer or if I simply accept it as my indifferent fate into which questions of suffering or acceptance do not enter.

I always wanted to please and always found other people's indifference wounding. As an orphan of Fortune I have, like all orphans, a need to be the object of someone's affection. I've always been starved of the realization of that need. I've grown so accustomed to this inevitable hunger that, at times, I'm not even sure I still feel the need to eat.

With or without it, life still hurts me.

Others have someone who is devoted to them. I've never had anyone who even considered devoting themselves to me. That is for other people: me, they just treat decently.

I recognize in myself the capacity to arouse respect but not affection. Unfortunately, I've done nothing that in itself justifies that initial respect and so no one has ever managed fully to respect me either.

I sometimes think that I enjoy suffering. But the truth is I would prefer something else.

I don't have the right qualities to be either a leader or a follower. I don't even have the merit of being contented, which, if all else fails, is what remains.

Other people of lesser intelligence are in fact much stronger than me. They are better than I am at carving out their lives among other people, more skilled at administering their intelligence. I have all the necessary qualities to influence others, but not the art with which to do so, nor even the will to want to do so.

If one day I were to love someone, I would not be loved in return.

It's enough for me to want something for that thing to die. My destiny, however, is not potent enough to prove deadly to just anything. It has the unfortunate disadvantage of being deadly only to those things that I want.

140 [1917?]

I have always experienced actual sensations less intensely than the sensation of having those sensations. I have always found my awareness of suffering more painful than the suffering itself.

Early on, the life of my emotions moved to the seat of thought, and there I enjoyed a broader emotional knowledge of life.

And since thought, when it gives refuge to emotion, becomes more demanding than emotion itself, the regime of consciousness in which I experienced what I was feeling made the manner in which I felt more day-to-day, more superficial, more titillating.

By thinking, I made of myself both echo and abyss. By going deeper inside myself, I became many. The slightest incident—a change in the light, the coiling fall of a dry leaf, a yellowing petal detaching itself, a voice from the other side of the wall, or the footsteps of the person doing the talking alongside the footsteps of the person listening, the door to the old garden left ajar, the courtyard opening through an arch onto the houses clustered together in the moonlight—all those things, which do not belong to me, bind me to my delicate meditations with bonds of resonance and nostalgia. In each one of those sensations, I am a different "I"; I painfully renew myself in each indefinite impression.

I live on impressions that do not belong to me, I am a squanderer of renunciations, always different in my way of being me.

141 [1917?]

To speak is to show too much consideration for others. The fish and Oscar Wilde both died by the mouth.

142 [1917?]

Even writing has lost its sweetness for me. It's become such a banal act, not just the process of giving expression to my feelings but even the pleasure of turning an elegant phrase; I write now in the way others eat or drink, abstracted and bored, only half paying attention, with no enthusiasm, no spark.

143 [1917?]

Humanity's childish instinct makes even the proudest of us—if we're men and in our right mind—yearn, holy Father, for a fatherly hand to guide us somehow, it doesn't matter how, through the mystery and confusion of the world. Each one of us is a speck of dust that the wind of life lifts up, then lets fall. We need to find a support, to place our small hand in another larger hand, because the hour is always uncertain, the heavens are always far away, and life always an alien thing.

Those of us who have risen highest merely know from closer to how hollow and uncertain everything is.

We may be guided by an illusion, but one thing is sure, it is not our consciousness that guides us.

144 [1917?]

The pagan idea of the perfect man was the perfection of the man who exists; the Christian idea of the perfect man is the perfection of the man who does not exist; the Buddhist idea of the perfect man is the perfection of no man at all.

Nature is the difference between the soul and God.

Everything that man pronounces or expresses is a marginal note in a text that has been totally erased. From the meaning of the note, we can more or less work out the meaning of that vanished text, but there is always a doubt, and many possible meanings.

145 [1918?]

When Christianity passed over our souls like a storm that raged into the small hours, people could feel the invisible damage it had caused; however, the ruins it left behind could be fully seen only once it had passed completely. Some thought the ruins were caused by its departure, but it was simply that the damage done was only revealed once it was gone.

What was left then, in this world of souls, were those visible ruins, that clear disaster, without the darkness that once covered it with its false affection. Souls saw themselves for precisely what they were.

A disease sprang up in those newly exposed souls, a disease called Romanticism, a Christianity that lacked both illusions and myths, pared down to its stark, sickly essence.

The trouble with Romanticism is that it confuses what we need and what we want. We all *need* those things that are vital to life, its preservation and its continuation; we all *want* a more perfect life, a more complete happiness, the realization of our dreams and [...]

It is human to want what we need, and it is human to want what we don't actually need, but want. What is unhealthy is to want with equal intensity what is necessary and what is desirable, and to suffer as intensely because our life is not perfect as we would if there were no bread. The Romantic malaise is this: wanting the moon as if there were actually some way of getting it.

"You can't have your cake and eat it."

The same malaise is to be found in the lower spheres of politics, as it is in the private arena of the soul.

The pagan knew nothing of this unhealthy sense of things and self. Being human, he, too, wanted the impossible, but not at the expense of all else. His religion was [...] and the transcendent ideas taught by religions, which fill the soul with the emptiness of the world, these were only to be found in the deepest depths of the mystery, and were taught only to the initiates, far from the ordinary people and the [...]

146 [1918?]

The misery of a man who feels the tedium of life while sitting on the terrace of his luxury villa is one thing; it's quite another matter for someone like me contemplating the view from my fourth-floor room in the Baixa, unable to forget that he is an assistant bookkeeper. "*Tout notaire a rêvé des sultanes*" ...

At official meetings, whenever I have to give my profession as office clerk, I take a certain private pleasure in the irony of that undeserved ridicule, which goes unnoticed by anyone else. I don't know quite how or why, but my name appears thus in the *Commercial Register*:

Guedes (Vicente), office clerk, Rua dos Retrozeiros, 17, 4º
COMM. REG. of Portugal

This mania for the absurd and the paradoxical is the animal joy of the sad. Normal men tell jokes and clap each other on the back out of sheer zest for life, while those incapable of enthusiasm or joy can only indulge in intellectual somersaults, and their cold manner takes the place of any warm, friendly gestures.

On evenings lit by oil lamps in large, empty provincial houses, the elderly aunts of those of us who had elderly aunts would pass the time, while the maid dozed and the kettle came to the boil, by methodically, sensibly, nostalgically playing a game of patience. Someone who takes my place inside me feels a quiet nostalgia for that pointless peace. The tea is served, and the old deck of cards is placed neatly on one corner of the table. The vast china cabinet makes the darkness still darker in the already gloomy dining room. The drowsy maid sweats as she hurries to finish her work. I see all this in me with an anguish and a yearning that bear no relation to anything else. And unwittingly, I find myself pondering the state of mind of someone playing patience.

147 [1918?]
Even if I wanted to create ...

The only true art is that of *construction*. However, the modern world makes it impossible for constructive qualities to appear in the mind.

That is why science was developed. The only thing in which construction plays a part today is the machine; the only logical argument is a mathematical proof.

The power to create needs a support, the crutch of reality.

Art is a science ...

It suffers rhythmically.

I cannot read anything because my hypercritical faculties see only defects, imperfections, possible improvements. I cannot dream because I feel the dream so intensely that I compare it with reality, and then feel, at once, that it is not real; and thus it loses all its value. I cannot forget myself in the innocent contemplation of things and men because I inevitably feel a desire to go deeper, and since my interest cannot exist without that desire, it either dies at the hands of that desire or withers away [...]

I cannot amuse myself with metaphysical speculations because I know all too well from my own experience that all systems are defensible and intellectually possible; and in order to enjoy the intellectual art of constructing systems, I lack the ability to forget that the aim of all metaphysical speculation is the search for the truth.

A happy past whose memory would make me happy again, with nothing in the present that might bring me joy or arouse my interest, with no dream or hypothetical future that could be different from this present, or that could have any other past than that past—here lies my life, a conscious specter of a paradise I never knew, the newborn cadaver of my future hopes.

Happy are those who suffer in unity! Those whom anxiety troubles but does not divide, who believe, even if only in unbelief, and who have no reservations about sitting in the sun.

148 [1918?]

The basest of all human needs is the need to confide, to confess. It is the soul's need to go outside itself.

All right, confess, but confess only what you do not feel. Free your soul from the weight of all your secrets by speaking them out loud; better never to have had the secrets you reveal. Lie to yourself rather than utter that truth. To express oneself is always a mistake. Be aware of this and make self-expression the twin of lying.

I am one of those souls whom women claim to love, and yet whom they never recognize when they actually meet; I am one of those souls who, were a woman to recognize me, she would still not recognize me. I put up with the delicacy of my feelings with disdainful attention. I have all the qualities that are admired in Romantic poets, even the lack of those same qualities that make one a genuine Romantic poet. I find myself (partly) described in various novels as the protagonist of various plots, but the essence of my life, and of my soul, is never to be a protagonist.

I have no clear idea of myself, not even an idea that consists of having no idea of myself. I am a nomad of my own consciousness of myself. The flocks of my inner riches all scattered during the first watch.

The only tragedy is not being able to conceive of ourselves as tragic. I have always had a very clear vision of my coexistence with the world. I never really felt my lack of coexistence with it, which is why I have never been a normal person.

To act is to rest.

All problems are insoluble. The essence of any problem is the absence of a solution. To go looking for a fact means that there is no fact. To think is not to know how to exist.

I sometimes spend hours beside the river on Terreiro do Paço vainly meditating. My impatience is constantly trying to draw me out of that quiet mood, and my inertia constantly keeps me firmly fixed there. I meditate then in a kind of physical torpor, which only resembles voluptuousness in the way a whispering wind resembles voices, in the eternal insatiability of my vague desires, in the perennial instability of my impossible yearnings. I suffer, principally, from being able to suffer. I lack something I do not want, and suffering for that lack is not really suffering.

The quayside, the afternoon and the sea air all form part of my anxiety. The pipes of impossible shepherds are no sweeter than the absence of pipes that reminds me of them here. In this analogous hour, I am pierced by distant idylls spent beside streams […]

150   [1918?]

Which uncertain queen waits beside her lake, keeping watch over the memory of my broken life? I was pageboy to the tree-lined avenues that proved too mediocre for the avian hours of my blue peace. Distant ships completed the sea, whose waves I watched from my terraces, and in the southern clouds I lost my soul, like a carelessly dropped oar.

151   [1918?]

I am astonished at my own capacity for anguish. Not being, by nature, a metaphysician, I have spent whole days in intense, even physical, anguish, unable to reach a conclusion about certain metaphysical and religious problems…

I quickly saw that, for me, solving a religious problem meant finding a rational solution to an emotional problem.

152   [1918?]

The River of Possession
It is axiomatic of our humanity that we are all different. We only look alike from a distance and, therefore, when we are least ourselves. Life, then, favors the undefined; only those who lack definition, and who are all equally nobodies, can coexist.

Each one of us is two, and whenever two people meet, get close or join forces, it's rare for those four to agree. If the dreamer in each man of action frequently falls out with his own personal man of action, he's sure to fall out with the other person's dreamer and man of action.

Each life is a force in itself. Each of us tends towards our own self by way of other people. If we have enough self-respect to find ourselves interesting […] All close encounters are also potential conflicts. The other person is always an obstacle for those in search of something or someone. Only nonsearchers are happy, because only those who do not seek will find, given that those who do not seek already have what they want, and to already have, whatever it is, is to be happy, just as not to think is the happiest part of being rich.

Inside myself, I look at you, my imagined bride, and we have already fallen out even before you exist. My habit of clear-sighted dreaming gives me a very fair notion of reality. Anyone who dreams too much needs to give reality to his dreams. Anyone who gives reality to his dreams has to give to his dreams the equilibrium of reality. Anyone who gives to his dreams the equilibrium of reality suffers as much from the reality of dreaming as from the reality of life and from the unreality of dreaming as much as from his sense of life as unreal.

I am daydreaming and waiting for you in our room with two doors, and I dream that you are arriving and that you enter my dream and come towards me through the right-hand door; if, when you enter, you enter through the left-hand door, there is already a difference between you and my dream. All of human tragedy lies in that small example of how those we think about are never the people we think they are.

Love requires us to be both identical and different, which isn't possible in logic, still less in life. Love wants to possess, to make its own something that must remain outside in order for it to be able to distinguish between the something it has made its own and its own self. To love is to surrender oneself. The greater the surrender, the greater the love. However, to surrender completely is to surrender one's consciousness to the other person. The greatest love, therefore, is death or oblivion or renunciation—all loves are the abomination of love.

On the terrace of the old palace, high above the sea, we were pondering in silence the differences between us. On that terrace by the sea, I was a prince and you a princess. Our love was born at our first meeting, just as beauty sprang from the encounter between moon and water.

Love wants to possess, but does not understand what possession means. If I am not mine, then how can I be yours or you mine? If I do not possess my own being, how can I possess someone else's being? If I am already different from the person to whom I am identical, how can I be identical to someone from whom I am entirely different?

Love is a mysticism that wants to be put into practice, an impossibility that according to our dreams should be possible.

Mere metaphysics. But all of life is metaphysics in the dark, with, in the background, the murmuring gods and our complete ignorance of the way ahead as the only possible way ahead.

The worst trick my decadence plays on me is my love of good health and clarity. I have always felt that the beautiful body and blithe gait of a young person have more right to be in the world than any dream of mine. Sometimes, in the afternoons—with the joy of the old in spirit, but without a flicker of envy or desire—I watch the couples strolling arm in arm towards their brimful consciousness of being young. I enjoy them as I enjoy a truth, regardless of whether it has anything to do with me or not. If I compare them with myself, I still enjoy them, but like someone enjoying a painful truth, combining the pain of the wound with the balm of having understood the gods.

I am the opposite of those symbolist platonists, for whom all being, all action, is the shadow of a reality that is itself merely a shadow.

For me, everything is a point of departure, not a point of arrival. For the occultist, everything ends in everything; for me, everything begins in everything.

Like them, I proceed by analogy and suggestion, but the small garden that, to them, suggests the order and beauty of the soul, to me merely recalls the bigger garden where, far from mankind, this unhappy life could be happy. Each thing suggests to me not the reality of which it is the shadow, but the reality to which it is the path.

The Estrela garden in the afternoon suggests to me an ancient garden dating from the century that preceded the soul's disenchantment.

153 [1918?]

Whenever I travel, I travel very far. I feel as weary after a train journey to Cascais as if I had, in that brief time, traversed the landscapes and cities of four or five different countries.

I imagine myself living in every house I pass, every villa, every small, isolated cottage, whitewashed and silent; I imagine being first happy, then bored, then tired, and, having abandoned it, I carry with me the enormous nostalgia for the time I lived there. And so every journey is a painful, happy harvest of great joys, vast tediums, and innumerable false nostalgias.

Then, as I pass by houses, villas, chalets, I live inside myself all the lives of the people living there. I live all those domestic lives simultaneously. I am, at one and the same time, the father, the mother, the children, the cousins, the maid and the maid's cousin, thanks to the special gift I have for simultaneously feeling several different sensations, for experiencing the lives of various people simultaneously, all the while seeing them outside me and feeling them inside me.

I created various personalities inside myself. I create them constantly. Every dream I have is immediately, as soon as it is dreamed, made flesh in another person, who then goes on to dream that dream, not me.

In order to create, I destroyed myself; I have externalized myself so much inside that, inside, I exist only externally. I am the bare stage on which various actors perform various plays.

154 [1918?]

One day
Instead of having lunch—a need I have to force myself to feel each day—I went down to see the Tejo, and then wandered back along the streets without even imagining that I might find it useful to my soul to have seen the river. Nevertheless . . .

Living is pointless. Only looking is worthwhile. If I could look without living, I would achieve happiness, but that's impossible, as is everything we dream about. How ecstatic the ecstasy that did not involve life! . . .

If only we could at least create a new pessimism, a new negation of life, so that we could have the illusion that something of us, even something bad, would remain!

155 [8 Oct 1919]

Nothing so intimately reveals, so fully interprets, the substance of my innate misfortune as my favorite type of daydream, the balm that I most frequently choose for my personal existential angst. The essence of what I desire is this—to sleep my life. I love life too much to want it to be over; I love not living it too much to feel an overly importunate desire to live it.

This, then, is my most favorite of dreams. Sometimes at night, when the house is still, because the owners have gone out or have fallen silent, I close my bedroom windows, close the heavy shutter doors; then, wearing a shabby old suit, I sink into my deepest armchair, and launch into the dream that I am a retired major in a provincial hotel, lingering on after supper, for no reason, along with a couple of other more sober guests.

I imagine I was born like that. I'm not interested in the youth of that retired major, nor how he rose up the ranks to arrive at the position I so long for. Independent of Time and Life, the major I imagine myself to be has no past life, no parents; he exists eternally in that provincial hotel, weary now of the anecdotes told to him by the other lingering guests.

156 [1919?]

I sometimes think with sad pleasure that if, one day in a future to which I will not belong, these sentences I write should meet with praise, I will at last have found people who "understand" me, my own people, a real family to be born into and to be loved by. But far from being born into that family, I will have been long dead by then. I will be understood only in effigy, and then affection can no longer compensate the dead person for the lack of love he felt when alive.

One day, perhaps, they will understand that I fulfilled, as did no other, my inborn duty as interpreter of one particular period of our century; and when they do, they will write that I was misunderstood in my own time; they will write that, sadly, I lived surrounded by coldness and indifference, and that it is a pity it should have been so. And the person writing, in whatever future epoch he or she may live, will be as mystified by my equivalent in that future time as are those around me now. Because men only learn in order to teach their great-grandfathers who died long ago. We are only able to teach the real rules of life to those already dead.

On this afternoon on which I am writing, the rain has finally stopped. A joyfulness in the air chills the skin. The day is ending not in grayness but in pale blue. Even the cobblestones in the streets reflect that vague blueness. It hurts to be alive, but only with a distant ache. Feeling is unimportant. The lights in one or two shop windows come on. I can see, high up in another window, that the people there have just finished work. The beggar who brushes past me would be afraid if he knew me.

The blue, growing slowly less pale and less blue, is reflected on the buildings as this indefinable hour falls further into evening.

It falls lightly, the definite end of this day, on which those who believe and blunder are caught up in their usual work and who, in the midst of their own pain, enjoy the bliss of unconsciousness. It falls lightly, this wave of dying light, the melancholy of the spent evening, the thin mist that enters my heart. It falls lightly, gently, this indefinite lucid blue pallor of the aquatic evening; light, gentle, sad, it falls on the cold and simple earth. It falls lightly, like invisible ashes, a tortured monotony, an active tedium.

157 [c. 12 Jan 1920]
[Funeral March?]
How often, in the history of all the various worlds, must a stray comet have put an end to one of them! Such a physical catastrophe is linked to the fate of many an intellectual project. Death is watching, like a sister of the intellect, and Fate [...]

Death means being subject to some external reality, and we, in each and every moment of our lives, are both a reflection and an effect of what surrounds us.

Death underlies every living gesture. We are born dead, we live dead, and we enter death already dead.

Composed of living cells and in a state of permanent dissolution, we are made of death.

158 [1920?]
Funeral March
What does any of us do in this world to trouble or change it? For every worthy man is there not another equally worthy? One ordinary

man is worth as much as another; a man of action is worth whatever energy he gives off; thinking men are worth what they create.

Whatever you created for humanity is at the mercy of the cooling Earth. Whatever you left behind for posterity is either so imbued with your own ideas that no one will understand it or else it is so typical of the age you are living in that other ages will not understand it, or else it will appeal to all ages, but will not be understood by the final abyss, into which all ages finally plunge.

We, mere shadows, make gestures in the darkness. Behind us, the Mystery [...]

We are all mortal, made to last only for a certain amount of time. Neither more nor less. Some die as soon as they die, others live on for a while in the memories of those who saw and heard them; others remain in the memory of the nation in which they were born; some fill the memory of the civilization that owned them; a rare few people bridge the contrary impulses of different civilizations ... However, we are all of us surrounded by the abyss of time, which, in the end, consumes us; yes, we all fall into the jaws of the abyss, which [...]

To live for ever is a Desire, to be eternal an illusion.

We are death and we live death. We are born dead, we exist in death, and we enter Death already dead.

Everything that lives, lives because it changes; it changes because everything passes; and because everything passes, it dies. Everything that lives perpetually becomes something else, constantly denying and eluding life.

Life, then, is an interval, a nexus, a link, but a link between what happened and what will happen, a dead interval between Death and Death.

... intelligence, a fiction composed solely of surface and error.

The material life is either pure dream or a mere jumble of atoms that knows nothing of the conclusions drawn by our intelligence or the motives of our emotions. Thus the essence of life is an illusion, an appearance, and there is only being or not-being, and since illusion and appearance are not, they must, therefore, be not-being, which means that life is death.

How entirely vain are our efforts to build and create with our eyes fixed on the illusion that we will not die! "An eternal poem," we say, "words that will never die." But the cooling of earthly matter will carry off not only the living who inhabit its surface, along with [...]

A Homer or a Milton is no more than a comet colliding with the earth.

159 [1920?]

Cenotaph

Neither widow nor son placed on his tongue the coin he paid to Charon. Forever veiled to us are the eyes with which he crossed the Styx and nine times saw reflected in the infernal waters the face we do not know. The shade now wandering the banks of those underworld rivers has no name among us; his name, too, is a shade.

He died for his Country, not knowing how or why. His sacrifice had the glory of going unrecognized. He gave his life with his whole soul: out of instinct, not duty; out of love for his country, not as a conscious act. He defended it as we might defend a mother, whose children we are by birth rather than logic. Faithful to the primeval secret, he did not think or want, he died his death as instinctively as he had lived his life. The shade he now wears makes him brother to those who fell at Thermopylae, faithful in flesh to the oath to which they were born.

He died for his Country as surely as the sun rises every day. He was, by nature, what Death would make of him.

He did not die a slave to an ardent faith, he was not killed fighting for that vile thing, a great ideal. With no base hope for better days for humanity, he did not fall in defence of some political idea, or the future of humanity, or some new religion. Far from that belief in another world with which the believers in Christ and the followers of Rome deceive themselves, he saw death arrive with no hope that it would bring a new life, he saw life pass with no hope for a better life beyond.

He died naturally, as does the wind or the day, taking with him the soul that had been his alone. He plunged into the darkness like someone going through a door, having reached his destination. He died for his Country, the only thing superior to us that we can know and understand as such. Neither the Christian nor the Muslim paradise nor the Buddhist's transcendent oblivion were reflected in his eyes when the flame of earthly life was snuffed out in them.

He did not know who he was, just as we do not know who he is. He did his duty without knowing that he was. He was guided by the same thing that makes the roses bloom and the falling of leaves sad. Life has no better reason, nor death a better reward.

Now, if the gods allow, he will be visiting those regions where there is no light, past Cocytus, the river of wailing, and the fiery river of Phlegethon, and will hear in the night the soft lapping of the pale waters of Lethe.

He is as anonymous as the instinct that killed him. He did not think he would die for his Country, he simply did. He did not set out to do his duty, he simply did. It is fitting that we do not ask of someone who had neither name nor soul what name was given to his body. He was Portuguese, and not being any particular Portuguese man, he is all Portuguese men.

His place is not beside the creators of Portugal, who enjoy a different stature and a different consciousness. Nor does he belong in the company of those demigods, whose boldness carved more and longer paths through the sea and discovered more land than we could grasp.

No statue and no tombstone tell us who he was, this man who was all of us; and since he is all people, he should have the whole earth for his tomb. We should bury him in his own memory, with only his example as tombstone.

160 [c. 13 Jan 1920]

Knowing how tormenting I can find even the smallest things, I deliberately avoid them. Imagine how someone like me, who suffers when even a cloud obscures the sun, must suffer in the dark day that has always been his life!

My isolation is not a search for happiness, which I do not have soul enough to achieve, nor for tranquillity, which no one achieves unless they never lost it in the first place; it is a search for sleep, extinction, and a modest renunciation.

The four walls of my poor room are, simultaneously, cell and distance, bed and coffin. My happiest hours are those during which I think nothing and want nothing, when I do not even dream, lost in the vegetable torpor of the moss that grows on the surface of life. I enjoy without bitterness my absurd consciousness of being nothing, this foretaste of death and extinction.

I never had anyone whom I could call "Master." No Christ died for me. No Buddha indicated the path I should take. No Apollo or Athena appeared to me in my dreams to illumine my soul.

161 [1920?]

All modern men, at least those whose moral stature and intellect surpass that of a pygmy or a peasant, love, when they do love, with a romantic love. Romantic love is the extreme product of century upon century of Christian influence; and both its substance and its evolution can be explained to anyone who doesn't understand it by comparing it to a waistcoat or suit created by the soul or the imagination to clothe any creatures that may happen along and that the mind thinks it will fit.

But since suits are not eternal, a suit only lasts as long as it lasts; and soon, from beneath that increasingly ragged ideal suit, there emerges the real body of the human being we put it on.

Romantic love, therefore, is a sure path to disillusion, unless that disillusion is embraced right from the start and allowed constantly to vary its ideal and, in the workshops of the soul, constantly to produce new suits, thus constantly renewing the appearance of the creature they clothe.

162 [1920?]

A philosophy of aesthetic quietism that prevents the insults and humiliations inflicted on us by life and the living from ever becoming more than a despicable periphery around our sensibility, beyond the outer wall of the conscious soul.

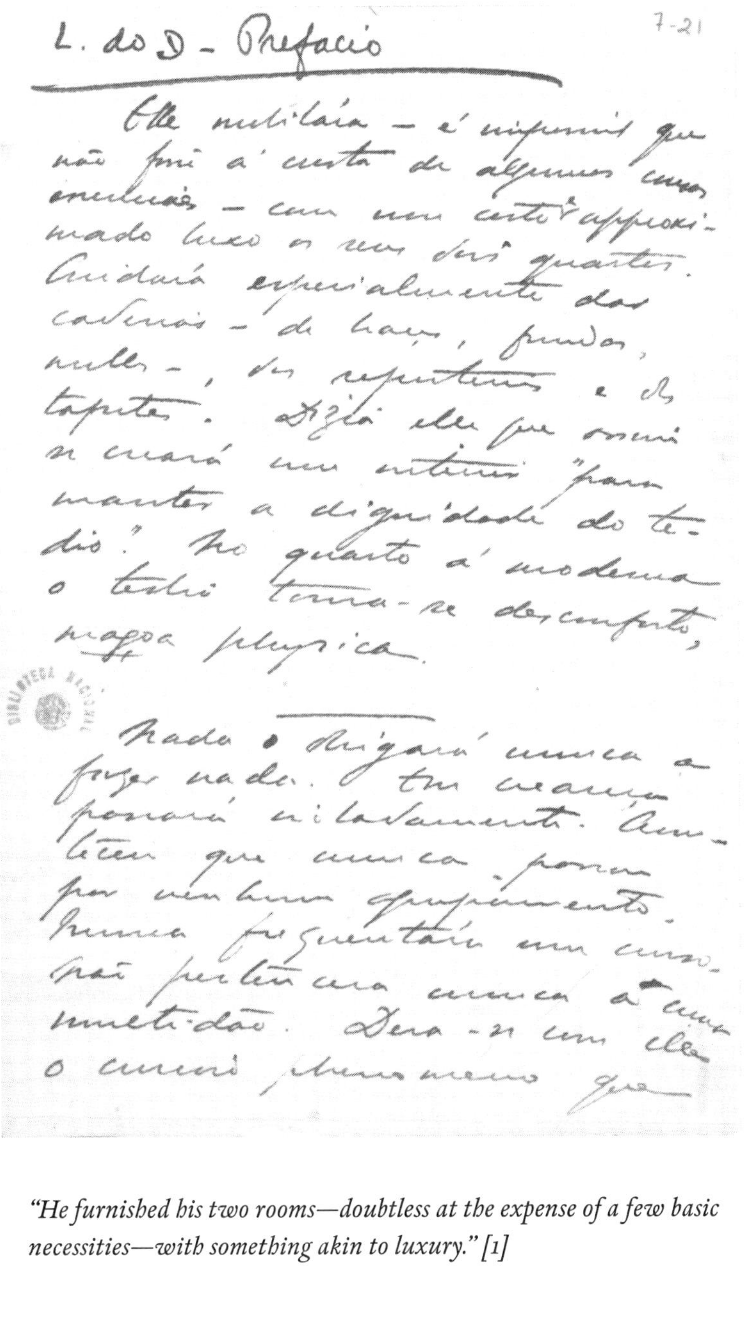
L. do D. – Prefacio 7-21

Elle mobilára — é de suppôr que
não fosse á custa de algumas cousas
essenciaes — com um certo approxi-
mado luxo os seus dois quartos.
Cuidára especialmente das
cadeiras — de braços, fundas,
molles —, dos reposteiros e dos
tapetes. Dizia elle que assim
se criava um interior "para
manter a dignidade do te-
dio." No quarto á moderna
o tedio torna-se desconforto,
magoa physica.

Nada o obrigára nunca a
fazer nada. Em creança
passara isoladamente. Acon-
teceu que nunca passou
por nenhum agrupamento.
Nunca frequentára um curso.
Não pertencera nunca a uma
multidão. Dera-se com elle
o curioso phenomeno que

"He furnished his two rooms—doubtless at the expense of a few basic necessities—with something akin to luxury." [1]

"He had never had to deal with the demands of state or society. He even avoided the demands of his own instincts." [1]

vendo tudo attenc... de ... interni digno de um psycho-
logo, que figui do mesmo
modo amigo d'elle e dedicado
ao ~~meu~~ fim para que elle
me approximou de si — a
publicação d'este seu livro.

Até ... — é' comuni ...
... o — as ~~sante~~ circumstan...
pant ante ella quem, do
meu caracter, lhe pudésse
servir, lhe friam formavas

"I did remain his friend, a friend devoted to the reason he had drawn me to him in the first place, that is, the publication of this his book." [1]

— Adia tudo. Nunca se deve fazer hoje o que se pode deixar de fazer também amanhã. [o que se pode ~~deixar para~~ fazer amanhã]. nem mesmo é necessário que o faças quer hoje, quer amanhã.

— Nunca penses no que vaes fazer. Não o faças.

— Vive a tua vida. Não ~~sejas~~ sujes a tua vida por ella. Na verdade e no erro, no gozo e no mal-estar, sê o teu próprio ser.

— Despreza tudo, mas de modo que o desprezar te não incommode. Não te julgues em ~~perigo~~ ao desprezar. A arte do desprezo ...

Só poderás fazer com sonhos, porque a tua vida-real, a tua vida humana é aquella que não é tua, mas dos outros. Assim, substituirás o sonho á vida e cuidarás apenas em que sonhes ~~ao~~ ~~cuidadosamente~~ com perfeição. ~~Desde nascer até morrer~~ Em todos os teus actos da vida-real, desde o de nascer até ao de morrer, tu não ages: és agido; não vives: és vivido apenas.

Torna-te, para os outros, uma esphynge absurda. Fecha-te, mas sem bater com a porta, na tua torre de marfim. E a tua torre de marfim és tu próprio.

"Postpone everything. Never do today what you can put off until to-morrow. You don't have to do anything, tomorrow or today." [39]

"I so regret never having been the Madame of a harem!" [73]

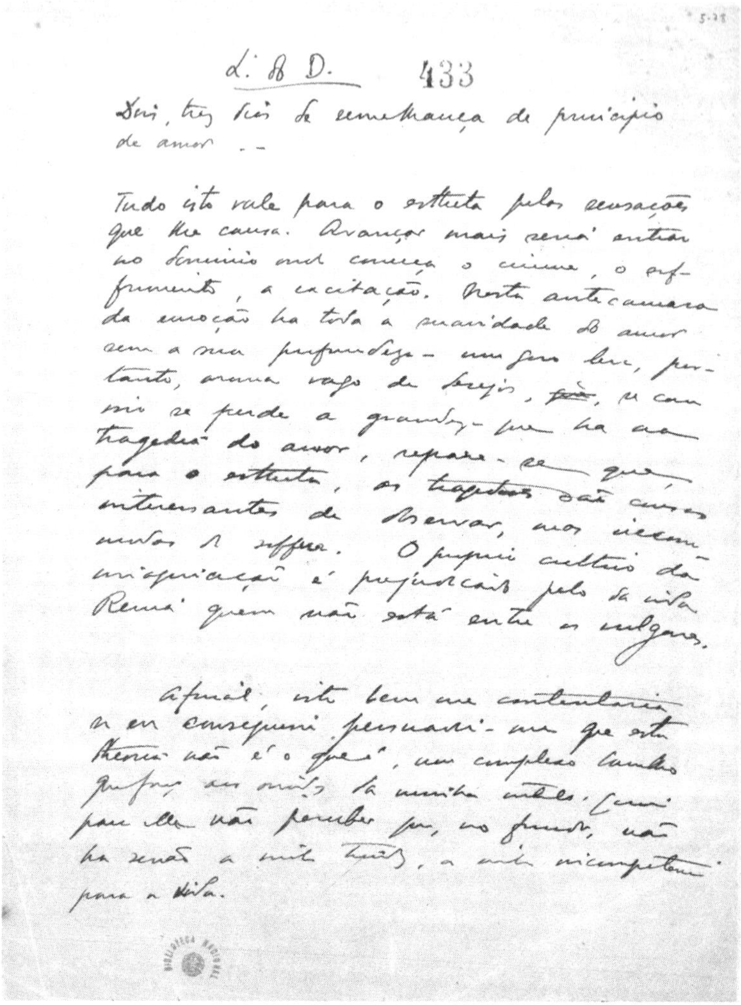

[handwritten manuscript in Portuguese]

"The cultivation of the imagination is hindered by the cultivation of life." [96]

"To be published = the socialization of the self. What a base necessity!"
[98]

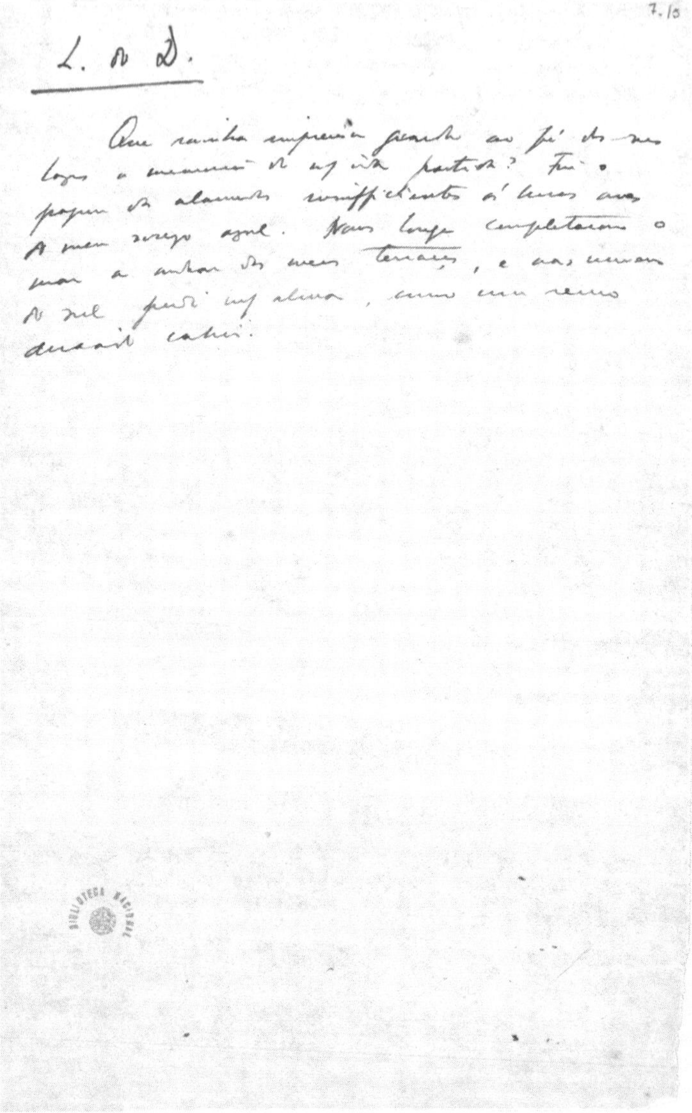
7.10

L. do D.

Que rainha imprecisa guarda ao pé dos seus lagos a memoria da minha vida partida? Fui o pagem de alamedas insufficientes ás horas aves do meu socego azul. Naus longe completaram o mar á sombra dos meus terraços, e nas nuvens do sul perdi minha alma, como um remo deixado cahir.

"Which uncertain queen waits beside her lake, keeping watch over the memory of my broken life?" [150]

The Book of Disquiet

Second Phase

from *The Book of Disquiet*
composed by Bernardo Soares,
assistant bookkeeper in the city of Lisbon
by Fernando Pessoa

163*   [29 Mar 1930]

I was born at a time when most young people had lost their be-
lief in God for much the same reason that their elders had kept
theirs—without knowing why. And so, because the human spirit
tends naturally to criticize because it feels rather than because it
thinks, most of those young people chose Humanity as a substitute
for God. I belong, however, to that species of man who is always on
the edge of the thing he belongs to, who sees not only the crowd of
which he forms a part, but also the great spaces all around. That's
why I did not abandon God as wholeheartedly as they did, nor did
I ever accept Humanity as a replacement. I considered that God,
because unlikely, just might exist and might therefore deserve to
be worshipped, but that Humanity, being a mere biological idea
designating nothing more than the human race itself, was no more
deserving of worship than any other animal species. This worship
of Humanity, with its rituals of Liberty and Equality, always struck
me as being like a revival of the ancient cults, in which animals
were gods or the gods bore the heads of animals.

   Thus, not knowing how to believe in God and being unable
to believe in a herd of animals, I maintained, like others on the
sidelines, that attitude of distance towards everything, which is
commonly called Decadence. Decadence is the total absence of un-
consciousness, for unconsciousness is the very foundation of life.
If the heart could think it would stop beating.

   To someone like myself, and to the few like me who live without
knowing they live, what remains except renunciation as a way of

life and contemplation as destiny? Ignorant of the meaning of a religious life and unable to discover it through reason, unable to have faith in the abstract concept of man and not even knowing what to do with it, all that remains for us as a justification for having a soul is the aesthetic contemplation of life. And so, insensitive to the solemnity of the world, indifferent to the divine and despising humankind, we give ourselves vainly over to a purposeless sensationism crossed with a refined form of epicureanism suited to our cerebral nerves.

From science we took only its central precept that everything is subject to laws of fate against which no independent action is possible because all action is merely reaction. We observed that this law fitted in well with that other more ancient law of the divine fatality of things and, like feeble athletes abandoning their training, we gave up the struggle and, with all the scrupulous attention of genuine erudition, we concentrated instead on the book of sensation.

Unable to take anything seriously and believing that we were given no other reality than that of our feelings, we took shelter in them and explored them as if they were great undiscovered lands. And if we work assiduously not just at aesthetic contemplation but at finding expression for its modes and consequences, it is because the prose or poetry we write, stripped of the desire to influence another's perceptions or change someone else's mind, has become rather like someone reading out loud in order to give a heightened objectivity to the subjective pleasure of reading.

We know only too well that every work is doomed to imperfection and that there is no aesthetic contemplation less assured than the aesthetic contemplation of what we ourselves write. But everything is imperfect; there is no sunset, however lovely, that could not be more so, no gentle breeze lulling us to sleep that could not lull us into a still deeper sleep. Thus, equally contented contemplating mountains or statues, poring over the days as if they were books, above all dreaming everything in order to convert it into something intimately ours, we, too, will write descriptions and analyzes which, once written, will become alien objects that we can enjoy as if they had simply arrived along with the dusk.

This is not the thinking of pessimists like Vigny, for whom life was a prison in which he wove straw to pass the time. To be a pessimist one has to view life as a tragedy, which is an exaggerated, uncomfortable attitude to take. It's true that we do not have any concept of value that we can place on the work we produce. It's true we produce that work in order to pass the time, but we do so not like the prisoner weaving straw to distract himself from his destiny, but like the little girl embroidering pillowcases to entertain herself and nothing more.

For me life is an inn where I must stay until the carriage from the abyss calls to collect me. I don't know where that carriage will take me because I know nothing. I could consider this inn to be a prison since I'm compelled to stay here; I could consider it a kind of club, because I meet other people here. However, unlike others, I am neither impatient nor sociable. I leave those who shut themselves in their rooms and wait, lying limply on their beds unable to sleep; I leave those who chatter in the lounges, from where the cozy sound of music and voices reaches me. I sit at the door and fill my eyes and ears with the colors and sounds of the landscape and slowly, just for myself, sing vague songs that I compose while I wait.

Night will fall on all of us and the carriage will arrive. I enjoy the breeze given to me and the soul given to me to enjoy it and I ask no more questions, look no further. If what I leave written in the visitors' book is one day read by others and entertains them on their journey, that's fine. If no one reads it or is entertained by it, that's fine too.

164 [after 15 Jan 1929]

On these lingering summer evenings, I love the quiet of this, the commercial part of town, all the more because it's such a contrast with the noisy bustle that fills it during the day. Rua do Arsenal,

Rua da Alfândega—the sad roads that reach out to the east where the Alfândega ends—and the long, solitary line of quiet quays: they comfort me with sadness on those evenings when I choose to share their solitude. I'm transported back to a time long before the one in which I actually live. I like to imagine myself a contemporary of Cesário Verde* and feel within myself, not more verses like the ones he wrote, but the substance of his verses. The life I drag around with me until night falls is not dissimilar to that of the streets themselves. By day, they're full of meaningless bustle and, by night, full of an equally meaningless lack of bustle. By day, I am nothing, by night, I am myself. There's no difference between me and the streets around the Alfândega, except that they are streets and I am a human soul, and this, when weighed against the essence of all things, might also count for little. Men and objects share a common abstract destiny: to be of equally insignificant value in the algebra of life's mystery.

But there is something else … In those slow, empty hours a sense of the sadness of all existence rises from my soul to my mind, the bitter sense that everything is at once both felt by me and external to me, and that I am powerless to change it. How often have I seen my own dreams take physical shape, assailing me from without in the form of a tram turning the corner at the far end of the street, or the voice of a street seller at night (selling who knows what) singing an Arab melody, a sudden gush of sound breaking the monotony of the evening, not in order to provide me with a substitute reality but to declare themselves equal in their independence from my will.

165   [1929?]
The weariness of all illusions and of everything that illusions involve—the loss of them, the pointlessness of having them, the

---

* Cesário Verde (1855–1886), one of the forerunners of modern Portuguese poetry, worked most of his life as a clerk. Pessoa felt a deep affinity with his poetry and shared his love of Lisbon.

anticipatory weariness of having to have them in order to lose them, the pain of having had them, the intellectual shame of having had them knowing how they would end.

The consciousness of the unconsciousness of life is the greatest martyrdom imposed on the intelligence. There are unconscious intelligences—flashes of brilliance, currents of understanding, mysteries and philosophies—that behave as automatically as bodily reflexes, much as the liver and the kidneys deal with their secretions.

166   [22 Mar 1929]

In the bay, between the woods and the meadows, there rose out of the uncertainty of the blank abyss the inconstancy of flaming desire. There was no need to choose between the wheat and the myrtles, and the distance continued to recede among the cypresses.

The magical power of words, whether isolated or brought together to form a musical chord, full of intimate resonances and meanings that diverge even as they converge, the pomp of sentences placed in between the meanings of other sentences, malicious vestiges, hopeful woods, and nothing but the peaceful pools in the childhood gardens of my subterfuges ... Thus, between the high walls of absurd audacity, among the lines of trees and the startled shivers of things withering, someone other than me would hear from sad lips the confession denied to the more insistent. Not even if the knights were to ride back down the road visible from atop the castle wall would there be more peace in the Castle of the Last Lost Men, where once lances clashed and clanged in the courtyard; nor would anyone recall another name on this side of the road, apart from the one that used to enchant us nightly, like the tale about the Moorish ladies, and the child who died afterwards from life and wonder.

Along the furrows in the grass, where footsteps left hollows in the waving greenery, the passing of the last lost men echoed faintly, slowly, like memories of the future. Those to come would all be old, while the young would never come. There was a rumble of drums beside the road, and the bugles hung silently in weary hands that would have dropped them if they'd had the strength to drop anything.

Then, again, as a consequence of the magic, the dead shouts rang out again, and the dogs could be seen hovering and havering on the garden paths. It was like an absurd wake, and the princesses of other people's dreams strolled endlessly about at their ease.

167 [1929?]

I feel sorrier for those who dream the probable, the legitimate and the near-at-hand than for those who daydream about the distant and the strange. Those who dream on a grand scale or who are mad and believe in their dreams and are happy, or who are simple daydreamers, for whom the daydream is music to the soul, a meaningless balm. But those who dream the possible have a real possibility of experiencing real disappointment. It may not weigh very heavily on me that I never became a Roman emperor, but it might pain me never to have spoken to the seamstress who, at about nine o'clock each morning, appears around the corner to the right of my window. The dream that promises us the impossible has already prevented us from achieving it, but the dream that promises us the possible interferes with real life and leaves it to life to provide a solution. The former lives exclusively and independently, the latter submits to the contingencies of what might happen.

That is why I love impossible landscapes and the great empty expanses of plains I will never visit. Past historical ages are a marvel too because there is no chance that I will ever be part of them. I sleep when I dream what does not exist; I will wake when I dream what does exist.

In the deserted office at midday, I look out of the balcony window at the street below, and while I can sense the movement of people with my eyes, I am too steeped in my own thoughts to actually see them. I sleep with the balustrade digging painfully into my elbows and am aware of nothing but a great sense of promise. With a strange detachment I can make out the details of the stopped street filled with passersby: the crates piled on a cart, the sacks outside the warehouse next door, and in the window of the grocery on the far corner a glimpse of the bottles of that port wine I imagine no one could possibly afford. My spirit separates itself off from the purely material. I probe more deeply with my imagination. The people walking down the street are always the same as the people who walked by shortly before, always the same fluctuating figures, blurred movements, hesitant voices, things that pass but never happen.

I note all this with my consciousness of my senses rather than with my actual senses … The possibility of other things … And, suddenly, behind me, I hear the metaphysically abrupt presence of the office boy. I could kill him for interrupting the "I" that I wasn't even thinking. I spin round and shoot him a silent look of loathing tense with latent homicidal tendencies. I can already hear the voice he will use when he speaks. He smiles at me from the far end of the office and says "Good afternoon." I hate him as I hate the whole universe. My eyes are heavy with imagining.

168 [1929?]

History rejects certainty. There are orderly times when everything is wretched, and disorderly times when everything is sublime. Decadent times can be intellectually fertile, and authoritarian times fertile only in feeblemindedness. Everything intermingles and intersects, and the only truth that exists is in one's imagination.

So many noble ideas fallen onto the dungheap, so many authentic desires lost in the mire!

As far as I can see, in the prolix confusion of uncertain fate all gods and all men are equal. In the obscure fourth-floor room where I live, they file past me in a succession of dreams, and they are no more to me than they were to those who believed in them. The fetishes of Negroes with frightened, bewildered eyes, the animal gods of savages from tangled wildernesses, the figures the

Egyptians made into symbols, the bright divinities of the Greeks, the upright gods of the Romans, Mithras, lord of the Sun and of all emotion, Jesus lord of consistency and charity, various interpretations of that same Christ, new saints, the gods of the new towns, all file past to the slow march (is it a pilgrimage or a funeral?) of error and illusion. On they all march, and behind them come the empty shadows, the dreams that the more inept dreamers believe must have come down to live on earth, simply because they cast shadows. Pathetic concepts with neither soul nor face—Freedom, Humanity, Happiness, a Better Future, Social Science—they trail through the solitude of the dark like leaves dragged along beneath the train of a regal cloak, in the eternal exile of kings, a cloak stolen by the beggars who occupied the gardens of the house of defeat.

169 [1929?]

...

Thoughts can be lofty without being elegant, but the more inelegant the less influential. Force without finesse is mere matter.

170 [1929?]

Reading the newspapers, always painful from an aesthetic point of view, is often morally painful too, even for one with little time for morality.

When one reads of wars and revolutions—there's always one or the other going on—one feels not horror but boredom. It isn't the cruel fate of all those dead and wounded, the sacrifice of those who die as warriors or onlookers, that weighs so heavy on the heart; it's the stupidity that sacrifices lives and possessions to anything so unutterably vain. All ideals and ambitions are just the ravings of gossiping men. No empire merits even the smashing of a child's doll. No ideal merits even the sacrifice of one toy train. What empire is really useful, what ideal really profitable? Everything comes from humanity and humanity is always the same—changeable but incapable of perfection, vacillating but incapable of progress.

Given this irredeemable state of affairs, given a life we were given we know not how and will lose we know not when, given the ten thousand chess games that make up the struggles of life lived in society, given the tedium of vainly contemplating what will never be achieved [...]—what can the wise man do but beg for rest, for a respite from having to think about living (as if having to live were not enough), for a small space in the sun and the open countryside and at least the dream that somewhere beyond the mountains there is peace.

171 [1929?]

The distinction that revolutionaries draw between the bourgeoisie and the people, between the nobility and the people, or between governors and governed, is a crass and grievous error. The only true distinction one can make is between those who adapt or conform to society and those who do not; the rest is literature and bad literature at that. The beggar, were he to adapt to society, could be king tomorrow, but would thereby lose his standing as a beggar. He would have crossed the frontier and lost his nationality.

This thought consoles me here in this poky office, whose grimy windows look out onto a joyless street. It consoles me to think that I have as brothers the creators of the consciousness of the world— the unruly playwright William Shakespeare, the schoolmaster John Milton, the vagabond Dante Alighieri [...] and even, if I'm allowed to mention him, Jesus Christ himself, who was so little in this world that some even doubt his historical existence. The others are a different breed altogether—Councillor of State Johann Wolfgang von Goethe, Senator Victor Hugo, heads of state Lenin and Mussolini.

It is we in the shadows, among the errand boys and barbers, who constitute humanity.

On one side sit the kings with their prestige, the emperors with their glory, the geniuses with their aura, the saints with their haloes, the leaders of peoples with their power, the prostitutes, the prophets and the rich ... On the other side sit we—the errand boy from around the corner, the unruly playwright William Shakespeare, the barber who tells stories, the schoolmaster John Milton, the shop assistant, the vagabond Dante Alighieri, those whom death either forgets or consecrates and whom life forgot and never consecrated.

172 [1929?]

Today my body felt afflicted by the old anguish that occasionally wells up inside me, and at the restaurant or eating-house, whose upstairs room provides some basis of continuity to my existence, I neither ate properly nor drank as much as I would normally drink. When I left, the waiter, noticing that the bottle of wine was still half full, turned to me and said: "Goodnight, Senhor Soares. Hope you feel better tomorrow."

Just as if the wind had suddenly dispersed the clouds obscuring the sky, the clarion call of that simple phrase eased my soul. And then I realized something I have never fully recognized before: that I have a spontaneous, natural sympathy with these waiters in cafés and restaurants, with barbers and street-corner errand boys, which I cannot honestly say I feel for those with whom I have more intimate relations, if "intimate" is the right word ...

Fraternity is a very subtle thing.

Some govern the world, others are the world. Between an American millionaire, a Caesar or Napoleon, or Lenin and the Socialist boss of a village there is no qualitative difference, only quantitative. Below them come us, the amorphous ones, the unruly dramatist William Shakespeare, the schoolteacher John Milton, that vagabond Dante Alighieri, the boy who ran an errand for me yesterday, the barber who always tells me stories, and the waiter who, simply because I drank only half my bottle of wine, proffered the fraternal hope that I would feel better tomorrow.

Whenever, under the influence of my dreams, my ambitions reared up above the daily level of my life and I felt myself riding high for a moment, like a child on a swing, just like that child, I always had to swing back down to the municipal gardens and recognize my defeat with no fluttering banners to carry into battle and no sword I would have the strength to unsheath.

I would guess—to judge by the silent movements of their lips and the vague indecisiveness in their eyes or the way they raise their voices when they pray together—that most of the people I pass at random in the streets carry within them similar ambitions to wage vain war with just such a bannerless army. And like me, all of them—I turn round to contemplate their vanquished backs—will meet utter and humiliating defeat, miserable and ignorant amongst the slime and the reeds, with no moonlight shining on the banks nor poetry to be found amidst the marshes.

Like me, they all have sad, exalted hearts. I know them well: some work in shops, others in offices, some have small businesses, others are the heroes of cafés and bars, unwittingly glorious in the ecstasy of their egotistical chatter or content to remain egotistically silent, having nothing to say anyway. But all of them, poor things, are poets and seem to me (as I must to them) to drag with them the same misery of our common incongruousness. Like me, their future is already in the past.

At this moment, alone and idle in the office now that everyone else has gone to lunch, I'm peering through the grubby window at the old man tottering slowly down the pavement on the other side of the road. He's not drunk, just a dreamer. He's awake to the nonexistent; perhaps he still has hopes. The gods, if they are just in their injustice, preserve our dreams for us however impossible and give us good dreams however petty. Today, when I am not yet old, I can dream of South Sea islands and impossible Indias; tomorrow, perhaps the same gods will give me the dream of being the proprietor of a small tobacconist's shop, or of retiring to a house in the suburbs. All dreams are the same, because they are dreams. May the gods change my dreams, but not my talent for dreaming.

While thinking this, I forgot about the old man. I can't see him now. I open the window to try to catch him, but he's out of sight. He's gone. For me he performed the function of a visual symbol; once he'd done that, he simply turned the corner. If someone were to tell me that he had turned a corner of the absolute and that he was never even here, I would accept it with the same gesture with which I now close the window …

To succeed? …

Poor apprentice demigods who can conquer empires with words and noble intentions, but still need money to pay for room and board! They're like the troops of a disbanded army, whose commanders had a dream of glory of which all that remains for these soldiers lost in the mud of the marshes is the notion of greatness, the knowledge that they were once an army, and the emptiness of not even having known what the commander they never saw actually did.

Thus everyone at some time dreams of being the commander of the army from whose rearguard they fled. Thus everyone, amidst the mud on the banks, salutes the victory that no one can enjoy and of which all that remained were the crumbs on a stained tablecloth no one bothered to shake out.

They fill the cracks of daily life the way dust fills the cracks in furniture that doesn't get dusted properly. In the ordinary light of every day they show up against the red mahogany or the oilcloth like gray worms. You can scrape them out with a small nail. But no one has the patience to do that.

My poor companions with their lofty dreams, how I envy and despise them! I'm on the side of the others, the poorest, who have only themselves to tell their dreams to and to make of those dreams what would be poems if they wrote them down; poor devils, with only the literature of their own souls […] who die suffocated by the mere fact of existing, without ever having taken that strange, transcendental examination that qualifies one to live.

Some are heroes who laid out five men at once on yesterday's street corner. Others are seducers, irresistible even to women who have never existed. They believe it when they say it and they all say it because they believe it. Other, baser dreamers listen and accept what they hear. Others […] As far as they're concerned, the victors of this world are simply people like them.

Like eels in a bowl they become so entangled with one another that they can never escape. They may occasionally get a mention in the newspapers. The newspapers speak of others more often—but they never achieve fame.

They are the happy ones because they are given the […] dream of stupidity. But as for those, like me, who have dreams without illusions […]

174 [1929?]

It starts as a noise that sets off another noise in the dark pit of things. Then it becomes a vague howling joined in turn by the rasp of swaying shop signs in the street. Then the roaring voice of space falls suddenly silent. Everything trembles, then stops and there is quietness amidst all this fear, like a silent fear seeing another mute fear passing by.

Afterwards, there is only the wind, just the wind, and I notice sleepily how the doors strain at their hinges and the glass in the windows moans resistance.

I do not sleep. I half-exist. Scraps of consciousness float to the surface. I am heavy with sleep but unconsciousness eludes me. I know nothing. The wind … I wake and drift back to sleep without as yet having slept. There is a landscape of loud and terrible noise beyond which I do not know myself. I timidly enjoy the possibility of sleeping. I do in fact sleep, but without knowing that I do. In everything I judge to be sleep there is always another noise heralding the end of everything, the wind in the dark and, if I listen harder, the sound of my own lungs and heart.

175 [1929?]
In the east rises the blond light of the golden moon. The swathe it cuts across the wide river makes serpents on the sea.

176 [1929?]
The instinctive persistence of life over and above any intelligence is something that provides matter for some of my most intimate and most constant reflections. The unreal disguise of consciousness serves only to emphasize to me the existence of the undisguised unconscious.

From birth to death man lives enslaved by the same external concept of self as do the animals. He does not live his life, he merely vegetates on a higher, more complex level. He follows norms he neither knows exist nor knows himself to be guided by, and his ideas, his feelings, his actions are all unconscious—not because they lack consciousness but because they do not contain two consciousnesses.

Occasional hints that they might be deluding themselves—that and only that is what most men experience.

I pursue with my desultory thoughts the ordinary story of ordinary lives. I see how in everything men are slaves to their unconscious temperament, to external circumstances, to impulses to be with people or to be alone that collide in and with that temperament as if it were nothing.

How often I've heard them come out with the one phrase that symbolizes the absurdity, the nothingness, the utter ignorance of their lives. It's the phrase they use to talk of any material pleasure: "You have to grab it while you can." Grab it and take it where? What for? Why? It would be sad to rouse them from the shadows they inhabit by asking them such questions ... For there speaks a materialist, because any man who talks like that is, even if only subconsciously, a materialist. What is it he expects to wrench from life and how? Where will he take the pork chops, the red wine and the girlfriend of the moment? To a heaven in which he doesn't even believe? To what earth other than this one which leads inevitably to the slow putrefaction his life has always been? I know of no other phrase more tragically, more utterly revealing of human nature. It's what plants would say if they were conscious of enjoying the sun. It's what animals inferior to man in their ability to express themselves would say of their somnambulant pleasures. And who knows but that I, now, in writing these words with the illusory idea that they might endure, do not also think that the memory of having written them is what I "grab from life." Like the useless corpse of the average man being lowered into the common ground, the equally useless corpse of my prose, written while I wait, is lowered into a general oblivion. What right have I to make fun of another man's pork chops, red wine and girlfriend?

Brothers in our ignorance, different vessels for the same blood, different forms of the same inheritance—which of us can deny the other? Deny your wife but not your mother, your father, or your brother.

177 [1929?]

… as wretched as the aims we live for, aims we never chose.

Most if not all men live wretched lives, even their joys are wretched, as are almost all their sorrows, except those related to death, because Mystery plays a part in those.

From outside come intermittent sounds, sifted through my inattention, fluid and scattered, like interleaving waves, as if they came from another world: the cries of street vendors selling natural things like cabbages or social things like lottery tickets; the rumble of wheels—jolting carts and wagons; cars, heard more in the approach than in their passing; the shaking of something like a rag out of a window; a boy whistling; loud laughter from the top floor; the metallic groan of the tram in the next street; the confusion of sounds from the crossroads; a variety of loud sounds and soft sounds and silences; the faltering thunder of traffic; a few footsteps; the beginnings, middles and ends of voices—and all of this exists for me, as I sleep-think it, like a stone hidden among the grass and somehow peering out from its hiding place.

Then, through the wall comes a flood of sounds that merge with the others: footsteps, the clatter of crockery, a broom sweeping, a fragment of song (a fado perhaps?); an evening rendezvous beneath a balcony; a cry of irritation when something is missing from the dining table; someone asking to be brought the cigarettes he left on the dresser—this is reality, the anaphrodisiac reality that fails to penetrate my imagination.

The light footsteps of the new young maid, her slippers, which I picture as having scarlet and black braid; the firm, confident, booted steps of the son of the house going out and calling a loud goodbye, the slamming of a door cutting short the echo of the "bye" that follows the "good"; quiet, as if the world ended in this fourth-floor room; the sound of dishes being placed in the sink; water running; "I've told you before..." and from the river a siren silence.

But on I drowse, digesting and imagining, in between synesthesias. And it's extraordinary to think that, if I was asked now, I would not want more for my brief life than these long minutes, this absence of thought, emotion, action, even sensation, this inner sunset of disparate desire. And then I think, almost without thinking, that, to a greater or lesser extent, most if not all men live like this, whether standing still or moving forward, but feeling the same drowsy apathy when it comes to ultimate aims, the same indifference to future plans, the same diluting of life. Whenever I see a cat lying in the sun, I am reminded of a man lying in the sun. Whenever I see anyone sleeping, I am reminded that everything is sleep. Whenever someone tells me they had a dream, I wonder if he is aware that he has never done anything other than dream. The noise from the street grows louder, as if a door had opened, and the doorbell clangs.

It was nothing, because the door immediately closed again. The footsteps stop at the end of the corridor. The washed dishes raise their watery, crockery voices. Does the air tremble? A truck passes, making the whole house shake, and since all things must come to an end, I get up from my thinking.

178 [1929?]

Most men spontaneously live a fictitious, alien life. Most people are other people, said Oscar Wilde, and he was quite right. Some spend their lives looking for something they don't want; others earnestly look for something they do want, but that is of no use at all; still others lose themselves [...]

However, most men are happy and enjoy life anyway. In general, men weep little and, when they do complain, they make literature out of it. Pessimism is not really viable as a democratic formula. Those who bemoan the ills of the world are an isolated few—they are only bemoaning their own ills. If a Leopardi or an Antero de Quental has no beloved, no lover, then the universe is a terrible place.* If Vigny feels unwell or unloved, the world is a prison. If Chateaubriand longs for the impossible, then human life is a bore. If Job is covered in boils, then the whole earth is covered in boils. If you tread on a sad man's corns, then woe betide the feet of the sun and the stars.

Indifferent to this, and grieving only as much as he needs to and for as little time as possible—over the death of a son, for example, whom he will forget as the years pass, except on his birthday; over the loss of money, which he mourns until he gets some more or becomes used to the loss—humanity continues digesting and loving. Life recovers and carries on. The dead are buried. Losses forgotten.

---

* Antero de Quental (1842–1891), Portuguese poet and philosopher. Pessoa wrote of him: "Properly speaking there has been no Portuguese literature before Antero de Quental; before that there has been either a preparation for a future literature, or foreign literature written in the Portuguese language."

179 [1929?]

Any effort we make, regardless of the goal in view, will inevitably have to adapt to the changes imposed on it by life; it then becomes a different kind of effort, with different goals, and may even achieve the exact opposite of what it set out to achieve. Only a paltry goal is worth aiming for, because only a paltry goal stands any chance of being achieved. If I want to put all my efforts into earning a fortune, I will, up to a point, achieve it, since all such paltry, quantitative goals, whether personal or not, are attainable and verifiable. But how do I set about achieving my aim of serving my country or enriching human culture, or improving humanity as a whole? I can never be sure that what I'm doing is right, nor that my goal has been achieved; [...]

180 [1929?]

And then there are the friends, great lads all of them, it's fun talking to them, having lunch with them, having supper with them, and yet also, somehow or other, so sordid, so despicable, so petty, still so tied to the workplace even when you're out in the street, still with your nose in the accounts book even when you venture abroad, still with the boss standing over you even in the infinite.

Open and adorned, everything awaits the King who will come, who is about to arrive, for the dust from his retinue forms a new mist in the slowly dawning east and in the distance the lances shine out their own bright dawn.

181 [1929?]

The trivialities natural to life, the insignificancies of the normal and vulgar, lie like a layer of dust, tracing a blurred, grotesque line beneath the squalor and meanness of my human existence.

The accounts book lying open before eyes whose life dreams of all the worlds of the Orient; the office manager's inoffensive joke that offends against the whole universe; the boss being told it's his girlfriend on the phone, Senhora So-and-so, in the middle of my meditation on the most asexual part of a theory that is purely aesthetic and intellectual.

But all dreamers, even if they don't do their dreaming in an office in the Baixa, or in front of a balance sheet for a textile company—each of them has an accounts book open before them whatever it may be, whether it's the woman they married or administering a future they've inherited, whatever it might be as long as it clearly is.

Everyone has a boss always ready with some inappropriate joke and a soul out of touch with the universe. Everyone has a boss and a boss's girlfriend and a telephone call that always comes at an inopportune moment just on the edge of the splendid fall of evening and mistresses now revealed as mistresses are speaking on a girlfriend's phone to say that they're at a chic tea party like all the other ladies.

All of us, we who dream and think, are assistant bookkeepers in a textile company or dealing in some other merchandise in some other Baixa. We draw up the accounts and make a loss; we add up the figures and pass on; we close the account and the invisible balance is never in our favor.

Though I smile as I write these words, my heart feels as if it would break, would break the way things break, into fragments, into shards, into so much rubbish to be dumped in the dustbin and carried shoulder-high to the eternal dustcart of all municipal councils.

182   [1929?]

From my fourth-floor room looking out over the infinite, in the plausible intimacy of the coming evening, at my window opening onto the beginning of the stars, my dreams—in rhythmic agreement with the distance before me—set off on journeys to unknown or imagined or simply impossible countries.

183 [after 31 May 1929]

Funeral march

Hieratic figures from unknown hierarchies are lined up waiting for you in the corridors—fresh-faced, fair-haired pageboys, young men in [...] a scattering of glinting blades and helmets and lofty adornments, somber glimpses of dull gold and silks.

Everything that the imagination infects, imbuing all ceremonies with a funereal solemnity that weighs on us even in victory, the mysticism of the void, the asceticism of absolute renunciation.

The Ganges also flows down Rua dos Douradores. All ages exist in this narrow room—the mixture
the multicolored shifts in manners,
the distances between different peoples,
and the vast variety of nations.

And there, in ecstasy, in a single street, I await Death among swords and battlements.

Not the six feet of cold earth that closes over closed eyes beneath the hot sun and beside the green grass, but the death that goes beyond our life and is itself a life—a dead presence in someone, the unknown god whom the Gods may remember.

184 [1929?]

With an enormous effort I rise from my seat only to find that I still seem to be carrying it around with me, only now it's even heavier because it's become the seat of my own subjectivity.

185 [1929?]

My conscious mind is filled by a drowsiness that I can't explain but which frequently attacks me, if something so shadowy can be said to attack. I walk along a street as if I were in fact still seated in an armchair and my attentive mind, though alert to everything, is

still filled by the inertia of a body in repose. I would be incapable of avoiding an oncoming passerby. I would be unable to respond in words, or even formulate an answer in my head, to a question put by some casual passerby taking advantage of my chance presence in the street. I would be incapable of harboring a desire, a hope, or anything that could be construed as a movement not necessarily of the will of my whole being but, if I can put it this way, of the partial and individual will of each of the elements I can be broken down into. I would be incapable of thinking, feeling, wanting. And yet I walk, I move on, I drift. Nothing in my movements (I know this because no one else seems to notice) betrays my stagnant state. And this lack of soul which would be comfortable, even correct, in someone lying down or recumbent, is singularly uncomfortable, even painful, in a man walking down a street.

It's like being drunk on inertia, a drinking spree as utterly joyless in itself as in its cause. It's an illness from which there is no hope of recovery. It is a cheerful death.

186 [1929?]

Sometimes when I raise my heavy head from the books in which I keep track of other people's accounts and of the absence of a life of my own, I feel a physical nausea. It may come from sitting so bent over but it goes beyond a mere question of numbers and disillusion. Life sickens me like a dose of bad medicine. And it's then, with immense clarity of vision, that I see how easy it would be to remove myself from this tedium if I just had the strength truly to want to do so.

We live through action, that is, through the will. Those of us— be we geniuses or beggars—who do not know how to want are brothers in our shared impotence. What's the point of calling myself a genius when in fact I'm just an assistant bookkeeper? When Cesário Verde had himself announced to the doctor not as Senhor Verde, commercial clerk, but Cesário Verde, poet, he was using one of those expressions of futile pride that stink of vanity. Poor man, he was never anything but Senhor Verde, commercial clerk. The poet was born only after he died, because it was only after his death that his poetry came to be appreciated.

To act, that is true intelligence. I will be what I want to be. But I have to want whatever that is. Success means being successful, not just having the potential for success. Any large area of land has the potential to be a palace, but where's the palace if no one builds there?

My pride stoned by blind men and my disillusion trampled on by beggars.

"I want you only so that I can dream you," they say to their beloved in poems they never send, those who dare not say anything to her. The line "I want you only so that I can dream you" is from an old poem of mine. I register this memory with a smile, and do not even comment on the smile.

187   [Spring 1929?]

Facing me on the sloping desk are the two large pages of the heavy accounts ledger; I look up with weary eyes, my soul even wearier than my eyes. Beyond the nothing that this represents is the warehouse in Rua dos Douradores with its rows of ordinary shelves and ordinary employees, human order and the peace and quiet of the vulgar. Through the window come diverse noises, and those diverse noises are as vulgar as the peace and quiet of the shelves.

I look with new eyes at the two white pages, on which my careful numbers record the company's results. And I smile to myself as I think that life, which includes these pages bearing the names of fabrics and various sums of money, blank spaces, ruled lines and letters, also includes the great navigators, the great saints, the poets of every age, none of whom appear in this book, a whole vast progeny excluded by those who determine what is of value in the world.

As I write the name of a fabric I do not even know, the doors of the Indus and of Samarkand open up to me; and—belonging to neither place—the poetry of Persia with its quatrains and unrhymed third lines provides a distant support for my disquiet. I make no mistakes, though, I write, I add up, and the accounts continue to be kept, carried out as usual by an employee of this office.

188 [1929?]

Today, during one of those periods of daydreaming which, though devoid of either purpose or dignity, still constitute the greater part of the spiritual substance of my life, I imagined myself free for ever of Rua dos Douradores, of my boss Vasques, of Moreira the bookkeeper, of all the other employees, the errand boy, the post boy, even the cat. In dreams, that freedom felt to me as if the South Seas had proffered up a gift of marvelous islands as yet undiscovered. Freedom would mean rest, artistic achievement, the intellectual fulfillment of my being.

But suddenly, even as I imagined this (during the brief holiday afforded by my lunch break in a café), a feeling of displeasure erupted into the dream: I would, I felt, be sad. Yes, I say it quite seriously: I would be sad. For my boss Vasques, Moreira the bookkeeper, Borges the cashier, all the lads, the cheery boy who takes the letters to the post office, the errand boy, the friendly cat—they have all become part of my life. I could never leave all that behind without weeping, without realizing, however displeasing the thought, that part of me would remain with them and that losing them would be akin to death.

Moreover, if I left them all tomorrow and discarded this Rua dos Douradores suit of clothes I wear, what else would I do? Because I would have to do something. And what suit would I wear? Because I would have to wear another suit.

We all have a Senhor Vasques; sometimes he's a tangible human being, sometimes not. In my case he really is called Vasques and he's a pleasant, healthy chap, a bit brusque at times but he's no double-dealer. He's selfish but basically fair, much fairer than many of the great geniuses and many of the human marvels of civilization on both left and right. For many people Vasques takes the form of vanity, a desire for greater wealth, for glory or immortality ... Personally I prefer to have Vasques as my real-life boss since, in times of difficulty, he's easier to deal with than any abstraction the world has to offer.

The other day a friend, who's a partner in a prosperous company that does business throughout the country and who considers my salary to be distinctly on the low side, said to me: "You're being exploited, Soares." This made me realize that indeed I am; but since it's the fate of everyone in this life to be exploited, my question would be: is it any worse being exploited by Senhor Vasques and his textile company than by vanity, glory, resentment, envy or the impossible? Some, the prophets and saints who walk this vacuous world, are exploited by God himself.

And I return, as if to someone else's house, to the spacious office in Rua dos Douradores, the way some return to their homes. I approach my desk as if it were a bulwark against life. I feel such an overwhelming sense of tenderness that my eyes fill with tears for my books that are in reality the books of other people whose accounts I keep, for the old inkwell I use, for Sergio's stooped shoulders as, not far from me, he sits writing out bills of lading. I feel love for all this, perhaps because I have nothing else to love or perhaps too, because even though nothing truly merits the love of any soul, if, out of sentiment, we must give it, I might just as well lavish it on the smallness of my inkwell as on the grand indifference of the stars.

189   [1929?]

I asked for so little from life and life denied me even that. Part of a ray of sunlight, a nearby field, some peace and quiet and a mouthful of bread, not to feel the knowledge of my existence weigh too heavily on me, to demand nothing of others and have them demand nothing of me. That was denied me, like someone denying the beggar not out of malice, but merely so as not to have to unbutton his jacket.

Sad, in my quiet room, alone as I have always been and as I always will be, I sit writing. And I wonder if that seemingly feeble thing, my voice, does not perhaps embody the substance of thousands of voices, the hunger to speak out of thousands of lives, the patience of millions of souls who, like me, have submitted in their daily lives to vain dreams and evanescent hopes. In moments like these my heart beats faster simply because I am conscious of it. I live more intensely because I live more fully. I feel in my person a religious force, a form of prayer, something like a clamor of voices. But the reaction against myself begins in my intellect ... I see myself in the fourth-floor room in Rua dos Douradores and feel drowsy; on the half-written page, I observe rather unlovely writing, the cheap cigarette in my left hand as it rests on the old blotter. Here I am, in this fourth-floor room, demanding answers from life! Pronouncing on what other souls feel! Writing prose as if I were a real genius, a famous writer! Me, here, like this!

190 [1929?]

The search for the truth—whether the subjective truth of one's own convictions, the objective truth of reality or the social truth of money or power—always brings with it, if the searcher in question deserves the prize, the ultimate knowledge that the truth does not exist. Life's biggest lottery prize goes only to those who happened to buy tickets.

The value of art is that it takes us away from here.

191 [1929?]

Normality is like a home to us and everyday life a mother. After a long incursion into great poetry, into the mountains of sublime aspiration, the cliffs of the transcendent and the occult, it is the sweetest thing, savoring of all that is warm in life, to return to the inn where the happy fools laugh and joke, to join with them in their drinking, as foolish as they are, just as God made us, content with the universe that was given us, and to leave the rest to those who climb mountains and do nothing when they reach the top.

It doesn't shock me that people should say of a man I consider mad or stupid that he is better than some other person whose life and achievements are merely ordinary. When seized by a fit, epileptics are extraordinarily strong; paranoiacs have reasoning powers beyond those of most normal people; religious maniacs in their delirium attract larger crowds of believers than (almost) any demagogue and give an inner strength to their followers that demagogues never can. But all this proves nothing except that madness is madness. I prefer to fail having known the beauty of flowers than to triumph in a wilderness, for triumph is the blindness of the soul left alone with its own worthlessness.

How often has some futile dream left me filled with a horror of the inner life, with a physical nausea for mysticisms and meditations. I rush from my home, where I have dreamed these things, and go to the office, where I gaze on Moreira's face like a voyager finally reaching port. All things considered, I prefer Moreira to the astral world; I prefer reality to truth; in fact, I prefer life to the God who created it. This is how he presented it to me, so this is how I will live it. I dream because I dream, but I don't insult myself by giving to dreams a value they do not have, apart from that of being my own personal theatre, just as I do not call wine (from which I still do not abstain) "food" or "one of life's necessities."

192 [1929?]

If I have no other virtue at least there exists in me the unending novelty of liberated sensation.

Today, walking down Rua Nova do Almada, I suddenly noticed the back of the man walking ahead of me: the ordinary back of an ordinary man, the jacket of a modest suit on the back of a chance passerby. He was carrying an old briefcase under his left arm and, with each step he took, he tapped the pavement with the point of the rolled umbrella he carried in his right hand.

Suddenly I felt something approaching tenderness for that man. I felt in him the tenderness one feels for human ordinariness, for the banal daily life of the head of a family on his way to work, for his humble, happy home, for the sad and joyous pleasures that no doubt make up his life, for the innocence of living unreflectively, for the animal naturalness of that clothed back.

I looked again at the man's back, the window through which I saw these thoughts.

It was exactly the same feeling that comes over you in the presence of someone sleeping. When someone sleeps they become a child again, perhaps because in sleep one can do no evil and one is unaware even of one's own existence. By some natural magic, the worst criminal, the most inveterate egotist, is made sacred by sleep. I can see no perceptible difference between killing a child and killing someone while they sleep.

That man's back sleeps. Every part of the man walking ahead of me, at the same speed as me, is asleep. He moves unconsciously. He lives unconsciously. He sleeps just as we all sleep. All of life is a dream. No one knows what he does, no one knows what he wants, no one knows what he knows. We sleep our lives away, the eternal children of Fate. That's why, if I think with that feeling, I experience an immense, boundless tenderness for all of infantile humanity, for the somnambulist lives people lead, for everyone, for everything.

What sweeps over me in such moments is a pure humanitarianism that draws no conclusions and knows no ulterior motives. I'm overwhelmed by tenderness as if I saw all this with the eyes of a god. I see everyone with the compassion of the only conscious being alive: poor men, poor humanity. What is it all doing here?

From the simple rise and fall of our lungs to the building of cities and the drawing up of imperial frontiers, I consider every movement, every motivating force in life, to be a form of sleep, to be dreams or intervals that occur involuntarily in the pauses between one reality and the next, between one day of the Absolute and the next. And at night, like some abstractly maternal figure, I bend over the beds of both good and bad children, made equal in the sleep that makes them mine. My tenderness for them has the generosity of some infinite being. I shift my gaze away from the back of the man immediately in front of me to look at everyone else, at everyone walking down this street, and I consciously include them all in the same absurd, cold tenderness provoked in me by the back of the unconscious being in whose steps I follow. They are all like him: the girls chatting on their way to the workshop, the young clerks laughing en route to the office, the maids returning home laden with shopping, the boys out running their first errands of the day—all of this is just one unconsciousness wearing different faces and bodies, puppets moved by strings pulled by the fingers of the same invisible being. They give every appearance of consciousness but, because they are not conscious of being conscious, they are conscious of nothing. Whether intelligent or stupid, they are all in fact equally stupid. Whether young or old, they all share the same age. Whether men or women, they all belong to the same nonexistent sex.

193 [1929?]

I have often tried in dreams to be the kind of imposing individual the Romantics imagined themselves to be, and whenever I have, I've always ended up laughing out loud at myself for even giving house-room to such an idea. After all, the *homme fatal* exists in the dreams of all ordinary men, and romanticism is merely the turning inside out of our normal daily selves. In the most secret part of their being, all men dream of ruling over a great empire, with all men their subjects, all women theirs for the asking, adored by all the people and (if they are inferior men) of all ages ... Few are as accustomed to dreaming as I am and so are not lucid enough to laugh at the aesthetic possibility of nurturing such dreams.

The most serious criticism of romanticism has not yet been made, namely, that it represents the inner truth of human nature, an externalization of what lies deepest in the human soul, but made concrete, visible, even possible, if being possible depends on something other than Fate, and its excesses, its absurdities, its various ploys for moving and seducing people, all stem from that.

Even I who laugh at the seductive traps laid by the imagination often find myself imagining how wonderful it would be to be famous, how gratifying to be loved, how thrilling to be a success! And yet I can never manage to see myself in those exulted roles without hearing a guffaw from the other "I" I always keep as close to me as a street in the Baixa. Do I imagine myself famous? Only as a famous bookkeeper. Do I fancy myself raised up onto the thrones of celebrity? This fantasy only ever comes upon me in the office in Rua dos Douradores, and my colleagues inevitably ruin the effect. Do I hear the applause of the most variegated multitudes? That applause comes from the cheap fourth-floor room where I live and clashes horribly with the shabby furnishings, with the surrounding vulgarity, humiliating both me and the dream. I never even had any castles in Spain, like those Spaniards we Portuguese have always feared. My castles were built out of an incomplete deck of grubby playing cards; and they didn't collapse of their own accord, but had to be demolished with a sweeping gesture of the hand, the impatient gesture of an elderly maid wanting to restore the tablecloth and reset the table, because teatime was calling like some fateful curse. Even that vision is of little worth, because I don't have a house in the provinces or old aunts at whose table, at the end of a family gathering, I sit sipping a cup of tea that tastes to me of repose. My dream failed even in its metaphors and figurations. My empire didn't even go as far as a pack of old playing cards. My victory didn't even include a teapot or an ancient cat. I will die as I lived, among the bric-a-brac of my room, sold off by weight among the postscripts of things lost.

May I at least take with me into the immense possibilities to be found in the abyss of everything the glory of my disillusion as if it were that of a great dream, the splendor of my unbelief like a flag of defeat—a flag held aloft by feeble hands, but dragged through the mud and blood of the weak and held on high as we sink into the shifting sands, whether in protest or defiance or despair no one knows ... No one knows because no one knows anything, and the sands swallow up those with flags and those without ... And the sands cover everything, my life, my prose, my eternity.

I carry with me the knowledge of my defeat as if it were a flag of victory.

194 [1929?]

Everything there is broken, anonymous, orphaned. There I witnessed generous gestures of tenderness that seemed to reveal to me the depths of poor sad souls; I discovered that those gestures lasted only as long as the words that expressed them, and—as I often observed with the wisdom of the silent—they had their roots in something analogous to pity, but that faded as quickly as my surprise on first noticing it, or else vanished with the wine drunk during that temporarily compassionate person's supper. There was always a clear relation between that humanitarian impulse and the amount of brandy consumed, and many grand gestures suffered from that one glass too many or from the pleonasm of thirst.

Those creatures had all sold their soul to a devil from hell's hoi polloi, a devil greedy for all things sordid and lewd. They lived on an intoxicating brew of vanity and idleness, and died limply among cushions of words and a tangle of scorpions with venom for spit.

The most extraordinary thing about all those people was their utter meaninglessness. Some wrote for important newspapers and yet still managed not to exist; others held public posts recorded in the professional registers and yet managed to do nothing in life; others were celebrated poets, but the same ashen dust smeared their foolish faces with gray, as if in a tomb of embalmed corpses, with, as in life, their hands behind their backs.

From the brief time in which I stagnated in that intellectual exile, I recall a few genuinely funny and enjoyable moments, and many more sad and monotonous ones, a few profiles silhouetted against the void, a few gestures directed at whatever waiter happened to be serving us; in short, a physically nauseating tedium and the memory of a few witty anecdotes.

Interspersed like blank spaces among the others were a few older men, some of whom told hackneyed jokes and were just as bad as the others when it came to speaking ill of others; indeed, they spoke ill of the very same people.

I never felt so sympathetic towards minor figures in the public eye as when I saw them criticized by these nobodies, even though they had never sought their pathetic public glory. I understood that the reason the pariahs of Greatness could triumph was because they triumphed over those nobodies and not over humanity as a whole.

Poor devils, always hungry, either for lunch or fame or for life's desserts. Any stranger hearing them speak would think he was listening to Napoleon's teachers or to Shakespeare's tutors.

There are those who triumph in love, those who triumph in politics and those who triumph in art. The first have the advantage of being able to come up with their own version of their amorous triumphs without anyone knowing what really happened. However, when hearing one of these individuals describing his sexual marathons, one does tend to feel a touch suspicious when he reaches his seventh deflowering. Those who are the lovers of titled ladies or famous women (as almost all of them are) get through so many countesses that a list of their conquests would shake the gravity and composure of even the great-grandmothers of young women of title.

Others specialize in physical conflict and claim to have slain all the boxing champions of Europe one drunken night on the corner of the Chiado. Some have influence with all the ministers in all the ministries, and their claims are slightly more plausible simply because they are less repellent.

Some are great sadists, others are great pederasts, others proclaim in loud, mournful tones that they beat women, whom they have whipped along the paths of life. And they always leave someone else to pay the bill.

Then there are the poets, the [...]

I know of no better cure for this great excremental torrent of shadows than being in direct contact with ordinary human life in all its commercial reality; for example, life in the office in Rua dos Douradores. What a relief it was to leave that madhouse of puppets for the authentic presence of Moreira, my superior and a genuinely knowledgeable bookkeeper, who, though shabby and badly dressed, is nevertheless something those others could never be, what we call a man ...

195 [1929?]

Whenever they can, they sit opposite the mirror and, while speaking to us, gaze at themselves with doting eyes. Sometimes, as with all such infatuations, they get distracted. I've always felt a certain sympathy for them, because my aversion for my own adult appearance has always taught me to sit with my back to mirrors. They instinctively recognized this and were kind to me; I was the good listener who left them free to indulge their vanity and their taste for oratory.

They were not bad lads, some better, some worse. They sometimes even surprised me, a close observer of the average man, with unsuspected displays of generosity and kindness, but they could also be base and sordid in ways that ordinary people would never notice. Mean, envious and delusional, that's how I would sum them up, and the same words could be applied to whatever part of that particular milieu has leached into the work of decent men who got caught in the undertow of that sea of the self-deluded. (It's there in Fialho's work, flagrant envy, out-and-out vulgarity, a repellent lack of elegance ...*)

---

* Fialho de Almeida (1857–1911) was a Portuguese writer and journalist, who initially embraced Naturalism, but later tended more towards Decadentism.

Some are funny, others are *only* funny, others do not yet exist. Café humour divides itself into witty remarks about those who aren't there and insolent remarks made to those who are. This kind of wit is just plain rude. There is no clearer indicator of poverty of spirit than a person's inability to be funny except at other people's expense.

I came, I saw and, unlike them, I conquered. Because my victory consisted in seeing. I saw that those inferior beings were no different from any other group of inferior beings: I found here, in the house where I rent a room, the same sordid soul I had found in the cafés, except, all the gods be praised, for the idea of taking Paris by storm. In her more ambitious moments, the landlady here may dream of moving to a posher part of town, but she has no ambitions to conquer Paris, and that touches my heart.

From my time spent at that graveside of the will I retain only a sense of utter tedium and a few amusing anecdotes.

They're on their way to the cemetery, and it seems that they left the past behind them in the café, because they make no mention of it now.

… and posterity will know nothing of them, hidden for ever beneath the rotting heap of flags won in victories that never happened.

196 [1929?]

The most contemptible thing about dreams is that everyone has them. In the dark, the errand boy dozes away the day as he leans against the lamp-post in the intervals between chores, immersed in thoughts about something or other. I know what he's daydreaming about: the same dreams I plunge into between entries in the summer tedium of the utterly still, silent office.

197 [1929?]

Apart from those vulgar dreams, which flow shamefully down the soul's sewers, and to which no one would dare confess, and which haunt our sleepless nights like grubby ghosts, the slimy, greasy, seething detritus of our repressed sensibility, what absurd, horrifying, unspeakable things the soul can, with a little effort, find in its hidden corners!

The human soul is a madhouse of caricatures. If a soul could reveal itself entirely, if its need for concealment did not go far deeper than all its known and named acts of ignominy, it would, as people say of the truth, be a very deep well indeed, a sinister well, full of vague echoes, inhabited by ignoble lives, dead slime, lifeless slugs, the snot of subjectivity.

198 [1929?]

We know that the book we will never write will be bad. Even worse will be the one we put off writing. At least the book that has been written exists. It may not be very good, but it exists, like the miserable little plant in the lone flowerpot belonging to my crippled neighbor. That plant is her pride and joy, and sometimes it's mine too. What I write, knowing that it's bad, might also offer a few moments of distraction from worse things to another sad or wounded soul. That is enough, or, rather, it isn't, but it nonetheless helps in some way, and that's how it is with life.

A tedium that contains only the prospect of more tedium; the anticipated sadness of feeling sad about having felt sad today—great tangles of feelings that lack utility or truth, great tangles ...

... where, sitting hunched on a bench at a railway station, my contempt drowses beneath the cape of my own dullness ...

... the world of dreamed images that make up, in equal parts, my knowledge and my life ...

An awareness of the present moment is not something that really bothers me. I'm hungry for time in all its long duration, and to be unconditionally myself.

199 [1929?]

… in the sad dishevelment of my confused emotions …

A twilight sadness composed of weariness and false renunciations, a sense of boredom with feeling anything at all, a pain like a suppressed sob or a truth suddenly grasped. Unfurling before me in my inattentive soul is this landscape of abdications—avenues of abandoned gestures, tall borders of dreams that were not even well dreamed, contradictions like box hedges separating deserted paths, suppositions like old pools unrefreshed by fountains, everything seems so tangled and pathetic in the sad dishevelment of my confused emotions.

200 [1929?]

I find it so irritating, the happiness of all those men unaware of their unhappiness. Their human life is full of everything that would constitute a whole series of anxieties for any truly sensitive soul. However, since their real life is purely vegetative, any pain they feel passes by without even touching their soul, and they live a life that can only be compared to that of a rich man who occasionally suffers from toothache, but takes plenty of aspirin—the genuine good fortune of being alive without realizing it, which is the greatest gift the gods can give, because it is the gift of being similar to them, and, like them, superior (albeit in a different way) to those incidents called joy and pain.

That is why, despite everything, I love them all. My beloved vegetables!

201 [1929?]

Isolation made me in its own image. The presence of another person—one person is all it takes—immediately slows down my thinking and, just as in a normal person contact with others acts as a stimulus to expression and speech, in me that contact acts as a counter-stimulus, if such a word exists. When I'm alone I can come up with endless bon mots, acerbic ripostes to remarks no one has made, sociable flashes of wit exchanged with no one; but all this disappears when I'm confronted by another human being. I lose all my intelligence, I lose the power of speech and after a while all I feel like doing is sleeping. Yes, talking to people makes me feel like sleeping. Only my spectral and imagined friends, only the conversations I have in dreams, have reality and substance, and in them the spirit is present like an image in a mirror.

The whole idea of being forced into contact with someone oppresses me. A simple invitation to supper from a friend produces in me an anguish difficult to put into words. The idea of any social obligation—going to a funeral, discussing something with someone at the office, going to meet someone (whether known or unknown) at the station—the mere idea blocks that whole day's thoughts and sometimes I even worry about it the night before and sleep badly because of it. Yet the reality, when it comes, is utterly insignificant, and certainly doesn't justify so much fuss, yet it happens again and again and I never learn.

"My habits are those of solitude not of men." I don't know if it was Rousseau or Senancour who said that, but it was some spirit belonging to the same species as me, though I could not perhaps say of the same race.

202 [1929?]

... Here I am caught between the life I scornfully love and the death I find both frightening and fascinating. I'm afraid of the nothingness that could turn out to be something else, and I'm afraid of it simultaneously as nothingness and as something else, as if it might combine both nonexistence and the horrible unknown, as if, in the coffin, they might stop the eternal breathing of a corporeal soul, as if they would slam down the lid on the impersonal. The idea of hell, which only a satanic soul could have invented, seems to me to derive from that confusion, that mixture of two contradictory, contaminating fears.

203

There are days when each person I meet, especially the people I have to mix with on a daily basis, take on the significance of symbols, either isolated or connected, which come together to form occult or prophetic writings, shadowy descriptions of my life. The office becomes a page on which the people are the words; the street is a book; words exchanged with acquaintances, encounters with strangers, are sayings that appear in no dictionary but which my understanding can almost decipher. They speak, they communicate, but it is not of themselves that they speak, nor themselves that they communicate; as I said, they are words that reveal nothing directly but rather allow meaning to be revealed through them. But, with my poor crepuscular vision, I can only vaguely make out whatever it is that those windowpanes suddenly appearing on the surface of things choose to show of the interiors they both guard and reveal. I understand without knowledge, like a blind man to whom people speak of colors.

Sometimes, walking down the street, I hear snatches of private conversations and they are almost all about another woman, another man, the son of some third party or someone else's lover […]

Just hearing these shadowy fragments of human discourse, which are after all what most conscious lives are taken up with, I carry away with me a tedium born of disgust, a terror of being exiled among illusions and the sudden realization of how bruised I am by other people; I am condemned by the landlord and by the other tenants, to being just one more tenant among many, peering disgustedly through the bars on the window at the back of the warehouse at other people's rubbish piling up in the rain in the inner courtyard that is my life.

204

God created me to be a child and left me to be a child for ever. But why did he let life beat me and take away my toys and leave me alone at playtime, to crumple up in feeble hands the blue pinafore streaked with tears? Since I cannot live without affection, why was that affection taken from me? Whenever I see a child in the street crying, a child exiled from the others, it hurts me more than the sadness of the child I see in the unsuspected horror of my exhausted heart. I hurt in every inch of my lived life, and the hands crumpling the hem of the pinafore, the mouth contorted by real tears, the weakness and the solitude are all mine, and the laughter of passing adults is like the flame of a match struck on the sensitive tinder of my own heart.

205 [1929?]

And at last—I see it in my mind's eye—over the darkness of the shining roofs, the cold light of the warm morning breaks like a torment out of the Apocalypse. Once more the immense night of the growing brightness. Once more the same horror—another day, life and its fictitious usefulness and vain activity; my physical personality, visible, social, communicable through words that mean nothing, usable by other people's thoughts and gestures. I am me again, exactly as I am not. With the coming of the dark light that fills with gray doubts the chinks of the shutters (so very far from being hermetic!), I begin to feel that I will be unable to remain much longer in my refuge, lying on my bed, not asleep but with a sense of the continuing possibility of sleep, of drifting off into dreams, not knowing if truth or reality exist, lying between the cool warmth of clean sheets, unaware, apart from the sense of comfort, of the existence of my own body. I feel ebbing away from me the happy lack of consciousness with which I enjoy my consciousness, the lazy, animal way I watch, from between half-closed eyes, like a cat in the sun, the logical movements of my unchained imagination. I feel slipping away from me the privileges of the penumbra, the slow rivers that flow beneath the trees of my half-glimpsed eyelashes, and the whisper of waterfalls lost among the sound of the slow blood pounding in my ears and the faint persistent rain. I slowly lose myself into life. I don't know if I'm asleep or if I just feel as if I were. I don't dream this precise interval, but I notice, as if I were beginning to wake from a waking dream, the first stirrings of life in the city, rising like a tide of words from that indefinite well down below, from the streets that God made. They are joyous sounds, filtered by the sad rain that falls, or was falling, for I can't hear it now … I can tell from the excess of gray in the splintered light in the far distance, in the shadows cast by a hesitant brightness, that it is unusually dark for this time in the morning, whatever time that is. The sounds I hear are joyful, scattered. They make my heart ache as if they had come calling me to go with them to an examination or an execution. Each day that I hear the dawn, from the bed on which I lie empty of knowledge, seems to me the day of some great event in my life that I will lack the courage to confront. Each day I feel it rise from its bed of shadows, scattering bedclothes along the streets and lanes below, in order to summon me to some trial. Each day that dawns I will be judged. And the eternal condemned man in me clings to the bed as if to his lost mother, and strokes the pillow as if my nanny could defend it from those other boys.

The great beast's untroubled siesta in the shade of trees, the weariness of the street urchin amidst the cool of tall grasses, the heavy drowsiness of the Negro in some warm, far-off afternoon, the pleasure of the yawn that closes languid eyes, the quiet comfort of our resting heads: everything that rocks us from forgetting into sleep slowly closes the windows of the soul in the anonymous caress of sleep.

To sleep, to be far off without even realizing it, to lay oneself down, to forget one's own body, to enjoy the freedom of unconsciousness, that refuge by a forgotten lake stagnating amongst the leafy trees of vast, remote forests.

A nothing that seems to breathe, a little death from which one wakes feeling fresh and revived, a yielding of the fibers of the soul as it is massaged by oblivion.

But, like the renewed cries of protest of an unconvinced listener, I hear again the sudden clamor of rain drenching the slowly brightening universe. I feel cold to my hypothetical bones, as if I were afraid. Crouching, desolate and human, all alone in the little dark that remains to me, I weep, yes, I weep for my solitude and for life and for my pain that lies abandoned by the roadside of reality, along with the dung, useless as a cart without wheels. I cry for everything, for the loss of that lap I used to sit on, the death of the hand held out to me, the arms that could not hold me, the shoulder to weep on that was never there ... And the day that finally breaks, the pain that dawns in me like the crude truth of day, everything that I dreamed, thought and forgot in me—all this, in an amalgam of shadows, fictions and remorse, is tumbled together in the wake of passing worlds and falls among the detritus of life like the skeleton of a bunch of grapes, eaten on the corner by the young lads who stole it.

Like the sound of a bell calling people to prayer, the noise of the human day grows suddenly louder. Indoors, like an explosion, I hear the sound of someone softly closing the first door to open onto life today. I hear the sound of slippers walking down an absurd corridor that leads straight to my heart. And with an abrupt gesture, like someone at last finding the resolve to kill himself, I throw off the heavy bedclothes that shelter my stiff body. I'm awake. Somewhere outside, the sound of the rain moves farther off. I feel happier. I have fulfilled some unknown duty. With sudden bold decisiveness I get up, go to the window and open the shutters to a day of clear rain that drowns my eyes in dull light. I open the windows. The cool air is damp on my hot skin. Yes, it's raining, but even if everything remains just the same, in the end what does it matter! I want to feel refreshed, I want to live and I lean out of the window as if to bow my neck to life, as if to bear the weight of God's abstract yoke.

I can only comprehend the perennial inertia in which I allow my monotonously uneventful life to lie, like a layer of dust or dirt on the surface of a resolute unchangeability, as a lack of personal cleanliness.

We should bathe our destinies as we do our bodies, change our lives just as we change our clothes—not to keep ourselves alive, which is why we eat and sleep, but out of the disinterested respect for ourselves which can properly be called cleanliness.

There are many people in whom a lack of cleanliness is not an act of will but an intellectual shrug of the shoulders. And there are many people for whom the dullness and sameness of their lives are not what they would have chosen for themselves nor a natural conformity with that lack of choice, but rather a snuffing out of self-knowledge, an automatic irony of the understanding.

There are pigs who, however disgusted they may feel at their own filth, fail to remove themselves from it, frozen by the same extremity of feeling that prevents the terrified from removing themselves from the path of danger. There are those, like me, pigs by destiny, who do not attempt to escape the daily banality of life, mesmerized by their own impotence. They are birds fascinated by the absence of the snake; flies who, unaware, hover above the branches until they come within the sticky reach of the chameleon's tongue.

So each day I promenade my conscious unconsciousness along my particular branch of the tree of routine. I promenade my destiny which trots ahead without waiting for me and my time that advances even when I don't. And the only thing that saves me from the monotony is these brief notes I make about it. I am merely glad that in my cell there are glass panes this side of the bars, and in large letters, in the dust of necessity, I write my daily signature on my contract with death.

Did I say my contract with death? No, not even with death. Anyone who lives the way I do does not die: he comes to an end, withers, merely ceases to vegetate. The space he occupied continues to exist without him, the street he walked along remains though he's no longer seen there, the house where he lived is inhabited by not-him. That is all and we call it nothing; but, were we to put it on, not even this tragedy of denial would be guaranteed applause, for we do not know for certain that it is nothing, we who are as much the vegetables of truth as we are of life, the dust that covers the windowpanes both inside and out, the grandchildren of Destiny and the stepchildren of God, who married Eternal Night when she was left a widow by Chaos, our true father.

To leave Rua dos Douradores for the Impossible ... To get up from my desk and set off into the Unknown ... A journey intersected by Reason—what the French call the Great Book.

207 [1929?]

As with all tragedies, the real tragedy of my life is just an irony of Fate. I reject life because it is a prison sentence, I reject dreams as being a vulgar form of escape. Yet I live the most sordid and ordinary of real lives and the most intense and constant of dream lives. I'm like a slave who gets drunk during his rest hour—two miseries inhabiting one body.

With the clarity afforded by the lightning flashes of reason that pick out from the thick blackness of life the immediate objects it is composed of, I see with utter lucidity all that is base, flaccid, neglected and factitious in this Rua dos Douradores that makes up my entire life: the squalid office whose squalor seeps into the very marrow of its inhabitants' bones, the room, rented by the month, in which nothing happens except the living death of its occupant, the grocer's shop on the corner whose owner I know only in the casual way people do know each other, the boys standing at the door of the old tavern, the laborious futility of each identical day, the same characters constantly rehearsing their roles, like a drama consisting only of scenery and in which even that scenery is facing the wrong way ...

But I also see that in order to flee from all this I must either master it or repudiate it. I do not master it because I cannot rise above reality and I do not repudiate it because, whatever I may dream, I always remain exactly where I am.

And what of my dreams? That shameful flight into myself, the cowardice of mistaking for life the rubbish tip of a soul that others only visit in their sleep, in that semblance of death through which they snore, in that calm state in which, more than anything, they look like highly evolved vegetables!

Unable to make a single noble gesture other than to myself, or to have one vain desire that isn't utterly vain!

Caesar gave the ultimate definition of ambition when he said: "Better to be the chief of a village than a subaltern in Rome." I enjoy no such position either in a village or in Rome. At least the grocer merits some respect on the block between Rua da Assumpção and Rua da Victoria; he's the Caesar of the whole block. Am I superior to him? In what respect, when nothingness confers no superiority, no inferiority, and permits no comparisons?

The grocer is the Caesar of a whole block and the women, quite rightly, adore him.

And so I drag myself along, doing things I don't want to do and dreaming of what I cannot have […], as pointless as a public clock that's stopped …

This tenuous but steady sensibility, this long but conscious dream […], which, together, form my privileged position here in the shadows.

208 [1929?]

The morning, half-cold, half-warm, winged its way over the scarce houses on the slopes of the hills at the outer edge of the city. On those drowsing slopes, a faint mist, full of awakening light, was gradually dissolving into nebulous shreds. (It wasn't cold, apart from the chilly business of having to resume life.) And all of that—all that slow, light morning coolness—was like a joy he had never been able to feel.

The tram was making its slow way to the avenues. As it approached the more densely built-up areas, he was gripped by a vague sense of loss. Human reality was beginning to stir.

In those morning hours, when the shadows had vanished, but not as yet their light weight, the spirit that allows itself to be carried along by the impulse of the moment longs to arrive, and to arrive in the ancient, sunny port. What would cheer one up is not so much for this moment to remain fixed and forever, as when one gazes at a solemn landscape or at the moonlight shining serenely on the river, but for life to have been something else, so that this moment would have had for him a different, more recognizable savor.

The uncertain mist was growing still thinner. The sun was spreading. The sounds of life were growing louder.

At such an hour, it would be best never to arrive at the human reality for which our life is destined. To be left hanging weightlessly between the mist and the morning, hovering above real life, not in one's spirit, but in one's spiritualized body, that, more than anything, would satisfy our longing to find a refuge, even if we have no reason to seek such a refuge.

Feeling everything very subtly makes us indifferent, except to those things we cannot have—sensations that our soul is still in too embryonic a form to feel, human activities in keeping with deep feelings, with passions and emotions lost among other kinds of achievement.

The trees, lined up along the avenues, had nothing to do with all this.

That moment came to an abrupt halt, just as the bank on the other side of the river does when the boat touches the quay. Before that, it carried imprinted on its hull the landscape of the other shore, which vanished with the sound of the hull scraping the quayside. The man with his trousers rolled up to his knees caught hold of the rope, and that natural gesture was definitive and conclusive. It brought metaphysical closure to the impossibility of our soul continuing to enjoy the pleasure of a hesitant anxiety. The boys on the quay looked at me as they would look at anyone, at someone who does not experience such inappropriate emotions while watching the practical business of a boat docking.

209 [1929?]

It's just a rather mediocre lithograph. I stare at it without knowing if I actually see it. There are others in the shop window and there is this one. It's in the middle, at the point that blocks my view of the stairs.

She's clasping the primrose to her breast, and the eyes that stare out at me are sad. Her smile has the same brilliance as the glossy paper and her cheek is touched with red. The sky behind her is bright blue. She has a rather small, curved mouth and above its picture-postcard expression her eyes fix me with a look of terrible sorrow. The arm pressing the flowers to her breast reminds me of someone else's arm. The dress or blouse has an open neckline that falls slightly to one side. Her eyes are very sad: they watch me from their background of lithographed reality expressing something like a truth. She arrived with the spring. She has large, sad eyes but that isn't why she seems sad. I drag my feet away from the window. I cross the road and then turn round in impotent rebellion. She's still holding the primrose they gave her, and her eyes reflect the sadness of everything I lack in life. Seen from a distance, the lithograph is more colorful. The figure has a pinker ribbon tied round its hair; I hadn't noticed that before. Even in lithographs there is something terrible about human eyes: the unavoidable proof of the existence of a consciousness, the clandestine cry that they too have a soul. With a great effort, I haul myself out of the trance into which I have sunk and, like a dog, shake off the dank darkness of the fog. And above my awakening, in a farewell to something else altogether, those eyes expressive of all of life's sadness, of the metaphysical lithograph we contemplate from afar, regard me as if I had some real notion of God. A calendar is attached to the bottom of the engraving. It's framed above and below by two broad, black, badly painted convex lines. Between the upper and lower boundaries, above the green paper bearing the obsolete calligraphy covering the inevitable first of January, the sad eyes smile ironically back at me.

Oddly enough, I do already know that figure. There's an identical calendar, which I've often seen, in the office, in a corner at the back. But by some mystery, to do with both the lithograph and me, the calendar in the office doesn't have sad eyes. It's just a lithograph. (It's printed on shiny paper and sleeps away its dull life above the head of Alves, the left-handed clerk.)

I would like simply to laugh this off, but I feel terribly uneasy. I feel the chill of a sudden sickness in my soul. I haven't the strength to rebel against this absurdity. Which window onto which of God's secrets have I unwittingly approached? What does the window on the landing actually look out on? Whose eyes looked out at me from that lithograph? I'm almost trembling. Involuntarily I look over to the far corner of the office at the real lithograph. Again and again I raise my eyes to look.

210   [1929?]

I hate reading. I feel a kind of anticipatory tedium at the prospect of all those unread pages. I can only read books I already know. My bedside reading is Father Figueiredo's book on rhetoric, in which, each night, I read for the thousandth time the description in clear, monastic Portuguese of the various rhetorical figures, whose names, read a thousand times before, I have still not memorized.* But the language soothes me [...] and I would sleep badly if I did not read those precise words with their old-fashioned spellings.

---

* António Cardoso Borges de Figueiredo (1792–1878) was a Portuguese priest who wrote a number of books for schools. A well-thumbed and annotated copy of his *Rhetoric* was found in Pessoa's personal library.

However, I owe to Father Figueiredo's book, with its exaggerated purism, the relative care I take—insofar as I can—over writing the language in which I express myself with the propriety that [...]
And I read:
(a passage by Father Figueiredo)
—beginning, middle and end,
and this consoles me for being alive.
Or else
(a passage on rhetorical figures)
that takes me back to the preface.

I'm not exaggerating a single verbal inch: I really feel all this.

Just as others read passages from the Bible, I read his book on rhetoric. I enjoy the advantage of repose and a lack of religious devotion.

211 [1929?]

In those occasional moments of detachment in which we become aware of ourselves as individuals whom other people perceive as other, it has always bothered me to imagine the sort of moral and physical figure I must cut in front of those who see and talk to me whether daily or from time to time.

We are all accustomed to think of ourselves as essentially mental realities and of others as merely physical realities; because of the way others respond to us, we do vaguely think of ourselves as physical beings; we vaguely think of other people as mental beings, but only when we find ourselves in love or conflict with another do we really take in the fact that others have a soul just as we do.

That's why I sometimes lose myself in futile imaginings about the kind of person I am for those who see me, what my voice sounds like, what kind of impression I leave on the involuntary memory of others, how my gestures, my words, my outward life engrave themselves on the retina of other people's interpretations.

I've never managed to see myself from outside. There is no mirror that can show us to ourselves as exteriors, because no mirror can take us outside ourselves. We would need another soul, another way of looking and thinking. If I were an actor captured on film or could record my speaking voice on disc I'm sure that I would still be a long way from knowing how I seem from outside because, whether I like it or not, record what I will of myself, I remain stuck here inside the high-walled garden of my consciousness of me.

I don't know if other people feel the same, or if the science of life does not indeed consist essentially in being so alienated from oneself that one instinctively achieves the alienation necessary to be able to participate in life as if unaware of one's own consciousness; or if others, even more inward-looking than me, are not entirely given over to the brutishness of just being themselves, living entirely outwardly through that miracle whereby bees form societies better organized than any human nation and ants communicate in a language of tiny twitching antennae far superior to our complex ability to misunderstand one another.

The geography of our consciousness of reality is one of complicated coastlines, lakes and rugged mountains. And to me, if I think about it too long, it begins to seem like the sort of map one finds in the Pays du Tendre or in *Gulliver's Travels*, a joke drawn up with precision in some fantastic or ironic book for the diversion of superior beings who know where lands are really lands.*

For those who think, everything is complex, and thought, no doubt purely for its own pleasure, only complicates things further. But any thinking person has a need to justify his abdication with a vast manifesto of understanding, embellished, like the excuses given by liars, with the excess of detail which, when shaken off like earth from a plant, reveals the root of the lie.

---

* The "Carte du Tendre" is an allegorical map showing the region of the "tender sentiments," drawn up by Madeleine de Scudéry (1607–1701).

Everything is complex or perhaps it's just me who is. But in the end it doesn't matter because nothing really matters. All this, all these considerations that have strayed from the main highway, vegetate in the gardens of the excluded gods like climbing plants growing too far from the walls they should be climbing. And in this night that sees the end but not the conclusion of my disjointed thoughts, I smile at the essential irony that causes them to rise in a human soul orphaned since before the stars were made from Destiny's grand motives.

212 [1929?]

In order to understand, I destroyed myself. To understand is to forget to love. I know nothing at once so false and so meaningful as that saying of Leonardo da Vinci's that one can only love or hate something once one has understood it.

Solitude torments me; company oppresses me. The presence of another person distracts me from my thoughts; I dream their presence in a peculiarly abstracted way that none of my analytical thoughts can define.

213 [1929?]

I find the idea of traveling only vicariously seductive, as if it were an idea more likely to seduce someone other than myself. The whole vast spectacle of the world fills my awakened imagination with a wave of brilliant tedium; like someone grown weary of all gestures, I sketch out a desire and the anticipated monotony of possible landscapes disturbs the surface of my stagnant heart like a rough wind.

And as with journeys so with books, and as with books so with everything else ... I dream of an erudite life in the silent company of ancients and moderns, renewing my emotions through other people's, filling myself with contradictory thoughts that spring from the contradictions of real thinkers and those who have only half-thought, in other words, the majority of those who write. But the minute I pick up a book from the table my interest in reading vanishes; the physical fact of having to read it negates the desire to read ... In the same way the idea of traveling atrophies if I happen to go anywhere near a place whence I could in fact embark. And, being myself a nonentity, I return to the two negatives of which I am certain—my daily life as an anonymous passerby and the waking insomnia of my dreams.

And as with books so with everything else ... Given that anything can be dreamed up to serve as a real interruption to the silent flow of my days, I raise eyes of weary protest to the sylph who is mine alone, to the poor girl who, had she only learned to sing, could perhaps have been a siren.

214 [1929?]

Any change in one's usual timetable fills the spirit with a cold novelty, a slightly discomforting pleasure. Someone who normally leaves the office at six but one day happens to leave at five immediately experiences a kind of mental holiday, followed almost at once by a feeling bordering on distress because he doesn't quite know what to do with himself.

Yesterday, because I had some business out of the office, I left at four o'clock and by five had completed my errand. I'm not used to being out in the streets at that hour and so I found myself in a different city. The slow light on the familiar shopfronts had a sterile sweetness, and the usual passersby walked in a city parallel to mine, like sailors given shore leave the night before.

Since the office was still open at that hour, I hurried back there to the evident surprise of the other employees whom I had already said goodbye to for the day. Back already? Yes, back already. I was free to feel again, alone with those people who accompanied me in all but spirit ... It was in a way like being at home, that is, in the one place where one does not have feelings.

I woke very early this morning in a sudden tangle of confusion and slowly sat up in bed feeling suffocated by an incomprehensible sense of tedium. It was provoked neither by a dream nor by any reality. It was a feeling of absolute, utter tedium that had its roots in something or other. In the dark depths of my soul, invisible unknown forces engaged in a battle in which my being was the battleground, and the whole of me was shaken by this secret struggle. With my waking was born a physical nausea for all of life. A horror at having to live awoke and sat up with me in bed. Everything rang hollow to me and I was filled with the cold realization that every problem, whatever it might be, would prove insoluble.

A terrible anxiety gripped and shook my smallest gesture. I felt afraid I might go mad, not from madness, but just from being there. My whole body was a suppressed scream. My heart was beating as if it were sobbing.

In my bare feet, in long, faltering strides that I vainly tried to make other than they were, I walked the short length of my room and traced an empty diagonal across the room beside mine, which has a door in the corner that opens onto the corridor. As my movements became more uncontrolled and imprecise, I accidentally knocked the brushes on the dressing table, bumped against a chair and, once, my swinging hand struck the harsh iron of the bedstead. I lit a cigarette that I smoked without thinking and only when I saw that ash had fallen on the pillow—but how could it when I hadn't even lain down there?—did I realize that I was possessed (or at least in some state analogous in effect if not in name) and that the consciousness I would normally have had of myself had become fused with the void.

I received the coming of morning, the tenuous cold light that lends a vague bluish whiteness to the emergent horizon, like a grateful kiss from the world. For that light, that true day, freed me, freed me from something, offered a supportive arm to my as yet unvisited old age, patted my false childhood on the head, gave shelter to the beggarly repose of my overflowing sensibility.

What a morning this is that wakes me both to the brutishness of life and to its overwhelming tenderness! I could almost cry to see the light growing before and beneath me in the old narrow street, and when the shutters on the grocer's shop on the corner turn a dirty brown in the almost glaring light, my heart feels a fairy-tale sense of relief, and the security of not feeling begins to seep back into me.

What a morning this pain brings with it! And what shadows retreat before it? What mysteries were unfolded? None: just the sound of the first tram like a match illuminating the darkness of my soul, and the firm steps of my first passerby, the friendly voice of physical reality telling me not to upset myself so.

216 [25 Dec 1929]

Once the last of the rain had dwindled until only intermittent drops fell from the eaves of roofs, and the reflected blue of the sky appeared along the cobbled center of the street, the traffic took up a different song, louder and gayer, and there was the sound of windows being opened to greet the return of the forgetful sun. Then, down the narrow street, from the next corner along, came the loud cry of the lottery seller, and the sound of nails being hammered into boxes in the shop next door reverberated about the bright space.

It was like an optional holiday, quite legal, but observed by no one. Rest and work lived alongside one another, and I had absolutely nothing to do. I'd got up early and lingered over my preparations for existence. I walked from one side of the room to the other, dreaming out loud of unconnected, impossible things—gestures I had forgotten to make, impossible ambitions only randomly realized, long, steadfast conversations which, had I had them, would have taken place. And in this reverie devoid of all grandeur and calm, in this hopeless, endless dawdling, my pacing feet wasted away my free morning, and my words, uttered out loud in a quiet voice, multiplied as they reverberated round the cloister of my simple isolation.

Seen from outside, my human figure appeared ridiculous in the way that everything human is when seen in private. Over the simple vestments of abandoned sleep I'd put on an ancient overcoat that I wear for these morning vigils. My old slippers, especially the left one, were badly split. And, with long decisive steps, my hands in the pockets of my posthumous coat, I walked the avenue of my small room, enjoying in those vain thoughts a dream much the same as everyone else's.

In the coolness entering through my one window, you could still hear plump drops falling from the rooftops, the accumulated waters of the rain now gone. There was still a hint of the sweet air it had left behind. The sky, however, was an all-conquering blue, and the clouds left behind by the defeated, weary rain withdrew over the castle walls, yielding up all legitimate paths to the sky.

It was a time to be happy, yet something weighed on me, an obscure longing, an undefined but not entirely despicable desire. Perhaps it just took me time to accustom myself to the sensation of being alive. And when I leaned out of the high window over the street I looked down at without seeing, I suddenly felt like one of those damp cloths used to clean grimy objects in the house that gets taken to the window to dry, but instead is left there, screwed up on the sill it slowly stains.

217 [1929?]

I envy—although I'm not sure if envy is the right word—those people about whom one could write a biography, or who could write their autobiography. Through these deliberately unconnected impressions I am the indifferent narrator of my autobiography without events, of my history without a life. These are my Confessions and if I say nothing in them it's because I have nothing to say.

What could anyone confess that would be worth anything or serve any useful purpose? What has happened to us has either happened to everyone or to us alone; if the former, it has no novelty value and if the latter, it will be incomprehensible. I write down what I feel in order to lower the fever of feeling. What I confess is of no importance because nothing is of any importance. I make landscapes out of what I feel. I make a holiday of sensation. I understand women who embroider out of grief and those who crochet because life is what it is. My old aunt passed the infinite evenings playing patience. These confessions of my feelings are my game of patience. I don't interpret the cards the way some do to know the future. I don't scrutinize them because, as in games of patience, the cards have no value in themselves. I unwind myself like a length of multicolored yarn, or make cat's cradles out of myself, like the ones children weave around stiff fingers and pass from one to the other. Taking care that my thumb doesn't miss the vital loop, I turn it over to reveal a different pattern. Then I start again.

Living is like crocheting patterns to someone else's design. But while one works, one's thoughts are free and, as the ivory hook dives in and out amongst the wool, all the enchanted princes that ever existed are free to stroll through their parks. The crochet of things ... A pause ... Nothing ...

For the rest, what qualities can I count on in myself? A horribly keen awareness of sensation and an all too deep consciousness of feeling ... A sharp self-destructive intelligence and an extraordinary talent for dreams to entertain myself with ... A defunct will and a reflective spirit in which to cradle it like a living child ... In short, crochet ...

218 [1929?]

The clock in the depths of the deserted house, deserted because everyone's asleep, slowly lets fall the clear quadruple sound of four o'clock in the morning. I haven't yet slept, nor do I expect to. With nothing to distract me and keep me from sleeping, or weigh on my body and prevent my resting, I lay down the dull silence of my strange body in the shadow that the vague moonlight of the street lamps makes even more solitary. I'm too tired even to think, too tired even to feel.

All around me is the abstract, naked universe, composed of nothing but the negation of night. I am split between tiredness and restlessness and reach a point where I physically touch a metaphysical knowledge of the mystery of things. Sometimes my soul softens and then the formless details of everyday life float up to the surface of my consciousness and I draw up a balance sheet on the back of my insomnia. At other times I wake within the half-sleep in which I lie stagnating, and vague images in random poetic colors let their silent spectacle slide by my inattentive mind. My eyes are not quite closed. My weak sight is fringed with distant light from the street lamps still lit below, in the abandoned regions of the street.

To cease, to sleep, to replace this intermittent consciousness with better, more melancholy things uttered in secret to a stranger! … To cease, to flow, fluid as a river, as the ebb and flow of a vast sea along coasts seen in a night in which one could really sleep! … To cease, to be unknown and external, the stirring of branches in remote avenues, the tenuous falling of leaves that one senses without hearing them fall, the subtle sea of distant fountains, and the whole indistinct world of gardens at night, lost in endless complexities, the natural labyrinths of the dark! … To cease, to end once and for all, but yet to survive in another form, as the page of a book, a loose lock of hair, a swaying creeper outside a half-open window, insignificant footsteps on the fine gravel on the curve of a path, the last twist of smoke high above a village as it falls asleep, the idle whip of the waggoner stopped by the road in the morning … Absurdity, confusion, extinction—anything but life …

And I do sleep in this vegetative life of conjecture, after a fashion, that is, without sleeping or resting, and over my unquiet eyelids there hovers, like the silent foam of a grubby sea, the far-off gleam of the dumb street lamps down below.

I sleep and half-sleep.

Beyond me, beyond where I lie, the silence of the house touches the infinite. I hear time falling, drop by drop, but do not hear the drops themselves fall. My own heart physically oppresses my memory, reduced to nothing, of everything that was and that I was. I feel my head resting on the pillow in which I've made a hollow. The contact of the pillowcase is like skin touching skin in the shadows. The ear on which I lie stamps itself mathematically on my brain. My eyelids droop with weariness and my eyelashes make a tiny, almost inaudible sound on the sensitive whiteness of the plump pillow. I breathe out, sighing, and my breath just happens, it is not mine. I suffer without feeling or thinking. In the house, the clock, occupying a precise place in the heart of things, strikes the half-hour, sharp, futile. It is all too much, too deep, black and cold!

I pass through time, through silences, as formless worlds pass through me.

Suddenly, like a child of the Mystery, innocent of the existence of night, a cock crows. I can sleep now because it is morning in me. And I feel my lips smile, pressing lightly into the soft folds of the pillow that cradles my face. I can abandon myself to life, I can sleep, I can forget about me ... And through the new sleep washing darkly over me I remember the cock that crowed, either that or it really is him, crowing a second time.

219 [1929?]

In the first few days of this sudden autumn, when the darkness seems in some way premature, it feels as if we have lingered too long over our daily tasks and, even in the midst of the daily round, I savor in advance the pleasure of not working that the darkness brings with it, for darkness means night and night means sleep, home, freedom. When the lights go on in the big office, banishing the darkness, and we move seamlessly from day to evening shift, I am assailed by an absurd sense of comfort, like the memory of another time, and I feel as contented with what I write as if I were sitting reading myself to sleep in bed.

We are all of us the slaves of external circumstance: even at a table in some backstreet café, a sunny day can open up before us visions of wide fields; a shadow over the countryside can cause us to shrink inside ourselves, seeking uneasy shelter in the doorless house that is our self; and, even in the midst of daytime things, the arrival of darkness can open out, like a slowly spreading fan, a deep awareness of our need for rest.

But we don't get behind in our work because of this, rather it cheers us on. We're not working any more; we're enjoying ourselves performing the task to which we are condemned. And suddenly, there on the vast ruled sheet of my bookkeeper's destiny, stands my old aunts' house, quite shut off from the world, where the tea is still brought in at the sleepy hour of ten o'clock, and the oil lamp of my lost childhood, its pool of light illuminating only the tablecloth, plunges into darkness my vision of Moreira, infinitely far from me, lit now by a black electricity. Tea is served—by the maid who's even older than my aunts and who brings it in with the slightly sleepy demeanour and the tetchily patient tenderness of very old servants—and across the whole of my dead past I faultlessly write a number or a sum. I am reabsorbed into myself again, I lose myself in me, I forget myself in those far-off nights, unpolluted by duty and the world, virginally pure of mystery and future.

And so gentle is this feeling distracting me from my debit and credit columns that if someone asks me a question, I reply with equal gentleness, as if my very being were hollow, as if I were nothing but a typewriter that I carry with me, a portable version of my own open self. Such an interruption of my dreams does not jar; so gentle are they that I continue to dream them even while I speak, write, answer, carry on a conversation. At last, the lost teatime draws to an end and it's time for the office to close. I slowly shut the book and raise my eyes, weary with unshed tears, and of all the mingled feelings this arouses, I feel more than anything a sense of sadness that the closing of the office may mean the ending of my dream; that the gesture of my hand closing the book may mean covering up my own irreparable past; that I will go to the bed of life not in the least tired, but companionless and troubled, caught in the ebb and flow of my confused consciousness, twin tides flowing in the black night, at the outer limits of nostalgia and desolation.

220   [5 Feb 30]

lt isn't the shabby walls of my ordinary room, or the old writing desks in the office, or even the poverty of the usual Baixa streets separating room and office (and which I've walked so often they already seem to have achieved a fixity beyond that of mere irreparability) that provoke in me my frequent feelings of disgust for the grubby everydayness of life. It's the people around me who leave this knot of physical disgust in my spirit, the souls who know nothing about me but, in their daily contact and conversations with me, treat me as if they did. It's the monotonous squalor of these lives that run parallel to my own external life, it's their inner certainty of being my equal that straps me in the straitjacket, locks me in the prison cell, makes me feel apocryphal and beggarly.

There are moments when every detail of the ordinary interests me in its own right and I feel affectionate towards everything because I can read it all so clearly. Then—as Sousa describes Vieira saying—I perceive the singularity of the ordinary, and I am a poet with the kind of soul that, among the Greeks, produced the intellectual age of poetry.* But there are also moments, like now, when I feel too oppressed and too aware of myself to be conscious of external things and everything then becomes for me a night of rain and mud, alone and lost in an abandoned railway station, where the last third-class train left hours ago and the next has yet to arrive.

In common with all virtues and indeed all vices, my inner virtue—my capacity for objectivity that deflects me from thoughts of

---

* Frei Luis de Sousa (c. 1555–1632) was a Dominican friar, a writer and biographer. António Vieira (1608–1697) was a Jesuit priest, who worked as a diplomat in Europe and as a missionary in Brazil, where he died. He was a great orator and one of Portugal's major baroque prose writers.

self—suffers from crises of confidence. Then I wonder at my ability to survive, at my cowardly presence here among these people, on terms of perfect equality, in genuine accord with all their trite illusions. All the solutions spawned by my imagination flash upon my mind like beams from a distant lighthouse: suicide, flight, renunciation, in short, the grand aristocratic gestures of our individuality, the cloak-and-dagger of existences like mine with no balconies to climb.

But the ideal Juliet of the finest reality has closed the high windows of literary discourse on the fictitious Romeo in my blood. She obeys her father; he obeys his. The feud between the Montagues and the Capulets continues; the curtain falls on what did not happen; and, my office worker's collar turned unselfconsciously up around the neck of a poet, my boots, which I always buy in the same shop, instinctively skirting the puddles of cold rainwater, I return home (to that room where the absent mistress of the house is as sordid a reality as the rarely seen children and the office colleagues I will meet again tomorrow), feeling a slight, confused concern that I may have lost for ever both my umbrella and the dignity of my soul.

221 [21 Feb 1930]

Suddenly, as if destiny had turned surgeon and, with dramatic success, operated on an ancient blindness, I raise my eyes from my anonymous life to the clear knowledge of the manner of my existence. And I see that everything I have done, everything I have thought, everything I have been, is a sort of delusion and madness. I marvel that I did not see it before. I am surprised by everything I have been and that I now see I am not.

I look down on my past life as if it were a plain stretched out beneath the sun just breaking through the clouds, and I notice, with a metaphysical shock, how all my most assured gestures, my clearest ideas and my most logical aims were, after all, nothing but an innate drunkenness, a natural madness, an immense ignorance.

I did not act the part. It acted me. I was merely the gestures, never the actor.

Everything that I have done, thought and been has been a series of subordinations either to a false entity I took to be myself, because all my actions came from him, or to the force of circumstance that I took to be the air I breathed. In this visionary moment, I am suddenly a solitary man realizing he is in exile from the country of which he had always considered himself a citizen. In the very heart of everything I thought, I was not me.

I am overwhelmed by a sarcastic terror of life, a dejection that overflows the bounds of my conscious being. I know that I was never anything but error and mistake, that I never lived, that I existed only in the sense that I filled up time with consciousness and thought. And my sense of myself is that of a person waking up after a sleep full of real dreams, or like someone freed by an earthquake from the feeble light of the prison to which he had become accustomed.

It weighs on me, this sudden notion of the true nature of my individual being that did nothing but make somnolent journeys between what was felt and what was seen, it weighs on me as if it were a sentence not to death but to knowledge.

It is so difficult to describe the feeling one has when one feels that one really does exist and that the soul is a real entity, that I do not know what human words I can use to define it. I don't know if I'm really as feverish as I feel or if instead I have finally recovered from the fever of slumbering through life. Yes, I am like a traveler who suddenly finds himself in a strange town with no idea of how he got there, and I'm reminded of cases of amnesiacs, who, losing all memory of their past lives, for a long time live as other people. For many years—from the time I was born and became a conscious being—I too was someone else and now I wake up suddenly to find myself standing in the middle of the bridge, looking out over the river, knowing more positively now than at any moment before that I exist. But I do not know the city, the streets are new to me and the sickness incurable. So, leaning on the bridge, I wait for the truth to pass so that I can regain my null and fictitious, intelligent and natural self.

It lasted only a moment and has passed now. I notice the furniture around me, the design on the old wallpaper, the sun through the dusty panes. For a moment I saw the truth. For a moment I was, consciously, what great men are throughout their lives. I recall their actions and their words and I wonder if they too were tempted by and succumbed to the Demon Reality. To know nothing about oneself is to live. To know a little about oneself is to think. To know oneself precipitately, as I did in that moment of pure enlightenment, is suddenly to grasp Leibniz's notion of the dominant monad, the magic password to the soul. A sudden light scorches and consumes everything. It strips us naked even of our selves.

It was only a moment, but I saw myself. Now I cannot even say what I was. And, after it all, I just feel sleepy because, though I don't really know why, I suspect that the meaning of it all is simply to sleep.

222 [14 Mar 1930]

The silence that emanates from the sound of the falling rain spreads in a crescendo of gray monotony along the narrow street I'm gazing down at. I'm sleeping on my feet, leaning against the window as if there were nothing else in the world. I search myself to find out what feelings I have before this unraveling fall of dark, luminous water standing out clearly against the grubby façades and, even more clearly, against the open windows. And I don't know what I feel, I don't know what I want to feel, I don't know what I think or what I am.

Before my unfeeling eyes, the repressed bitterness of my whole life peels off the suit of natural joy it wears in the prolonged randomness of every day. I realize that I'm always sad, however happy or content I may often feel. And the part of me that realizes this stands a little behind me, as if it were leaning over me standing at the window, and stares out, with more piercing eyes than mine, over my shoulder and over my head at the slow, slightly undulating rain that filigrees the brown, evil air.

One should abandon all duties, even those not demanded of us, reject all cozy hearths, even those that are not our own, live on what is vague and vestigial, among the extravagant purples of madness and the false lace of imagined majesties ... To be something that does not feel the weight of the rain outside, or the pain of inner emptiness ... To wander with no soul, no thoughts, just pure impersonal sensation, along winding mountain roads, through valleys hidden among steep hills, distant, absorbed, ill-fated ... To lose oneself in landscapes like paintings. To be nothing in distance and in colors ...

Safe behind the windowpanes, I do not feel the soft gust of wind that tears and fragments the perpendicular fall of the rain. Somewhere a section of the sky clears. I know this because behind the half-cleaned window immediately opposite I can just make out the calendar on the wall that I couldn't see before.

I forget. I stop seeing, stop thinking.

The rain stops, but lingers a moment longer in a cloud of tiny diamonds like crumbs shaken off a great blue tablecloth somewhere up above. You can sense now that part of the sky is already blue. Through the window opposite I can see the calendar more clearly now. It bears the face of a woman and I recognize it as an advertisement for one of the more popular brands of toothpaste.

But what was I thinking about before I lost myself in looking? I don't know. The will? Effort? Life? From the spreading light I can tell that the sky must be almost completely blue again. But there is no peace—nor will there ever be!—in the depths of my heart, that old well at the far corner of the estate long since sold, the memory of childhood locked up under the dust of an attic in someone else's house. There is no peace and, alas for me, not even a desire to find it ...

238

223

I see my dreamed landscapes as clearly as I see the real ones. When I lean over to look into my dreams, I am leaning over something real. When I see life passing, I am also dreaming something.

Someone said of someone else that, for him, the people in his dreams were as sharply defined as the people in real life. I could understand someone applying those same words to me, but I would not agree. The people in my dreams are not the same as those in real life. They are parallel. Each life—that of dreams and that of the world—has its own reality, the same but different. Like things that are close and things that are distant. The people in my dreams are closer to me, but […]

224   [23 Mar 1930]

There is such a thing as a weariness of the abstract intelligence, which is the most terrible of all wearinesses. It does not weigh on you like physical weariness, nor does it trouble you like a weariness of the emotions. It is the consciousness of the weight of the whole world, an inability in the soul to breathe.

In that moment, as if they were clouds blown by the wind, every idea through which we have experienced life, all the ambitions and plans on which we have founded our hopes for the future, are torn apart, ripped open, carried far off like the gray remnants of mists, the tatters of what never was nor ever could be. And in the wake of that defeat arises the black, implacable solitude of the deserted, starry sky in all its purity.

Life's mystery wounds and frightens us in many ways. Sometimes it comes to us as a formless phantasm, the monstrous incarnation of nonbeing, and our soul trembles in the most terrible of fears. At other times it—the whole truth in all the horror of our inability ever to know it—lurks behind us, visible only so long as we do not turn round to see it.

But the horror that racks me today is at once less noble and more corrosive. It is a wish not to think, a desire never to have been anything, a conscious despair in every cell of my soul. It is a sudden sense of being locked up in an infinite prison. Where can one even think of fleeing, if the prison cell is all there is?

And then there comes over me an absurd and irresistible desire, a kind of satanism predating Satan, that one day—a day outside of all time and matter—we might find a way of fleeing beyond God so that whatever constitutes the deepest part of us might cease entirely (though how I don't know) to participate in either being or nonbeing.

225   [c. 23 Mar 1930]
Having nothing to do or to even think of doing, I am going to set down on this piece of paper a description of my ideal:

A note.

The sensibility of Mallarmé in the style of Vieira; to dream like Verlaine in the body of Horace; to be Homer by moonlight.

To feel everything in all possible ways; to be able to think with the emotions and feel with the intellect; to desire nothing very much except with the imagination; to suffer coquettishly; to see clearly in order to write precisely; to know oneself through simulation and tactics; to become naturalized as an entirely different person, with all the correct documentation; in short, to experience all sensations inside oneself, stripping them down to God, but wrapping them up again and putting them back in the shop window just as the sales assistant I can see now is doing with small tins of a new brand of shoe polish.

Whether possible or impossible, they all come to nothing, these ideals, and if there were any others, I've forgotten them. I have reality before me—and it isn't even the sales assistant, but the isolated creature that is his hands, the absurd tentacle of a soul with a family and a fate making the gestures of a spider without a web as it reaches into the window opposite.

And then one of the tins fell, like this note of mine.

226 [c. 23 Mar 1930]

The office boy was tying up the day's parcels in the crepuscular cool of the vast office. "Hark at that thunder," he said to no one, as loudly and cheerily as if he were saying "Good morning," the cruel devil. My heart began to beat again. The apocalypse had passed. There was a pause underlined by the scratching of a pen.

And with what relief—a bright flash, a pause, a thunderclap—did that thunder, now near at hand, now moving off, relieve us of what had been. God was retreating. I felt myself filling my lungs. I noticed how airless the office was. I noticed that there were other people present too, as well as the office boy. Everyone had fallen silent. Then a crisp, tremulous sound, Moreira abruptly turning a large, thick page of the ledger as he checked some figures.

227 [24 Mar 1930]

I reread passively those simple lines by Caeiro, the natural conclusion he draws from the smallness of his village, receiving from them what I feel to be both inspiration and liberation. According to him, because his village is small, you can see more of the world there than you can in the city, and in that sense his village is larger than the city ...

> *Because I am the size of what I see*
> *And not the size of my own stature.*

Lines such as these, which seem to have come spontaneously into existence as if not requiring any human will to dictate them, cleanse me of all the metaphysics I spontaneously add to life. After reading them, I go over to the window that looks out onto the narrow street. I look up at the great sky and the many stars and the beating wings of a splendid freedom shakes my whole body.

"I am the size of what I see!" Each time I think this phrase with every nerve of my being, I'm filled by an even stronger conviction of its ability to reorganize the heavens into new constellations. "I am the size of what I see!" What mental energy springs up from the well of deep emotions to the high stars it reflects and which, in some way, inhabit it.

And right now, conscious of my ability to see, I look at the vast objective metaphysics of the skies with a certainty that makes me want to die singing. "I am the size of what I see!" And the vague moonlight, entirely mine, begins to mar with its vagueness the almost black blueness of the horizon.

I feel like throwing up my arms and shouting out things of unheard-of savagery, exchanging words with the high mysteries, proclaiming to the vast spaces of empty matter the existence of a new expansive personality.

But I pull myself together and calm myself. "I am the size of what I see!" The phrase still fills my whole soul, I rest every emotion I have on it, and the indecipherable peace of the harsh moonlight beginning to spread as night comes falls on me, in me, as it does on the city beyond.

228   [29 Mar 1930]

In contrast to the vivid white wings of the seagulls' restless flight, the dark sky to the south of the Tejo was a sinister black. There was, however, no storm as yet. The heavy threat of rain had passed over to the opposite shore, and the Baixa, still damp from the brief rainfall, smiled up from the earth at a sky that was slowly, palely, turning blue again to the north. There was a chill in the cool spring air.

At such empty, fathomless moments, I like to guide my thoughts into a meditation, which is nothing in itself, but retains in its empty lucidity something of the solitary cold of the brightening day with its backdrop of distant black clouds and certain intuitive feelings which, like the seagulls, evoke by way of contrast the mystery of everything in the gloom.

Suddenly, contrary to my personal literary aims, the black sky in the south evokes another sky—whether it's a real or imagined memory I cannot tell—a sky seen perhaps in another life, over a small river in the north full of sad reeds and far from any city. Without understanding how or why, a landscape of wild ducks gradually spreads through my imagination and with the clarity of a strange dream I feel very close to that imagined scene.

In this land of reeds and rushes by the banks of rivers—a land made for hunters and for fear—the ragged banks push out like small grubby promontories into the leaden yellow waters and retreat to form muddy bays for boats as small as toys, and shores where the water shines on the surface of the concealed mud among the greenish-black stems of rushes too dense to walk through.

The desolation is that of a dead gray sky which here and there crumples up into clouds even blacker than itself. Though I cannot feel it, a wind is blowing, and I see that what I had thought was the other bank is, in fact, a long island behind which one can make out, in the flat distance, across the great, desolate river, the other bank, the real one.

No one goes there, no one ever will. Even though, via a contradictory flight through time and space, I can escape from this world into that landscape, no one else will ever go there. I would wait in vain for something I did not even know I was waiting for, and, in the end, there would be nothing but the slow fall of night in which everything would slowly take on the color of the blackest clouds and lose itself little by little in the negation of the sky.

And here, suddenly, I feel the cold from there. It seeps into my body from my bones. I take a deep breath and wake up. The man who passes me beneath the Arcade by the Stock Exchange looks at me with uncomprehending distrust. The black sky, now even darker, hangs still lower over the southern shore.

229   [c. 4 Apr 1930}

However much I belong, in my soul, to the Romantics, I can only find repose in reading the classics. Their very narrowness, through which their clarity finds expression, brings me a kind of comfort. I take from them a glad sense of a larger life that looks out upon ample spaces without ever venturing into them. Even the pagan gods find rest there from the mystery.

An over-curious analysis of sensations—sometimes purely imaginary—the identification of the heart with the landscape, the anatomical laying bare of the nerves, replacing will with desire and thought with aspiration—all these things are too familiar to seem novel in someone else's words or to bring me peace. Whenever I feel them, I wish, precisely because I am feeling them, that I was feeling something else. And reading a classical author gives me that something else.

I confess this frankly and unashamedly ... There is no passage from Chateaubriand, no lyric by Lamartine—passages that so often seem to voice my own thoughts, lyrics that so often seem to have been written so that I might know myself—that transports and raises me up in the way a piece of prose by Vieira does or an ode written by one of the few Portuguese classical writers who were true disciples of Horace.

I read and I am set free. I gain objectivity. I have ceased to be my usual disparate self. And what I read, rather than being a near-invisible suit that sometimes weighs on me, becomes instead the great clarity of the outside world, in which everything is worthy of note, the sun that everyone can see, the moon that weaves a web of shadows on the still earth, the vast spaces that open out into the sea, the dark solidity of the trees waving aloft their green branches, the solid peace of ponds in gardens, the paths thick with vines on the terraced slopes of the hills.

I read like someone abdicating from life. And since the crown and the royal mantle never look as grand as when the departing King deposits them on the ground, I set down on the mosaic floor of the antechambers all my past triumphs of tedium and dreams, and ascend the steps wearing only the nobility of seeing.

I read like someone who just happens to be passing. And it is in the classics, with those who are calm of mind and who, if they suffer, do not speak of it, that I feel myself to be a sacred passerby, an anointed pilgrim, a purposeless observer of a purposeless world, a Prince of the Great Exile, who, as he left, made of his desolation a final gift of alms to the last beggar.

230 [5 Apr 1930]

The firm's sleeping partner, a man much troubled by obscure ailments, was suddenly taken with the notion (a caprice that came on him, it seems, between afflictions) that he wanted to have a group photograph taken of the office staff. So, the day before yesterday, following the instructions of the jolly photographer, we all lined up against the grubby white partition that serves as a rickety wooden division between the general office and Senhor Vasques' office. In the center stood Vasques himself; on either side of him, according to a hierarchy that began logically enough but rapidly broke down, stood the other human souls who gather here each day, in body, to perform the small tasks, the ultimate aim of which is a secret known only to the gods.

Today, when I arrived at the office, a little late and having in fact completely forgotten about the frozen moment captured twice by the photographer, I found Moreira, an unexpectedly early bird, and one of the clerks poring over some blackish objects that I recognized with a start as being the first prints of the photographs. They were, in fact, two copies of the same photo, the one that had come out best.

I experienced the pain of truth when I saw myself there, because, inevitably, it was my face I looked for first. I have never had a very high opinion of my physical appearance, but never before have I felt such a nonentity as I did then, comparing myself with the other faces, so familiar to me, in that line-up of my daily companions. I look like a rather dull Jesuit. My thin, inexpressive face betrays no intelligence, no intensity, nothing whatever to make it stand out from the stagnant tide of the other faces. But they're not a stagnant tide. There are some really expressive faces there. Senhor Vasques is exactly as he is in real life—the firm, likable face, the steady gaze, all set off by the stiff moustache. The energy and intelligence of the man—qualities which are after all utterly banal and to be found in thousands of other men all over the world—are stamped on that photograph as if it were a psychological passport. The two traveling salesmen look superb; the clerk has come out well but he's half hidden behind Moreira. And Moreira! My immediate superior Moreira, the embodiment of monotony and routine, looks much more human than I do! Even the office boy—I detect in myself, without being able to suppress it, a feeling that I hope is not envy—has a directness in his smile that far outshines the insignificant dullness of my face, of me, the sphinx of the stationery cupboard.

What does all this mean? Is it true that the camera never lies? What is this truth documented by a cold lens? Who am I that I possess such a face? And then to add insult to injury, Moreira suddenly said to me: "It's a really good one of you." And then, turning to the traveling salesman, "It's the absolute image of him, isn't it?" The salesman's happy and companionable agreement signaled my final relegation to the rubbish heap.

231 [5 Apr 1930]

And today, thinking about my life, I feel like some living creature being carried in a basket on someone's arm, between two suburban stations. It's a stupid image, but then the life it describes is even more stupid. Those baskets usually have two lids, each a half-oval, which lift up slightly at either of the curved ends if the creature inside gets agitated. However, the arm carrying the basket and resting lightly on the hinges in the middle doesn't allow such a feeble creature to do anything more than vainly lift those ends, like the wings of a dying butterfly.

I forgot that I was talking about me when I described that basket. I can see it clearly, as well as the plump, sunburned arm of the maid carrying it. I can see only the maid's arm and its downy hairs. I can't get comfortable—then, suddenly, a cool breeze from … from … those white strips of willow and fabric that the baskets are made of, and where I, the creature, wriggle about as I'm transported between those two stations. Between stations, I rest on what seems to be a bench, and I can hear people talking outside. It's quiet and so I sleep, until they lift me up again when we reach the stop.

232 [6 Apr 1930]

Atmosphere constitutes the soul of things. Each thing has its own mode of expression and that expression comes from without.

Each thing is the intersection of three lines which, together, shape that thing: a quantity of material, the way in which we interpret it and the atmosphere in which it exists. This table at which I'm writing is a piece of wood, it is a table and one of the pieces of furniture in this room. My impression of this table, if I wanted to transcribe it, would have to be made up of various notions: that it is made of wood, that I call it a table and attribute to it certain uses and purposes, and that in it are reflected or inserted the objects in whose presence it acquires its external soul, the things that are imposed on it and that transform it. And the color it was given, the way that color has faded, the knots and splits it contains, all of this, you will notice, comes from without and, more than its innate woodenness, these are what give it soul. And the inner kernel of that soul, the being a table, that is, its personality, also comes from without.

I think, therefore, that it is not just a human or a literary mistake to attribute a soul to the things we call inanimate. To be a thing is to be the object of an attribution. It might be wrong to say that a tree feels, that a river runs, that a sunset is poignant or that the calm sea (as blue as the sky it does not contain) smiles (because of the sun above it). But it is equally wrong to attribute beauty to an object, to attribute color, form, perhaps even being to an object. This sea is salt water. This sunset is just the fading of the sun's light from this particular longitude and latitude. This child playing before me is an intellectual bundle of cells, but he is also a timepiece made up of subatomic movements, a strange electrical conglomeration of millions of solar systems in microscopic miniature.

Everything comes from without and even the human soul is perhaps no more than the ray of sunlight shining in and picking out on the floor the dungheap that is the body.

These considerations might contain the seeds of a whole philosophy for anyone strong enough to draw conclusions from them. I'm not that person. Intent but vague thoughts about logical possibilities surface in me, and everything fades in the vision of a single golden ray of sun shining on a dungheap like dark, damp, crushed straw on the almost black earth next to a stone wall.

That's how I am. When I want to think, I see. When I want to step out of my soul, I stop suddenly, absentmindedly, on the first step of the steep spiral staircase, looking out of this top-floor window at the fading sun lighting in tawny gold the diffuse jumble of rooftops.

233   [10 Apr 1930]

The whole life of the human soul is just a movement in the half-light. We live in a twilight of consciousness never sure about what we are or what we think we are. Even in the best of us there exists some feeling of vanity about something, some error whose dimensions we cannot calculate. We are something that happens in the interval of a play; sometimes, through certain doors, we glimpse what may only be the scenery. The whole world is confused, like voices in the night.

I've just reread these pages, in which I write with a clarity that will last only as long as they last, and I ask myself: What is this, and what is it for? Who am I when I feel? What dies in me when I am me?

Like someone high on a peak trying to make out the lives of those living in the valley, I look down and see myself, along with everything else, as just a blurred, confused landscape.

At times like this, when my soul is plunged into the abyss, even the tiniest detail grieves me as if it were a letter of farewell. I feel I

am always on the eve of an awakening. Beneath a suffocating wel-
ter of conclusions I struggle within an outer covering that is me.
I would cry out if I thought anyone would hear. But all I feel is a
great drowsiness that shifts from one feeling to another like a suc-
cession of clouds, the sort that leave patterns of sunlight and green
on the almost sad grass of long meadows.

I'm like someone engaged in a random search for an object no
one has yet described to him. We play hide-and-seek alone. Some-
where there is a transcendent reason for all this, some fluid divin-
ity, heard but not seen.

Yes, I reread these pages representative of empty hours, of mi-
nor moments of tranquillity or illusion, great hopes turned into
landscapes, griefs like rooms no one enters, a few voices, a great
weariness, the gospel yet to be written.

Everyone is vain about something, and the vanity of each of us
consists in our forgetting that there are others with souls like ours.
My vanity consists in a few pages, a few paragraphs, certain doubts
…

Did I say I reread these pages? I lied. I daren't reread them. I
can't. What good would it do me? It's some other person there. I
no longer understand any of it …

234   [10 Apr 1930]
I feel physically sickened by ordinary humanity, which is, besides,
the only kind there is. And I sometimes play at provoking that nau-
sea, the way one can sometimes make oneself vomit in order to
relieve the urge to vomit.

On mornings when I dread the banality of the day ahead as
keenly as someone might dread prison, one of my favorite walks
is to proceed slowly along the streets, before the shops and ware-
houses are open, and eavesdrop on the snatches of conversation ex-
changed by groups of girls or boys or of girls and boys, and which
fall, like ironic alms, into the invisible begging bowl of my street
meditations.

And it's always the same sequence of phrases … "And then she said …" and the tone gives a hint of the intrigue to come. "It wasn't him, it was you …" and the voice that answers is raised in a protest I can no longer hear. "No, you said it …" and the seamstress's strident voice declares "My mother says she doesn't want …" "Me?" and the astonishment expressed by the boy carrying his lunch wrapped in greaseproof paper doesn't convince me, nor can it possibly convince the grubby blonde he's speaking to. "Perhaps it was …" and the laughter from three of the four girls nearby obscures the obscenity that […] "No kidding, Zé, I go up to the guy and look him straight in the eye …" and the poor devil is lying, because the office manager—who I don't know personally, but I know it must have been him, given what the other contender said—did not confront that straw gladiator in the arena of the office. "And then I went and had a smoke in the gents," giggles the small boy with dark patches sewn on the seat of his trousers.

Others, who walk by on their own or together, don't speak or, if they do, I don't hear them, but the voices, when they reach me, do so through a kind of faulty, transparent intuition of mine. I dare not say—I don't even dare say it to myself in writing, even if I were to erase it at once—what I have seen in those casual glances, that unwitting baseness, those murky dealings. I don't dare to because, when you do make yourself sick, you only want to do it once.

"The guy was so pissed he didn't even notice there were any steps." I look up. At least the boy is describing something. And when these people describe a thing, they do so far better than when they merely feel, because when someone is describing something, he forgets about himself. My nausea passes. I see the guy. I see him photographically. I'm even cheered by his slangy way of speaking. He's like a fresh breeze cooling my brow, that guy who was so pissed he didn't even notice the steps, perhaps it was the steps up which humanity stumbles, groping and blundering its way up the ordered falsity of the slope.

Intrigue, gossip, boasting about what no one actually dared to

do, the contentment of each poor wretch dressed in the uncon-
scious consciousness of his own soul, all that unwashed sexuality,
the jokes they tell, like a monkey scratching itself, the horrifying
ignorance of their own unimportance … All this leaves me with the
impression of a vile, monstrous animal created out of the unwitting
dreams of the soggy crusts of desire, the chewed-over remains of
sensations.

235 [12 Apr 1930]

Often, captivated by the bewitching surface of things, I feel like
a man. Then I live joyfully with other people and there's a clarity
about my existence. I float on the surface of things. And it's a plea-
sure to me to receive my wages and go home. I feel the weather
without seeing it, and I'm pleased by anything organic. If I medi-
tate, I don't think. On such days I really enjoy gardens and parks.

I don't know what it is, this strange, poor thing that exists in the
inner substance of city parks and which I can only feel when I'm
feeling well in myself. A garden is a summation of civilization—an
anonymous modification of Nature. There are plants, but there are
also streetlike paths. Trees grow, but there are benches placed in
their shade. On the four walkways turned to face the four sides of
the city, the benches are larger and nearly always crowded with
people.

I don't hate the regularity of flowers in beds. I do, however, hate
the public use of flowers. If the beds were in enclosed parks, if the
trees were growing on feudal estates, if there were no one sitting
on the benches, then I could console myself with the futile contem-
plation of a garden. Orderly, useful, city gardens are, for me, like
cages, in which the colorful spontaneities of trees and flowers have
only just enough space—from which there is no escape—and their
own beauty, but without the life that goes with beauty.

But there are days when that is the only landscape that belongs to
me, and which I enter like an actor in a tragicomedy. On such days, I
feel I am wrong, but at least, in a way, I am happier. If I forget myself

for a moment, I imagine that I really do have a home to go back to. If I forget myself, I am normal, reserved for some particular purpose, I brush down another suit and read a newspaper from front to back.

That illusion doesn't last long, though, both because it doesn't last and because night falls. And the color of the flowers, the shade of the trees, the paths and the beds, all fade and shrink. Above my sense of error and of feeling that I'm just an ordinary man, there appears—as if the daylight were a hidden theatre curtain suddenly raised—the great backdrop of the stars. And then my eyes, with all the excitement of a child at the circus, forget the amorphous public and I wait for the first actors to come on.

I am free and lost.

I feel. I shiver feverishly. I am I.

236 [13 Apr 1930]

I think what creates in me the deep sense I have of living out of step with others is the fact that most people think with their feelings whereas I feel with my thoughts.

For the average man, to feel is to live, and to think is to know that one lives. For me, to think is to live, and to feel just provides food for thought.

My capacity for enthusiasm being minimal, it's odd that I'm more drawn to those opposed to me in temperament than to those of the same spiritual species as myself. In literature I admire no one more than the classical writers with whom I have least in common. If I had to choose as my only reading between either Chateaubriand or Vieira, I wouldn't think twice about choosing Vieira.

The more different someone is from me, the more real they seem, because they depend less upon my subjectivity. That is why the constant object of my close study is precisely that vulgar humanity I reject and from which I distance myself. I love it because I hate it. I enjoy observing it because I hate actually feeling it. The landscape one admires so much as a picture generally makes for an uncomfortable bed.

When we reach the bare summits of nature's peaks, we have a sense of privilege. With our own height added in, we are higher than the highest pinnacle. Nature's highest point, at least in that one place, lies beneath our feet. We are, as we stand there, the kings of the visible world. Everything around us is lower down: life is a downward slope, a recumbent plain, and we are the very apogee.

We, however, are all accident and artifice, and the height we enjoy when standing on a mountain is not ours to enjoy; we are no higher on that summit than we would be normally. It is the thing we are standing on that raises us up, that makes us seem taller.

One breathes more easily when one is rich; one is freer if one is famous; even having an aristocratic title automatically places one on a small hillock. It's all artifice, but an artifice that isn't even ours. We climb that hill or else are carried up it, or are born in the house on the hill.

The truly great man is the one who believes that the difference in the distance from valley to sky or from mountain to sky makes no difference at all. When the flood waters rise, we would be safer in the hills, but when God's curse takes the form of Jupiter's lightning bolts or Aeolus' winds, we would be better off staying in the valley and keeping our heads down.

The wise man has in his muscles the ability to climb to great heights and, in his mind, the refusal to do so. From where he stands, he can see all the mountains and all the valleys. The sun that gilds the peaks looks more golden to him than it does to someone actually on the peak exposed to that bright light; and the palace built high up in the woods is far more beautiful to someone looking at it from the valley than to someone imprisoned in its grand rooms.

I console myself with these thoughts, since I cannot console myself with life. And the symbol fuses with reality when I, a passerby in body and soul along these low streets leading down to the Tejo, see the city's hills aglow, like a glory belonging to someone else, with the various colors and lights left behind by a sun that has already set.

Some feelings are like dreams that pervade every corner of one's spirit like a mist, that do not let one think or act or even be. Some trace of our dreams persists in us as if we had not slept properly, and a daytime torpor warms the stagnant surface of the senses. It is the intoxication of being nothing, when one's will is a bucket of water kicked over in the yard by some clumsy passing foot.

One looks but does not see. The long street crowded with human creatures is like a fallen inn sign on which the jumbled letters no longer make sense. The houses are merely houses. Although one sees things clearly, it's impossible to give meaning to what one sees.

The ringing hammer blows coming from the box-maker's shop have a familiar strangeness. Each blow is separated in time, each with its echo and each utterly vain. The passing carts sound the way they do on days when thunder threatens. Voices emerge not from people's throats but from the air itself. In the background, even the river seems weary.

It is not tedium that one feels. It is not grief. It is not even tiredness that one feels. It is a desire to go to sleep clothed in a different personality, to forget, dulled by an increase in salary. You feel nothing except the mechanical rise and fall of your legs as they walk involuntarily forward on feet conscious of the shoes they're wearing. Perhaps you don't even feel that much. Something tightens inside your head, blinding you and stopping up your ears.

It's like having a cold in the soul. And with that literary image of illness comes a longing for life to be like a long period of convalescence, confined to bed; and the idea of convalescence evokes the image of large villas on the outskirts of the city, but deep in the heart of them, by the hearth, far from the streets and the traffic. No, you can't hear anything. You consciously pass through the door you must enter, you go through it as if asleep, unable to make your body go in any other direction. You pass through everything. Where's your tambourine now, sleeping bear?

Fragile as something just begun, the salt breeze hovered over the Tejo and grubbily infiltrated the fringes of the Baixa. It blew cool and rank over the torpor of the warm sea. Life became something lodged in my stomach, and my sense of smell inhabited some space behind my eyes. High up, perching on nothing at all, thin skeins of cloud dissolved from gray into false white. The atmosphere was like a threat made by a cowardly sky, like inaudible thunder, full of nothing but air.

Even the gulls as they flew seemed static, lighter than the air itself, as if someone had simply left them hanging there. But it wasn't oppressive. Evening fell on our disquiet; the air grew intermittently cool.

My poor hopes, born of the life I've been forced to lead! They are like this hour and this air, vanished mists, inept attempts at stirring up a false storm. I feel like shouting out, to put an end to this landscape and this meditation. But the salt smell of the sea fills all my good intentions, and the low tide has laid bare in me the muddy gloom which only my sense of smell tells me is there.

What a lot of nonsense just to satisfy myself! What cynical insights into purely hypothetical emotions! All this mixing up of soul and feelings, of my thoughts with the air and the river, just to say that life wounds my sense of smell and my consciousness, just because I do not have the wit to use the simple, all-embracing words of the Book of Job: "My soul is weary of my life!"

239   [23 Apr 1930]

An uncertain evening breeze touches my brow and my consciousness with something like a vague caress, all the gentler for not being a caress. I know only that suddenly, just for a moment, my tedium feels more comfortable, like an item of clothing that stops chafing against a sore.

A poor sensibility that depends on such a minimal movement of the air to achieve, however intermittently, a little peace! But that is the nature of all human sensibilities, and I do not believe it has any more weight for other human beings than receiving a sudden windfall or an unexpectedly warm smile, which, for other people, are the equivalent of that brief, passing breeze.

I can think about sleeping. I can dream about dreaming. I can see more clearly the objectivity of everything. I feel more comfortable with the sense of that life outside me. And all this because, when I was almost at the corner of the street, a slight shift in the air made my skin shiver with joy.

Everything we love or lose—things, people, meanings—brushes our skin and thus reaches our soul, and, in God's eyes, that is no more or less than the breeze that brought me nothing except the imagined relief, the propitious moment, and the ability to lose everything splendidly.

240   [25 Apr 1930]
Whirls and whirlpools in the fluid futility of life! In the big square in the city center, the soberly multicolored flow of people passes, changes course, forms pools, breaks up into streams, embraces brooks. My eyes watch distractedly, and I construct in myself that aqueous image which, better than any other—and because I thought it was about to rain—fits this uncertain movements.

When I wrote that last sentence, which describes exactly what I saw, I thought it might be useful to place at the end of my book, when it's published, underneath any "Errata," a few "Non-Errata" and to say: the words "this uncertain movements" on page so-and-so is correct, with the noun in the plural and the demonstrative pronoun in the singular. But what has that to do with what I was thinking? Nothing, which is why I allow myself to think it.

The trams growl and clang around the edges of the square, like large, yellow, mobile matchboxes, into which a child has stuck a spent match at an angle to act as a mast; as they set off they emit a loud, iron-hard whistle. The pigeons wandering about around the central statue are like dark, ever-shifting crumbs at the mercy of a scattering wind. On their small feet the plump birds take tiny steps.

Seen from close to, everyone is monotonously diverse. Vieira said of Frei Luiz de Sousa that he wrote about the ordinary in a singular way. These people are ordinarily singular, contrary to the style of *The Life of the Archbishop*. All this is both saddening and a matter of utter indifference. I came here for no reason, as with everything in life.

Towards the east, the part of the city I can see appears to rise almost vertically as if launching a static assault on the castle. The pale sun sets a moist, vague halo around that sudden heap of houses hiding it from view. The sky is a damp, whitish blue. Yesterday's rain may return today, only gentler. The wind seems to be coming from the east, perhaps because here, suddenly, it smells vaguely of the ripe greenness of the hidden market. There are more foreigners on the eastern side of the square than on the west. Like muffled gunshots, the corrugated metal blinds are lowered upwards; I don't know why, but that's what the sound suggests to me. It's perhaps because they make more noise when being lowered, even though, at the moment, they are being raised. There's an explanation for everything.

Suddenly, I am alone in the world. I see all this while looking down from a mental rooftop. I am alone in the world. To see is to be distant. To see clearly is to stop. To analyze is to be foreign. People pass without even touching me. I have only air around me. I feel so isolated that I'm aware of the distance between me and my suit. I'm a child carrying a flickering candle and crossing, in my nightshirt, the big, deserted house. Living shadows surround me—only shadows, the daughters of dead things and the light accompanying me. They surround me here too in the sun, but they are people. And yet they are shadows too, shadows ...

241   [25 Apr 1930]

Today, in a break from feeling, I was meditating on the form of prose I use, in short, on how I write. Like many other people, I had the perverse desire to establish a system and a norm, even though up until now I've always written without the need for any such norm or system; in that, too, I'm no different from anyone else.

However, when I was analyzing myself this afternoon, I discovered that my stylistic system rests on two principles and, following in the footsteps of the classical authors, I at once made of those two principles the general foundations of all style: first, to say what one feels exactly as one feels it—clearly, if it is clear; obscurely, if it is obscure; and confusedly, if it is confused; secondly, to understand that grammar is a tool not a law.

Let's suppose that I see before me a rather boyish young girl. An ordinary person would say of her: "That girl looks like a boy." Another ordinary person, more conscious of the difference between speaking and saying, would put it differently: "That girl is a boy." Another, equally aware of the rules of expression, but more informed by a love of brevity, which is the luxury of thought, would say: "That boy." I, on the other hand, would say: "She's a boy," thus violating the most elementary of grammatical rules that demands agreement of gender between personal pronoun and noun. And I would be right; I would have spoken absolutely, photographically, stepping outside of all vulgar norms and beyond the commonplace. I will not merely have uttered words: I will have spoken.

Grammar, in defining usage, makes divisions which are sometimes legitimate, sometimes false. For example, it divides verbs into transitive and intransitive; however, someone who understands what is involved in speaking often has to make a transitive verb intransitive, or vice versa, if he is to convey exactly what he feels, and not, like most human animals, merely to glimpse it obscurely. If I wanted to talk about my simple existence, I would say: "I exist." If I wanted to talk about my existence as a separate soul, I would say: "I am me." But if I wanted to talk about my existence as an entity that both directs and forms itself, that exercises within itself the divine function of self-creation, I would have to invent a transitive form and say, triumphantly and ungrammatically supreme, "I exist me." I would have expressed a whole philosophy in three small words. Isn't that preferable to taking forty sentences to say nothing? What more can one ask of philosophy and language?

Only those who are unable to think what they feel obey grammatical rules. Someone who knows how to express himself can use those rules as he pleases. There's a story they tell of Sigismund, King of Rome, who, having made a grammatical mistake in a public speech, said to the person who pointed this out to him: "I am King of Rome and therefore above grammar." And history tells that he was known thereafter as Sigismund "supragrammaticam." What a marvelous symbol! Anyone who knows how to say what he wants to say is, in his own way, King of Rome. The title is regal and the reason for it impossible.

242 [c. 4/1930]

I often wonder what kind of person I would be if I had been protected from the cold wind of fate by the screen of wealth, and my uncle's moral hand had never led me to an office in Lisbon, and I had never moved on from there to other offices and reached the tawdry heights of being a good assistant bookkeeper in a job that is about as demanding as an afternoon nap and offers a salary that gives me just enough to live on.

I know that had that nonexistent past existed, I would not now be capable of writing these pages, which, though few, are at least better than all the pages I would undoubtedly have just daydreamed about given more comfortable circumstances. For banality is a form of intelligence, and reality, especially if it is brutish and rough, forms a natural complement to the soul.

Much of what I feel and think I owe to my work as a bookkeeper since the former exists as a negation of and flight from the latter.

If I had to fill in the space provided on a questionnaire to list one's formative literary influences, on the first dotted line I would write the name of Cesário Verde, but the list would be incomplete without the names of Senhor Vasques, Moreira the bookkeeper, Vieira the traveling salesman and António the office boy. And after each of them I would write in capital letters the key word: LISBON.

In fact, they were all as important as Cesário Verde in providing corrective coefficients for my vision of the world. I think "corrective coefficients" is the term (though, of course, I'm unsure of its exact meaning) that engineers use of a methodology applying mathematics to life. If it *is* the right term, that's what they were to me. If it isn't, let it stand for what might have been, and my intention serve in place of a failed metaphor.

When, with all the clarity I can muster, I consider what my life has apparently been, I imagine it as some brightly colored scrap of litter—a chocolate wrapper or a cigar ring—that the eavesdropping waitress brushes lightly from the soiled tablecloth into the dustpan, among the crumbs and crusts of reality itself. It stands out from those things whose fate it shares by virtue of a privilege that is also destined for the dustpan. The gods continue their conversations above the sweeping, utterly indifferent to these incidents in the world below.

Yes, if I had been rich, cosseted, carefully groomed and ornamental, I would never have known that brief moment as a pretty piece of paper among the breadcrumbs; I would have been left on one of fortune's trays—'Not for me, thank you'—and returned to the sideboard to grow old and stale. Discarded once my useful center has been eaten, I am thus relegated to the rubbish bin, along with the crumbs of what remains of Christ's body, unable even to imagine what will come after, and under what stars; but I know there will be an "after."

243 [c. 4/1930]
The burden of feeling! The burden of having to feel!

244 [c. 4/1930]
I never wanted to be understood by other people. To be understood is akin to prostituting oneself. I prefer to be taken seriously

as what I am not and, with decency and naturalness, to be ignored as a person.

Nothing would displease me more than to have my colleagues in the office think me different. I want to savor the irony of their not doing so. I want the penance of having them think me the same as them. I want the crucifixion of their not thinking me any different. There are more subtle martyrdoms than those recorded among saints and hermits. There are torments of the intellect just as there are of the body and of desire. And as in other torments, these contain their own voluptuousness [...]

245   [c. 4/1930]
Forest
But, ah, not even the bedroom was right—it was the old bedroom of my lost childhood! Like a mist, it moved off, actually passed through the white walls of my real room, which emerged from the shadows smaller but very clear, like life and the day, like the passing of the wagon and the faint sound of the whip that puts standing-up muscles into the prone body of the sleepy horse.

246   [6 May 1930]
I always thought of metaphysics as a prolonged form of latent madness. If we knew the truth, we would see it; everything else is just empty systems and vain trappings. We should, if we think about it, be content with the incomprehensibility of the universe; the desire to understand makes us less than human, for to be human is to know that one does not understand.

They bring me faith wrapped up like a parcel and borne on someone else's tray. They want me to accept it, but not open it. They bring me science, like a knife on a plate, with which I will cut the pages of a book of blank pages. They bring me doubt, like dust inside a box; but why do they bring me the box if all it contains is dust?

I write because I lack knowledge; and, depending on the demands of a particular emotion, I use other people's rotund phrases about Truth. If it is a clear, irrevocable emotion, I speak of the *Gods*, and thus frame it in a consciousness of the multiple world. If it is a deep emotion, I speak, naturally, of God and thus fix it in a consciousness of the singleness of the world. If the emotion is a thought, I speak, again naturally, of Fate and thus let it flow by like a river, the slave of its own river bed.

Sometimes the actual rhythm of the phrase will demand "God" and not "the Gods"; at others, the two syllables of "the Gods" will simply impose themselves on a phrase, and I then verbally change universes; at still other times, in contrast, the need of an internal rhyme, a shift in rhythm or an emotional shock, will tip the balance and then either polytheism or monotheism will fit itself to the moment and be preferred. The Gods are simply a function of style.

247   [14 May 1930]

Recognizing that reality is a kind of illusion, and that illusion is a kind of reality, is simultaneously necessary and pointless. Even to exist, the contemplative life must consider objective accidents as the disparate premises of an unreachable conclusion; but it must, at the same time, consider the chance content of dreams as somehow worthy of the attention we pay them, and which is what makes contemplatives of us.

Depending on how you look at it, anything can be both astonishing and an obstacle, everything and nothing, a way forward or a cause for concern. Looking at something differently each time means renewing it and multiplying it. That is why the contemplative soul who never left his village nevertheless has at his disposal the entire universe. The infinite lies in a cell or in a desert. One can sleep cosmically resting on a stone.

There are, however, times—and this happens to all those who meditate—when everything, however new, seems old and worn and hackneyed, because, however hard we meditate on anything— and, by meditating, transform it—we can only ever transform it into something that can be used as further matter for meditation. We are assailed then by a desire to live, to know things without knowing them, to meditate only with the senses or to think in a tactile or sensitive way, from within the object we are thinking about, as if it were a sponge and we were water. Then, too, we have our night, and the weariness of all emotions grows even deeper because they are thought emotions, which are, in themselves, deep. But it is a night without repose, without moonlight, without stars, a night in which everything seems to have been turned inside out—the infinite is transformed into a tight, constraining interior, and the day has become the black lining of a suit we have never seen before.

Yes, far better to be always the human slug that loves in blithe ignorance, the leech unaware of its own repugnant nature. Ignorance as a way of living! Sensation as a way of forgetting! How many adventures lost in the white-green wake of those vanished ships, like a cold gobbet of spit off the tall rudder that served as a nose beneath the eyes of the old cabins!

248 [15 May 1930]

A glimpse of countryside over a suburban wall gives me a keener sense of freedom than a whole journey might to another person. The point at which we stand to view something forms the apex of an inverted pyramid whose base is indeterminable.

There was a time when the very things that today make me smile used to irritate me intensely. One of them, of which I am reminded almost every day, is the way normal, active men persist in laughing at poets and artists. Although newspaper philosophers would have us believe otherwise, ordinary men do not always laugh at us with an air of superiority. They often do so affectionately. But it's always rather like the pat on the head an adult would give a child, someone unconvinced of life's certainty and exactitude.

This used to irritate me because I thought ingenuously—for I was ingenuous then—that the smile they bestowed on other people's preoccupation with dreaming and with describing their dreams was the effluvium of a deep sense of superiority. In fact, it's just a blunt recognition of difference. And while I used to consider that smile an insult because it implied some kind of superiority, now I consider it to be the admission of an unconscious doubt; just as grown men often recognize in children a sharper wit than their own, so they recognize in us, in those who dream and speak of our dreams, a difference that they distrust because it is strange. I'd like to think that often the more intelligent among them glimpse our superiority and then smile in order to conceal that fact.

But our superiority is not what many dreamers have considered it to be. The dreamer is not superior to the active man because dreaming is essentially superior to reality. The superiority of the dreamer lies in the fact that dreaming is much more practical than living, and in the fact that the dreamer derives a greater and more multifarious pleasure from life than the man of action. To put it more succinctly, it's the dreamer who is the true man of action.

Since life is essentially a mental state and everything that we do or think is only as valuable as we think it is, it depends on us for any value it may have. The dreamer is a distributor of banknotes and these notes are passed around the city of his spirit just as they would be in reality. What does it matter to me if the paper money of my soul can never be converted into gold, since there is no gold in the factitious alchemy of life. After us the deluge, but only after all of us. The truly superior (and the happiest) men are those who, perceiving that everything is a fiction, make up their own novel before someone else does it for them and, like Machiavelli, don courtly robes in order to write in secret.

249 [18 May 1930]

To live is to be other. Even feeling is impossible if one feels today what one felt yesterday, for that is not to feel, it is only to remember today what one felt yesterday, to be the living corpse of yesterday's lost life.

To wipe everything off the slate from one day to the next, to be new with each new dawn, in a state of perpetually restored virginity of emotion—that and only that is worth being or having, if we are to be or to have what we imperfectly are.

This dawn is the first the world has seen. Never before has this pink light dwindling into yellow then hot white fallen in quite this way on the faces that the windowpaned eyes of the houses in the west turn to the silence that comes with the growing light. Never before have this hour, this light, my being existed. What comes tomorrow will be different, and what I see will be seen through different eyes, full of a new vision.

Tall mountains of the city! Great buildings, rooted in, raised up upon, steep slopes, an avalanche of houses heaped indiscriminately together, woven together by the light out of shadows and fire—you are today, you are me, because I see you, you are what [you will not be] tomorrow, and, leaning as if on a ship's rail, I love you as ships passing one another must love, feeling an unaccountable nostalgia in their passing.

250 [12 June 1930]

There are times when everything wearies us, even those things that would normally bring us rest. Obviously what wearies us does so because it's tiring; what is restful tires us because the thought of having to obtain it is tiring. Behind all anguish and pain lie certain debilities of the soul; the only people who remain unaware of these are, I believe, those who shrink from human anguish and pain and tactfully conceal from themselves their own tedium. Since in this way they armor themselves against the world, it is not surprising that at some stage in their self-consciousness they feel suddenly crushed by the whole weight of that armor, and life is revealed to them as an anguish in reverse, an absent pain.

That's how I feel now, and I write these lines like someone struggling to know that he is at least alive. Up until now I've worked the whole day as if half asleep, dreaming my way through accounts, writing out of my own listlessness. All day I've felt life like a weight on my eyelids and temples—my eyes heavy with sleep, constant pressure on my temples, an awareness of all this in the pit of my stomach, feelings of nausea and despair.

Living seems to me a metaphysical mistake on the part of matter, an oversight on the part of inaction. I don't even look to see what kind of day it is, to see if there might be something to distract me from myself and, by describing it here, cover with words the empty cup of my self-love. I don't even look out at the day but sit, shoulders hunched, not knowing whether or not there's sun down there in the subjectively sad street, in the deserted street where nonetheless I hear the sounds of people walking by. I know nothing and my heart aches. I've finished work, but I don't want to move from here. I look at the off-white expanse of blotter glued at the corners to the ancient surface of the sloping desk. I stare attentively at the blur of doodles, the result of self-absorption or of simple distraction. My signature appears several times upside down and back to front, as do certain figures and a few meaningless sketches, the creations of my distracted mind. I look at all this like a yokel who has never seen a blotter before, like someone staring at the latest novelty, with my whole brain inert (except for the areas to do with seeing).

I feel an inner drowsiness so great it overflows the bounds of self. And I want nothing, prefer nothing, there is nothing I can escape into.

251 [13 June 1930]

I live always in the present. I know nothing of the future and no longer have a past. The former weighs me down with a thousand possibilities, the latter with the reality of nothingness. I have neither hopes for the future nor longings for what was. Knowing what my life has been up until now—so often so contrary to the way I wished it to be—what assumptions can I make about my life except that it will be neither what I presume nor what I want it to be, that it will be something that happens to me from outside, even against my own will? Nothing in my past life fills me with the vain desire to repeat it. I have never been anything more than a mere vestige, a simulacrum of myself. My past is everything I never managed to become. Not even the feelings associated with past moments make me nostalgic; what one feels is of the moment; once that is past the page turns and the story continues, but not the text.

Brief, dark shadow of a city tree, the light sound of water falling into a sad pool, the green of smooth grass—a public park on the edge of dusk—in this moment you are the whole universe to me, because you entirely fill my every conscious feeling. I want nothing more from life than to feel it ebbing away into these unexpected evenings, to the sound of other people's children playing in gardens fenced in by the melancholy of the surrounding streets, and above, the high branches of the trees, vaulted by the ancient sky in which the stars are just beginning to reappear.

252 [c. 13 June 1930]

Thunderstorm

A low sky of unmoving clouds. The blue of the sky was sullied with transparent white.

The office boy at the other end of the room paused for a moment in his eternal tying up of parcels ... "Just listen to that [...]," he said appreciatively.

A cold silence. The sounds from the street stopped as if cut with a knife. For what seemed an age one sensed a malaise in everything, a cosmic holding of breath. The whole universe stopped. Minutes and minutes passed. The darkness grew black with silence.

Then, suddenly, the flash of bright steel [...].

How human the metallic clanking of the trams seemed! How joyful the landscape of simple rain falling in streets dragged back from the abyss!

Oh, Lisbon, my home!

Life for us is whatever we imagine it to be. To the peasant with his one field, that field is everything, it is an empire. To Caesar with his vast empire which still feels cramped, that empire is a field. The poor man has an empire; the great man only a field. The truth is that we possess nothing but our own sensations; it is on them, then, and not on what they perceive, that we must base the reality of our life.

But all this is apropos of nothing.

I've dreamed a lot. I'm tired now from dreaming but not tired of dreaming. No one tires of dreaming, because to dream is to forget, and forgetting does not weigh on us, it is a dreamless sleep throughout which we remain awake. In dreams I have achieved everything. I've also woken up, but what does that matter? How many countless Caesars I have been! And yet how mean-spirited are the glorious! Saved from death by the generosity of a pirate, Caesar subsequently searched long and hard for that same man, arrested him and ordered him to be crucified. When Napoleon drew up his last will and testament on St. Helena, he left a legacy to a criminal who had tried to assassinate Wellington. Such greatness of soul is about on a par with that of their squint-eyed neighbor! O great men born of another world's cook! How many countless Caesars have I been and still dream of being!

How many countless Caesars have I been, yet I was never like the real Caesars. I was truly imperial in my dreams and for that reason came to nothing. My armies were defeated, but it was a thing of no importance and no one died. No flags were taken. I never dreamed the army to the point where those flags might hove into view around the corner of my dreaming gaze. How many countless Caesars have I been right here in Rua dos Douradores. Those Caesars still live in my imagination, but the real Caesars are all long dead, and Rua dos Douradores, that is, Reality, would not now recognize them.

I toss an empty matchbox out into the abyss that is the street beyond the sill of my high window. I sit up in my chair and listen. As if the fact were significant, the empty matchbox sends back a clear echo telling me the street is deserted. There is no sound apart from the sounds made by the entire city. Yes, the sounds of the entire city—so many indecipherable sounds and each in its way right.

How little of the real world one needs as a starting point for the best meditations: arriving late for lunch, running out of matches and throwing the empty box out into the street, feeling slightly indisposed after eating lunch late, it being Sunday with nothing in the air but the promise of a poor sunset, my being no one in this world, and other such metaphysical matters.

But oh how many Caesars I have been!

254 [June/July 1930]

They were strange hours, successive unconnected moments, that I spent on my walk at night by the solitary shore of the sea. In my walking meditation, all the thoughts that have made men live, all the emotions that men have allowed to exist, passed through my mind like an obscure summary of history.

I suffered in myself, with myself, the aspirations of every era and all the unrest of all time strolled alongside me by the thunderous shore. What men wanted to do but did not and what they destroyed in so doing, what became of their souls and was never spoken of—all that formed part of the sensitive soul accompanying me along the night shore. And what lovers found wanting in each other, the truth about herself that the wife always hid from her husband, what the mother thought of the child she never had, things that found expression only in a smile or an opportunity, in a moment that was not the right one or in an absent emotion—all of this came with me on my walk and returned with me while the vast waves crashed out the accompaniment that lulled me to sleep.

We are who we are not, and life is swift and sad. The sound of waves at night is a nocturnal sound, and how many have heard it in their own soul like the constant hope breaking in the dark in a dull thud of dense foam! What tears were shed by those who failed, what tears were spent by those who reached their goal! In my stroll by the sea, all this came to me like the secrets of the night, the whispered confidences of the abyss. How many we are, how many of those selves we deceive! What seas break in us, in the night of our being, along beaches that we only sense in the full flood of our emotion!

What we lost, what we should have loved, what we got and were, by mistake, contented with, what we loved and lost and, once lost, saw that we had not loved but loved it still just because we had lost it; what we believed we thought when we felt something; what we believed to be an emotion and was in fact only a memory; and, as I walked, the whole sea came rolling in, cool and clamorous, from the deepest reaches of the dark, to etch itself delicately along the sands ...

Who knows what he thinks or what he desires? Who knows what meaning he really has for himself? How many things are suggested to us by music and how comforting to know those things can never be! How many things the night recalls and how we weep for them though they never were! Like a voice unleashed from the long peaceful line of the sea, the wave arches, crashes and dies, leaving behind the sound of its waters licking the invisible shore.

How I die if I allow myself to feel for all things! How much I feel if I let myself drift, incorporeal and human, my heart quiet as a beach, and, in the night in which we live, in my endless nocturnal walk along its shore, the sea of all things beats loud and mocking, then grows calm.

255   [16 July 1930]
You can feel life like a sickness in the pit of the stomach, the existence of your own soul like a muscular cramp. Desolation of the spirit, when sharply felt, creates distant tides in the body and hurts by proxy.

I am conscious that in myself today the pain of consciousness is, as the poet says:

languor, nausea
and a terrible yearning.

256 [20 July 1930]

Whenever I've dreamt a lot, I go out into the street with my eyes open but I'm still wrapped in the safety of those dreams. And I'm amazed how many people fail to recognize my automatism. For I walk through daily life still holding the hand of my astral mistress, and my footsteps in the street are concordant and consonant with the obscure designs of my sleeping imagination. And yet I walk straight down the street; I don't stumble; I react as I should; I exist.

But whenever there's an interval in which I don't have to watch where I'm going in order to avoid cars or passersby, when I don't have to talk to anyone or dodge into some nearby doorway, I let myself drift off once more like a paper boat on the waters of the dream and I revisit the dying illusion that warmed my vague awareness of the morning stirring into life amidst the sounds of carts carrying vegetables to market.

It is there, in the midst of life, that the dream becomes like a vast cinema screen. I go down a dream street in the Baixa and the reality of the dream-lives inhabiting it gently binds a white blindfold of false memories about my eyes. I become a navigator through an unknown me. I conquer all in places I have never even visited. And it's like a fresh breeze, this somnolent state in which I walk, leaning forward, in my march on the impossible.

Each of us is intoxicated by different things. There's intoxication enough for me in just existing. Drunk on feeling, I drift but never stray. If it's time to go back to work, I go to the office just like everyone else. If not, I go down to the river to stare at the waters, again just like everyone else. I'm just the same. But behind this sameness, I secretly scatter my personal firmament with stars and therein create my own infinity.

257

I write with a strange sense of grief, I make use of a certain intellectual asphyxia, which comes to me from the perfection of the evening. This exquisitely blue sky fading into pale pink on a soft, steady breeze fills my consciousness of myself with an urge to scream. I am, after all, writing in order to flee and flee again. I avoid ideals. I forget precise expressions, and they come to me in the physical act of writing, as if the pen itself were producing them.

From what I thought, from what I felt, there survives obscurely a futile desire to weep.

258

We never love anyone. We love only our idea of what someone is like. We love an idea of our own; in short, it is ourselves that we love.

This is true of every kind of love. In sexual love we seek our own pleasure through the intermediary of another's body. In nonsexual love, we seek our own pleasure through the intermediary of an idea we have. The onanist may be an abject creature but in truth he is the logical expression of the lover. He is the only one who neither disguises nor deludes himself.

Relations between one soul and another, expressed through such uncertain, divergent things as words exchanged and gestures made, are of a strange complexity. The very way in which we come to know each other is a form of unknowing. When two people say "I love you" (or perhaps think or reciprocate the feeling), each one means by that something different, a different life, even, perhaps, a different color and aroma in the abstract sum of impressions that constitute the activity of the soul.

I am as lucid today as if I had altogether ceased to exist. My thought is laid bare like a skeleton, divested of the carnal rags of the illusion of communication. And these thoughts, which I first shape and then abandon, are born of nothing, of nothing at all, at least not of anything that exists in the pit of my consciousness.

Perhaps the disappointment in love that our salesman experienced over the girl he was going out with, perhaps some phrase taken from an account of a love affair that newspapers here reprint from the foreign press, perhaps a vague nausea I carry within me and which I have not managed to expel physically …

The commentator on Virgil was wrong. It's perfectly understandable that what we feel above all else should be weariness. To live is not to think.

259 [c. 27 July 1930]

The sense of smell is like a strange way of seeing. It evokes sentimental landscapes out of a mere sketch in our subconscious minds. I've often felt that. I walk down a street. I see nothing, or rather, though I look at everything, I see only what everyone sees. I know that I'm walking down a street, but I'm not conscious of it comprising two sides made up of different houses built by human beings. I walk down a street. From a baker's comes the almost sickeningly sweet smell of bread and from a district right on the other side of town my childhood rises up and another baker's appears before me from that fairy kingdom which is everything we have lost. I walk down a street. Suddenly it smells of the fruit on the stand outside a narrow little shop, and my short time in the country—I no longer know when or where it was—plants trees and quiet comfort in my heart, for a moment indisputably that of a child. I walk down a street. I'm overcome, quite unexpectedly, by the smell of the wooden crates being made by the box-maker: ah, Cesário, you appear before me and at last I am happy because, through memory, I have returned to the one truth that is literature.

260 [27 July 1930]

Their inability to say what they see or think is a cause of suffering to most people. They say there is nothing more difficult than to define a spiral in words; it's necessary, they say, to describe it in the air, with one's illiterate hands, using gestures spiraling slowly upwards to show how that abstract form, peculiar to coiled springs and certain staircases, appears to the eye. But as long as we remember that to speak means to renew language, we should have no difficulty whatsoever in describing a spiral: it is a circle that rises upwards but never closes upon itself (I know perfectly well that most people wouldn't dare to define it thus, because they imagine that to define something one should say what other people want, and not what one needs to say in order to produce a definition). I would go farther: a spiral is a virtual circle which repeats itself as it rises but never reaches fulfillment. But, no, that's still abstract. If I make it concrete all will become clear: a spiral is a snake, which is not a snake, coiled vertically around nothing.

All literature consists of an effort to make life real. As everyone knows, even when they act as if they did not, in its physical reality, life is absolutely unreal; fields, cities, ideas are all totally fictitious, the children of our complex experience of ourselves. All impressions are incommunicable unless we make literature of them. Children are naturally literary because they say what they feel and do not speak like someone who feels according to someone else's feelings. Once I heard a child on the point of tears say not "I feel like crying," which is what an adult, i.e. a fool, would say, but: "I feel like tears." And this phrase, absolutely literary, to the point where it would be considered affectation on the lips of a famous poet (were he capable of inventing it), refers resolutely to the hot presence of tears behind eyelids burning with the bitter liquid. "I feel like tears." That child produced a fine definition of his particular spiral.

To say things! To know how to say things! To know how to exist through the written voice and the intellectual image! That's what life is about: the rest is just men and women, imagined loves and fictitious vanities, excuses born of poor digestion and forgetting, people squirming beneath the great abstract boulder of a meaningless blue sky, the way insects do when you lift a stone.

261 [10 Dec 1930]

I go through periods of great stagnation. By this I don't mean that, like most people, it takes me days and days to reply on a postcard to an urgent letter someone wrote to me. I don't mean that, again like other people, I put off indefinitely something easy that might prove useful to me, or something useful that might give me pleasure. My misunderstanding with myself is more subtle than that. I stagnate in my very soul. I suffer a suspension of will, emotion and thought that lasts for days at a time; I can only express myself to others and, through them, express myself to me in the purely vegetative life of the soul, through words, gestures, habits.

In these shadowy times, I am incapable of thinking, feeling or wanting. The only things I manage to write are numbers or mere strokes of the pen. I feel nothing, and even the death of someone I love would seem as far removed from me as if it had taken place in a foreign language. I can do nothing; it's as if I slept and my gestures, words and actions were just a surface breathing, the rhythmical instinct of some organism.

Thus days and days pass; how much of my life, were I to add up those days, I couldn't say. Sometimes I think that when I finally slough off these stagnant clothes, I may not stand as naked as I imagine and some intangible vestments may still clothe the eternal absence of my true soul; it occurs to me that to think, feel or want may also be stagnant forms of a more personal way of thinking, of feelings more intimately mine, of a will lost somewhere in the labyrinth of who I really am.

Whatever the truth, I let it be. And to whatever gods or goddesses may exist, I hand over what I am, resigned to whatever fate may send and whatever chance may offer, faithful to some forgotten promise.

262 [1930?]

I don't really believe in the happiness of animals, except when I want to use it as a frame for some feeling that supports that supposition. To be happy it is necessary to know that one is happy. The only happiness one gets out of enjoying a dreamless sleep is waking up and knowing that one has slept without dreaming. Happiness exists outside itself.

There is no happiness without knowledge, but the knowledge of happiness brings unhappiness, because to know one is happy is to know that one is passing through happiness and, therefore, will soon be obliged to leave it behind. In happiness as in everything, knowledge kills. Not to know, however, is not to exist.

Only Hegel's absolute managed, over several pages, to be two things at once. In the feelings or motivating forces of life, not-being and being never become fused or confused; through some process of inverse synthesis the two things remain mutually exclusive.

So what should one do? Isolate the moment as if it were a physical object and be happy now, in the moment in which one feels happiness, without even thinking about what one feels, simply shutting out everything else. Cage up thought in feeling [...]

the bright maternal smile of the bounteous earth, the dense splendor of the dark above [...]

That is what I believe, this afternoon. Tomorrow morning it will be different, because tomorrow morning I will be different. What kind of believer will I be tomorrow? I don't know, because to know that I would need to have been there already. Tomorrow or today not even the eternal God I believe in now will know, because today I'm me and tomorrow he may perhaps never have existed.

263 [1930?]

I'm always astonished whenever I finish anything. Astonished and depressed. My desire for perfection should prevent me from ever finishing anything; it should prevent me even from starting. But I forget that and I do begin. What I achieve is a product not of the application but of a giving in of the will. I begin because I do not have the strength to think; I finish because I do not have the heart just to abandon it. This book is my cowardice.

The reason I so often break off from a thought to insert a description of a landscape, which in some real or imagined way fits in with the general scheme of my impressions, is that the landscape is a door through which I can escape from the knowledge of my own creative impotence. In the middle of the conversations with myself that make up this book, I often feel a sudden need to talk to someone else, so I address the light hovering, as it does now, above the roofs of the houses that shine as if damp, or the tall trees, apparently so near, swaying gently on a city hillside rehearsing the possibility of their own silent downfall, or the posters pasted one on top of the other on the walls of the steep houses with windows for words, where the dead sun turns the still-wet glue golden.

Why write if I can't manage to write any better? But what would become of me if I didn't write what I do manage to write, however far below my own standards I fall? I'm a plebeian in my aspirations because I try to create; I fear silence the way others fear entering a dark room alone. I'm like those people who value the medal more than the effort it took to win it and see glory in the gold braid on dress uniforms.

For me, to write is to despise myself, but I can't stop writing. Writing is like a drug I detest but keep taking, a vice I despise and for which I live. There are necessary poisons and there are very subtle ones made up of ingredients of the soul, herbs gathered in the corners of ruined dreams, black poppies found near the graves of intentions, the long leaves of obscene trees that wave their branches on the noisy banks of the infernal rivers of the soul.

Yes, to write is to lose myself, but everyone gets lost, because everything in life is loss. But unlike the river flowing into the estuary for which, unknowing, it was born, I feel no joy in losing myself, but lie like the pool left on the beach at high tide, a pool whose waters, swallowed by the sands, never more return to the sea.

264

The uncertain, silent city lies spread out beneath my nostalgic gaze. The houses, all different, stand together in a tightly packed crowd, and the equally uncertain moonlight puddles this dumb, jostling confusion with mother-of-pearl. Nothing but rooftops and night, windows and a faint medieval air. Nothing else. A breath of the far-away hovers over everything. From where I stand, what I see lies cradled in the dark branches of trees. I hold the whole sleeping city in my poor, dispirited heart. Lisbon in the moonlight and my weariness at the prospect of another day!

What a night! May whoever created the tiny details of this world give me no better state, no sweeter melody than this singular lunar moment in which I both know and unknow myself.

No breeze, no people interrupt my nonthoughts. Drowsing and living are one and the same. Except that I can feel something pressing on my eyelids. I can hear my own breathing. Am I asleep or awake?

Leaden-footed and leaden-sensed, I walk home. The caress of all-extinguishing sleep, the flower of sheer futility, my never-spoken name, my disquiet lapped between two shores, the pleasure of relinquished duties, and, at the last bend in the path through the ancient park, that other century like a rose garden.

265

However hard his life may be, the ordinary man does at least have the pleasure of not thinking. Living life as it comes, externally, like a cat or a dog—that is what most men do, and that is how you should live if you want to be as contented as a cat or a dog.

To think is to destroy. Thought itself is destroyed by the very process of thinking, because to think is to de-compose. If men were able to ponder the mystery of life, if they were able to feel the thousand complexities that spy on the soul in every detail of every action, they would never act at all—they wouldn't even live. They would kill themselves out of pure fear, in the way some men kill themselves in order not to be guillotined the next day.

More than once, while out strolling in the evening, the strange presence of things and the way they are organized in the world has often struck my soul with sudden, surprising violence. It's not so much the natural things that affect me, that communicate that feeling so powerfully, it's rather the arrangement of the streets, shop signs, the people talking to one another, their clothes, jobs, newspapers, the intelligence underlying everything. Or, rather, it's the fact of the very existence of streets, shop signs, jobs, men and society, all getting on together, following familiar routes and setting out along new ones.

I look hard at man and I see that he is as unconscious as a cat or a dog; the unconsciousness out of which he speaks and orders his life in society is utterly inferior to that employed by ants and bees in their social life. But then, beyond the existence of organisms, beyond the existence of rigid, intellectual and physical laws, what is revealed to me in a blaze of light is the intelligence that creates and impregnates the world.

Whenever I feel that, the old phrase of a Scholastic, whose name I've forgotten, immediately springs to mind: *Deus est anima brutorum*. God is the soul of the beasts. That was how the author of this marvelous sentence tried to explain the certainty with which instinct guides the lower animals in whom one sees no sign—or at best only a glimmer—of intelligence. But we are all lower animals; speaking and thinking are just new instincts, less accurate than the others because they are so new. And the Scholastic's words, so apt in their beauty, can be expanded to read: God is the soul of everything.

I have never understood how anyone, having once intuited the great fact of this universal timepiece, could deny the watchmaker in whom not even Voltaire could disbelieve. I understand that when one looks at certain apparently mistaken facets of a plan (and it would be necessary to know what the plan was in order to know that these were indeed mistakes) one could attribute to that supreme intelligence some element of imperfection. I understand that, although I don't accept it. I understand that, seeing the evil that exists in the world, one might feel unable to accept the idea of the infinite goodness of that all-creating intelligence. That, too, I understand, although again without accepting it. But to deny the existence of that intelligence, of God, strikes me as just one of those foolish whims that so often afflict one part of the intelligence of men who, in every other respect, are quite superior; such as those who can't add up or even (throwing into the arena the intelligence implicit in artistic sensibility) those who have no feeling for music or painting or poetry.

I accept neither the theory of the imperfect watchmaker nor the theory of the cruel watchmaker. I reject the former because, without knowing the whole plan, we cannot say whether the details of the way in which the world is governed and arranged are the lapses or mistakes that they seem to be. We clearly see a plan in everything; we see some things that seem wrong, but we must consider that if there is a reason for everything, there must also be a reason for the things that are apparently wrong. We see the reason but not the plan; if we do not know what the plan is, how can we say that certain things fall outside it? Just as a poet, say, a master of subtle rhythms, may introduce a dissonant line into a poem for reasons of rhythm, that is, for a reason that seems entirely contrary to its nature (and which a more prosaic critic would denounce as wrong), so the Creator may interpose in the majestic flow of his metaphysical rhythms things that our narrow reasoning perceives as mistakes.

Neither, as I said, do I accept the theory of the cruel watchmaker. I agree it's a more difficult argument to answer but only apparently so. We can say that we don't really know what "bad" means, and cannot therefore state categorically that a thing is good or bad. What is certain is that pain, even if it is for our own good, is in itself bad and is in itself sufficient proof of the existence of evil in the world. One toothache is enough for us to disbelieve in the benevolence of the Creator. Now the essential defect of this argument would seem to lie in our complete ignorance of God's plan, and our equal ignorance of what, as an intelligent being, the Intellectual Infinite might be like. The existence of evil is one thing, the reason for its existence quite another. The distinction is perhaps subtle to the point of sophistry, but it is accurate. We cannot deny the existence of evil, but we can reject the idea that the existence of evil is in itself evil. I recognize that the problem remains, but only because of our own continuing imperfection.

267 [1930?]

I know no pleasure like that of books, and yet I read little. Books act as introductions to dreams, and such introductions are unnecessary to someone who can so easily and instinctively enter into conversation with dreams. I've never been able to surrender myself to a book; at every step, my intelligence or my imagination would make some comment that got in the way of the narrative. After a matter of minutes, I would become the person writing, and the words on the page would be nowhere to be found.

What I like most is to read and reread the rather banal books that sleep next to me on my bedside table. There are two in particular that never leave me—Father Figueiredo's *Rhetoric* and Father Freire's *Reflections on the Portuguese Language*.* Rereading these books is always a pleasure, and although I have read them many times, I have never read either of them all the way through. I owe these books a discipline I thought almost impossible in me, namely, that one must always write objectively and rationally.

Father Figueiredo's affected, monastic, fusty style is a discipline that delights my understanding. Father Freire's diffuse, often undisciplined style amuses my mind without wearying it, and instructs without provoking any feelings of anxiety. They are both calm, erudite minds who provide proof of my utter lack of inclination to be like them—or like anyone else.

---

* Francisco José Freire (1719–1773) wrote under the pen name Cândido Lusitano and was a founding member of a literary group known as the Arcadians.

I read and I abandon myself, not to reading, but to myself. I read and fall asleep, and, as if among dreams, I follow Father Figueiredo's descriptions of rhetorical figures, and in marvelous forests, I hear Father Freire telling me that I should say Magdalena, because only common people say Madanela.

268 [1930?]

One of the great tragedies of my life—though it is one of those tragedies that take place amidst shadows and subterfuge—is that of being unable to feel anything naturally. I am as capable as anyone of love and hate, of fear and enthusiasm, but neither my love nor my hate, neither my fear nor my enthusiasm, is exactly what it seems. They either lack some element or have had something added to them. What is certain is that they are something else, and what I feel is out of step with life.

In those spirits we so aptly call "calculating," feelings are defined and limited by calculation and by selfish scruples, and therefore seem different. You can see the same dislocation of natural instincts in those we call "scrupulous." In me there is the same muddying of clear feelings yet I'm neither calculating nor scrupulous. I have no excuse for being bad at feeling. This denaturing of instincts is utterly instinctive in me. Without even wanting to, I want mistakenly.

269 [1930?]

As in the hours during which a storm is brewing and the noises in the street speak in one solitary voice.

The street puckered beneath the intense, pale light, and from east to west, the grubby blackness trembled as a boom of thunder rolled out like a great echoing cackle of laughter ... The harsh sadness of the brutal rain only made the dark air more intensely ugly. Cold, warm, hot—all at the same time—everywhere, the air felt wrong. And then, in the ample room, a metallic light drove a wedge into the repose of our human bodies, and, like an icy shock, a gravelly sound beat down upon us, slicing through everything to create a single large silence. The sound of the rain dwindled, as if adopting a gentler tone of voice. The noise in the streets grew worryingly quiet. A new, swift, yellow light veiled the silent darkness, but there was just time to catch one's breath before the fist of sound suddenly echoed out from somewhere else; as if bidding an angry farewell, the thunderstorm was beginning not to be here.

[…] with a slurred, dying whisper, dark in the growing light, the rumble of thunder was moving off into the far distance—somewhere near Almada—[…]

A sudden splintering, a blaze of light, exploding inside minds and thoughts. Everything stopped. Hearts stopped. Like sensitive souls. The silence terrifies as if a death had just occurred. The sound of the rain growing louder brings a sense of relief like tears copiously shed. The air is leaden.

270 [1930?]

A kind of looming anticipation hung in the air like a dark hope: even the rain seemed intimidated; a dull blackness bore down upon us. And suddenly, like a shout, a terrifying day broke. A light from some fake hell filled everything, every mind, every corner. Everyone was stunned. Then came a deep intake of breath because the blow had passed. The brutal rain was joyful in its almost human noise. Hearts resumed their normal rhythm, and even thinking made us dizzy. A vaguely religious feeling filled the office. No one was who they were, and the boss Vasques appeared in the doorway in order to think of saying something. Moreira smiled, still bearing on the outskirts of his face the yellow of sudden fear. And his smile was saying that the next thunder clap would probably be a long way off. A cart trotting noisily past drowned out the sounds from the street. Involuntarily the phone shivered. Instead of withdrawing to his room, my boss Vasques went over to the phone in the big office. There was a moment of repose and silence, while the rain fell nightmarishly hard. Then Vasques forgot about the phone, which had stopped ringing. At the far end of the room, the office boy stirred into life like some cumbersome object.

A great joy, full of repose and liberation, took us all by surprise. We resumed our work feeling almost lightheaded, and were spontaneously pleasant and sociable with each other. Unbidden, the office boy flung open the windows. A fresh, damp smell entered the room. The rain was falling only lightly now, almost humbly. The noises from the street were the same, but different. We could hear the voices of the drivers of carts, and they were the voices of real people. In the next street, the clear, clanging bells on the trams seemed to join in our jollity. A chuckle from a lone child sang out like a canary in the washed-clean air. The light rain was fading.

It was six o'clock. The office was closing. From the half-open door of his room, my boss Vasques said: "You can all go home now," and he said this as if he were bestowing on us a commercial blessing. I immediately got to my feet, shut the ledger and put it away. I ostentatiously replaced my pen in its inkstand and, going over to Moreira, addressed him with an optimistic "see you tomorrow" and shook his hand as if he had just done me an enormous favor.

271 [1930?]

From the very beginning of that hot, deceitful day, dark, shaggy clouds had hung over the oppressed city. Above what we call the estuary, those dark clouds continued to pile up, cloud upon cloud, and they and the vaguely rancorous streets—at odds with the angry sun—gave off a sense of imminent tragedy.

It was midday and, as we left the office to have lunch, a sense of foreboding seemed to weigh upon the pale air. Scraps of ragged clouds grew still blacker. The sky near the castle was a clear but ominous blue. It was sunny, but not the kind of sun you could enjoy.

At half past one, when we were back in the office after lunch, the sky seemed clearer, but only over the older parts of the city. Near the estuary it was slightly overcast. To the north, however, the clouds had become a single black, implacable cloud, advancing slowly, reaching out its black arms and its blunt ash-gray talons. It would not be long before it covered the sun, and the sounds of the city seemed to grow muted in expectation. To the east, the sky was or seemed to be clearer, but the heat there was more oppressive. We were even sweating in the relative cool of the office. "There's a big storm coming," said Moreira, and turned a page in his ledger.

By three o'clock, the sun had been entirely obscured. We had to turn on the lights—a sad thing in summer—first, at the back of the big office, where the parcels were all ready to be sent off, then in the middle, where it was becoming hard to see clearly enough to fill in the remittance advices and note down on them the correct train numbers. Finally, at about four o'clock, even we privileged few with desks near the windows could not see to work. The whole office was lit up. My boss Vasques flung open the door to his room, came out and said: "Moreira, I was supposed to go to Benfica this afternoon, but I don't think I will now. Any moment, it's going to chuck it down." "Yes, and that's definitely where it's coming from," answered Moreira, who lived near the Avenida. The noises in the street suddenly stopped, then changed subtly, and for some reason, there was a melancholy note to the clanging of the tram bells in the street parallel to ours.

272 [1930?]

… the rain was still sadly falling, but less heavily, as if infected by a universal weariness; there was no lightning now and, from somewhere off in the distance, a brief roll of thunder would occasionally grumble then stop, as if it, too, had grown weary. Suddenly, the rain grew lighter still. One of the clerks opened the windows that give onto Rua dos Douradores. Into the room slipped a cool breeze with fading remnants of heat in it. The voice of my boss Vasques said loudly into the phone: "You mean the line's still busy?" And then there was the sound of a muttered expletive—an impatient remark addressed (presumably) to the receptionist on the other end.

273 [1930?]
Holiday prose

For those three days of holiday, the small beach, forming an even smaller bay cut off from the world by two miniature promontories, was my retreat from myself. You reached the beach by a rough staircase that started as wooden steps but halfway down became mere ledges cut out of the rock, with a rusty iron banister to hold on to. Every time I went down the old steps, especially the ones cut out of the rock, I left my own existence behind and found myself.

Occultists, at least some of them, say that there are supreme moments in the life of the soul when, by way of an emotion or a fragment of memory, the soul recalls a moment, an aspect or just the shadow of some previous incarnation. Then, since it returns to a time which is closer than the present to the origin and beginning of all things, it feels in some way a child again, it feels a sense of liberation.

You could say that when I slowly descended those rarely used steps to the small, always deserted beach, I was making use of a magical process in order to bring myself closer to the possible monad that is my self. Certain aspects and features of my daily life—represented in my constant self by desires, dislikes, worries—just disappeared from me as if chased away by the night patrol, simply melted into the shadows until one couldn't even make out their shapes, and I achieved a state of inner distance in which it became difficult even to remember yesterday, or to recognize as mine the being that inhabits me from day to day. My usual emotions, my regularly irregular habits, my conversations with other people, my adaptations to the social way of the world—all that seemed like things I had read somewhere, the dead pages of a printed biography, details from some novel, those intervening chapters that we read with our mind on something else, leaving the narrative thread to unravel and slither to the ground.

On the beach, where the only sounds were of the waves themselves or the wind passing high above like a great invisible aeroplane, I abandoned myself to new dreams—soft, shapeless things, marvels that impressed without images or emotions, as clear as the sky and the waters, trembling like the crumbling lace on the folds of the sea rising up from the depths of some great truth, a matt blue in the far distance, then, as it reached the shore, its transparency becoming stained by dull greens that shattered, hissing, drawing back a thousand broken arms across the darkened sand, leaving only a dribble of white foam, gathering in to itself all the retreating waves, the returns to an original freedom, divine nostalgias, memories—like my nebulous, painless memory of a happier time, happy either because it was genuinely good or simply because it was other, a body of nostalgia with a soul of foam—rest, death, the everything or nothing that, like a great sea, surrounds the island of shipwrecked souls that is life.

And I slept without sleeping, removed from what I saw with my senses, in the twilight of my own self, the sound of water among trees, the calm of wide rivers, the cool of sad evenings, the slow rise and fall of the white breast of the childlike sleep of contemplation.

274 [1930?]

A shrug of the shoulders

We generally give to our ideas about the unknown the color of our notions about what we *do* know: if we call death a sleep it's because it has the appearance of sleep; if we call death a new life, it's because it seems different from life. We build our beliefs and hopes out of these small misunderstandings with reality and live off husks of bread that we call cakes, the way poor children play at being happy.

But that's how all of life is; at least that's how the particular way of life generally known as civilization is. Civilization consists in giving an inappropriate name to something and then dreaming what results from that. And in fact the false name and the true dream do create a new reality. The object really does become other, because we have made it so. We manufacture realities. We use the raw materials we always used, but the form lent it by art effectively prevents it from remaining the same. A table made out of pinewood is a pine tree but it is also a table. We sit down at the table not at the pine tree. Although love is a sexual instinct, we do not love with that instinct, rather we presuppose the existence of another feeling, and that presupposition is, effectively, another feeling.

These meandering thoughts that I calmly record in the café I chanced to sit down in were evoked by something as I was walking down the street, quite what I don't know, a sudden subtle trick of the light, a vague noise, the memory of a perfume or a snatch of music, each strummed into being by some unknown influence from without. I don't know where I was going to lead those thoughts or where I would choose to lead them. There's a light mist today, damp and warm, unthreateningly sad, oddly monotonous. Some feeling I don't recognize aches in me; I feel as if I had lost the thread of some discussion; the words I write are utterly will-less. Sadness lurks beneath consciousness. I write, or rather scribble, these lines not in order to say anything in particular but to give my distraction something to do. With the soft marks made by a blunt pencil I haven't the heart to sharpen, I slowly fill the white paper the café uses to wrap up sandwiches (and which they provided me with because I required nothing better and anything would have done, as long as it was white). And I feel content. I lean back. Evening falls, monotonous and rainless, in a discouraged, uncertain sort of light … And I stop writing just because I stop writing.

275 [1930?]

That's how I am, frivolous and sensitive, capable of impulses that can be violent and all-consuming, good and bad, noble and base, but they never contain any lasting feeling, any enduring emotion that really penetrates the substance of my soul. Everything in me

288

is a tendency to be about to become something else; an impatience of the soul with itself, as if with an importunate child; a disquiet that is always growing and always the same. Everything interests me and nothing holds my attention. I listen to everything while constantly dreaming; I notice the tiniest facial tics of the person I'm talking to, pick up minimal changes in the intonation of what they say; but when I hear, I do not listen, for I'm thinking about something else, and I come away from any conversation with little idea of what was said, either by me or by the other person. So I often find myself repeating to someone something I've already told him or asking again the very thing he's just told me; yet I can describe in four photographic words the set of his facial muscles as he said the words I no longer remember, or the attentive way he looked at me as I told him the story I now have no recollection of having told. I'm two people who mutually keep their distance—Siamese twins living separate lives.

276 [1930?]

If some day I should happen to have a secure life and all the time and opportunity in the world to write and publish, I know that I will be nostalgic for this uncertain life in which I scarcely write at all and publish nothing. I will feel nostalgic not only because this ordinary life is over and I will never have it again, but because there is in every kind of life a particular quality and a peculiar pleasure, and when we move on to another life, even if it is a better one, that peculiar pleasure is dimmed, that particular quality impoverished, they cease to exist and one feels their loss.

If one day I manage to carry the cross of my intentions to the ultimate calvary, I know that I will find another calvary within and will feel nostalgia for the days when I was futile, unpolished and imperfect. I will be in some way diminished.

I feel drowsy. I spent a boring day engaged on a particularly absurd task in an almost deserted office. Two of the staff are off sick and the others are simply not in today. I'm alone apart from the office boy, who is far away at the opposite end of the room. I feel nostalgia for the possibility of one day feeling nostalgia, regardless of how absurd that nostalgia may seem.

I almost pray to the gods to let me stay here, as if locked up in a safe, protected from both life's bitterness and its joys.

277 [1930?]

"What are you laughing about?" Moreira's voice asked mildly from behind the two shelves separating him from my lofty peak.

"Oh, I just got in a bit of a tangle with some names," I said, managing to quell my laughter.

"Ah," was all Moreira said, and the dusty peace descended once more on the office and on me.

Not even Bourget, poor soul, who is as hard work to read as a tall building with only stairs and no lift ... I turn back and lean out of the window to take another look at my personal Boulevard Saint-German, at the precise moment when the wealthy landowner next door is leaning out to spit into the street. Vicomte de Chateaubriand doing the accounts! Professor Amiel perched on a high royal stool! Comte Alfred de Vigny debiting the Grandela department store! Senancour in Rua dos Douradores! And in between thinking all this and smoking a cigarette, and not really connecting it all up, my mental laughter meets the smoke and gets tangled up in my throat, where it grows into a timid attack of audible laughter.*

---

* Paul Bourget (1852–1935), a French novelist and critic. François-René de Chateaubriand (1768–1848), a French writer, politician and historian, whose most famous works are his novella *René* and his autobiography *Mémoires d'outre-tombe*. Henri-Frédéric Amiel (1821–1881), a Swiss diarist and critic whose *Fragments d'un journal intime* was published between 1883 and 1887. Alfred de Vigny (1797–1863), the French Romantic poet and novelist, was the author of *Chatterton* (1835). For him, the world was a place of suffering, life a constant process of abnegation, and God (if he existed) a harsh Old Testament deity. Etienne Pivert de Senancour (1770–1846), a French essayist and philosopher, best known for his influential novel *Obermann*.

278

I'm tired of the street; no, I'm not—all of life is in the street. There's the tavern opposite, which I can see if I look over my right shoulder; and there's the box-maker's, which I can see if I look over my left shoulder; and in the middle, which I can only see if I turn around, is the cobbler occupying the entrance to the office of the Africa Company with his steadfast hammering. I'm not sure about the other floors. On the third floor there's a boarding house, none too salubrious, they say, but then you could say the same about life.

Tired of the street? I only get tired when I think. When I look out at the street or I feel it, then I don't think: I do my work with a great sense of inner repose, usefully filling my corner of the office, a clerical nobody. I have no soul, no one does—here it's all work, work, work. Far off, doubtless in some foreign place, where the millionaires swan around, there is work too, and, as here, no souls either. All that's left is a poet or two. If only I could leave behind me a phrase, a dictum, of which others would say "Brilliant!" like the numbers I'm writing, copying them down in the book of my entire life.

I don't think I will ever stop being a bookkeeper in a fabric warehouse. I fervently, sincerely hope never to be promoted to chief bookkeeper.

279

If in art there were such a thing as a perfecter, then I would have a function in life, at least as regards my art.

To have the work done by someone else, and merely having to do one's best to perfect it ... Perhaps that is how the *Iliad* was written ...

And not to have all the effort of creating something from scratch!

How I envy those who write novels, who begin them and write them and finish them! I can imagine a novel, chapter by chapter, sometimes with entire dialogues as well as the bits in between, but I would never be able to set down on paper those dreams of writing [...]

280 [1930?]

We worship perfection, because we cannot have it; and we would loathe it if we did. Perfection is inhuman, because to be human is to be imperfect.

We secretly hate paradise—our desire to reach it is like that of the poor wretch who hopes to find the countryside in heaven. It isn't abstract ecstasies or the marvels of the absolute that charm the sentient soul: its cozy firesides and gentle hills, green islands set in blue seas, tree-lined paths and long restful hours spent on ancestral estates, even ones we never owned. If there's no earth in heaven, then let's not bother with heaven. Far better for everything to turn out to be nothing and for this plotless novel to end there.

In order to achieve perfection a man would need a coldness that is alien to man, and then he would lack the human heart with which to love his own perfection.

We stand in awe of the great artists' desire for perfection. We love their attempt to achieve perfection, but we love it because it is only an attempt.

281 [1930?]

... and gazing down from these majestic dream-heights, here am I, an assistant bookkeeper in the city of Lisbon. Far from feeling crushed by this comparison, I feel liberated; indeed, the irony of it all is my life's blood. The very thing I ought to find humiliating has become my standard, which I proudly unfurl; and the mocking laughter with which I ought to greet my own thoughts is a bugle with which I welcome and create the aurora I have become.

The nocturnal glory of being great while being nothing! The

somber majesty of splendid anonymity. And suddenly, I experience the sublime joy of the monk in the wilderness, of the hermit in his cave, at one with the substance of Christ in the desert sands and caverns of the park's empty statuary ...

And seated at the desk of my absurdly ordinary room, I, a mere clerk, write words as if they were my soul's salvation, and adorn myself with the impossible sunset of tall, towering, distant pinnacles, with the priestly stole bestowed on me for pleasures received, with the renunciatory ring on my evangelical finger, the lone jewel of my endless self-disdain.

282 [1930?]

... the painful acuity of my sensations, even those that bring me joy; the joyful acuity of my sensations, even those that are sad.

I am writing late one Sunday morning, on a day full of soft light, on which above the rooftops of the interrupted city, the always astonishing blue of the sky clothes in oblivion the mysterious existence of the stars ...

It's Sunday inside me too ... My heart is also going to church, although quite where the church is it doesn't know, and it's wearing a little velvet suit, and, above a collar several sizes too big, its cheeks, flushed with the excitement of so many first impressions, positively beam, resolutely happy.

283 [1930?]

To subordinate oneself to nothing—be it another human being, someone we love, or an idea—to maintain that aloof independence that consists in not believing in the truth nor, were such a thing to exist, in the usefulness of knowing it: that, it seems to me, is the proper condition of the intellectual life of thinkers. To belong to something—that's banal. Creed, ideal, wife or profession: nothing but prison cells and shackles. To be is to be free. Even ambition is a burden if it is based only on futile pride and passion; we would not feel so proud of it if we realized that it is just the string we're tugged along by. No, no ties, even to ourselves! As free from ourselves as we are from others, contemplatives without ecstasy, thinkers without conclusions, the liberated slaves of God, we will live out the brief interlude that the absentmindedness of our executioners commutes into a temporary stay of execution. Tomorrow we face the guillotine or, if not tomorrow, then the day after. Let us spend this respite before the end walking in the sun, wilfully disregarding all aims and pursuits. The sun will burnish our smooth brows and the breeze bring coolness to he who abandons all hope.

I throw down my pen, and before I can pick it up again, it rolls back down the slope of the desk on which I write. All this came to me in a rush, and my happiness manifests itself in this gesture of an anger I do not feel.

284 [1930?]

Symphony of an unquiet night

Everything was sleeping as if the universe were simply a mistake, and the hesitant wind was a limp, unfurled flag on top of a nonexistent building. In the high, strong wind nothing at all was being ripped to shreds, while the window frames rattled the panes to make themselves heard inside. In the depths of everything, the soul was silently suffering, feeling sorry for God.

And suddenly, a new order of universal things imposed itself on the city; the wind whistled when the wind was silent, and there was a slumbering sense of great agitation up above. Then the night closed like a trapdoor, and the ensuing peace made me wish I had been sleeping.

285 [1930?]

A breath of music or of a dream, anything that might make me almost feel, anything that might make me stop thinking.

286 [1930?]

Give to each emotion a personality, to each state of mind a soul.

Around a bend in the road came a gaggle of girls. They were walking along singing, and the sound of their voices was a joyful one. I don't know who or what they were. I listened to them for a time from afar, without feeling anything in particular, then a kind of sadness for them settled in my heart.

For their future? For their innocent obliviousness? No, not directly for them, but perhaps, who knows, simply for myself.

The path leads to the mill, but effort leads nowhere.

It was late afternoon in the early autumn, when the sky has a kind of cold, dead warmth to it, and there are clouds that muffle the light in slow blankets.

The two things that Fate gave me: some accounts ledgers and the gift of dreaming.

287 [1930?]

He listened to me reading my poetry—and because I was distracted, I actually read rather well—and he said to me as simply as if he were stating a law of nature: "You know, if you were always like that, but with a different face, you would be a real charmer." It was the word "face" rather than what he had said that grabbed me by the collar of our native inability to know ourselves. I imagined the mirror in my room, reflecting my poor, unpoor beggar's face, and suddenly the mirror moved away, and the specter of Rua dos Douradores opened up before me like a nirvana for postmen.

The intensity of my sensations is almost like a disease that's quite separate from me. Someone else of whom I am the ailing part suffers from that disease, because I genuinely feel as though I were dependent on someone else's greater capacity to feel. I am merely a special tissue, or even a cell, responsible for a whole organism.

If I think, that is because I'm daydreaming; if I dream, that is because I'm awake. Everything in me gets tangled up, and has no way of knowing how to be.

288 [1930?]

I'm curious about everyone, greedy for everything, ravenous for ideas. It weighs on me like the loss of [...] the notion that not everything can be seen or read or thought ...

But I only see inattentively, read distractedly, and even think incoherently. In everything I am an intense, rather coarse dilettante.

My soul is too weak even to have the strength of its own enthusiasms. I am composed of the ruins of things unfinished, and the landscape that would define my being is one of resignations.

I daydream if I concentrate; everything in me is decorative and uncertain, like a great spectacle shrouded in dense mist.

This carnal tendency to convert all thought into expression or, rather, to think as an expression of all thought; to see all emotions in color and shape and even all negation in terms of rhythm [...]

I write with great intensity of feeling; I do not even know what I feel. I am half somnambulist and half nothing.

The woman I am when I actually know myself.

The opium of regal twilights and the marvel lying recumbent in the darkness, the hand that emerges from the rags.

Sometimes the concentrated flow of images and phrases filling my abstracted mind is so great, so fast, so abundant, that I rave and writhe and weep to have lost them—because I do lose them. Each one had its moment and cannot be recalled once that moment is gone. And just as a lover is left only with a nostalgia for a beloved face glimpsed, but never fixed, all that remains for me is the memory of my own being as if it were dead, of peering into the abyss of a fast-flowing past of images and ideas, dead figures swathed in the very mist they themselves are made of.

Fluid, absent, inessential, I lose myself as if I were drowning in nothing; I am entirely preterite, and that word, which speaks and then stops, says and is everything.

The rhythm of a word, the image it evokes, and its meaning as idea, necessarily combine into one word, but for me they combine separately. Just thinking of a word makes me understand the concept of the Trinity. I think the word "numberless" and I choose it as an example because it's abstract and mysterious. But if I hear it in my actual being, great waves roll in on a sound that does not stop in the endless sea; the skies glitter, not with stars, but with the music of all the waves glittering with sounds, and the idea of a fluid infinity opens up to me, like a flag unfurled, into the form of stars or the sounds of the sea, to an "I" that reflects all the stars.

If Dom Sebastião were to emerge now from the mist that would not contradict history.* All of history happens in the mist, and the great battles we are told about, the great ceremonies, all man's greatest achievements, are merely great spectacles shrouded in mist, cortèges glimpsed in the distance in the dim twilight.

The soul in me is expressive and material. I either stagnate in a state of social not-being, or I am awake, and if I am awake, I project myself into words as if they were my being's way of opening its eyes. If I think, thought rises up in my mind in the form of brief, rhythmic sentences, and I am never quite sure if I think before speaking those sentences or only once I have seen myself say them.

---

* Dom Sebastião (1554–1578) was King of Portugal from 1557–1578. He disappeared in the disastrous Battle of Alcácer Quibir, presumably killed in action. He was often referred to as O Desejado (*The Desired One*) by people believing that, were he to return, he would halt Portugal's perceived decline.

If I find myself dreaming, I immediately fill up with words. In me every emotion is an image, and every dream a painting set to music. What I write may be bad, but it is more me than what I think … Or so I sometimes believe …

All my life I have been narrating myself, and if I lean over to observe the very least of my tediums, it blossoms, by virtue of some magnetism of […], into flowers the colors of musical abysses.

289 [1930?]

When I consider the vast literary output—or if not vast then fairly extensive and complete—of many of the people I know or know of, I do feel a kind of envy, a scornful admiration, an incoherent blend of mixed emotions.

The ability to complete something, whether good or bad—and while it will never be entirely good, it will often not be entirely bad either—yes, the ability to complete something probably provokes more envy in me than anything else. It's like a child, as imperfect as all human beings are, but nevertheless our child.

My self-critical mind allows me to see only the defects and faults in my own work, and so I only have the courage to write snippets and snatches, brief notes on the theme of nonexistence, and yet even the little I write is imperfect. Best to produce either something complete, albeit bad, but which nonetheless exists, or else a complete absence of words, the blank silence of a soul that knows itself incapable of action.

290 [1930?]

I wonder if everything in life is not simply a degenerate form of something else, if our being is not simply an approximation—the eve or the outskirts of something …

Just as Christianity was merely a bastard form of a debased Neoplatonism—the Romanization of the Hellenic tradition via Judaism—so our timid, amorphous age is merely a multifaceted distortion of all the great philosophies, both convergent and contrary, out of whose failure emerged the accumulated negations by which we define ourselves.

We are living an entr'acte with orchestral accompaniment.

But what do I, living in this fourth-floor room, have to do with all those civilizations? It's all a dream to me, like the princesses of Babylon, and it's utterly futile to worry about humanity—a bibliomania of the illiterate, an archaeology of the present.

I will disappear into the mist, a foreigner to all things, a human island detached from the dream of the sea, a superfluous ship floating on the surface of everything.

291 [1930?]

I was only ever truly loved once. Everyone has always treated me kindly. Even the most casual acquaintance has found it difficult to be rude or brusque or even cool towards me. Sometimes with a little help from me, that kindness could—or at least might—have developed into love or affection. I've had neither the patience nor the concentration of mind to want to make that effort.

When I first noticed this in myself—so little do we know ourselves—I attributed it to some shyness of the soul. But then I realized that this wasn't the case; it was an emotional tedium, different from the tedium of life; an impatience with the idea of associating myself with one continuous feeling, especially if that meant steeling myself to make some sustained effort. Why bother? thought the unthinking part of me. I have enough subtlety, enough psychological sensitivity to know how, but the why has always escaped me. My weakness of will always began by being a weakness of the will even to have a will. The same happened with my emotions, my intelligence, my will itself, with everything in my life.

But on the one occasion that malicious fate caused me to believe I loved someone and to recognize that I really was loved in return, it left me at first as stunned and confused as if my number had come up on the lottery and I had won a huge amount of money in some inconvertible currency. Then, because I'm only human, I felt rather flattered. However, that most natural of emotions soon passed, to be overtaken by a feeling difficult to define but one in which tedium, humiliation and weariness predominated.

A feeling of tedium as if Fate had imposed on me a task to be carried out during some unfamiliar evening shift. As if a new duty—that of an awful reciprocity—were given to me, ironically, as a privilege over which I would have to toil, all the time thanking Fate for it. As if the flaccid monotony of life were not enough to bear without superimposing on it the obligatory monotony of a definite feeling.

And humiliation, yes, I felt humiliated. It took me a while to understand the justification for such an apparently unjustifiable feeling. The love of being loved no doubt surfaced in me. I probably felt flattered that someone had taken the time to consider my existence and conclude that it was that of a potentially lovable being. But apart from that brief moment of pride—and I'm still not entirely sure that astonishment did not outweigh pride—the feeling that welled up in me was one of humiliation. I felt as if I had been given a prize intended for someone else, a prize of great worth to the person who truly deserved it.

And, above all, I felt weary—the weariness that surpasses all tedium. Only then did I understand something that Chateaubriand wrote and which until then, because I lacked the necessary self-knowledge, had always puzzled me. Of his character René he says: *"on le fatiguait en l'aimant"* (people wearied him with their love) and I realized with a shock that this was exactly my experience, the truth of which I could not deny.

How wearisome it is to be loved, to be truly loved! How wearisome to be the object of someone else's bundle of emotions! To be changed from someone who wanted to be free, always free, into an errand boy with a responsibility to reciprocate those emotions, to have the decency not to run away, so that the other person won't think you are acting with princely disdain and rejecting the greatest gift the human soul can offer. How wearisome to let one's existence become something absolutely dependent on someone else's feelings; to have no option but to feel, to love a little too, whether or not it is reciprocated.

That episode passed me by just as it had come to me, in the shadows. Now not a trace of it remains either in my intelligence or in my emotions. It brought me no experience that I could not have deduced from the rules of human life, an instinctive knowledge of which I hold inside me simply by virtue of being human. It gave me neither pleasure that I could later remember with sadness, nor grief to be recalled with equal sadness. It feels like something I read somewhere, something that happened to someone else, in a novel of which I read only half, the other half being missing, not that I cared that it was missing, because what I had read up till then was enough and, although it made no sense, it was already clear that, however the plot turned out, the missing part would clarify nothing.

All that remains is a feeling of gratitude towards the person who loved me. But it's a stunned, abstract gratitude, more intellectual than emotional. I'm sorry that someone should have suffered because of me; I regret that, but nothing else.

It's unlikely that life will bring me another encounter with natural emotions. I almost wish it would just to see how I would feel the second time around, now that I have thoroughly analyzed that first experience. I might feel less; I might feel more. If Fate decrees it should happen, so be it. I feel curious about emotions. About facts, whatever they might be, I feel no curiosity whatsoever.

292 [1930?]

In the light morning mist of mid-spring the Baixa comes sluggishly awake, and even the sun seems to rise only slowly. A quiet joy fills the chilly air, and, in the gentle breath of a barely existent breeze, life shivers slightly in the cold that is already past, shivers at the memory of the cold rather than at the cold itself, shivers at the contrast with the coming summer rather than at the present weather.

Apart from cafés and dairies nothing is open yet, but the quietness is not the indolent quiet of Sunday mornings, it is simply quiet. The air has a blond edge to it and the blue sky reddens through the thinning mist. A few passersby signal the first hesitant stirrings of life in the streets and high up at a rare open window the occasional early-morning face appears. As the trams pass, they trace a yellow, numbered furrow through the air, and minute by minute the streets begin to people themselves once more.

I drift, without thoughts or emotions, attending only to my senses. I woke up early and came out to wander aimlessly through the streets. I observe them meditatively. I see them with my thoughts. And, absurdly, a light mist of emotion rises within me; the fog that is lifting from the outside world seems slowly to be seeping into me.

I realize with a jolt that I have been thinking about my life. I didn't know I had been, but it's true. I thought I was just seeing and listening, that in my idle wanderings I was nothing but a reflector of received images, a white screen onto which reality projected colors and light instead of shadows. But, though I was unaware of it, I was more than that. I was still my self-denying soul, and my own abstract observation of the street was in itself a denial.

As the mist lifts, the air covers itself in pale light in which the mist is somehow mingled. I notice suddenly that there is much more noise, that there are many more people about. The footsteps of this larger number of passersby seem less hurried. Making a reappearance on the street, in sharp contrast to the leisurely pace of everyone else, come the brisk steps of the women selling fish and the swaying stride of the bakers with their monstrous baskets. The diverse monotony of the sellers of other produce is broken only by what's in their baskets, varying more in color than in content. The milkmen rattle the miscellaneous metal cans of their meandering trade as if they were a bunch of absurd hollow keys. The policemen stand stolidly at the crossroads, civilization's uniformed denial of the imperceptibly rising day.

If only, I feel now, if only I could be someone able to see all this as if he had no relation with it other than that of seeing it, someone able to observe everything as if he were an adult traveler newly arrived today on the surface of life! If only one had not learned, from birth onwards, to give certain accepted meanings to everything, but instead was able to see the meaning inherent in each thing rather than that imposed on it from without. If only one could know the human reality of the woman selling fish and go beyond just labeling her a fishwife and the known fact that she exists and sells fish. If only one could see the policeman as God sees him. If only one could notice everything for the first time, not apocalyptically, as if they were revelations of the Mystery, but directly as the flowerings of Reality.

I hear the hour struck by some bell or clock tower—it must be eight o'clock though I don't count. The banal fact of the existence of time, the confines that social life imposes on continuous time—a frontier around the abstract, a limit on the unknown—brings me back to myself. I come to, look around at everything, which is full of life and ordinary humanity now, and I see that, apart from the patches of imperfect blue where it still lingers, the mist has cleared completely from the sky and seeped instead into my soul and into all things, into that part of them that touches my soul. I've lost the vision of what I saw. I'm blinded by sight. My feelings belong now to the banal realm of knowledge. This is no longer Reality: it is simply Life.

... Yes, Life to which I belong and which belongs to me; not Reality which belongs only to God or to itself and contains neither mystery nor truth and, given that it is real or pretends to be, exists somewhere in some fixed form, free from the need to be either transient or eternal, an absolute image, the ideal form of a soul made visible.

Slowly (though not as slowly as I imagine) I make my way back to my own door in order to go up to my room again. But I don't go in, I hesitate, then continue on. Praça da Figueira, replete with goods of various colors, fills with customers and peoples my horizon with vendors of all kinds. I advance slowly, a dead man, and my vision, no longer my own, is nothing now: it is merely that of a human animal who unwittingly inherited Greek culture, Roman order, Christian morality and all the other illusions that make up the civilization in which I live and feel.

What's become of the living?

293 [1930?]

I've come to the realization that I'm always thinking and listening to two things at the same time. I expect everyone does that a little. Some impressions are so vague that only when we remember them afterwards are we aware of them at all. I think these impressions form a part (the internal part perhaps) of this double attention we all pay to things. In my case the two realities I attend to have equal weight. In that lies my originality. In that, perhaps, lie both my tragedy and the comedy of my tragedy.

I write carefully, bent over the book in which I measure out in balance sheets the futile history of an obscure company and, at the same time and with equal attention, my thoughts follow the route of an imaginary ship through oriental landscapes that have never existed. The two things are equally clear, equally visible to me: the ruled page on which I meticulously write the lines of the epic commercial poem that is Vasques & Co. and the deck where, a little to one side of the lines made by the tarred spaces between the planks, I watch intently the rows of deckchairs and the stretched-out legs of people relaxing on the voyage.

The smoking room blocks my view, which is why I can see only legs.

I dip my pen in the inkwell and from the door of the smoking room—almost right next to the place where I feel I am standing—a stranger appears. He turns his back on me and goes over to join the others. He walks very slowly and his hips tell me very little. He's English. I begin another entry. What with all that looking, I've made a mistake. The Marques account should be debited not credited. (I can see him, fat and friendly and jokey, and in that moment, the ship disappears.)

(If l were knocked down by a child's bicycle, that bicycle would become part of my story.)

294 [1930?]

The carts go snoring down the street, the sound slow and distinct, in keeping, it seems, with my own somnolent state. It's lunchtime, but I've stayed behind in the office. The day is warm and slightly overcast. For some reason—possibly due to that somnolent state—the noises from the street reflect the kind of day it is.

295 [1930?]

Sometimes I think I will never leave Rua dos Douradores. Once written down, that seems to me like eternity.

Not pleasure, not glory, not power: just freedom, only freedom.

To move from the phantasms of faith to the specters of reason is merely a matter of changing cells. Art, while it frees us from the abstract idols of earlier times, also frees us from generous ideas and social concerns, which are also idols.

To find one's personality by losing it—faith itself subscribes to that sense of destiny.

296 [1930?]

Literature, which is art married to thought and the immaculate realization of reality, seems to me the goal towards which all human effort should be directed, as long as that effort is truly human and not just a vestige of the animal in us. I believe that to say a thing is to preserve its virtue and remove any fear it might arouse. Fields are greener when described than when they are merely their own green selves. If one could describe flowers in words that define them in the air of the imagination, they would have colors that would outlast anything mere cellular life could manage.

To move is to live, to express oneself is to endure. There is nothing real in life that isn't more real for being beautifully described. Small-minded critics often point out that such and such a poem, for all its generous rhythms, is saying nothing more profound than: it's a nice day. But it's not easy to say it's a nice day, and the nice day itself passes. Our duty, then, is to preserve that nice day in endless, flowering memory and garland with new flowers and new stars the fields and skies of the empty, transient external world.

Everything depends on what we are and, in the diversity of time, how those who come after us perceive the world will depend on how intensely we have imagined it, that is, on how intensely we, fantasy and flesh made one, have truly been the world. I do not believe that history, and its great faded panorama, is any more than a constant flow of interpretations, a confused consensus of absent-minded witnesses. We are all novelists and we narrate what we see, because, like everything else, seeing is a complex matter.

At this moment, I have so many fundamental thoughts, so many truly metaphysical things to say, that I feel suddenly tired and decide not to write any more, not to think any more, but to let the fever of saying lull me to sleep whilst, with closed eyes, I gently stroke, as I would a cat, all the things I might have said.

297 [1930?]

During one of those periods of sleepless somnolence in which we entertain ourselves intelligently enough without recourse to our intelligence, I reread some of the pages which, when put together, will make up my book of random impressions. And there rises from them, like a familiar smell, an arid sense of monotony. I feel that in describing all my different moods, I always use the same words; I feel that I am more like myself than I would care to think; that, when the final accounts are drawn up, I have tasted neither the joy of winning nor the excitement of losing. I am my own absence of balance, of an involuntary equilibrium that torments and weakens me.

Everything I wrote is so gray. It's as if my life, even my mental life, were a day of slow rain in which everything is eventlessness and shadow, empty privilege and forgotten reason. I mourn in torn silks. I don't recognize myself in this light and this tedium.

My humble attempt simply to say who I am, to set down, like a feeling machine, the tiniest details of my sharp, subjective life, all this emptied out of me like an overturned bucket and soaked the earth just like water. I painted myself in false colors and ended up with an attic room for an empire. Today, rereading with a different soul what I wrote on these distant pages, my heart, out of which I spun the great events of my lived prose, seems to me like a pump in some provincial garden, installed by instinct and set going by duty. I was shipwrecked beneath a stormless sky in a sea shallow enough to stand up in.

In this confused series of intervals between things that don't even exist, I ask what remains of my consciousness: what possible use was it to me to fill so many pages with words I believed to be mine, with emotions I felt to have been thought by me, with the flags and banners of armies that are, after all, just scraps of paper that the beggar's daughter sticks with her spit to the eaves?

I address what remains of me and ask what is the point of these useless pages, destined for the rubbish heap and for ruin, lost even before they come into being among the torn pages of Fate.

I ask and I continue. I write down the question, I wrap it up in new sentences, unravel it to form new emotions. And tomorrow I will return to my foolish book to coldly set down further thoughts on my lack of conviction.

Let them continue, just as they are. When the last domino is played and the game is won or lost, all the pieces are turned over and the game ends in darkness.

298

Day by day, in my deep but ignoble soul, I record the impressions that form the external substance of my consciousness of myself. I put them into errant words that desert me as soon as they're written and wander off independently down hills and across lawns of images, along avenues lined with conceits and lanes of confusions. This is of no use to me, for nothing is of any use. But it calms me to write, the way an invalid may breathe more easily even though his sickness has not passed.

Some people when they're distracted scribble lines and absurd names on the dog-eared blotter on their desk. These pages are the doodles of my intellectual unconsciousness of myself. I set them down in a torpor of feeling, like a cat in the sun, and reread them at times with a dull, belated pang, as if remembering something I had always previously forgotten.

Writing is like paying myself a formal visit. I have special rooms, recalled in the interstices of the imagination by someone else, where I enjoy myself analyzing what I do not feel and peer at myself as at a painting hung in the shadows.

I lost my ancient castle even before I was born. The tapestries of my ancestral palace were all sold before I even came into being. My mansion, built before I lived, has now crumbled into ruins and, only at certain times, when the moon rises in me over the reeds, do I feel the chill of nostalgia emanating from that site where the toothless remains of the walls stand silhouetted black against the sky whose dark blue gradually pales into milky yellow.

I divide myself up, sphinxlike. And the forgotten skein of my soul falls from the lap of the queen I lack, like a scene taken from her futile tapestry. It rolls beneath the inlaid chest and something of myself follows it, as if that something were my eyes, until the skein is lost amongst a general horror of tombs and endings.

299

Every stirring in our sensibility, however pleasurable, is merely the interruption of another state, quite what I don't know, but it constitutes the inner life of that same sensibility. It is not the major anxieties that distract us from ourselves, but the minor annoyances that can trouble the peace of mind to which we all unwittingly aspire.

We live almost entirely outside ourselves, and life itself is a perpetual dispersion. However, we are nonetheless drawn back to ourselves as if to a center around which we orbit, like the planets, tracing absurd, distant ellipses.

300 [1930?]

I am, I suppose, what people would call a decadent, someone whose spirit is externally defined by the sad glimmerings of a kind of bogus eccentricity that gives unexpected expression to an adroit but anxious soul. That, at least, is how I feel about myself, and I find myself absurd. And that is why, in imitation of some hypothetical classicism, I seek out an expressive mathematics with which to describe the decorative sensations of my counterfeit soul. When writing down my thoughts, there is always a point where I lose track of the focus of my attention—whether it's the disparate sensations I'm trying to describe as if they were unfamiliar tapestries or the words in which, as I try to describe my own description, I become entangled, lose my way and see other things. Other ideas and images and words come into my mind—all equally lucid and diffuse—and I am both saying what I feel and what I imagine I'm feeling, and I cannot distinguish what my soul is telling me from those images discarded by my soul and which somehow spring up from the ground, nor if the sound of some barbarous word or the rhythm of some interpolated phrase is merely a distraction from my already rather hazy subject matter or from some already abandoned sensation, thus absolving me from thinking and saying, as if these were long voyages intended to distract. And all of this, which, were I to repeat it, should fill me with a sense of futility, failure and suffering, instead gives me wings of gold. Whenever I speak of images, possibly even to condemn their overuse, other images are instantly born inside me; whenever I stand up to myself and repudiate what I do not feel, I am already feeling those feelings, and my own repudiation becomes another richly embroidered feeling; whenever, having lost all faith in my efforts, I want simply to let my mind roam free, a placid, unassuming turn of phrase, a sober, spatial adjective, like a bright shaft of sunlight, suddenly reveals to me the drowsily written page before me, and the letters traced by my pen have become an absurd map of magical signs. Then I put myself and my pen down, and I lean back and draw about me the cape of incoherence, distant, intermediate and passive, like a shipwreck victim drowning within sight of the marvelous islands set in the same golden-purple seas of which I really did once dream in some now distant bed.

301   [1930?]

There is an erudition of knowledge, which is what we usually mean by "erudition," and there is an erudition of understanding, which is what we call "culture." But there is also an erudition of sensibility.

This has nothing to do with one's experience of life. Like history, experience of life teaches us nothing. True experience consists in reducing one's contact with reality while at the same time intensifying one's analysis of that contact. In that way one's sensibility can widen and deepen since everything lies within us anyway; it is enough that we seek it out and know how to do so.

What is travel and what use is it? One sunset is much like another; you don't have to go to Constantinople in order to see one. And what of the sense of freedom that travel brings? I can enjoy that just going from Lisbon to Benfica and I can feel it more intensely than someone journeying from Lisbon to China because, in my opinion, if that sense of freedom is not in me, then it's nowhere. "Any road," said Carlyle, "this simple road to Entepfuhl, will lead you to the end of the world." But the road to Entepfuhl, if followed right to the end, would lead straight back to Entepfuhl, which means that Entepfuhl, where we started, is that "end of the world" we set out to find in the beginning.

Condillac begins his famous book with the words: "However high we climb and however low we fall we never escape our own feelings." We can never disembark from ourselves. We can never become another person, except by making ourselves other through the sensitive application of our imaginations to our selves. The true landscapes are those that we ourselves create, because, since we are their gods, we see them as they really are, that is, exactly as they were created. I'm not interested in nor can I truly see any of the seven zones of the world; I travel the eighth zone, which is my own.

Someone who has sailed every sea has merely sailed through the monotony of himself. I have sailed more seas than anyone. I have seen more mountains than exist on earth. I have passed through more cities than were ever built, and the great rivers of impossible worlds have flowed, absolute, beneath my contemplative gaze. If I were to travel, I would find only a feeble copy of what I have already seen without traveling.

When other travelers visit countries, they do so as anonymous pilgrims. In the countries I have visited I have been not only the secret pleasure felt by the unknown traveler but the majesty of the king who rules there, I have been the people who live there and their customs, and the whole history of that and other nations. I saw those landscapes and those houses because I was them, created in God from the substance of my imagination.

Renunciation is freedom. Not wanting is power.

What can China give me that my soul has not already given me? And if my soul cannot give me that, how can China, since it is with my soul that I would see China, were I ever to see it? I can go in search of riches in the Orient, but not the riches of the soul, because I am the riches of my soul, and I am where I am, with or without the Orient.

I can understand why people incapable of feeling like to travel. That's why travel books are always so lacking as books of experience, because they are only as good as the imagination of the person writing them. And if the writer has imagination, he can delight us as much with a detailed, photographic description of flags and landscapes as with the inevitably less detailed description of landscapes he only imagined he saw. We are all myopic, except when we look inside ourselves. Only in dreams do we truly see.

Basically, there are only two things that our experience of the world can give us—the universal and the particular. To describe the universal is to describe what is common to every human soul and to all human experience—the vast sky and the days and nights that emerge from it and exist within it; the flowing rivers—all with the same cool, nunlike water; the seas and the great undulating mountains, which keep the majesty of their great height in the secret of their depths; the fields, the seasons, houses, faces, gestures; clothes and smiles; love and war; the gods, finite and infinite; the formless Night, mother of the origin of the world; Fate, the intellectual monster that is everything ... Describing this, or any other universal thing, my soul is speaking a primitive, divine language, the Adamic language everyone understands. But what fragmented, Babelic language would I be speaking when describing the Elevador de Santa Justa, Reims Cathedral, Zouave trousers, the way Portuguese people pronounce Tras-os-Montes? These things are superficial accidents; they can be experienced by walking, but not by feeling. What is universal about the Elevador de Santa Justa is the helpful mechanical knowledge it brings to the world. What is true about Reims Cathedral is neither the Cathedral nor Reims, but the sacred majesty of buildings devoted to the knowledge of the depths of the human soul. What is eternal in those Zouave trousers is the colorful fiction of clothes, a human language that gives voice to a social simplicity which is, in its own way, a new nakedness. What is universal about local pronunciations is the homely timbre of the voices of people who live spontaneously, the diversity within groups of individuals, the multicolored panoply of customs, the differences between peoples, and the vast variety of nations.

We are eternal travelers of ourselves, and the only landscape that exists is what we are. We possess nothing, because we do not even possess ourselves. We have nothing because we are nothing. What hands will I reach out to what universe? The universe is not mine: it is me.

302   [1930?]

Outside, slowly in the moonlight of the slow night, the wind is shaking things that make shadows as they move. It may be nothing but the clothes hung out to dry on the floor above, but the shadow itself knows nothing of shirts and floats, impalpable, in mute accord with everything around it.

I left the shutters open so that I would wake early, but until now (and it is now so late that not a sound can be heard), I have managed neither to go to sleep nor to remain properly awake. Beyond the shadows in my room lies the moonlight but it does not enter my window. It is just there, like a day of hollow silver, and the roofs of the building opposite, which I can see from my bed, are liquid with inky whiteness. The hard light of the moon contains a sad peace, something resembling words of congratulation spoken from on high to someone unable to hear them.

And without looking, without thinking, my eyes closed now to absent sleep, I consider which words would best describe moonlight. The ancients would say that the moon is white or silver. But the false whiteness of the moon is of many colors. If I were to get up out of bed and look through the cold windowpanes I know that, high up in the lonely air, the moonlight would be grayish-white with a bluish tinge of faded yellow; that on the various rooftops, in diverse degrees of blackness, it now gilds the submissive buildings with dark white and now floods with colorless color the chestnut red of the roof tiles. Down below in the quiet chasm of the street, on the irregular roundnesses of the bare cobblestones, its only color is a blue that emanates perhaps from the gray of the stones themselves. It will be almost dark blue on the distant horizon, but quite different from the blue-black depths of the sky, and dark yellow where it touches the glass of windowpanes.

From here, from my bed, if I open my eyes filled with a sleep I do not as yet enjoy, the air is like snow made color in which float filaments of warm mother-of-pearl. And if I think the moonlight with my feelings, it is a tedium made white shadow that grows gradually darker as if my eyes were slowly closing on its vague whiteness.

303 [8 Jan 1931]

I haven't written anything for ages. Whole months have passed during which I haven't lived, but have merely endured, caught between the office and physiology, marooned in an inner stagnation of thinking and feeling. Alas, this is not a restful state to be in, for putrefaction inevitably involves fermentation.

Not only have I not written anything for ages, I haven't even existed. I'm not even sure I dream. The streets are just streets to me. I do my work in the office, my mind entirely on that, although I do occasionally become distracted, not meditating, but sleeping, and yet, behind my work, I am still someone else.

I haven't existed for ages. I feel utterly at peace. No one else can tell the difference between the two "I"s. I felt myself breathe just now as if I were belatedly practicing some new skill. I am beginning to be conscious of being conscious. Perhaps tomorrow I will wake up to myself and resume the course of my own existence. If I do, I don't know if I will be more or less happy. I don't know anything. I raise my pedestrian head and see that, over near the castle, dozens of windows are aflame with the reflected sunset, like a lofty echo of cold fire. Apart from those few hard, fiery eyes, the rest of the hill is bathed in the gentle evening light. I can at least feel sad and am aware that cutting across my sadness—noises seen with my ears—is the sudden clatter of a tram passing, the casual voices of young people chatting, the forgotten whisper of the living city.

I haven't been myself for ages.

304 [1 Feb 1931]

After endless rainy days the sky restores the blue, hidden until now, to the great spaces up above. There's a contrast between the streets, where puddles doze like country pools, and the bright, cold joy above them, which makes the dirty streets seem pleasant and the dull winter sky springlike. It's Sunday and I have nothing to do. It's such a lovely day, I don't even feel like dreaming. I enjoy it with a sincerity of feeling to which my intelligence abandons itself. I walk around like a traveling salesman with no wife to go home to. I feel old merely in order to have the pleasure of feeling myself grow young again.

Another type of day stirs solemnly in the great Sunday square. At the church of São Domingos people are coming out from one mass and another is about to begin. I watch those who are leaving and those who have not yet gone in and who, waiting for others to arrive, don't even notice the other people coming out.

None of these things is of any importance. Like all ordinary things in life, they are a dream of mysteries and castle battlements from which I look out upon the plain of my meditations like a herald who has delivered his message.

Years ago, when I was a child, I used to go to mass here (at least I think it was here, though it may have been somewhere else). Conscious of the importance of the occasion, I would put on my best suit and simply enjoy it all, even those things there was no reason to enjoy. I lived outwardly then and the suit I had on was brand new and spotless. What more could be wished for by someone who one day must die but who, holding tight to his mother's hand, as yet knows nothing of death?

Years ago I used to enjoy all this, perhaps that's why only now do I realize how much I did enjoy it. For me going to mass was like penetrating a great mystery and leaving it was like stepping out into a clearing in the woods. And that is how it really was, and how it still is. Only the unbelieving adult, whose soul still remembers and weeps, only he is but fiction and turmoil, confusion and the cold grave.

Yes, what I am would be unbearable if I could not remember the person I was. And this crowd of strangers still filing out of mass and the people gathering for the next mass, they are like ships that pass me by, a slow river flowing beneath the open windows of my home built on its banks.

Memories, Sundays, mass, the pleasure of having been, the miracle of time still present because it is past and which, because it was mine, never forgets ... By some maternal paradox of time, somehow surviving into the present along the absurd diagonal of possible sensations, beyond the noisy silences of the cars, the sound of cab wheels rattles into this precise moment, between what I am and what I lost, in the interval of the me that I call I ...

305   [2 Feb 1931]
The higher a man rises up the scale, the more things he must relinquish. On the mountain peak there is only room for that man alone. The more perfect, the more complete; the more complete, the less other he is.

These thoughts came to me after reading an article in a newspaper about the long, multifaceted life of a famous man. He was an American millionaire and had been everything. He had everything he could have wanted—money, love affairs, affection, devotion, travel, private art collections. Not that money can buy everything, but the magnetism that comes with great wealth can achieve almost anything.

When I put the newspaper down on the table in the café, I was already thinking that the same could be said, in his own sphere, of the traveling salesman, an acquaintance of mine, who has lunch every day, as he is today, at the table in the corner at the back. Everything that millionaire had, he has too; to a lesser degree, of course, but far more than befits his status. The two men have achieved exactly the same thing, there isn't even any difference in the degree of fame, because everything depends on context. Everyone in the world knows the name of the American millionaire, but everyone in this part of Lisbon knows the name of the man currently eating his lunch over there.

These two men have snapped up everything that lay within

their grasp. The length of their arms might be different, but otherwise they are the same. I've never been able to feel envious of such people. I always felt that virtue lay in getting what lay beyond one's reach, in living where you were not, in being more alive when dead than when alive, in achieving, in short, something difficult, something absurd, in overleaping—like an obstacle—the obstinate reality of the world.

If I were told that there is no pleasure to be had in enduring after you have ceased to exist, I would answer, firstly, that I don't know if that's true or not, because I don't know what happens after death; I would then say that the pleasure of future fame is a present pleasure—it's the fame that is future. And it is a pride as pleasurable as any material gains one might make. It might well be illusory, but even if it is, it lasts longer than the pleasure of enjoying only what is here. The American millionaire cannot expect posterity to appreciate his poems, because he hasn't written any; the traveling salesman cannot expect the future to take delight in his paintings, because he didn't paint any.

On the other hand, I, who am nothing in this transitory life, can savor the vision of the future reading this page, because I am actually writing it; I can pride myself, as if it were a child, on the fame I will enjoy, because I do at least have the means to achieve that fame. And when I think this, I rise from my table and, with an inner, invisible majesty, I also rise up above Detroit and Michigan and the whole commercial district of Lisbon.

I notice, however, that these were not the thoughts I began with. What I thought was how little we have to be in the world in order to survive. One thought is as good as another, though, because they come down to the same thing. Glory is not a medal, but a coin: on one side there's the head, and on the other the value of the coin. For larger values, there are no coins, only paper, and paper is never worth very much.

It is with such metaphysical psychologies that humble people like me console ourselves.

Just as some people work because they're bored, I sometimes write because I have nothing to say. My writing is just like the reverie in which someone avoiding thought would naturally immerse himself, with the difference that I am able to dream in prose. And I extract a great deal of sincere feeling and much legitimate emotion out of not feeling.

There are moments when the vacuity that comes with one's sense of being alive takes on the density of something concrete. Among the saints, who are the truly great men of action, for they act with all their emotions, not just some of them, this sense of the nothingness of life leads to the infinite. They garland themselves in night and stars, anoint themselves with silence and solitude. Among the great men of inaction, to whose ranks I humbly belong, the same feeling leads to the infinitesimal; feelings are pulled taut, like elastic bands, the better to observe the pores of their false, flabby continuity.

At such moments, both types of men long for sleep, just like the most ordinary of men, that mere reflection of the generic existence of the human species, who neither acts nor doesn't act. Sleep is fusion with God, Nirvana, or however you choose to define it; sleep is the slow analysis of sensations, whether applied like an atomic science of the soul or experienced through sleep like a music of the will, a slow anagram of monotony.

I write and linger over the words as if over window displays I can't quite see, and all that remains to me are half-meanings, quasi-expressions like the colors of fabrics I couldn't identify, a harmonious display composed of unknown objects. I rock myself as I write, like the crazed mother of a dead child.

I found myself in this world one day, I don't know when, and until then, from birth I presume, I had lived without feeling. If I asked where I was, everyone deceived me, everyone contradicted everyone else. If I asked them to tell me what to do, everyone lied and told me something different. If I became lost and stopped along the road, everyone was shocked that I did not just continue on to wherever the road led (though no one knew where that was), or did not simply retrace my steps—I, who did not even know whence I came, having only woken up at the crossroads. I realized that I was on a stage and did not know the words that everyone else picked up instantly even though they did not know them either. I saw that though I was dressed as a pageboy they had given me no queen to wait on and blamed me for that. I saw that I had in my hands a message to deliver and when I told them the paper was blank, they laughed at me. I still don't know if they laughed because all such pieces of paper are blank or because all messages are only hypothetical.

At last, as if before the hearth I did not have, I sat down on the milestone at the crossroads and, all by myself, began to make paper boats out of the lie they had given me. No one took me seriously, not even as a liar, and I had no lake on which to test my truth.

Lost, lazy words, random metaphors, chained to the shadows by a vague anxiety ... Traces of happier times, lived out in some avenue somewhere ... An extinguished lamp whose gold shines in the dark, a memory of the lost light ... Words scattered not to the winds but on the ground, dropped from fingers that can no longer grip, like dry leaves fallen from a tree invisibly infinite ... A nostalgic longing for the fountains that play in other people's gardens ... A feeling of tenderness for what never happened ...

To live! To live! With just the suspicion that perhaps only in Proserpina's garden would I sleep well.

307 [8 Apr 1931]

The whole desolate day, filled with light, warm clouds, was taken up with the news that there had been a revolution. Whether true or false, such news always fills me with a peculiar unease, a mixture of scorn and physical nausea. It pains my intelligence that someone should think they can alter anything through political agitation. I've always considered violence, of any type, a particularly cock-eyed example of human stupidity. All revolutionaries are stupid as are all reformers, albeit to a lesser degree, because less discomfiting.

Revolutionaries and reformers all make the same mistake. Lacking the power to master and reform their own attitude towards life, which is everything, or their own being, which is almost everything, they escape into wanting to change others and the external world. Every revolutionary, every reformer, is an escapee. To fight is proof of one's inability to do battle with oneself. To reform is proof that one is oneself beyond all help.

If a man of real sensitivity and correct reasoning feels concerned about the evil and injustice of the world, he naturally seeks to correct it first where it manifests itself closest to home, and that, he will find, is in his own being. The task will take him his whole lifetime.

For us everything lies in our concept of the world; changing our concept of the world means changing our world, that is, the world itself, since it will never be anything other than how we perceive it. The inner sense of justice that allows us to write one beautifully fluent page, the true reformation by which we bring to life our dead sensibilities—these are the truth, our truth, the only truth. All the rest is landscape, picture frames for our feelings, bindings for our thoughts. And that is the case whether the landscape is full of colorful things and people—fields, houses, posters and clothes—or a colorless landscape of monotonous souls rising to the surface for a moment to utter clichéd phrases or sketch tired gestures, only to sink back again to the bottom of the fundamental stupidity of all human expression.

Revolution? Change? What I most want, with every particle of my soul, is for the sluggish clouds that fill the sky with grubby lather to be gone; I want to see the blue beginning to show between them, a bright, clear truth, because it is nothing and wants nothing.

308   [c. 27 May 1931]
The only traveler with real soul I've ever met was an office boy who worked in a company where I was at one time employed. This

young lad collected brochures on different cities, countries and travel companies; he had maps, some torn out of newspapers, others begged from one place or another; he cut out pictures of landscapes, engravings of exotic costumes, paintings of boats and ships from various journals and magazines. He would visit travel agencies on behalf of some real or hypothetical company, possibly the actual one in which he worked, and ask for brochures on Italy or India, brochures giving details of sailings between Portugal and Australia.

He was not only the greatest traveler I've ever known (because he was the truest), he was also one of the happiest people I have had the good fortune to meet. I'm sorry not to know what has become of him, though, to be honest, I'm not really sorry, I only feel that I should be. I'm not really sorry because today, ten or more years on from that brief period in which I knew him, he must be a grown man, stolidly, reliably fulfillling his duties, married perhaps, some-one's breadwinner—in other words, one of the living dead. By now he may even have traveled in his body, he who knew so well how to travel in his soul.

A sudden memory assails me: he knew exactly which trains one had to catch to go from Paris to Bucharest; which trains one took to cross England; and in his garbled pronunciation of the strange names hung the bright certainty of the greatness of his soul. Now he probably lives like a dead man, but perhaps one day, when he's old, he'll remember that to dream of Bordeaux is not only better, but truer, than actually to arrive in Bordeaux.

And then again perhaps all this has some other explanation, perhaps he was just imitating someone else. Or perhaps ... Yes, sometimes, when I consider the huge gulf that exists between the intelligence of children and the stupidity of adults, I think that as children we must have a guardian angel who lends us his own astral intelligence and then, perhaps with sadness, but in accordance with a higher law, abandons us, the way female animals abandon their grown-up offspring, to become the fattened pigs it's our destiny to be.

309 [c. 27 May 1931]

I daydream the journey between Cascais and Lisbon. I went to Cascais in order to pay the tax on a house my boss Vasques owns in Estoril. I looked forward eagerly to the trip, an hour there and an hour back, a chance to watch the ever-changing face of the great river and its Atlantic estuary. On the way there, I lost myself in abstract thoughts, watching, without actually seeing, the waterscapes I was so looking forward to, and on the way back I lost myself in the analysis of those feelings. I would be unable to describe the smallest detail of the trip, the least fragment of what I saw. I've wrested these pages from oblivion and contradiction. I don't know if that's better or worse than whatever its contrary might be.

The train slows, we're at Cais do Sodré. I've arrived in Lisbon but not at any conclusion.

310 [18 June 1931]

If I look closely at the lives men lead I can find nothing that differentiates them from the lives of animals. Both men and animals are launched unconsciously into the midst of objects and into the world; both intermittently enjoy themselves; they daily follow the same physical path; neither group ever thinks beyond the thoughts that naturally occur to them nor experiences anything beyond what their lives happen to offer them. A cat lolls about in the sun and goes to sleep. Likewise a man lolls about in life with all its complexities and goes to sleep. Neither of them can free himself from the fate of being exactly what he is. Neither of them tries to escape from beneath the weight of being. The greatest among men love glory but they love it, not as if it meant immortality for themselves, but as an abstract immortality in which they may not even participate.

These thoughts, which I often have, arouse in me a sudden admiration for the kind of individual I instinctively reject. I mean the mystics and ascetics, all those solitary men living in Tibets all over the world, all those Simon Stylites standing on pillars. These men, though admittedly in the most absurd ways, do at least try to free themselves from the law of animals. In fact, however mad their methods, they do go against the law of life that tells them to loll around in the sun and wait unthinkingly for death. Even when they're stuck on top of a pillar, they are seeking something; even when they're locked in a windowless cell, they long for something; even if it means martyrdom and pain, they want what they do not know.

The rest of us, who live animal lives of greater or lesser complexity, cross the stage like extras with no lines to speak, content with the vain solemnity of the journey. Dogs and men, cats and heroes, fleas and geniuses, we all play at existence without even thinking about it (the best of us think only about thinking) beneath the great comforting quiet of the stars. The others—the mystics with all their suffering and sacrifice—at least feel the magical presence of the mystery in their own body and in their daily lives. They are free because they deny the visible sun; they are made full because they have emptied themselves of the vacuousness of the world.

Even I feel almost mystical when I speak of them but I would be incapable of being more than these words written under the influence of a chance mood. Like all of humanity, I will always belong to a Rua dos Douradores. In verse or prose, I will always be just another employee at his desk. With or without mysticism, I will always be parochial and submissive, the slave of my feelings and of the moment in which I feel them. Beneath the great blue canopy of the silent sky, I will always be a pageboy caught up in some incomprehensible ritual, clothed in life in order to take part in it, and blindly going through the different gestures and steps, poses and mannerisms, until the party or my role in it ends and I can go and eat the fancy food from the great stalls they tell me are set out at the bottom of the garden.

311 [20 June 1931]

After the last rains had passed over and gone south and only the wind that swept them away remained, the joy of the certain sun returned to the city's disorderly piles of houses, and white sheets suddenly appeared, hanging and dancing on the lines stretched between poles fixed outside the high windows.

I felt happy too, simply to exist. I left home with a great aim, namely to get to the office on time. But that day, my own vital impulse joined forces with that other worthy impulse by virtue of which the sun rises at the time ordained by one's latitude or longitude on the earth's surface. I felt happy not to be able to feel unhappy. I strolled down the street, feeling full of certainty, because the familiar office and the familiar people in it were themselves certainties. It's hardly surprising, then, that I felt free, though without knowing from what. Beneath the sun, in the baskets placed by the side of the pavement in Rua da Prata, the bananas on sale were a magnificent yellow.

I really need very little to feel content: the rain having stopped, the good sun of the happy South, some yellow bananas, all the yellower for having black spots, the people who chatter as they sell them, the pavements of Rua da Prata, the blue touched with green and gold of the Tejo beyond this domestic corner of the Universe.

A day will come when I'll no longer see this, when the bananas by the side of the pavement will continue to exist without me, as will the voices of their canny sellers and the daily newspapers that the young lad has laid out side by side on the corner of the pavement opposite. I know they will not be the same bananas, nor the same sellers; and, for the person bending to look at them, the newspapers will bear a different date from today's, but because they are inanimate, they will remain the same, even though their form may change; on the other hand, because I live, I will pass on yet remain the same.

I could easily consecrate this moment by buying some bananas, for it seems to me that the natural floodlight of the day's sun has poured all of itself into them. But I feel ashamed of rituals and symbols, of buying things in the street. They might not wrap the bananas properly, they might not sell them to me as they should be sold because I don't know how to buy them as they should be bought. My voice might sound odd when I ask the price. Far better to write than dare to live, even if living means no more than buying bananas in the sunshine, as long as the sun lasts and there are bananas to sell.

Later, perhaps ... Yes, later ... Another, perhaps ... Maybe ...

312 [10 June 1931]

Today is one of those days when the monotony of everything closes about me like a prison. The monotony, though, is just the monotony of being me. Each face, even if it belongs to someone we saw only yesterday, is different today simply because today is not yesterday. Each day is the day it is, and there will never be another like it in the world. Only in the soul is there the absolute identity (albeit a false identity) in which everything resembles everything else and everything is simplified. The world is made up of promontories and peaks, but all our myopic vision allows us to see is a thin all-pervading mist.

I'd like to run away, to flee from what I know, from what is mine, from what I love. I want to set off, not for some impossible Indies or for the great islands that lie far to the south of all other lands, but for anywhere, be it village or desert, that has the virtue of not being here. What I want is not to see these faces, this daily round of days. I want a rest from, to be other than, my habitual pretending. I want to feel the approach of sleep as if it were a promise of life, not rest. A hut by the sea, even a cave on a rugged mountain ledge, would be enough. Unfortunately, my will alone cannot give me that.

Slavery is the only law of life, there is no other, because this law must be obeyed; there is no possible rebellion against it or refuge from it. Some are born slaves, some become slaves, some have slavery thrust upon them. The cowardly love we all have of freedom— which if it were given to us we would all repudiate as being too new and strange—is the irrefutable proof of how our slavery weighs upon us. Even I, who have just expressed my desire to have a hut or a cave where I could be free from the monotony of everything, that is to say from the monotony of being myself, would I really dare to go off to this hut or cave, knowing and understanding that, since the monotony exists in me alone, I would never be free of it? Suffocating where I am and because I am where I am, would I breathe any better there when it is my lungs that are diseased and not the air about me? Who is to say that I, longing out loud for the pure sun and the open fields, for the bright sea and the wide horizon, would not miss my bed, or my meals, or having to go down eight flights of stairs to the street, or dropping in at the tobacconist's on the corner, or saying good morning to the barber standing idly by?

Everything that surrounds us becomes part of us, it seeps into us with every experience of the flesh and of life and, like the web of the great Spider, binds us subtly to what is near, ensnares us in a fragile cradle of slow death, where we lie rocking in the wind. Everything is us and we are everything, but what is the point if everything is nothing? A ray of sun, a cloud whose own sudden shadow warns of its coming, a breeze getting up, the silence that follows when it drops, certain faces, some voices, the easy smiles as they talk, and then the night into which emerge, meaningless, the broken hieroglyphs of the stars.

313   [1 July 1931]

No one likes us when we've slept badly. The sleep we missed carried off with it whatever it was that made us human. There is, it seems, a latent irritation in us, in the empty air that surrounds us. Ultimately, it is we who are in dispute with ourselves, it is within ourselves that diplomacy in the secret war breaks down.

All day I've dragged my feet and this great weariness around the streets. My soul has shrunk to the size of a tangled ball of wool and what I am and was, what is me, has forgotten its name. Will there be a tomorrow? I don't know. I only know that I didn't sleep, and the jumble of half-slept interludes fills with long silences the conversation I hold with myself.

Ah, the great parks enjoyed by others, the gardens taken for granted by so many, the marvelous avenues belonging to people who will never know me! Between sleepless nights I stagnate like someone who never dared to be superfluous and what I meditate upon wakes up, startled, with one closing dream.

I am a widowed house, cloistered in upon itself, darkened by timid, furtive specters. I am always in the room next door, or they are, and all around me great trees rustle. I wander around and I find things and I find things because I wander. My childhood days stand before me dressed in a pinafore!

And in the midst of all this, made drowsy by my wanderings, I drift out into the street, like a leaf. The gentlest of winds has swept me up from the ground and I wander, like the very close of twilight, through whatever the landscape presents to me. My eyelids grow heavy, my feet drag. Because I'm walking I would like to sleep. I keep my mouth pressed tight shut as if to seal my lips. I am the shipwreck of my own wanderings.

No, I didn't sleep, but I'm better when I haven't slept and can't sleep. I am more truly myself in this random eternity, symbolic of the half-souled state in which I live deluding myself. Someone looks at me as if they knew me or thought they knew me. With painful eyes beneath sore eyelids I feel myself look back at them; I don't want to know about the world out there.

I'm just sleepy, so so sleepy!

314 [13 July 1931]

In the vague shadows cast by the dying light before the evening turns to early darkness, I enjoy wandering, unthinking, through what the city is becoming, and I walk as if everything were lost. The vague sadness that goes with me is more pleasing to my imagination than to my senses. I drift, and in myself, I leaf through, without actually reading it, a book whose text is interspersed with rapid images, out of which I indolently build a never-completed idea.

Some people read as quickly as they look, and so, inevitably, they can't take everything in. And so from the book I'm leafing through in my soul I pluck a story, any story, the memoirs of another wanderer, brief descriptions of twilight evenings and moonlit nights, interspersed with tree-lined paths and various silken figures passing by, passing by.

I make no distinction between tediums. I continue simultaneously down the street, through the evening and that dreamed reading, and I really do travel those paths. I emigrate and rest, as if I were standing on the deck, and the ship was already on the high seas.

Suddenly, the dead street lamps all spring into light on either side of the long, curved street. With a jolt, my sadness increases. I have finished the book. In the airy damp of that abstract street, there is only an external thread of feeling, like the drool of an idiot Destiny dripping onto my soul's conciousness.

Another life, that of the city as night falls. Another soul, that of someone looking at the night. I remain uncertain and allegorical, unreally sentient. I am like a tale told by someone else and told so well that it took on a little flesh in this novel-world, at the beginning of a chapter: "At that hour, a man could be seen walking slowly down Rua de …"

What do *I* have to do with life?

315 [22 Aug 1931]

Before summer ends and autumn arrives, in that warm interval in which the air weighs heavy and the colors soften, the afternoons tend to wear a suit redolent of false glory. They are comparable to imaginative artifices in which one feels a nostalgia for nothing, and they drag on like the endlessly snaking wakes of ships.

On such afternoons, I am filled, like the sea at high tide, by a feeling worse than tedium, but for which there is no other word than tedium—a feeling of desolate desolation, as if my entire soul were shipwrecked. I feel that I have lost an omnipotent God, that the Substance of everything has died. And the tangible universe is, for me, a corpse that I loved when it was life; but everything has turned to nothing in the still-warm glow of the last colorful clouds.

My tedium takes on a horrific aspect; my boredom becomes fear. I do not break out in a cold sweat, but it feels cold nonetheless. I experience no physical malaise, but so intense is the malaise in my soul that it seeps through the pores of my body and chills that too.

So great is my tedium, so overwhelming the horror of being alive, that I cannot imagine what could possibly serve as a palliative, an antidote, a balm, a source of oblivion. The idea of sleeping horrifies me too. As does the idea of dying. Leaving or staying are the same impossible thing. Hoping and doubting are equally cold and gray. I am a shelf full of empty bottles.

And yet, if I allow my vulgar eyes to receive the dying greeting of the bright day's end, what a longing I feel to be no one else but me! What a grand funeral for hope in the still-golden silence of the lifeless skies, what a cortège of vacuums and voids parades past the reddish blues growing paler on the vast plains of empty white space!

I don't know what I want or don't want. I no longer know what it is to want, or how to want, or how to recognize the emotions or thoughts by which we usually know that we do want something or want to want something. I don't know who or what I am. Like someone buried under the rubble of a wall, I lie beneath the fallen vacuity of the entire universe. And thus I continue, in my own wake, until night falls and the slight soothing caress of being different wafts, like a breeze, through the beginning of my own unconsciousness of myself.

Ah, the round, high moon of these placid nights, warm with anxiety and disquiet! The sinister peace of that celestial beauty, the cold irony of the warm air, the dark blue misted with moonlight and already timidly starry.

29/3/1930.

L. do D.
-------- (trecho inicial).   309

Nasci em um tempo em que a maioria dos jovens haviam
perdido a crença em Deus, pela mesma razão que os seus maio-
res a haviam tido - sem saber porquê. E então, porque o
espirito humano tende naturalmente para criticar porque
sente, e não porque pensa, a maioria d'esses jovens esco-
lheu xxxxxxxxxxx a Humanidade para succedaneo de Deus.
Pertenço, porém, aquella especie de homens que estão sem-
pre na margem d'aquillo a que pertencem, nem teem só a
multidão xxxxxx de que são, senão tambem os grandes espa-
ços que ha ao lado. Porisso nem abandonei Deus tam ampla-
mente como elles, nem acceitei nunca a Humanidade. Consi-
derei que Deus, xxx sendo improvavel, poderia ser; que a
Humanidade, sendo uma mera idéa biologica, e não xxxxxxxx
xxxxxxxxxx significando mais que a especie animal xxxxxx
Humana, não era mais digna de adoração do que qualquer ou-
tra especie animal. xxxxxxxxxxxxxxxxx Este culto da Huma-
nidade, com seus ritos de Liberdade e Egualdade, parecue-
me sempre uma reviviscencia dos cultos antigos, em que os
animaes xxx eram deuses, e os deuses tinham cabeças de ani-
maes.

/podendo
pois dever
ser adora-
do; mas

Assim, não sabendo crer em Deus, e não podendo crer
na somma xx xxxxxx dos animaes meus passos, fiquei, como
outros da orla das gentes, naquella distancia de tudo a
que communmente se chama a Decadencia. A Decadencia é a
perda total da inconsciencia; porque a xxxxxxxx inconsci-
encia é o fundamento da vida. O coração, se pudesse pen-
sar, pararia.

A quem, como eu, assim, vivendo, não sabe ter vida,
que resta senão, como a meus xxxxx poucos pares, a renun-
cia por modo e a contemplação por destino. (?) Não sa-
bendo o que é a vida religiosa, nem podendo sabel-o, por-
que se não tem fé com a razão; não podendo ter fé na abstracta
especie humana, nem sabendo mesmo que fazer d'ella peran-
te nós, ficava-nos, como motivo de ter alma a contempla-
ção esthetica da vida. E, assim, alheios á solemnidade
de todos os mundos, indifferentes ao xxx é desprezadores
xxxxxxxx do humano, entregamo-nos futilmente á sensação
sem proposito, cultivada num epicurismo subtilizado, co-
mo convém aos nossos nervos cerebraes.

Retendo, da sciencia, sómente aquelle seu preceito
central, de que tudo é sujeito a leis fataes, contra as
quaes se não reage independentemente, por que reagir é
ellas terem feito que reagissemos; e verificando como es-
se preceito se ajusta ao outro, mais antigo, da fatali-
dade das coisas, abdicamos do exforço como os debeis do
entretimento dos athletas, e curvamo-nos sobre o livro
das sensações com um grande escrupulo de erudição sentida.

"Decadence is the total absence of unconsciousness, for unconsciousness
is the very foundation of life. If the heart could think it would stop
beating." [163]

Não tomando nada a serio, nem considerando que nos ~~fôr~~
fôsse dada, por certa, outra realidade que não as nossas
sensações, nellas nos abrigamos, e a ellas exploramos
como grandes paizes desconhecidos. E, se nos empregamos
assiduamente, não só na contemplação esthetica, mas tambem
na expressão dos seus modos e resultados, é que a prosa ou
o verse que escrevemos, destituidos de vontade de querer
~~operar sobre~~ o alheio entendimento ou mover a alheia von-
tade, é apenas como o fallar alto de quem lê, feito para
dar plena objectividade ao prazer subjectivo da leitura.

Sabemos bem que toda a obra tem que ser imperfeita,
e ~~x~~ que a menos segura das nossas contemplações estheti-
cas será a de aquillo que escrevemos. Mas imperfeito é
tudo, nem ha poente tam bello que o não pudesse ser mais,
~~brisa~~ ou brisa leve que nos dê somno que não pudesse
dar-nos um somno mais calmo ainda. E assim, contemplado-
res eguaes das montanhas e das estatuas, gosando os dias
como os livros, sonhando tudo, sobretudo, para o conver-
ter na nossa intima substancia, faremos tambem descrip-
ções e analyses, que, uma vez feitas, passarão a ser coi-
sas alheias, que podemos gosar como se viessem na tarde.

Não é o conceito dos pessimistas, como aquelle de
Vigny, que a vida é uma cadeia, e elle tecia ~~all~~ palha
para se distrahir. Ser pessimista é tomar qualquer coisa
como tragico, e essa attitude é um exaggero e um incommo-
do. Não temos, é certo, um conceito de valia que applique-
mos á obra que produzimos. Produzimol-a, é certo, para
nos distrahir, porém não como o preso que tece a palha,
~~produzimol-a, é certo, para~~ para se distrahir do Desti-
no, senão da menina que borda almofadas, para se distra-
hir, sem mais nada.

Considero a vida uma estalagem onde tenho que me
demorar até que chegue a diligencia do abysmo. Não sei onde
ella me levará, porque não sei nada. Poderia considerar
esta estalagem uma prisão, porque estou compellido a
aguardar nella; poderia consideral-a um logar de socia-
veis, porque aqui me encontro com outros. Não sou, porém,
nem impaciente nem commum. Deixo ao que são os que se
fecham no quarto, deitados molles na cama onde esperam;
deixo ao que fazem os que conversam nas salas, de onde
as musicas e as vozes chegam commodas até mim. Sento-me
á porta e embebo meus olhos e ouvidos nas cores e nos
sons da paisagem, e canto lento, para mim só, vagos can-
tos que componho emquanto espero.

Para todos nós descerá a noite e ~~chegará~~ chegará a
diligencia. Goso a brisa que me dão e a alma que me de-
ram para gosal-a, e não interrogo mais nem procuro. Se
o que deixar escripto no livro dos viajantes puder, reli-
do um dia por outros, entrebel-os tambem na passagem,
será bem. Se não o lerem, nem se entretiverem, será bem
tambem.

"We know only too well that every work is doomed to imperfection."
[163]

Vejo as paisagens sonhadas com a mesma clareza com
que fito as reaes. Se me debruço sobre os meus sonhos e sobre
qualquer cousa que me debruço. Se vejo a vida passar, sonho
qualquer cousa.

De alguem alguem disse que para elle as figuras dos
sonhos tinham o mesmo relevo e recorte que as figuras da vida.
Para mim, embora comprehendesse que se me applicasse phrase
similhante, não a acceitaria. As figuras dos sonhos não são pa-
ra mim eguaes ás da vida. São parallelas. Cada vida - a dos
sonhos e a do mundo - tem uma realidade egual e propria, mas
differente. /As figuras dos sonhos estão mais, proximas de mim,
mas

Como as cousas proximas e as cousas remotas.

L. do D.

O olfacto é uma vista estranha. Evoca paysagens sentimen-
taes por um desenhar subito do subconsciente. Tenho sentido
isto muitas vezes. Passo numa rua. Não vejo nada, ou, antes,
olhando tudo, vejo como toda a gente vê. Sei que vou
por uma rua e não sei que ella existe com lados feitos de casas
diffrentes e construidas por gente humana. Passo numa rua. De
uma padaria sahe um cheiro a pão que nauseia por doce no chei-
ro d'elle: e a minha infancia ergue-se de determinado bairro
distante, e outra padaria me surge d'aquelle reino das fa-
das que é tudo que senos morreu. Passo numa rua. Cheita de
repentexas fructas do taboleiro inclinado da loja estreita;
e a minha breve vida de campo, não sei já quando nem onde, tem
arvores ao fim e socego no meu coração, indiscutivelmente me-
nino. Passo uma rua. Transtorna-me, sem que eu espere, um
cheiro aos caixotes do caixoteiro: ó meu Cesario, appa-
reces-me e eu sou emfim feliz porque regressei, pela recordação,
á unica verdade, que é a literatura.

"Through memory, I have returned to the one truth that is literature."
[259]

"All this is pure dream and phantasmagoria, and it matters little whether the dream is an entry in an accounts ledger or a piece of superb prose." [373]

Floresce alto na solidão nocturna um candieiro
incognito por traz de uma janella. Tudo mais na
cidade que vejo está escuro, salvo onde reflexos
frouxos da luz das ruas sobe vagamente e faz um
luar inverso, muito pallido. Na negrura da noite
a propria casaria destaca pouco, entre si, as suas
diversas cores, ou tons de cores: só differenças va-
gas, dir-se-hia abstractas, irregularisam o conjunc-
to atropellado.

Um fio invisivel me liga ao dono anonymo do
candieiro. Não é a commum circumstancia de estarmos
ambos accordados: não ha nisso uma reciprocidade
possivel, pois, estando eu à janella no escuro, el-
le nunca poderia ver-me. É outra cousa, minha só,
que se prende um pouco com a sensação de isolamen-
to, que participa da noite e do silencio, que esco-
lhe aquelle candieiro para ponto de appoio porque
é o unico ponto de appoio que ha. Parece que é por
elle estar filuxixuxxu acceso que a noite é tam es-
cura. Parece que é por eu estar disperto, sonhando
na treva, que elle está allumiando.

Tudo que existe existe talvez porque outra
coisa existe. Nada é, tudo coexiste: talvez assim
seja certo. Sinto que eu não existiria nesta hora
- que não existiria, ao menos, do modo em que es-
tou existindo, com esta consciencia presente de
mim, que por ser consciencia e presente é neste
momento inteiramente eu - se aquelle candieiro
não estivesse acceso além, algures, pharol não
indicando nada num falso privilegio de altura.
Sinto isto porque não sinto nada. Penso isto por-
que isto é nada. Nada, nada, parte da noite e do
silencio e do que com elles eu sou de nullo, de
negativo, de intervallar, espaço entre mim e mim,
esquecimento de qualquer deus...

12 8/9/1933.

"High up in the lonely night an unknown lamp blooms behind a win-
dow." [417]

Desde que possamos considerar este mundo uma illusaõ
e um phantasma, poderemos considerar tudo que nos aconte-
ce como um sonho, coisa que fingiu ser porque dormiamos.
E então nasce em nós uma indifferença subtil e profunda
para com todos os desaires e desastres da vida. Os que
morrem viraram uma esquina, e porisso os deixámos de vêr;
os que soffrem passam perante nós, se sentimos, como um
pesadello, se pensamos, como um devaneio ingrato. E o nos-
so proprio soffrimento não será mais que esse nada. Neste
mundo dormimos sobre o lado esquerdo, e ouvimos nos sonhos
a existencia/do coração.
            oppressa

    Mais nada... Um pouco de sol, um pouco de brisa, umas
arvores que emmolduram a distancia, o desejo de ser feliz,
a magua de os dias passaram, a sciencia sempre incerta e
a verdade sempre por descobrir... Mais nada, mais nada...
Sim, mais nada...

                      21-6-1934.

"And our own suffering will be nothing more than that nothingness."
[428]

Unknowingly, I have been a witness to the gradual wasting away of my life, to the slow shipwreck of everything I ever wanted to be. I can say, with the truth that requires no wreaths to remind it of its own demise, that there is not one thing I have wanted or in which I have even for a moment placed my momentary dream that has not fallen and shattered beneath my window and lain like the dusty remains of a clump of soil fallen from a flowerpot on a balcony high above the street. It even seems that Fate has always tried, first and foremost, to make me love or want the very thing that, the following day, Fate itself has ordained I will see that I did not and would not have.

However, as an ironic spectator of myself, I have never lost my interest in observing life. And now, knowing beforehand that each tentative hope will be crushed, I suffer the special pleasure of enjoying the disillusion together with the pain, a bittersweetness in which the sweetness predominates. I am a somber strategist who has lost every battle and now, on the eve of each new engagement, draws up the details of the fatal retreat, savoring the plan as he does so.

That fate of being unable to desire without knowing beforehand that I will not be granted my desire has pursued me like some malign creature. Whenever I see the figure of a young girl in the street and just for a moment wonder, however idly, how it would be if she were mine, every time, just ten paces on from my daydream, that girl meets a man who is obviously her husband or her lover. A romantic would make a tragedy of this, a stranger a comedy; I, however, mix the two things, for I am both a romantic and a stranger to myself, and I simply turn the page to enjoy the next irony.

Some say there's no life without hope, others that hope makes life meaningless. For me, bereft of both hope and despair, life is just a picture in which I am included but that I watch as if it were a play with no plot, performed merely to please the eye—an incoherent ballet, the stirring of leaves on a tree, clouds that change color with the changing light, random networks of ancient streets in odd parts of the city.

I am, for the most part, the very prose that I write. I shape myself in periods and paragraphs, I punctuate myself and, in the unleashed chain of images, I make myself king, as children do, with a crown made from a sheet of newspaper or, in finding rhythms in mere strings of words, I garland myself, as madmen do, with dried flowers that in my dreams still live. And, above all this, I am as calm as a doll stuffed with sawdust which, becoming conscious of itself, every now and then gives a nod so that the bell on top of the pointed hat sewn to its head rings out: the jingle of life in a dead man, a tiny warning to Fate.

How often, though, right in the midst of my quiet dissatisfaction, has not a sense of the emptiness and tedium of this way of thinking crept slowly into my conscious emotions! How often, like someone hearing voices emerging from amongst other intermittent noises, have I felt the essential bitterness of this life so alien to human life, a life in which the only thing that happens is its own consciousness of itself. How often, waking from myself, have I glimpsed from the exile that is me, how much better to be the ultimate nobody, the fortunate man who at least feels real bitterness, the contented man who feels tiredness not tedium, who suffers rather than merely imagining he suffers, who actually kills himself instead of just slowly dying.

I've become a character in a book, a life already read. Quite against my wishes, what I feel is felt in order for me to write it down. What I think appears later set down in words, mixed up with images that merely undo it all, set out in rhythms that mean something else altogether. With all this rewriting, I have destroyed myself. With all this thinking, I am now just my thoughts, not myself. I plumbed the depths of myself but dropped the plumb line; I spend my life wondering whether or not I am deep, with only my own eyes to gauge the depth, and all they show me, clearly, in the black mirror of the great well, is my own face watching me watching it.

I'm like a playing card that belongs to some ancient and un-known suit, the only remnant of a lost pack. I have no meaning, I do not know my value, I have nothing to compare myself with in order to find myself, I have no purpose in life by which to know myself. And thus, in the successive images I use to describe my-self—not untruthful but not truthful either—I become more im-age than me, talking myself out of existence, using my soul as ink, whose sole purpose is to write. But that reaction fades and I resign myself again. I return to myself as I am, even though that is nothing. And something like dry tears burns in my staring eyes; something like a never-felt anxiety catches in my dry throat. But, alas, I don't know what I would have wept for if I had cried, nor why it was I did not weep. The fiction cleaves as close to me as my shadow. All I dream of is to sleep.

317   [3 Sep 1931]

The most painful feelings, the most piercing emotions, are also the most absurd ones—the longing for impossible things precisely be-cause they are impossible, the nostalgia for what never was, the desire for what might have been, one's bitterness that one is not someone else, or one's dissatisfaction with the very existence of the world. All these half-tones of the soul's consciousness create a raw landscape within us, a sun eternally setting on what we are. Our sense of ourselves then becomes a deserted field at nightfall, with sad reeds flanking a boatless river, bright in the darkness growing between the distant shores.

I don't know if these feelings are some slow madness brought on by hopelessness, if they are recollections of some other world in which we've lived—confused, jumbled memories, like things glimpsed in dreams, absurd as we see them now, although not in their origin if we but knew what that was. I don't know if we were once other beings, whose greater completeness we sense only incompletely today, being mere shadows of what they were, beings that have lost their solidity in our feeble two-dimensional imaginings of them among the shadows we inhabit.

I know that these thoughts born of emotion burn with rage in the soul. The impossibility of imagining something they might correspond to, the impossibility of finding some substitute for what in visions they embrace, all this weighs on one like a judgement given one knows not where, by whom, or why.

But what does remain of all this is a distaste for life and all its manifestations, a prescient weariness with all its desires and ways, an anonymous distaste for all feeling. In these moments of subtle pain, it becomes impossible for us, even in dreams, to be a lover or a hero, even to be happy. It is all empty, even the idea of its emptiness. It is all spoken in another language, incomprehensible to us, mere sounds of syllables that find no echo in our understanding. Life, the soul and the world are all hollow. All the gods die a death greater than death itself. Everything is emptier than the void. It is all a chaos of nothing.

If I think this and look around me to see if reality will quench my thirst, I see inexpressive houses, inexpressive faces, inexpressive gestures. Stones, bodies, ideas—everything is dead. All movement is a kind of standing still, everything lies in the grip of stasis. Nothing means anything to me. Everything looks unfamiliar, not because I find it strange but because I don't know what it is. The world is lost. And in the depths of my soul—the only reality of the moment—there is an intense, invisible pain, a sadness like the sound of someone weeping in a dark room.

318 [10 and 11 Sep 1931]

Contrary to the sunny custom of this bright city, the successive rows of houses, the empty plots, the ragged outline of roads and buildings have, since early morning, been wrapped in a light blanket of mist that the sun has slowly turned to gold. Towards midmorning the soft fog began to unravel and, tenuously, in shadowy gusts like the lifting of veils, to vanish. By ten o'clock, the only remaining evidence of the vanished mist was the tenuously tarnished blue of the sky.

As the mask of veils fell away, the features of the city were reborn. The day, which had already dawned, dawned anew, as if a window had been suddenly flung open. The noises in the streets took on a slightly different quality, as if they too had only just appeared. A blueness insinuated itself even into the cobblestones and the impersonal auras of passersby. The sun was hot, but gave off a humid heat as if filtered through the now nonexistent mist.

I've always found the awakening of a city, whether wreathed in mists or not, more moving than sunrise in the country. There is a stronger sense of rebirth, more to look forward to; instead of merely illuminating the fields, the silhouettes of trees and the open palms of leaves with first dark then liquid light and finally with pure luminous gold, the sun multiplies its every effect in windows, on walls, on roofs [...]—so many windows, so many different walls, so many varied rooftops—a splendid morning, diverse among all those diverse realities. Seeing dawn in the countryside does me good, seeing dawn in the city affects me for both good and ill and therefore does me even more good. For the greater hope it brings me contains, as does all hope, the far-off, nostalgic aftertaste of unreality. Dawn in the countryside just exists; dawn in the city overflows with promise. One makes you live, the other makes you think. And, along with all the other great unfortunates, I've always believed it better to think than to live.

319 [14 Sep 1931]

The coming of autumn was announced in the aimless evenings by a certain softening of color in the ample sky, by the buffetings of a cold breeze that arose in the wake of the first cooler days of the dying summer. The trees had not yet lost their green or their leaves, nor was there yet that vague anguish which accompanies our awareness of any death in the external world simply because it reflects our own future death. It was as if what energy remained had grown weary so that a kind of slumber crept over any last attempts at action. Ah, these evenings are full of such painful indifference it is as if the autumn were beginning in us rather than in the world.

Each autumn that comes brings us closer to what will be our last autumn; the same could be said of late spring or summer, but autumn, by its very nature, reminds us of the ending of everything, so easy to forget in kinder seasons. It is still not yet quite autumn, and the air is not yet filled with the yellow of fallen leaves or the damp sad weather that will eventually turn to winter. But there is an anticipation of sadness, some intimate grief dressed and ready for the journey, in one's sense of being aware, however vaguely, of the diffuse colors of things, of a different tone in the wind, of an ancient quiet which, as night falls, slowly invades the unavoidable presence of the universe.

Yes, we will all pass, everything will pass. Nothing will remain of the person who put on feelings and gloves, who talked about death and local politics. The same light falls on the faces of saints and the gaiters of passersby, and the dying of that same light will leave in darkness the utter nothingness that will be all that remains of the fact that some were saints and others wearers of gaiters. In the vast vortex, in which the whole world indolently wallows as if in a whirl of dry leaves, the dresses run up by seamstresses have as much value as whole kingdoms; the fair plaits of children are swept up in the same mortal jig as the scepters that once symbolized empires. All is nothing and in the atrium of the Invisible, whose door swings open only to reveal another closed door beyond, every single thing, large or small, which formed for us and in us the system we understood to be the universe, everything dances in thrall to the wind that stirs all but touches nothing. It is nothing but lightly mixed shadow and dust, there is not even a voice, only the sound the wind makes as it scoops up and sweeps along, there is not even silence except when the wind allows it. Some are whirled up through the atrium like light leaves, less bound to the earth because of their lightness, and they fall outside the circle of heavier objects. Others, indistinguishable unless seen close to, form a single layer within the vortex, almost invisible, like dust. Others again, tree trunks in miniature, are dragged into the circle only to be abandoned in different corners of the floor. One day, when all knowledge ceases, the door beyond will open and everything that we were—a mere detritus of stars and souls—will be swept from the house in order that whatever remains may begin again.

My heart aches as if it were not mine. My brain lulls to sleep everything I feel. Yes, it is the beginning of autumn that touches both the air and my soul with the same unsmiling light that edges with dull yellow the hazy contours of the few clouds at sunset. Yes, it is the beginning of autumn and, in this limpid hour, the beginning of a clear understanding of the anonymous inadequacy of all things. The autumn, yes, the autumn, as it is and always will be: an anticipation of weariness in every gesture, of disillusionment with every dream. What possible hopes can I have? In my thoughts, I already walk among the leaves and dust of the atrium, caught up in this senseless orbit around nothing, my footsteps the only human sound on the clean flagstones that an angular sun—from where I know not—burnishes with death. The autumn will take everything, everything I ever thought or dreamed, everything I did or did not do, spent matches scattered at random on the ground, discarded scraps of paper, great empires, all the religions and philosophies that the drowsy children of the abyss played at making. The autumn will take everything, everything, that is, that made up my soul, from my noblest aspirations to the ordinary house in which I live, from the gods I once worshipped to my boss Vasques. The autumn will take everything, will sweep everything up with tender indifference. The autumn will take everything.

320

We do not even know if the day now ending is actually drawing to an end in us like a pointless grief, or if what we are is a mere illusion in the growing gloom, in which there is only the great silence— without even the cries of wild ducks—that falls on the lakes where the reeds hold up their stiff, swooning blades. We know nothing, we do not even have the memory of childhood stories, now mere algae, or the belated caress of future skies, a breeze whose vagueness slowly opens into stars. The votive lamp flickers hesitantly in the temple that no one visits, the pools grow stagnant in the sun of deserted gardens, we can no longer make out the name someone once carved on the trunk, and the privileges of the ignorant were swept, like torn bits of paper, down windy roads, until they met whatever obstacles blocked their way. Others will lean from the same windows; those who have forgotten about shadowy fears are sleeping, nostalgic for the sun they never knew; and I myself, who dares but does not act, will end up, with no regrets, among those soggy reeds made muddy by the nearby river and by my own flaccid inertia, beneath the vast autumn skies of evening, in impossibly far-flung places. And through it all, like the shrill whistle of naked anxiety, I will feel my soul in my dreams—a deep, pure howl, useless in the darkness of the world.

321

Fluidly, the departing day dies amid spent purples. No one will tell me who I am, nor knows who I was. I came down from the unknown mountain to the equally unknown valley, and my steps in the slow evening were just tracks left in the clearings of the forest. Everyone I loved abandoned me to the shadows. No one knew the time of the last boat. In the post there was no sign of the letter no one would write.

Yes, everything was false. No tales were told that others might have told before, and no one had any firm information about the person who left earlier in the hope of embarking on some illusory boat, child of the coming fog and of future indecision. Among the latecomers I have a name but that, like everything else, is mere shadow.

322 [7 Oct 1931]

The sunset is scattered with stray clouds that fill the whole sky. Soft reflected lights of every color fill the multifarious upper air and float, oblivious, among the great disquiet above. On the very tops of the tall roofs, half color, half shade, the last slow rays of the setting sun take on shades of colors that belong neither to them nor to the things on which they alight. A vast peace hovers above the noisy surface of the city that is itself slowly settling into quietness. Beyond all the color and sound everything takes in a deep, dumb breath of air.

The colors on the stuccoed houses out of sight of the sun gradually take on their stone-gray tones. There's something cold about that diversity of grays. A mild unease slumbers in the false valleys of the streets. It slumbers and grows quiet. And little by little the light on the lowest of the high clouds begins to turn to shadow; only on one small cloud, which hovers above everything like a white eagle, does the sun still smile, golden, distant.

I gave up everything I searched for in life precisely because I had to search for it. I am like someone distractedly looking for something in his dreams, having already forgotten what exactly it was. The present gesture of visible hands—that actually exist, each with their five long, white fingers—seeking, turning things over, picking things up and putting them down, becomes more real than the object of my search.

Everything I have ever had is like this lofty sky, diversely uniform, full of scraps of nothing touched by a distant light, fragments of a false life that death, from afar, touches with gold, with the sad smile of the whole truth. Yes, everything I have been came from my inability to look and find: the feudal lord of twilight marshes, the deserted prince of a city of empty tombs.

In these thoughts of mine and in the abrupt fall from light of that one high cloud, everything I am or was or whatever I think of what I am or was suddenly loses its grasp on the secret, the truth, perhaps even the danger there might be in whatever it is that uses life as its bed. This, like a truant sun, is all that remains to me; the changing light lets its hands slip from the tall roofs and the inner shadow of all things slowly appears on the rooftops.

Far off the first tiny star—a hesitant, tremulous drop of silver—begins to shine.

323   [16 Oct 1931]

I've always been an ironic dreamer, unfaithful to promises I made to myself. I've always savored the shipwreck of my daydreams as if I were someone else, a stranger, as if I were a chance participant in what I thought I was. I never gave much credence to any of my beliefs. I filled my hands with sand and called it gold, then let it all slip away through my fingers. The sentence was the only truth. Once the sentence was formed, everything was done; the rest was the sand it always had been.

Were it not for the fact that I am always dreaming and live in a state of perpetual foreignness to my own self, I could happily call myself a realist, that is, an individual for whom the external world is an independent nation. However, I prefer not to label myself but to be only briefly, obscurely who I am and to enjoy the piquancy of being unpredictable even to myself.

I have a kind of duty always to dream, for, since I am nothing more, nor desirous of being anything more, than a spectator of myself, I must put on the best show I can. So I deck myself in gold and silks and place myself in imaginary rooms on a false stage with ancient scenery, a dream created beneath the play of soft lights, to the sound of invisible music.

Like the recollection of a sweet kiss, I treasure the childhood memory of a theatre in which the blue, lunar scenery represented the terrace of an impossible palace. Painted round it was a vast park, and I put my whole heart into living all that as if it were real. The music that played quietly on that imaginary occasion in my experience of life lent the gratuitous scene a feverish reality.

The scenery was definitively blue and lunar. I don't remember who appeared on the stage, but the play I choose to set in that remembered landscape comes to me now in lines from Verlaine and Pessanha; it's not the play, now long forgotten, that was acted out on the real stage beyond that reality of blue music.* It's my own play, a vast, fluid, lunar masquerade, an interlude in silver and fading blue.

Then life intervened. That night they took me to have supper at the Leão. On the palate of my nostalgia I can still remember the taste of the steaks—steaks, I know or imagine, the like of which no one cooks today and the like of which I never eat. And all those things mingle in me—my childhood, lived somewhere in the distance, that night's delicious meal, the lunar scenery, the future Verlaine and the present me—in a diffuse refraction, in a false space between what I was and what I am.

324   [after 18 Oct 1931]

I prefer prose to poetry as an art form for two reasons, the first of which is mine alone, namely, that I have no choice, because I am incapable of writing poetry. The second reason, however, applies to everyone, and is not—I believe—a mere shadow of that first reason or the same reason in disguise. It's perhaps worth my while to dissect this second reason here, because it touches on the inner meaning of everything of value in art.

I consider poetry to be an intermediate thing, a transitional stage between music and prose. Like music, poetry is bound by rhythmic rules, which, although they are not the rigid rules of regular meter, do still exist as controls, constraints, automatic mechanisms of oppression and punishment. In prose we can speak freely. We can

---

* Camilo Pessanha (1871–1926) was a Portuguese symbolist poet.

include musical rhythms and yet still think. We can include poetic rhythms and yet still exist outside them. An occasional poetic rhythm does not get in the way of prose, but an occasional prosaic rhythm can cause poetry to stumble.

Prose encompasses all of art—partly because everything is contained in the word and partly because the unfettered word contains within it all possible ways of saying and thinking. Prose can, through transposition, convey everything: color and form, which painting can only do directly and with no inner dimension; rhythm, which music can only convey directly through itself, with no physical body, nor that other body—the idea; structure, which the architect has to make out of hard, already existing external objects, and which we construct out of rhythms, hesitations, pauses and cadences; reality, which the sculptor has to leave in the world, with no aura or transubstantiation; and finally, poetry, in which the poet, like an initiate into some occult order, plays the willing slave to an order and a ritual.

I truly believe that, in a perfectly civilized world, the only art would be prose. We would allow sunsets to be sunsets, taking pains only to understand them verbally, communicating them through an intelligible music of color. We would not make sculptures of bodies, which could keep all their soft, warm, supple curves to be seen and touched. We would build houses only to be lived in, which is, after all, what they are intended for. Poetry would remain the domain of children, as a preparation for writing prose in the future; because there is something childish about poetry, something mnemonic, something auxiliary and elementary.

Even the minor arts, if I can call them that, are the murmuring echoes of prose. There is prose that dances, sings, declaims. There are verbal rhythms that can be danced, and in which the idea sinuously lays itself bare with perfect, translucent sensuality. You can also find in prose the subtle gestures with which a great actor, the Verb, rhythmically transmutes the intangible mystery of the universe into its own corporeal substance.

Clouds … I'm very conscious of the sky today, though there are days when, although I feel it, I don't see it, living as I do in the city and not out in the country where the sky is always so present. Clouds … They are the principal reality of the day and I'm as pre-occupied with them as if the clouding over of the sky were one of the great dangers that fate has in store for me. Clouds … From the river up to the castle, from west to east, they drift along, a disparate, naked tumult. Some are white, the tattered vanguard of some un-known army; others, more ponderous and almost black, are swept slowly along by the audible wind; besmirched with white, they seem inclined to linger and plunge into darkness the illusion of space afforded to the serried ranks of houses by the narrow streets, a darkness provoked more by their approach than by any actual shadow they cast.

Clouds … I exist unconsciously and I'll die unwillingly. I am the interval between what I am and what I am not, between what I dream and what life has made of me, the abstract, carnal halfway house between things, like myself, that are nothing. Clouds … How disquieting it is to feel, how troubling to think, how vain to want! Clouds … They continue to pass, some so large (though just how large it's hard to judge because of the houses) they seem about to take over the whole sky; others, of uncertain size, which could be two clouds together or one about to split into two, drift, direc-tionless, through the high air across the weary sky; to one side, in grand and chilly isolation, are other smaller clouds that look like the playthings of powerful creatures, irregularly shaped balls to be used in some absurd game.

Clouds … I question myself, but do not know myself. I've done nothing nor will I ever do anything useful to justify my existence. The part of my life not wasted in thinking up confused interpreta-tions of nothing at all has been spent making prose poems out of the incommunicable feelings I use to make the unknown universe my own. Both objectively and subjectively speaking, I'm sick of myself.

I'm sick of everything, and of everything about everything. Clouds ... Today they are everything, dismantled fragments of heaven, the only real things between the empty earth and the nonexistent sky, indescribable scraps of a tedium I impose on them, mist condensed into bland threats, soiled tufts of cotton wool in a hospital without walls. Clouds ... They are, like me, a ruined road between sky and earth, at the mercy of some invisible impulse, they may or may not thunder, they gladden the earth with their whiteness, sadden it with their darkness, fictions born of empty intervals and aimless meanderings, remote from earthly noises, but lacking the silence of the sky. Clouds ... They continue to drift past, on and on, as they always will, like a constantly interrupted winding and unwinding of dull yarns, the diffuse prolongation of a false, fragmented sky.

326   [after 18 Oct 1931]

I enjoy using words. Or rather: I enjoy making words work. For me words are tangible bodies, visible sirens, sensualities made flesh. Perhaps because real sensuality has no interest for me whatsoever—not even in thoughts or dreams—desire has become transmuted into the part of me that creates verbal rhythms or hears them in other people's speech. I tremble if I hear someone speak well. Certain pages in Fialho or in Chateaubriand make life tingle in my veins, make me quietly, tremulously mad with an unattainable pleasure already mine. Moreover, some pages by Vieira, in all the cold perfection of his syntactical engineering, make me shiver like a branch in the wind, in the passive delirium of something set in motion.

Like all great lovers, I enjoy the pleasure of losing myself, that pleasure in which one suffers wholeheartedly the delights of surrender. And that's why I often write without even wanting to think, in an externalized daydream, letting the words caress me as if I were a little girl sitting on their lap. They're just meaningless sentences, flowing languidly with the fluidity of water that forgets itself as a stream does in the waves that mingle and fade, constantly reborn, following endlessly one on the other. That's how ideas and images, tremulous with expression, pass through me like a rustling procession of faded silks amongst which a sliver of an idea flickers, mottled and indistinct in the moonlight.

Though I weep for nothing that life might bring or take away from me, certain pages of prose can reduce me to tears. I remember, as if it were yesterday, the night when, still a child, I picked up an anthology and read for the first time Vieira's famous passage on King Solomon. "Solomon built a palace ..." I read on to the end, trembling and confused, then burst into joyful tears that no real happiness could have provoked, tears that no sadness in my life will ever provoke. The stately rhythm of our clear, majestic language, the expression of ideas in words that flowed as inevitably as water down a hillside, that vocalic thrill by which every sound takes on its ideal color: all this intoxicated me as instinctively as some great political passion. And, as I said, I wept; I still cry when I remember it today. It isn't nostalgia for my childhood, for which I feel no nostalgia: it's nostalgia for the emotion of that moment, it's the pain of never again being able to read for the first time that great symphonic certainty.

I have no political or social sense. In a way, though, I do have a highly developed patriotic sense. My fatherland is the Portuguese language. It wouldn't grieve me if someone invaded and took over Portugal as long as they didn't bother me personally. What I hate, with all the hatred I can muster, is not the person who writes bad Portuguese, or who does not know his grammar, or who writes using the new simplified orthography; what I hate, as if it were an actual person, is the poorly written page of Portuguese itself; what I hate, as if it were someone who deserved a beating, is the bad grammar itself; what I hate, as I hate a gob of spit independently of its perpetrator, is modern orthography with its preference for *i* over *y*.

For orthography is just as much a living thing as we are. A word is complete when seen and heard. And the pomp of the Greco-Roman transliteration clothes it for me in the true royal mantle that makes it our lady and our queen.

Yes, it's sunset. I walk, leisurely and distracted, down Rua da Alfân-
dega towards the Tejo and, as Terreiro do Paço opens out before
me, I can clearly see the sunless western sky. To the left, above the
hills on the far shore of the river, a bank of brownish, dull pink
mist crouches in the sky and there the colors shade from greenish
blue to grayish white. A great sense of peace that I do not possess
is scattered in the cold, abstract autumn air. Not having it, I let
myself suffer the vague pleasure of imagining its existence. But in
reality there is neither peace nor a lack of it, there is only sky, a sky
made up of every fading color—blue-white, blue-green, a pale gray
that is neither green nor blue, the faded remote colors of clouds
that are not clouds, yellows darkened with blanched reds. And all
of this is just a vision that dies the instant it is conceived, a fleeting
interval between nothing and nothing, placed on high, prolix and
undefined, painted in the colors of heaven and of grief.

I feel and I forget. A sense of nostalgia invades me, like an opiate
borne on the cold air, the nostalgia that everyone feels for every-
thing. I am filled with an intimate, illusory ecstasy of seeing.

At the estuary mouth where the last moments of the sun linger
to an end, the light finally ebbs away in a livid white that turns blue
as it mixes with the cold green. There is a torpor in the air of things
unfulfilled. Above, the landscape of the sky falls silent.

At this moment, when I almost overflow with feeling, I would
like to have the wit simply to speak out and have as my destiny the
capricious freedom of a style. But no, there is only the vast, remote
sky slowly canceling itself out, and the emotion I feel—a mixture
of many confused emotions—is nothing but the reflection of that
empty sky in a lake within myself, silent as a dead man's gaze, a
hidden lake amidst tall rocks, in which the oblivious sky contem-
plates itself.

Now, as many times before, I am troubled by my own experience
of my feelings, by my anguish simply to be feeling something, my
disquiet at simply being here, my nostalgia for something never

known, the setting of the sun on all emotions, this fading, in my external consciousness of myself, from yellow into gray sadness.

Who will save me from existence? It isn't death I want, or life: it's the other thing that shines at the bottom of all longing like a possible diamond in a cave one cannot reach. It's the whole weight and pain of this real and impossible universe, of this sky, of this standard borne by some unknown army, of these colors that grow pale in the fictitious air, out of which there emerges in still, electric whiteness the imaginary crescent of the moon, silhouetted by distance and indifference.

The absence of a true God has become the empty corpse of the vast sky and the closed soul. Infinite prison, because you are infinite no one can escape you!

328   [after 18 Oct 1931]

Just as, whether we know it or not, we all have a metaphysics, so also, whether we like or not, we all have a morality. I have a very simple morality—to do neither good nor evil to anyone. To do no evil because I not only recognize in others the same right I believe myself to have, which is not to be bothered by them, but also because I think there are enough natural evils in the world without my adding to them. In this world we're all travelers on the same ship that has set sail from one unknown port en route to another equally foreign to us; we should treat each other, therefore, with the friendliness due to fellow travelers. And I choose to do no good because I don't know what good is, nor whether I really am doing good when I think I am. How am I to know what evils I may cause when I give alms, or if I attempt to educate or instruct? In case of doubt, I abstain. I believe, moreover, that to help or clarify is, in a way, to commit the evil of intervening in someone else's life. Kindness is a temperamental caprice and we do not have the right to make others the victims of our caprice however humane or tender-hearted. Favors are things imposed on others; that's why I so thoroughly detest them.

If, for moral reasons, I choose to do no good, neither do I demand that anyone else should do good to me. What I hate most when I fall ill is obliging someone to look after me, because it's something I would hate to do for someone else. I've never once visited a sick friend. Whenever I've been ill and people have visited me, I felt each visit to be an inconvenience, an insult, an unjustifiable violation of my chosen privacy. I don't like people giving me things; they seem then to be obliging me to give them something too—to them or to others, it doesn't matter to whom.

I'm extremely sociable in an extremely negative manner. I'm inoffensiveness incarnate. But I'm no more than that, I don't want to be more than that, nor can I be more than that. I feel for everything that exists a visual tenderness, an intelligent affection, but nothing heartfelt. I have no faith in anything, no hope in anything, no charity for anything. I feel nothing but aversion and disgust for the sincere adherents of every kind of sincerity and for the mystics of every kind of mysticism, or rather for the sincerities of all sincere people and for the mysticisms of all mystics. I feel an almost physical nausea when those mysticisms turn evangelical, when they try to convince another intelligence or another will to find the truth or change the world.

I consider myself fortunate to no longer have any relatives, for I am thus free of the obligation, which would inevitably weigh on me, of having to love someone. My only nostalgias are literary ones. My eyes fill with tears at the memory of my childhood, but they are rhythmical tears in which some piece of prose is already in preparation. I remember it as something external to me and remember it through external things; I remember only external things. It isn't the cozy warmth of provincial evenings that fills me with tender feelings for my childhood, but the way the table was laid for tea, the shapes of the furniture placed around the house, people's faces and physical gestures. My nostalgia is for certain pictures of the past. That's why I feel as much tenderness for my own childhood as for someone else's: lost in some indefinite past, they are both purely visual phenomena that I perceive with my literary mind. I do feel tenderness, not because I remember, but because I see.

I've never loved anyone. What I have loved most have been sensations—the scenes recorded by my conscious vision, the impressions captured by attentive ears, the perfumes by which the humble things of the external world speak to me and tell me tales of the past (so easily evoked by smells)—that is, their gift to me of a reality and emotion more intense than the loaf baking in the depths of the bakery as it was on that far-off afternoon on my way back from the funeral of the uncle who so adored me and when all I felt was the vague tenderness of relief, about what I don't know.

That is my morality or my metaphysics or me myself: a passerby in everything, even in my own soul, I belong to nothing, I desire nothing, I am nothing except an abstract center of impersonal sensations, a sentient mirror fallen from the wall, but still turned to reflect the diversity of the world. I don't know if this makes me happy or unhappy, and I don't much care.

329 [c. 21 Oct 1931]

Having touched the feet of Christ is no excuse for faulty punctuation.

If a man writes well only when he is drunk, I would tell him: Drink. And if he were to tell me that his liver suffers as a consequence, I would say: And what is your liver? It is a dead thing that lives only while you live, whereas there is no "while" about the poems you write.

330 [c. 21 Oct 1931]

True wealth is closing one's eyes and puffing on an expensive cigar.

With the aid of a cheap cigarette I can return, like someone revisiting a place where they spent their youth, to the time in my life when I used to smoke cheap cigarettes. The light tang of that cigarette smoke is enough for me to relive the whole of my past life.

At other times, a certain type of sweet might serve the same purpose. One innocent chocolate can rack my nerves with the profusion of memories it provokes. Childhood! And as my teeth bite into the soft, dark mass, I bite into and savor my humble joys as contented companion to a lead soldier, as competent horseman with a stick for a horse. My eyes fill with tears, and the taste of chocolate mingles with the taste of my past happiness, my lost childhood, and I cling voluptuously to that sweet pain.

The simplicity of this ritual tasting does not detract from the solemnity of the occasion.

But it is cigarette smoke that most subtly rebuilds past moments for me. It just barely touches my consciousness of having a sense of taste and that's why, part wrapped in gauze, part transparent, it evokes hours to which I am now dead, makes far-off times present, makes them mistier the closer they wrap about me, more ethereal when I make them flesh. A mentholated cigarette or a cheap cigar can bathe in tenderness almost any moment from my past. With what subtle plausibility I use that combination of taste and smell to reconstruct dead scenes and perform the comedies from my past, as distant, bored and malicious as the eighteenth century, as irredeemably lost to me as the Middle Ages.

331 [c. 21 Oct 1931]

We can die of loving too meanly.

332 [4 Nov 1931]

Anyone wanting to make a catalogue of monsters would need only to photograph in words the things that night brings to somnolent souls who cannot sleep. These things have all the incoherence of dreams without the unacknowledged excuse of sleep. They hover like bats over the passivity of the soul, or like vampires that suck the blood of our submissiveness.

They are the larvae of decline and waste, shadows filling the valley, the last vestiges of fate. Sometimes they are worms, repellent to the very soul that cossets and nourishes them; sometimes they are ghosts sinisterly haunting nothing at all; sometimes they emerge like cobras from the bizarre grottoes of lost emotions.

They are the ballast of falsehood, their only purpose is to render us useless. They are doubts from the deep that settle in cold, sleepy folds upon the soul. They are as ephemeral as smoke, as tracks on the ground, and all that remains of them is the fact of their once having existed in the sterile soil of our awareness of them. Some are like fireworks of the mind that glitter for a moment between dreams, the rest are just the unconsciousness of the consciousness with which we saw them.

Like a bow that's come undone, the soul does not in itself exist. The great landscapes all belong to a tomorrow we have already lived. The interrupted conversation was a failure. Who would have guessed life would be like this?

The moment I find myself, I am lost; if I believe, I doubt; I grasp hold of something but hold nothing in my hand. I go to sleep as if I were going for a walk, but I'm awake. I wake as if I slept, and I am not myself. Life, after all, is but one great insomnia and there is a lucid half-awakeness about everything we think or do.

I would be happy if only I could sleep. At least that's what I think now when I can't sleep. The night is an immense weight pressing down on my dream of suffocating myself beneath the silent blanket. I have indigestion of the soul.

Always, after everything, day will come, but it will be late, as usual. Everything except me sleeps and is contented. I rest a little without daring to sleep. And, confusedly, from the depths of my being the enormous heads of imaginary monsters emerge. They are oriental dragons from the abyss, with illogically scarlet tongues and lifeless eyes that stare at my dead life which does not look back.

Someone, please, close the lid on all this! Let me be done with unconsciousness and life! Then, fortunately, through the cold window with the shutters thrown back, I see a wan thread of pallid light beginning to disperse the shadows on the horizon. Fortunately, what is about to break upon me is the day bringing rest, almost, from the weariness of this unrest. Absurdly, right in the city center, a cock crows. The pale day begins as I drift into vague sleep. At some point I will sleep. The noise of wheels evokes a cart passing by. My eyelids sleep, but I do not. In the end, there is only Fate.

333 [29 Nov 1931]

If there is one thing life gives us, apart from life itself, and for which we must thank the gods, it is the gift of not knowing ourselves: of not knowing ourselves and of not knowing one another. The human soul is an abyss of viscous darkness, a well whose depths are rarely plumbed from the surface of the world. No one would love himself if he really knew himself and thus, without vanity, which is the life blood of the spirit, our soul would die of anaemia. No one knows anyone else and it's just as well, for if we did, be they mother, wife or son, we would find lurking in each of them our deep, metaphysical enemy.

The only reason we get on together is that we know nothing about one another. What would happen to all those happy couples if they could see into each other's soul, if they could understand each other, as the romantics say, unaware of the danger (albeit futile) in their words? Every married couple in the world is a mismatch because each person harbors, in the secret part of the soul that belongs to the Devil, the subtle image of the man they desire but who is not their husband, the nubile figure of the sublime woman their wife never was. The happiest are unaware of these frustrated inner longings; the less happy are neither aware nor entirely unaware of them, and only the occasional clumsy impulse, a roughness in the way they treat the other, evokes, on the casual surface of gestures and words, the hidden Demon, the old Eve, the Knight or the Sylph.

The life one lives is one long misunderstanding, a happy medium between a greatness that does not exist and a happiness that cannot exist. We are content because, even when thinking or feeling, we are capable of not believing in the existence of the soul. In the masked ball that is our life, it's enough to feel that we're wearing a costume, which is, after all, what matters in the dance. We are the slaves of lights and colors, we launch ourselves into the dance as if it were truth itself, and, unless we are left alone and do not dance, we have no knowledge of the vast and lofty cold of the night outside, of the mortal body beneath the rags that outlive it, of everything which, when alone, we believe to be essentially us, but in the end is just a personal parody of the truth of what we imagine ourselves to be.

Everything we do or say, everything we think or feel, wears the same mask and the same fancy dress. However many layers of clothing we take off, we are never left naked, for nakedness is a phenomenon of the soul and has nothing to do with taking off one's clothes. Thus, dressed in body and soul, with our multiple outfits clinging to us as sleek as feathers, we live out the brief time the gods give us to enjoy ourselves happily or unhappily (or ignorant of quite what our feelings are), like children playing earnest games.

Someone, freer or more accursed than the rest of us, suddenly sees (though even he sees it only rarely) that everything we are is what we are not, that we deceive ourselves about what is certain and are wrong about what we judge to be right. And this individual, who, for one brief moment, sees the universe naked, creates a philosophy or dreams a religion, and the philosophy is listened to and the religion resonates, and those who believe in the philosophy wear it like an invisible garment, and those who believe in the religion put it on like a mask which they then forget they are wearing.

And so, ignorant of ourselves and of everyone else, and therefore happily able to get along with one another, we are caught up in the folds of the dance or the conversations in the intervals, human, serious and futile, dancing to the sound of the great orchestra of the stars, beneath the scornful, distant gaze of the organizers of the show.

Only they know that we are the prisoners of the illusion they created for us. But what is the reason for this illusion, and why does this or any illusion exist and why is it that they, as deluded as we are, chose this illusion to give to us? That, of course, even they do not know.

334 [November 1931]

Many people have come up with definitions of man and, generally, they define him by contrast with the animals. That's why in such definitions they often make use of the phrase "man is a ... animal," and add the appropriate adjective, or "man is an animal that ..." followed by an explanation of the kind of animal man is. "Man is a sick animal," said Rousseau, and in part it's true. "Man is a rational animal," says the Church and in part that's true. "Man is a tool-using animal," says Carlyle, and in part that's true too. But these definitions, and others like them, are always imperfect and one-sided. And the reason is very simple: it's not easy to distinguish man from the animals; there's no foolproof criterion by which to do so. Human lives pass by in the same profound unconsciousness as the lives of animals. The same deep-rooted laws that rule from without the instincts of the animals rule the intelligence of man, which seems to be nothing more than an instinct in the making, as unconscious as any instinct, and less perfect because as yet unformed.

According to the Greek rationalists: "Everything has its source in unreason." And everything does come from unreason. Apart from mathematics, which has nothing to do with anything except dead numbers and empty formulae and can therefore be perfectly logical, science is nothing but a game played by children in the twilight, a desire to catch hold of the shadows of birds, to fix the shadows of grasses swaying in the wind.

And it's very strange that, though it's by no means easy to find words that truly distinguish man from the animals, it's easy to find a way of differentiating the superior man from the common man.

I have never forgotten that phrase of the biologist, Haeckel, whom I read in the infancy of my intelligence, at that age when one reads scientific publications and arguments against religion. The phrase goes more or less like this: the superior man (a Kant or a Goethe, I think he says) is farther removed from the common man than the common man is from the monkey. I've never forgotten the phrase because it's true. Between myself, of little significance amongst the ranks of thinkers, and a peasant in Loures there is a greater distance than between that peasant and, I won't say a monkey, but a cat or a dog. None of us, from the cat up, actually leads the life imposed on us or the fate given to us; we all derive from equally obscure origins, we are all shadows of gestures made by someone else, effects made flesh, consequences with feelings. But between me and the peasant there is a qualitative difference, deriving from the existence in me of abstract thought and disinterested emotion; whereas between him and the cat, at the level of the spirit, there is only a difference of degree.

What distinguishes the superior man from the inferior man and from the latter's animal brothers is the simple quality of irony. Irony is the first indication that consciousness has become conscious, and it passes through two stages: the stage reached by Socrates when he said "I only know that I know nothing," and the stage reached by Sanches,* when he said "I do not even know that I know nothing." The first stage is that point at which we dogmatically doubt ourselves and it's a point that every superior man will reach. The second stage is the point at which we doubt both ourselves and our doubt, and, in the brief yet long curve of time during which we, as humans, have watched the sun rise and the night fall over the varied surface of the earth, that is a stage very few men have reached.

To know oneself is to err, and the oracle who said "Know thyself" proposed a task greater than all of Hercules' labors and an enigma even more obscure than that of the Sphinx. To consciously unknow oneself, that is the right path to follow. And to consciously unknow

---

* Francisco Sanches (1551–1623) was a Portuguese humanist and philosopher and forerunner of Descartes.

oneself is the active task of irony. I know no greater nor more proper task for the truly great man than the patient, expressive analysis of ways of unknowing ourselves, the conscious recording of the unconsciousness of our consciousnesses, the metaphysics of us as autonomous shadows, the poetry of the twilight of disillusion.

But something always eludes us, there is always some analysis that slips our grasp; the truth, albeit false, is always just around the corner. That's what tires one more than life when life grows wearisome, and more than any knowledge of or meditation on life, which are never less than exhausting.

I get up from the chair where, leaning distractedly on the table, I've been amusing myself setting down these rough and ready impressions. I get up, I make my body get up, and go over to the window, high above the rooftops, from where I can see the city settling to sleep in the slow beginnings of silence. The big, bright white moon sadly points out the ragged line of the terraced roofs and its icy light seems to illuminate all the mystery of the world. It seems to reveal everything and that everything is just shadows intermingled with dim light, false intervals, erratically absurd, the incoherent mutterings of the visible world. The absence of any breeze only seems to increase the mystery. I'm sick of abstract thoughts. I will never write a single page that will reveal myself or anything else. The lightest of clouds hovers vaguely above the moon as if it were the moon's hiding place. Like these rooftops, I know nothing. Like all of nature, I have failed.

335   [1 Dec 1931]

Art consists in making others feel what we feel, in freeing them from themselves, by offering them our own personality as a liberation. What I feel, in the actual substance in which I feel it, is totally incommunicable; and the more profoundly I feel something, the more incommunicable it becomes. In order for me to be able to transmit what I feel to someone else, I have to translate my feelings into his language, that is, to say those things as if they were what I feel, and for him, reading them, to feel exactly what I felt. And since that other person is, in terms of art, not this or that person, but everyone, that is, the person common to all people, what I have to do in the end is to convert my feelings into a typical human feeling, even if that perverts the true nature of what I felt.

All abstractions are hard to understand, because it's hard for abstractions to hold the attention of the person reading. Let me give a simple example, which will make those abstractions easier to grasp. Imagine that, for some reason—possibly when I'm fed up with poring over the accounts ledger or having nothing to do—I am assailed by a vague sadness about life, an anxiety that troubles and disturbs me. If I want to translate that emotion into words that fit tightly, the tighter the fit, the more I give of myself and the less, therefore, I will communicate to others. And if I cannot communicate with others, then it would be better and easier just to feel the emotion and not bother writing it down.

Imagine, though, that I want to communicate that emotion to other people, that is, make it into art, because art means communicating one's own sense of identity with them, without which there can be neither communication nor the need to communicate. I try to track down the general human emotion that has the tone, type and form of the emotion I'm feeling now for the inhuman and particular reason that I'm a weary bookkeeper or a bored citizen of Lisbon. And I discover that the type of ordinary emotion that produces that same emotion in an ordinary soul is a nostalgia for our lost childhood.

Then I have the key to the door of my subject. I write and weep over my lost childhood; I linger touchingly over details of the people and furniture that inhabited that old house in the provinces; I evoke the joy of having no rights and no duties, of being free because I did not know how to think or feel—and that evocation, if successfully and vividly transposed into prose, will awaken in my reader precisely the emotion I was feeling, and which had nothing to do with childhood.

Was I lying? No, I simply understood. Because a lie—apart from the childish, spontaneous lie born of a desire to dream—is merely a recognition that other people exist and an acknowledgement of the need to shape that existence to our own, which cannot be shaped to theirs. A lie is simply the ideal language of the soul, for just as we use words—which are sounds articulated in an absurd manner—to translate into real language the most intimate and subtle movements of emotion and thought, which words alone could never translate, so we make use of lies and fictions in order to understand and get along with other people, which we would never be able to do with our own very personal and untransmittable truth.

Art lies because it is a social thing. And there are only two great forms of art—one is addressed to our deep soul, the other to our attentive soul. The first is poetry, the second the novel. The structure of the former is in itself a lie; and the very intention of the latter is a lie. One sets out to give us the truth by means of metered lines, which go against the inherent nature of speech; the other sets out to give us the truth through a reality that we know very well never existed.

To pretend is to love. I never see a sweet smile or a meaningful look, regardless of who the smile or the look belongs to, without probing deep into the soul of the person smiling or looking in search of the politician hoping to buy us or the prostitute hoping that we will buy her. And yet the politician who bought us at least loved the act of buying us; and the prostitute whom we bought at least loved the act of being bought by us. Much as we would like to, we cannot escape the universal brotherhood of man. We all love each other, and the lie is the kiss we exchange.

336 [1 Dec 1931]

Since I'm so given to tedium, it's odd that until today I've never really thought much about what it actually consists of. Today I'm in that intermediate state of mind in which I feel no interest in life or in anything else. And I take advantage of the sudden realization that I've never really thought about this feeling to dream up an inevitably somewhat artificial analysis of it, using my thoughts and half-impressions on the subject.

I don't honestly know if tedium is just the waking equivalent of the somnolence of the inveterate idler or something altogether nobler than that particular form of listlessness. I often suffer from tedium but, as far as I can tell, it follows no rules as to when and why it appears. I can spend a whole vacuous Sunday without once experiencing tedium, yet sometimes, when I'm hard at work, it comes over me, suddenly, like a cloud. I can't link it to any particular state of health or lack of health; I can't see it as the product of causes in any apparent part of myself.

To say it is a metaphysical anguish in disguise, an ineffable disappointment, a secret poem of the bored soul leaning out of the window that opens on to life, to say that, or something similar, might lend color to the tedium, the way a child draws something then clumsily colors it in, blurring the edges, but to me it's just words echoing around the cellars of thought.

Tedium ... It is thinking without thinking, yet requires all the effort involved in having to think; it is feeling without feeling, yet stirs up all the anguish that feeling normally involves; it is not wanting something but wanting it, and suffering all the nausea involved in not wanting. Although tedium contains all of these things, they are not themselves tedium, they provide only a paraphrase, a translation. Expressed as direct sensation, it is as if the drawbridge over the moat around the soul's castle had been pulled up, leaving us with but one power, that of gazing impotently out at the surrounding lands, never again to set foot there. We are isolated within ourselves from ourselves, an isolation in which what separates us is as stagnant as us, a pool of dirty water surrounding our inability to understand.

Tedium ... It is suffering without suffering, wanting without will, thinking without reason ... It's like being possessed by a negative demon, bewitched by nothing at all. They say that witches and some minor wizards, by making images of us which they then torment, can reproduce those same torments in us by means of some sort of astral transference. Tedium arises in me, in the transposed feeling of such an image, like the malign reflection of some fairy demon's spell cast not upon the image but upon its shadow. It is on my inner shadow, on the surface of the interior of my soul, on which they glue papers or stick pins. I am like the man who sold his shadow or, rather, like the shadow of the man who sold it.

Tedium ... I work quite hard. I fulfill what practical moralists would call my social duty, and fulfill that duty, or that fate, with no great effort or noticeable difficulty. But sometimes, right in the middle of work or leisure (something which, according to those same moralists, I deserve and should enjoy), my soul overflows with the bile of inertia and I feel weary, not of work or leisure, but of myself.

And why weary of myself, if I wasn't even thinking about myself? What else would I be thinking about? The mystery of the universe descending upon me while I toil over accounts or recline in a chair? The universal pain of living crystallized suddenly in the intermediary of my soul? Why thus ennoble someone who doesn't even know who he is? It's a feeling of utter vacuity, a hunger with no desire to eat, about as noble as the feelings you experience in your brain or stomach from having smoked or eaten too much.

Tedium ... Perhaps it's basically an expression of a dissatisfaction in our innermost soul not to have been given something to believe in, the desolation of the child all of us are deep down not to have been bought the divine toy. It is perhaps the insecurity of someone in need of a guiding hand, conscious of nothing on the black road of deep feeling but the silent night of one's inability to think, the deserted road of one's inability to feel ...

Tedium ... No one with a god to believe in will ever suffer from tedium. Tedium is the lack of a mythology. To the unbeliever, even doubt is denied, even scepticism does not give the strength to despair. Yes, that's what tedium is: the loss by the soul of its capacity to delude itself, the absence in thought of the nonexistent stairway up which the soul steadfastly ascends towards the truth.

337 [1 Dec 1931]

Today, suddenly, I reached an absurd but unerring conclusion. In a moment of enlightenment, I realized that I am nobody, absolutely nobody. When the lightning flashed, I saw that what I had thought to be a city was in fact a deserted plain and, in the same sinister light that revealed me to myself, there seemed to be no sky above it. I was robbed of any possibility of having existed before the world. If I was ever reincarnated, I must have done so without myself, without a self to reincarnate.

I am the outskirts of some nonexistent town, the long-winded prologue to an unwritten book. I am nobody, nobody. I don't know how to feel or think or love. I'm a character in a novel as yet unwritten, hovering in the air and undone before I've even existed, among the dreams of someone who never quite managed to breathe life into me.

I'm always thinking, always feeling, but my thoughts lack all reason, my emotions all feeling. I'm falling through a trapdoor, through infinite, infinitous space, in a directionless, empty fall. My soul is a black maelstrom, a great madness spinning around a vacuum, the swirling of a vast ocean around a hole in the void, and in the waters, more like whirlwinds than waters, float images of all I ever saw or heard in the world: houses, faces, books, crates, snatches of music and fragments of voices, all caught up in a sinister, bottomless whirlpool.

And I, I myself, am the center that exists only because the geometry of the abyss demands it; I am the nothing around which all this spins, I exist so that it can spin, I am a center that exists only because every circle has one. I, I myself, am the well in which the walls have fallen away to leave only viscous slime. I am the center of everything surrounded by the great nothing.

And it is as if hell itself were laughing within me but, instead of the human touch of diabolical laughter, there's the mad croak of the dead universe, the circling cadaver of physical space, the end of all worlds drifting blackly in the wind, misshapen, anachronistic, without the God who created it, without God himself, who spins in the dark of darks, impossible, unique, everything.

If only I could think! If only I could feel!

My mother died very young; I never knew her ...

338   [3 Dec 1931]

When I first came to Lisbon the sound of someone playing scales on a piano used to drift down from the apartment above, the monotonous piano practice of a little girl I never saw. Today, through processes of assimilation I fail to comprehend, I discover that if I open up the door to the cellars of my soul, those repetitive scales are still audible, played by the little girl who is now Mrs Someone-or-other, or else dead and shut up in a white place overgrown by dark cypresses.

I was a child then, now I am not. In my memory, though, the sound is the same as it was in reality and, when it raises itself up from the place where it lies feigning sleep, there it is, perennially present, the same slow scales, the same monotonous rhythm. Whenever I feel it or think of it, I am invaded by a diffuse, anguished sadness that is mine alone.

I do not weep for the loss of my childhood; I weep because everything, and with it my childhood, will be lost. What makes my mind ache with the repeated, involuntary recurrence of the piano scales from upstairs, so horribly distant and anonymous, is the abstract flight of time, not the concrete flight of time that affects me directly. It is the whole mysterious fact of nothing lasting which again and again hammers out the notes, notes that are not quite music, but rather a mixture of nostalgia and longing that lurks in the absurd depths of my memory.

Slowly, there rises before me the sitting room I never saw, where the pupil I never knew is even today playing, finger by careful finger, the same repetitive scales of something already dead. I look and see and, seeing, reconstruct the scene. And, full of a poignancy it lacked then, a vision of family life in the upstairs apartment emerges from my perplexed contemplation.

I suppose, though, that I am merely a vehicle for all this and that the longing I feel is neither truly mine nor truly abstract, but the intercepted emotion of some unknown third party for whom these emotions, which in me are literary, would be—as Vieira would say—literal. My hurt and anguish come from my imagined feelings, and it is only in my imagination and my sense of otherness that I think and feel this nostalgia, which nevertheless leaves my own eyes awash with tears.

And still, with a constancy born in the depths of the world, with a studied metaphysical persistence, the sound of someone practicing piano scales echoes and re-echoes up and down the physical spine of my memory. It evokes ancient streets thronged by other people, the same streets as today only different; they are the dead speaking to me through the transparent walls of their absence; they are feelings of remorse for what I did or didn't do, the rushing of streams in the night, noises downstairs in the still house.

In my head I feel like screaming. I want to stop, smash, break in two that intangible torturer, that impossible record playing inside my head, in someone else's house. I want to order my soul to stop and let me out, then drive on without me. I grow mad with hearing it. In the end, those notes are me—with my horribly sensitive mind, my skin covered in goose bumps, my nerves on edge—playing scales on the awful, inner piano of memory.

And always, always, as if in some part of my brain that had declared itself independent, the scales still play and play, drifting up to me from below, from above, from what was my first home in Lisbon.

339   [16 Dec 1931]
Today, the man we call the office boy left for his village, for good, they say; today, the same man whom I've come to consider part of

this human company, and therefore part of me and my world, left. When we met by chance in the corridor for the inevitable surprise of our farewells, he shyly reciprocated my embrace and I mustered enough self-control not to cry, as if in my heart, but without my heart's permission, this was what my burning eyes wanted.

Everything that was ours, simply because it was once ours, even those things we merely chanced to live with or see on a daily basis, becomes part of us. It was not the office boy who left today for some place in Galicia unknown to me, it was a part, vital because both visual and human, of the very substance of my life. Today I am diminished, no longer quite the same. The office boy left today.

Everything that happens in the world we live in happens in us. Anything that ceases to exist in the world we see around us, ceases to exist in us. Everything that was, assuming we noticed it when it was there, is torn from us when it leaves. The office boy left today.

As I sit down at the high desk and return to yesterday's accounts, I feel heavier, older, my will weaker. But today's vague tragedy interrupts what should be the automatic process of drawing up accounts with meditations that I have to struggle to suppress. The only way I can find the heart to work is by turning myself, through active inertia, into my own slave. The office boy left today.

Yes, tomorrow or another day or whenever the silent bell of death or departure tolls for me, it will be me who is no longer here, an old copybook to be tidied away into a cupboard under the stairs. Yes, tomorrow, or whenever Fate decrees, what was supposedly me will die. Will I go back to my native village? Who knows where I'll go. Today tragedy is made visible by an absence and made tangible because it barely deserves to be felt. Ah, but the office boy left today.

340 [20 Dec 1931]

I'm almost convinced now that I'm never truly awake. I'm not sure if it's that I don't dream when I live, or don't live when I dream, or if dreaming and living commingle and overlap in me and out of that interpenetration is formed my conscious being.

Sometimes, right in the middle of my active life, when I'm evidently as clear about myself as anyone else is, a strange feeling of doubt enters my imagination; I do not know if I exist, it seems possible to me that I might be someone else's dream; the idea occurs to me, with an almost carnal reality, that I might be a character in a novel, moving through the long waves of someone else's literary style, through the created truth of a great narrative.

I've often noticed that certain characters in novels take on for us an importance that our acquaintances and friends, who talk and listen to us in the real and visible world, could never have. And this thought provokes the dream question: is everything in the whole world just a series of interlocking dreams and novels like smaller boxes fitting inside larger ones—each one inside another—stories within a story, like *The Thousand and One Nights*, unwinding falsely into the eternal dark?

If I think, everything seems absurd to me; if I feel, everything seems strange; if I want, what I want is something in myself. Whenever something happens in me, I realize that it wasn't me it happened to. If I dream, I feel as if someone were writing me; if I feel, it's as if someone were painting me. If I want something, I feel as if I had been put in a cart, like merchandise to be transported, and simply let myself be carried along, rocked by a motion apparently my own, until we reach a place I didn't know I wanted to go to until after I had arrived.

How confusing everything is! Seeing is so superior to thinking, and reading so superior to writing! I may be deceived by what I see, but at least I never think it's mine. What I read may depress me, but at least I'm not troubled by the thought that I wrote it. How painful everything is if we think of it conscious of having the thought, like spiritual beings who have passed through that second evolution of consciousness by which we know that we know! However lovely the day, I can't help thinking like this ... To think or to feel, or is there some third possibility between the sets pushed to the side of the stage? Feelings of tedium brought on by twilight and neglect, fans clicked shut, the weariness of having had to live ...

341 [1931?]

For someone who has, like Dis, raped Proserpina, albeit in dreams, how can the love of some worldly woman ever be anything but a dream?

Like Shelley, I loved Antigone before time was: any temporal love always savored to me of the memory of what I lost.

342 [1931?]

... my hypersensitivity, whether to sensations or merely to the expression of those sensations, or, rather, to the intelligence that exists between the two, and which springs from my intention to express the factitious sensation that exists only in order to be expressed. (Perhaps in me this is merely the mechanism whose sole purpose is to reveal who I am not.)

343 [1931?]

Senhor Vasques. I often find myself mesmerized by Senhor Vasques. What does this man represent to me beyond the chance inconvenience of his being master of my time, of the daylight hours of my life? He treats me well, he always talks to me in a friendly enough manner except on the odd occasion when he's been offhand because of some private worry, but then he was offhand with everyone. So why do I think about him so much? Is he a symbol? A motive force? What is he to me?

Senhor Vasques. I remember him now as I will in the future with the nostalgia I know I will feel for him then. I'll be living quietly in a little house somewhere in the suburbs, enjoying a peaceful existence not writing the book I'm not writing now and, so as to continue not doing so, I will come up with different excuses from the ones I use now to avoid actually confronting myself. Or else I'll be interned in a poorhouse, content with my utter failure, mingling with the riff-raff who believed they were geniuses when in fact they were just beggars with dreams, mixing with the anonymous mass of people who had neither the strength to triumph nor the power to turn their defeats into victories. Wherever I am, I will think nostalgically of my boss Senhor Vasques and the office in Rua dos Douradores, and for me the monotony of my daily life will be like the memory of loves that never came my way and of triumphs that were never to be mine.

Senhor Vasques. I see him from that future perspective as clearly as I see him here today: medium height, thickset, coarse, with his particular limitations and affections, frank and astute, brusque and affable. It isn't only money that marks him out as a boss, you can see it in his slow, hairy hands marked by plump veins like small colored muscles, his neck, strong but not too thick, and his firm, rosy cheeks above the dark, neatly trimmed beard. I see him, see the deliberate but energetic gestures, his eyes reflecting from within his thoughts about the world without. I'm troubled if I displease him and my soul is gladdened by his smile, a broad, human smile, warm as the applause of a large crowd.

Perhaps the reason the ordinary, almost vulgar figure of Senhor Vasques so often tangles with my intelligence and distracts me from myself is simply because there's no one else in my life of greater stature. I think there's some symbolism in all this. I believe, or almost believe, that somewhere in a distant life this man was something more to me than he is today.

Ah, now I understand! Senhor Vasques is Life; Life, monotonous and necessary, commanding and unknowable. This banal man represents the banality of life. On the surface he is everything to me, just as, on the surface, Life is everything to me.

And if the office in the Rua dos Douradores represents Life for me, the fourth-floor room I live in on that same street represents

Art. Yes, Art, living on the same street as Life but in a different room; Art, which offers relief from life without actually relieving one of living, and which is as monotonous as life itself, but in a different way. Yes, for me Rua dos Douradores embraces the meaning of all things, the resolution of all mysteries, except the existence of mysteries themselves, which is something beyond resolution.

344 [1931?]

Only one thing surprises me more than the stupidity with which most men live their lives and that is the intelligence inherent in that stupidity.

To all appearances, the monotony of ordinary lives is horrific. I'm having lunch in this ordinary restaurant and I look over at the cook behind the counter and at the old waiter right next to me, serving me as he has served others here for, I believe, the past thirty years. What are these men's lives like? For forty years the cook has spent nearly all of every day in a kitchen; he has a few breaks; he sleeps relatively little; sometimes he goes back to his village whence he returns unhesitatingly and without regret; he slowly accumulates his slowly earned money, which he does not propose spending; he would fall ill if he had to abandon (for ever) his kitchen for the land he bought in Galicia; he's lived in Lisbon for forty years and he's never even been to the Rotunda, or to the theatre, and only once to the Coliseu (whose clowns still inhabit the inner interstices of his life). He got married, how or why I don't know, has four sons and one daughter and, as he leans out over the counter towards my table, his smile conveys a great, solemn, contented happiness. He isn't pretending, nor does he have any reason to. If he seems happy it's because he really is.

And what about the old waiter who serves me and who, for what must be the millionth time in his career, has just placed a coffee on the table before me? His life is the same as the cook's, the only difference being the four or five yards that separate the kitchen where one works from the restaurant dining room where the other works. Apart from minor differences like having two rather than five children, paying more frequent visits to Galicia, and knowing Lisbon better than the cook (as well as Oporto, where he lived for four years), he is equally contented.

I look again, with real terror, at the panorama of those lives and, just as I'm about to feel horror, sorrow and revulsion for them, I discover that the people who feel no horror or sorrow or revulsion are the very people who have the most right to, the people living those lives. That is the central error of the literary imagination: the idea that other people are like us and must therefore feel like us. Fortunately for humanity, each man is only himself and only the genius is given the ability to be others as well.

In the end, everything is relative. A tiny incident in the street, which draws the restaurant cook to the door, affords him more entertainment than any I might get from the contemplation of the most original idea, from reading the best book or from the most pleasant of useless dreams. And, if life is essentially monotonous, the truth is that he has escaped from that monotony better and more easily than I. He is no more the possessor of the truth than I am, because the truth doesn't belong to anyone; but what he does possess is happiness.

The wise man makes his life monotonous, for then even the tiniest incident becomes something marvelous. After his third lion the lion hunter loses interest in the adventure of the hunt. For my monotonous cook there is something modestly apocalyptic about every street fight he witnesses. To someone who has never been out of Lisbon the tram ride to Benfica is like a trip to the infinite and if, one day, he were to visit Sintra, he would feel as if he had journeyed to Mars. On the other hand, the traveler who has covered the globe can find nothing new for five thousand miles around, because he's always seeing new things; there's novelty and there's the boredom of the eternally new, and the latter brings about the death of the former.

The truly wise man could enjoy the whole spectacle of the world from his armchair; he wouldn't need to talk to anyone or to know how to read, just how to make use of his five senses and a soul innocent of sadness.

One must monotonize existence in order to rid it of monotony. One must make the everyday so anodyne that the slightest incident proves entertaining. In the midst of my day-to-day work, dull, repetitive and pointless, visions of escape surface in me, vestiges of dreams of far-off islands, parties held in the avenues of gardens in some other age, different landscapes, different feelings, a different me. But, between balance sheets, I realize that if I had all that, none of it would be mine. The truth is that Senhor Vasques is worth more than any Dream King; the office in Rua dos Douradores is worth more than all those broad avenues in impossible gardens. Because I have Senhor Vasques I can enjoy the dreams of the Dream Kings; because I have the office in Rua dos Douradores I can enjoy my inner visions of nonexistent landscapes. But if the Dream Kings were mine, what would I have to dream about? If I possessed the impossible landscapes, what would remain of the impossible?

May I always be blessed with the monotony, the dull sameness of identical days, my indistinguishable todays and yesterdays, so that I may enjoy with an open heart the fly that distracts me, drifting randomly past my eyes, the gust of laughter that wafts volubly up from the street somewhere down below, the sense of vast freedom when the office closes for the night, and the infinite leisure of my days off.

Because I am nothing, I can imagine myself to be anything. If I were somebody, I wouldn't be able to. An assistant bookkeeper can imagine himself to be a Roman emperor; the King of England can't do that, because the King of England has lost the ability in his dreams to be any other king than the one he is. His reality does not allow him to exist.

345 [1931?]

Now and then something happens in me, and when it does it usually happens suddenly, a terrible weariness with life imposes itself on all other feelings, a weariness so terrible as to defy all remedy. Suicide seems too uncertain and death, even if one assumes it guarantees oblivion, merely insignificant. What this weariness aspires to is not simply to cease to exist—which might or might not be possible—but, far more horrifying, far deeper than that, it wants never to have existed at all, and that, of course, cannot be.

I have caught occasional hints of something similar to this ambition (which outdoes in negativity even the void itself) in the often confused speculations of the Indians. But either they lack the keenness of feeling that would enable them to explain what they think or the acuity of thought to feel what they feel. The fact is that what I glimpse in them I cannot actually see. More to the point, I believe I am the first to put into words the sinister absurdity of this irremediable feeling.

Yet I exorcize it by writing about it. Provided it comes also from the intellect and isn't just pure emotion, there is no truly deep-seated affliction that won't succumb to the ironic cure of being written about. For the few this might be one of literature's uses, assuming, that is, that it has no other use.

Unfortunately, the suffering of the intellect is less painful than that of the emotions, and that of the emotions, again unfortunately, less than that of the body. I say "unfortunately" because human dignity would naturally demand the opposite. No anguished sense of the mystery of life hurts like love or jealousy or longing, chokes you the way intense physical fear can or transforms you like anger or ambition. But neither can any of the pains that lacerate the soul ever be as real a pain as that of toothache, or colic or (I imagine) childbirth …

We are so constituted that the intelligence that ennobles certain emotions or sensations, and raises them up above others, also downgrades them if it begins to make comparisons between them.

I write like someone asleep, and my whole life is like a receipt awaiting signature.

Inside the chicken coop from whence he will go to be killed, the cock sings hymns to freedom because they gave him two perches all to himself.

346 [1931?]

I would like to be in the countryside simply in order to enjoy being in the city. I always enjoy being in the city, but I would have double the enjoyment were I in the countryside.

347 [1931?]

Direct experience is the subterfuge, the hiding place, of those devoid of imagination. Reading about the risks taken by a hunter of tigers I experience all the risks worth taking, except the risk itself, which was worth so little that it has passed out of existence.

Men of action are the unwitting slaves of men of the intellect. Things only acquire value once they are interpreted. Some men, then, create things in order that others, by giving them meaning, make them live. To narrate is to create, whilst to live is merely to be lived.

348 [1931?]

On such a bright day even the soothing city sounds are pure gold. There's a gentleness about everything that happens. If I were told that war had broken out, I would deny it. On a day like today nothing can trouble that all-pervading gentleness.

349 [1931?]

… the world, a dungheap of instinctive impulses that somehow glitters in the shafts of sunlight, pale gold and dark gold.

As far as I can see, plagues, storms and wars are all products of the same blind force, which sometimes operates through unconscious microbes, sometimes through unconscious lightning bolts and floods, sometimes through unconscious men. I see no difference between an earthquake and a massacre, except in the way that murdering someone with a knife and murdering someone with a dagger can be considered different. The monster immanent in all things is as likely to deploy—to its own advantage or disadvantage, the monster doesn't seem to care which—a boulder falling from on high as a heart suddenly filling up with jealousy or greed. The boulder falls and kills a man; the greed or jealousy puts a weapon in someone's hand, and the hand kills a man. That is how the world is, a dungheap of instinctive impulses, that somehow glitters in the shafts of sunlight, pale gold and dark gold.

The mystics realized that repudiation was the best way of facing down the brutality of indifference, which constitutes the visible basis of things. To deny the world and turn away from it as if from the shore of a lake. To do as Buddha did and deny its absolute reality; to do as Christ did and deny its relative reality too; to deny [...]

All I asked of life was for life to ask nothing of me. At the door of the rustic cabin I never had, I sat in the sun that never shone, and enjoyed the future old age of my weary reality (savoring the pleasure of not yet having reached it). Not yet having died is enough for life's poor wretches, that and still being able to hope [...]

350 [1931?]

We are death. This thing we consider to be life is just the sleep of a real life, the death of what we truly are. The dead are born, they do not die. The two worlds have been switched. When we think we are alive, we are dead; let us live while we are dying.

The relationship between sleep and life is the same as that between what we call life and what we call death. We are sleeping, and this life is a dream, not in a metaphorical or poetic sense, but in a very real sense.

All the activities we consider to be superior participate in death, are death. What is an ideal but an admission that life is not good enough? What is art but the denial of life? A statue is a dead body carved so as to fix death in incorruptible matter. Even pleasure, which appears to be an immersion in life, is, rather, an immersion in ourselves, a destruction of the relationship between us and life, an animated shadow of death.

Living itself is dying, because each day we live means that we have one less day left to live.

We inhabit dreams, we are shadows wandering through impossible forests, in which the trees are houses, habits, ideas, ideals and philosophies.

Never finding God, never even knowing if God exists! Passing from world to world, from incarnation to incarnation, always in the embrace of comforting illusion, always caressed by erroneous belief.

Never reaching the truth, and never stopping! Never finding union with God! Never being entirely at peace, but always clinging to a little sliver of peace and always wanting more!

351 [1931?]

Sometimes, when I least expect it, the suffocating quality of the ordinary takes me by the throat and I feel physically sickened by the voices and gestures of my so-called fellow man. That genuine nausea, felt in my stomach and in my head, is the foolish wonderment of an alert sensibility ... Each individual who speaks to me, each face whose eyes meet mine, has the same impact on me as a direct insult or foul language. I overflow with a horror of everything. I grow dizzy feeling myself feel that.

And almost always, when I feel sick to my stomach like that, a man, or a woman, or even a child, rises before me like a representative of the very banality that afflicts me. They are not representative of any subjective, considered emotion of mine, but of an objective truth which, in its outward shape, conforms to what I feel inside and which arises by some analogical magic to provide me with the example for the general rule I happen to be thinking of.

352

Every day, the broad summer sky would wake up as a dull greenish blue and soon change to a blue that was tinged, first, with gray and then with a muted white. In the west, though, it was the color people usually use to describe the whole sky.

Telling the truth, finding what they hope for, denying that everything is an illusion, how many people resort to such things as the ground sinks and slips away beneath them, and how many famous names mark in capitals, like places on a map, the acute perceptions read on sober pages!

A cosmorama of future events that could never have happened! Lapis lazuli of intermittent emotions! Can you recall how many memories contain some factitious supposition, how many were mere imagination? And in a delirium interspersed with certainties, light, brief, soft, the murmurings of the water in every park spring up, pure emotion, from the depths of my consciousness of me. With no one sitting on the ancient benches, and the paths filled with the melancholy of empty streets.

Night in Heliopolis! Night in Heliopolis! Night in Heliopolis! Who will utter these futile words and compensate me for the blood and the indecision?

353

I don't remember my mother. She died when I was only one year old. If there is anything harsh or disjointed about my sensibility, it has its roots in that absence of warmth and in a vain nostalgia for kisses I cannot even recall. I'm a fraud. I always awoke on other breasts, warmed only obliquely.

Ah, it's the longing for the other person I could have been that unsettles and troubles me. Who would I be now had I but received the affection that wells up naturally from the womb to be bestowed as kisses on a baby's face?

I'm not sure whether my recognition of the human aridity of my heart makes me sad or not. I care more about an adjective than about any real cry from the soul. My master Vieira [...]

But sometimes I'm different and I weep real tears, hot tears, the tears of those who do not have or never had a mother; and my eyes, burning with those dead tears, burn too inside my heart.

Perhaps the nostalgia that comes from never having been someone's son has contributed to my emotional indifference. The person who clasped me to her when I was a child could not truly clasp me to her heart. The one person who could have done that was far away, laid in a tomb—the mother who would have been mine, had Fate wished it so.

They say that later, when told that my mother had been pretty, I said nothing. I was already grown in body and soul but ignorant of emotions, and for me speech was not yet mere information lifted from the inconceivable pages of another's book.

My father, who lived a long way from us, killed himself when I was three and I never knew him. I still don't know why he lived so far away. I never particularly wanted to know. I remember his death as a great cloak of seriousness over the first meals after we heard the news. I remember that every now and then they would look at me and I would look back, in clumsy comprehension. Then I would eat my food more carefully just in case, without my knowing, the others continued to look at me.

Whether I like it or not, in the confused depths of my fatal sensibility I am all these things.

354 [1931?]

Everything is absurd. One man spends his life earning money which he then saves even though he has no children to leave it to nor any hope that a heaven somewhere will offer him a divine reward. Another puts all his efforts into becoming famous so that he will be remembered once dead, yet he does not believe in a survival of the soul that would give him knowledge of that fame. Yet another wears himself out looking for things he doesn't even like. Then there is the man who …

One man reads in order to know, all in vain. Another enjoys himself in order to live, again all in vain.

I'm riding a tram and, as is my habit, slowly absorbing every detail of the people around me. By "detail" I mean things, voices, words. In the dress of the girl directly in front of me, for example, I see the material it's made of, the work involved in making it—since it's a dress and not just material—and I see in the delicate embroidery around the neck the silk thread with which it was embroidered and all the work that went into that. And immediately, as if in a primer on political economy, I see before me the factories and all the different jobs: the factory where the material was made; the factory that made the darker-colored thread that ornaments with curlicues the neck of the dress; and I see the different workshops in the factories, the machines, the workmen, the seamstresses. My eyes' inward gaze even penetrates into the offices, where I see the managers trying to keep calm and the figures set out in the account books, but that's not all: beyond that I see into the domestic lives of those who spend their working hours in these factories and offices … A whole world unfolds before my eyes all because of the regularly irregular dark green edging to a pale green dress worn by the girl in front of me of whom I see only her brown neck.

A whole way of life lies before me.

I sense the loves, the secrets, the souls of all those who worked just so that this woman in front of me on the tram could wear around her mortal neck the sinuous banality of a thread of dark green silk on a background of light green cloth.

I grow dizzy. The seats on the tram, of fine, strong cane, carry me to distant regions, divide into industries, workmen, houses, lives, realities, everything.

I leave the tram exhausted, like a sleepwalker, having lived a whole life.

355

For me, everything that is not my soul is, whether I like it or not, mere scenery, mere decor. Even if I recognize intellectually that a man is a living being like myself, my real, instinctive self has always felt him to be of less importance than a tree, if the tree is more beautiful than him. That is why I have always seen human events—the great collective tragedies of history or what we make of them—as colorful friezes, full of soulless figures. I've never been touched by tragic events in China. It's just a distant backdrop, even if it is one involving blood and plague.

I remember, with ironic sadness, a demonstration held by workers, although I can't vouch for the sincerity of those involved (I always find it hard to admit that anything done collectively can possibly be sincere, since the only truly sentient being is the individual). It was a small, disparate group of animated fools, who marched past my utter indifference shouting slogans. I felt suddenly sick. They weren't even very dirty. Those who really suffer don't form groups, don't go around in a gang. Those who suffer suffer alone.

What a crew! What a lack of humanity and pain! Their very reality made them unconvincing. No one would write a novel about them or even a descriptive scene. They flowed like rubbish down a river, the river of life. I felt sleepy just watching them, I felt both sick and superior.

356

Everything has become unbearable to me, except life—the office, my house, the streets—even their opposite, if such a thing existed—everything overwhelms and oppresses me. Only the totality affords me relief. Yes, any part of it is enough to console me. A ray of sunlight falling endlessly into the dead office; a street cry that soars up to the window of my room; the existence of people, of climates and changes in the weather; the terrifying objectivity of the world ...

Suddenly the ray of sun entered into me, by which I mean that

I suddenly saw it ... It was a bright stripe of almost colorless light cutting like a naked blade across the dark, wooden floor, enlivening everything around it, the old nails and the grooves between the floorboards, black-ruled sheets of nonwhiteness.

For minutes on end I observed the imperceptible effect of the sun penetrating into the still office ... Prison pastimes! Only the imprisoned, with the fascination of someone watching ants, would pay such attention to one shifting ray of sunlight.

357 [1931?]

With the soul's equivalent of a wry smile, I calmly confront the prospect that my life will consist of nothing more than being shut up for ever in Rua dos Douradores, in this office, surrounded by these people. I have enough money to buy food and drink, I have somewhere to live and enough free time in which to dream, write— and sleep—what more can I ask of the gods or hope for from Fate?

I had great ambitions and extravagant dreams, but so did the errand boy and the seamstress, for everyone has dreams; the only difference is whether or not we have the strength to fulfill them or a destiny that will fulfill them through us.

When it comes to dreams, I'm no different from the errand boy and the seamstress. The only thing that distinguishes me from them is that I can write. Yes, that's an activity, a real fact about myself that distinguishes me from them. But in my soul I'm just the same.

I know there are islands in the South and grand cosmopolitan passions and [...]

I'm sure that even if I held the world in my hand, I'd exchange it all for a tram ticket back to Rua dos Douradores.

Perhaps it's my destiny to remain a bookkeeper for ever and for poetry and literature to remain simply butterflies that alight on my head and merely underline my own ridiculousness by their very beauty.

I would miss Moreira, but what does missing someone matter compared with a chance for real promotion?

I know that the day I'm made chief bookkeeper to Vasques & Co. will be one of the greatest days of my life. I know it with a prescient bitterness and irony, but I know it with the intellectual finality that certainty can bring.

358 [1931?]

In flickering intervals a firefly pursues itself. All around, in the darkness, the countryside is a great absence of sound that almost smells good. The peace of it all hurts me and weighs on me. A formless tedium suffocates me.

I don't often go to the country, I hardly ever spend a day there or stay overnight. But today, because the friend in whose house I'm staying would not hear of me declining his invitation, I came, full of misgivings, like a shy man on his way to a big party. But I felt glad when I arrived; I enjoyed the fresh air and the open spaces; I lunched and dined well, but now, at dead of night, sitting in my lampless room, the uncertainty of the place fills me with anxiety.

The window of the room where I'll sleep gives onto the open countryside, onto an indefinite vastness, which is all the fields, onto the great, vaguely starry night where I can feel a silent breeze stirring. Sitting at the window I contemplate with my senses the nothingness of the universal life out there. The hour settles into an uneasy harmony that reigns over all, from the visible invisibility of everything to the wood (on the bleached window ledge on which I rest my left hand) that is slightly rough to the touch where the old paint has blistered.

How often, though, have my eyes longed for this peace from which now, were it easy or polite, I would flee! How often, down there among the narrow streets of tall houses, have I thought I believed that peace, prose and certainty could be found here, among natural things, rather than where the tablecloth of civilization makes one forget the varnished pine it rests on! And now, here, feeling healthy and healthily tired, I am ill at ease, trapped and homesick.

I don't know if it's only to me that this happens or to everyone for whom civilization has meant being reborn. But it seems that for me, or for people who feel as I do, the artificial has come to seem natural and the natural strange. No, that's not quite it: the artificial has not become natural; the natural has simply become different. I detest and could happily do without cars and the other products of science—telephones and telegrams—that make life easy, or the by-products of fantasy—gramophones and radios—which, to those who like them, make life fun.

I'm not interested in any of that; I want none of it. But I love the Tejo because of the great city on its banks. I enjoy the sky because I see it from a fourth-floor window in a street in the Baixa. Nothing in the countryside or in nature can give me anything to equal the ragged majesty of the calm moonlit city seen from Graça or São Pedro de Alcântara. For me no flowers can match the endlessly varied colors of Lisbon in the sunlight.

Only people who wear clothes find the naked body beautiful. The overriding value of modesty for sensuality is that it acts as a brake on energy.

Artificiality is a way of enjoying naturalness. What I enjoyed about these vast fields I enjoyed because I don't live here. Someone who has never known constraint can have no concept of freedom.

Civilization is an education in nature. The artificial provides an approach to the natural.

What we must never do, however, is mistake the artificial for the natural.

In the harmony between the natural and the artificial lies the essence of the superior human soul.

Nothing grates more on me than the vocabulary of moral intent and social responsibility. For a start, I find the word "duty" as disagreeable as an intruder into my home. And as for the terms "civic duty," "solidarity," "humanitarianism" and others of the same ilk, they are as repellent to me as a pile of rubbish that someone threw out of a window on top of me. What I find offensive is the implicit supposition that these expressions apply to me, that I find them not just valuable, but meaningful.

Not long ago, I saw something in a toy-shop window that reminded me of precisely those expressions: pretend plates full of pretend food for a doll's house. What does a real man, sensual, egotistical, vain, who wins friends because he has the gift of the gab and makes enemies because he has the gift of life, what does he have to gain from playing at dolls with those empty, hollow words?

Government is based on two things: restraint and deceit. The trouble with those sequined terms is that they neither restrain nor deceive. At most, they intoxicate, and that's quite a different matter.

If there is one thing I loathe, it's a reformer. A reformer is a man who sees the superficial ills of the world and proposes curing them by making the more deep-seated ills still worse. A doctor tries to adapt a sick body to a healthy one, but in society we don't know what is healthy and what is sick.

I see humanity as one of those fashionable schools of painting that favor decorative art painted *en plein air.* Basically, I cannot tell a man from a tree; in fact, I prefer whichever one is more decorative, more interesting to my thinking eyes. If I found the tree more interesting, I would grieve more over that tree being felled than over the man dying. There are fading sunsets that touch me more than the deaths of children. In order that I can feel, I always keep my own feelings to myself.

I feel almost guilty to be writing these semi-reflections at this late-afternoon hour when a light breeze is beginning to get up, taking on color as it does. No, not taking on color, it isn't the breeze that's doing that, it's the air on which it so hesitantly floats; but since it seems to me that it is the breeze taking on color, that is what I say, because, given that I am I, I have to say how it seems to me.

360 [1931?]

(Written at intervals and much in need of emendation)

Once the last stars had paled into nothingness in the morning sky and the breeze that blew in the slightly orange-yellow light falling on the few low clouds had grown less cold, I could at last, still not yet having slept, slowly raise my body (exhausted after doing nothing) from the bed from which I imagined the universe.

I went over to the window, my eyelids burning from not having closed all night. Among the crowded rooftops the light was experimenting with different shades of pale yellow. I stood there looking at everything with the great stupidity brought on by lack of sleep. On the erect masses of the tall houses the yellow was airy, barely perceptible. Far off in the west, towards which I was turned, the horizon was already a greenish white.

I know today is going to be tedious for me, as tedious as one's inability to understand something. I know that everything I do today will be infected not by the weariness brought on by lack of sleep, but by tonight's insomnia. I know that my customary state of somnambulism will be even more marked, even nearer the surface, not just because I didn't sleep, but because I couldn't sleep.

Some days are like whole philosophies in themselves that suggest to us new interpretations of life, marginal notes full of the acutest criticism in the book of our universal destiny. I feel that this is one such day. The foolish thought strikes me that my heavy eyes and my empty head are the absurd pencil shaping the letters of that futile and profound statement.

361 [1931?]

The greater the sensibility and the more subtle the capacity to feel, the more absurdly one trembles and quivers at the small things. It requires prodigious intelligence to be reduced to anguish by a day of lowering skies. Humanity, which is not very sensitive, doesn't get upset by the weather, because the weather is always with us; humanity only feels the rain when it's actually falling on its head.

It's a soft, dull day of humid heat. Alone in the office, I review my life, and what I see is like this day which oppresses and afflicts me. I remember myself as a child made happy by anything, as an adolescent with a hundred ambitions, as a man with no joy and no ambition. And all this happened softly, dully like the day that makes me see or remember it.

Which of us, turning to look back down the road along which there is no return, could say that we had walked that road as we should have?

362 [1931?]

I've always felt an almost physical repugnance for secret things—intrigues, diplomacy, secret societies, occultism. I find those last two things particularly unsettling—the way certain men arrogantly believe that, by reaching an understanding with Gods or Masters or Demiurges, they will discover—keeping their discovery to themselves, of course, and excluding the rest of us—the great secrets that are the very foundations of this world.

I can't believe that to be true, but I can believe that someone else might. Are all those people mad, deluded? Just because there are a lot of them proves nothing; there are such things as collective hallucinations.

What I find most shocking about those teachers and connoisseurs of the invisible is that, when they write about and describe their mysteries, they write really badly. It offends me that a man can master the Devil, but not the Portuguese language. Why should tackling devils be easier than tackling grammar? Why is it that, after all those prolonged exercises in concentration and willpower, someone can, or so he says, experience astral visions, but cannot, with far less investment of concentration and willpower, have a clear vision of syntax? What is it in the dogma and ritual of the Magical Arts that prevents someone from writing, not necessarily clearly, because obscurity may be part of the occult law, but at least elegantly and fluently, which is perfectly possible even when writing about abstruse subjects? Why spend all your soul's energy on studying the language of the Gods, and not have a tiny bit of energy left over with which to study the color and rhythm of the language of mankind?

I distrust teachers who cannot teach the most basic things. For me, they are like those strange poets who are incapable of writing like everyone else. I can accept that they are strange, but I would like them to prove to me that they are strange because they are superior to the norm rather than because they lack the ability to be otherwise.

People say there are great mathematicians who make mistakes when doing simple addition, but this isn't a matter of making mistakes, it's sheer ignorance. I can accept that a great mathematician might make two and two equal five; that could happen to anyone when distracted. What I cannot accept is that he didn't know what adding up was or how to do it. And that is the case with the vast majority of these teachers of the occult.

363 [1931?]

The idea of traveling makes me feel physically sick.

I've already seen everything I've never seen.
I've already seen everything I haven't yet seen.

The tedium of the constantly new, the tedium of discovering, beneath the transitory difference of things and ideas, the perennial sameness of everything, the absolute similarity between a mosque, a temple and a church, the absolute equivalence between a cabin and a castle, the same physical body in a king in all his finery and a naked savage, the eternal concordance of life with itself, the stagnation of everything that lives despite the constant changes to which it is eternally condemned.

Landscapes are repetitions. On an ordinary train journey, I divide myself pointlessly and nervously between not looking at the landscape and not looking at the book that would be keeping me amused if I were someone else. Life already gives me a vague sense of nausea, and movement only aggravates that.

The only nontedious landscapes and books are landscapes that don't exist and books I will never read. For me, life is a somnolence that does not affect the brain. I keep that free as a place in which to be sad.

Leave traveling to those who don't exist! Presumably for someone who is nothing, life, like a river, is a simple matter of flowing ever onwards. For those who think and feel, those who are awake, the ghastly experience of sitting on a train, in a car or in a ship lets them neither sleep nor wake.

I return from any journey, however short, as if from a sleep full of dreams—in a state of torpid confusion, with all my sensations glued together, drunk on what I have seen.

I can't rest because my soul is sick. I can't move because there's something lacking between body and soul; it's not movement I lack, but the desire to move.

I've often wanted to cross the river, the ten minutes it takes to go from Terreiro do Paço to Cacilhas. And I have almost always felt rather overcome by all those people, by myself and by my decision to go. I've made the journey a couple of times, and felt terrified all the way there and back and thrilled when I step onto dry land again on my return.

When one feels too intensely, the Tejo is an endless Atlantic, and Cacilhas another continent or even another universe.

364   [1931?]

You want to travel? To travel you simply need to exist. In the train of my body or of my destiny I travel from day to day, as from station to station, leaning out to look at the streets and the squares, at gestures and faces, always the same and always different as, ultimately, is the way with all landscapes.

If I imagine something, I see it. What more would I do if I traveled? Only extreme feebleness of imagination can justify anyone needing to travel in order to feel.

"Any road, this simple road to Entepfuhl, will take you to the end of the world." But the end of the world, once you've exhausted the world by going round it, is the same Entepfuhl from which you set out. In fact the end of the world, and its beginning, is merely our concept of the world. It is only within us that landscapes become landscapes. That's why if I imagine them, I create them; if I create them, they exist; if they exist, I see them just as I do other landscapes. So why travel? In Madrid, in Berlin, in Persia, in China, at the North and South Poles, where would I be other than inside myself, feeling my particular kind of feelings?

Life is whatever we make it. The traveler is the journey. What we see is not what we see but who we are.

365   [1931?]

Lucidly, slowly, piece by piece, I reread everything I have written. And I find it all worthless and feel it would have been better never to have written it. The very fact of completing or achieving anything, be it an empire or a sentence, contains what is worst about all real things: our knowledge that they will perish. But, as I slowly reread these pages, that isn't what I feel or what hurts me about what I've created. What hurts me is that it wasn't worth doing, and that all I gained from the time I wasted is the now shattered illusion that it was worth doing.

In seeking anything, we do so out of ambition, but we either fail to achieve that ambition and are the poorer, or we think we have achieved it and are merely rich madmen.

What hurts me is that even the best of it is bad and that someone else (if he existed and of whose existence I dream) would have done it better. Everything we do, in art and life, is the imperfect copy of what we intended. It betrays both external and internal ideals of perfection; it fails not only our concept of what it should have been, but also of what it could have been. We are hollow inside and out, pariahs of anticipation and promise.

Where did I find the strength in my solitary soul to write page after lonely page, to live out syllable by syllable the false magic not of what I was writing but of what I imagined I was writing? What spell of ironic witchery led me to believe myself the poet of my own prose, in the winged moment in which it was born in me, faster than my pen could write, like a sly revenge on life's insults! And rereading it today I watch my precious dolls ripped apart, see the straw burst out of them and see them scattered without ever having been ...

366 [1931?]

Everything about me is fading away. My whole life, my memories, my imagination and its contents, my personality, it's all fading away. I continually feel that I was someone else, that I felt and thought as another. I am present at a play with different scenery and the drama I watch is me.

Sometimes amidst the accumulated banality of my literary work stored randomly in various desk drawers, I come across things I wrote ten or even fifteen or more years ago. And many of them seem to me to have been written by a stranger; I don't recognize myself in them. Someone wrote them and it was me. It was me who felt them, but in another life from which I have now awoken as if from another's dream.

I often find things written by me when I was still very young, passages I wrote when I was seventeen or twenty years old. And some of them have a power of expression I do not remember having at that age. Certain phrases, certain sentences written when I was barely out of adolescence, seem the product of who I am now, educated by the passing years and by experience. I realize that I am the same as I was. And, having often thought that to get to where I am now I must have progressed a lot from what I was, I wonder in what that progress consists if I was the same then as I am now.

There's a mystery in this that undermines and oppresses me.

Only a few days ago I came across a short text written years ago, which really shook me. I know perfectly well that my (relative) scrupulousness about language dates from only a few years back, yet I found in a drawer a piece I had written long before, which was remarkable for this same linguistic scrupulousness. I genuinely could not understand that past self. How is it that I have advanced only to become what I already was? How could I know myself today when I did not yesterday? And everything becomes lost in a labyrinth in which I lose myself.

I let my thoughts drift and feel convinced that what I'm writing now I have already written. I remember and I ask the part of me that pretends to be me if there is not in the Platonic view of the senses another more oblique recollection, another memory of a previous life that is in fact this life ...

Dear God, who is this person I attend on? How many people am I? Who is me? What is this gap that exists between me and myself?

367 [1931?]

Once, I found a passage of mine written in French some fifteen years ago. I've never been to France and never had close contact with the French, and since I never practiced the language I could not, therefore, be said to have become unpracticed in it. Today I read as much French as ever. I'm older, more experienced; I should have progressed. And yet that passage from my far-off past has a sureness of touch in its use of French that I do not have today; the style has a fluidity I could not now reproduce in that language; there are whole paragraphs, whole sentences and turns of phrase, that demonstrate a fluency I have lost without even knowing I had it. How can one explain this? Whose place have I usurped within myself?

I know it's easy enough to come up with a theory of the fluidity of things and souls, to understand that we are an inner flow of life, to imagine that we are many, that we merely pass through ourselves, that we have been many people ... But there's something else going on here which is not the mere flowing of the personality between its own banks: there is here the absolute other, an alien being that was mine. That I should lose, as I grow older, imagination, emotion, a certain type of intelligence, a way of feeling, all that, whilst painful, would not shock me. But what is happening to me when I can read what I wrote as if it were written by a stranger? What shore can I be standing on that allows me to look down and see my own self at the bottom of the sea?

On other occasions I've found passages I can't remember having written, which is not so surprising, but to be unable to remember even having been capable of writing something, that terrifies me. Certain phrases belong to another way of thinking altogether. It's as if I had found an old portrait, clearly of myself, yet showing someone of a different stature, with unrecognizable features that are still indisputably, frighteningly mine.

368 [1931?]

Yesterday I saw and heard a great man.* I don't mean someone who is merely considered to be a great man, but a man who truly is. He has value, if there is such a thing in this world; other people know that and he knows they know. He therefore fulfills all the necessary conditions that allow me to call him a great man. And indeed that is what I do call him.

Physically he looks like a worn-out businessman. The signs of weariness on his face could as easily come from leading an unhealthy life as from thinking too much. His gestures are utterly unremarkable. There's a certain sparkle in his eyes—the privilege

---

* On the back of the sheet of paper is written the name "Jaeger," the name of Aleister Crowley's lover, Hanni Larissa Jaeger. Could he be "the great man"?

of one not afflicted with myopia. His voice is a little slurred as if a general paralysis were beginning to attack that particular manifestation of his soul, a soul that expressed views on party politics, the devaluation of the escudo and the more despicable aspects of his colleagues in greatness.

Had I not known who he was, I would never have guessed from his appearance. I know perfectly well that one should not succumb to the heroic ideas about great men that appeal to simple people: that a great poet should have Apollo's body and Napoleon's face or, rather less demanding, that he be a man of distinction with an expressive face. I know that such ideas are absurd, if natural, human foibles. However, it is not unreasonable to expect some sign of greatness. And when one moves from physical appearance to consider the utterances of the soul, whilst one can do without spirit and vivacity, one does expect intelligence with at least a trace of grandeur.

All this, all these human disappointments, make us question the truth of what is vulgarly called inspiration. It would seem that this body destined to be that of a businessman and this soul destined to be that of a man of culture are mysteriously invested with an outer and an inner quality respectively and, though they do not speak, something speaks through them and that voice utters words which, if said by the body or the soul alone, would be falsehoods.

But these are just vain, indolent speculations. I almost regret having indulged in them. I've neither diminished the value of the man nor improved his physical appearance by my remarks. The truth is that nothing changes anything and what we say or do only brushes the tops of the mountains in whose valleys all things sleep.

369 [1931?]
We strolled, still young, beneath the tall trees and the vaguely whispering forest. In the clearings that emerged suddenly along the path, the moon created lakes, and the tangled shores of those lakes were darker than the darkest night. The warm breeze of great

forests breathed softly about us. We talked of impossible things; and our voices were part of the night, the moonlight and the forest. We heard them as if they belonged to someone else.

That mysterious forest was not entirely without paths. There were trails which somehow we knew, and we walked uncertainly along them among the dappled shadows and the shafts of cold, hard moonlight. We were talking of impossible things, and that whole real landscape was equally impossible.

370   [1931?]

The farther we advance in life, the more we become convinced of two contradictory truths. The first is that, confronted by the reality of life, all the fictions of literature and art pale into insignificance. Though it's true that the latter afford us a nobler pleasure than life, in fact they are like dreams in which we experience feelings never felt in life and that conjure up shapes never seen; they are just dreams from which one awakens, not memories or nostalgic longings with which we might later live a second life.

The second is this: every noble soul wishes to live life to the full, to experience everything and every feeling, to know every corner of the earth and, given that this is impossible, life can only be lived to the full subjectively, only lived in its entirety once renounced.

These two truths are mutually irreducible. The wise man will refrain from trying to conflate them and will also refrain from repudiating one or other of them. He will, however, have to choose one and then live with his regret at not having chosen the other, or else reject both, and rise above himself to some personal nirvana.

Happy the man who demands no more from life than what life spontaneously gives him and who guides himself with the instinct of cats who seek the sun when there is sun and, when there is no sun, find what warmth they can. Happy the man who renounces his life in favor of the imagination and finds pleasure in the contemplation of other people's lives, experiencing not the impressions themselves but the external spectacle of those impressions. Happy the man, then, who renounces everything and from whom, therefore, nothing can be taken or subtracted.

The rustic, the reader of novels, the pure ascetic: these three are the truly happy men, because they have all renounced their personality—the first because he lives by instinct, which is impersonal, the second because he lives through his imagination, which is oblivion, and the third because he does not live and, not yet having died, sleeps.

Nothing satisfies me, nothing consoles me, everything—whether or not it has ever existed—satiates me. I neither want my soul nor wish to renounce it. I desire what I do not desire and renounce what I do not have. I can be neither nothing nor everything: I'm just the bridge between what I do not have and what I do not want.

371 [1931]

What do I care if no one reads what I write? I write to distract myself from living, and I publish because those are the rules of the game. If, tomorrow, all my writings were lost, I would feel sad, but I really don't think I would feel the mad, violent grief you might expect given that my whole life is contained in these writings. Is it not true that a mother, months after her child has died, can laugh again and be her old self? The great earth, which takes care of the dead, would also take care of my papers, albeit rather less maternally. Nothing matters, and there would, I think, have been those who would have had little patience with that child when awake and who would have longed for the peace and quiet that would reign when the child finally went to bed.

372 [1931?]

… the imaginative episode we call reality.

It's been raining for two days now and the rain that falls from the cold, gray sky is of a color that grieves the soul. Two days … I'm sad from too much feeling and reflect this back onto the window to the sound of water dripping and rain falling. My heart feels heavy and all my memories have turned to anguish. I'm not sleepy, nor is there any reason for me to feel sleepy, but I nevertheless feel a great desire to sleep. Once, when I was a child and happy, the voice of a brightly colored green parrot used to live in the neighboring courtyard. On rainy days, it never grew sad, but would transmit, doubtless from the shelter of its cage, some kind of constant feeling, which would hover in the gloom like a gramophone before its time.

What made me think of that parrot now? Because I'm feeling sad and my far-off childhood reminds me of it? No, I thought of it because, right now, from the courtyard on the borders of this present moment, I can hear the voice of a parrot calling out incomprehensible words.

Everything becomes mixed up in me. When I think I have remembered something, I'm actually thinking something else; if I look, I see nothing, yet when distracted, I see everything clearly.

I turn my back on the gray window, on the glass panes cold to the touch, and, by some trick of the penumbra, I carry with me the interior of the old house where, in the nearby courtyard, a parrot used to call; and my eyes close sleepily on the irreparable fact of having actually lived.

373 [1931?]

The wretchedness of my condition is in no way affected by the words I am writing, and out of which I am shaping, little by little, this random book of thoughts. I subsist, a mere nothing, at the bottom of all expression, like an indissoluble powder at the bottom of a glass that contained only water. I write my literature just as I write my entries in the accounts ledger—with careful indifference. Faced by the vast, starry sky and the enigma of so many souls, faced by the night of the unknown abyss and the chaos of utter ignorance—faced by all this, what I write in the ledger and what I write on this paper soul of mine remains stuck fast here in

Rua dos Douradores, and has little to do with the great millionaire expanses of the universe.

All this is pure dream and phantasmagoria, and it matters little whether the dream is an entry in an accounts ledger or a piece of superb prose. What is the point of dreaming about princesses rather than the door to the office? Everything we know is merely our impression, and everything we are is merely someone else's impression of us, a personal melodrama in which we are conscious of being our own spectators, our own gods, by kind permission of the local council.

374 [1931?]

Opportunity is like money, which is, in fact, neither more nor less than an opportunity. For those who act, opportunity is a thing of the will, and I'm not interested in the will. For someone like me, who never acts, opportunity is a song no sirens sing. It should be voluptuously scorned and put away somewhere high up as being of no use.

To have a chance ... This is the spot where they will erect a statue to renunciation.

O broad, sunlit fields, the spectator for whom you alone exist is contemplating you from the shade.

The alcohol of grand words and long sentences, which, like waves, rise with their rhythmic breathing and fall again smiling, ironic snakes of foam in the sad magnificence of the dark night.

375 [17 Jan 1932]

The world belongs to the unfeeling. The essential condition for being a practical man is the absence of any sensitivity. The most important quality in everyday life is that which leads to action, that is, a strong will. Now there are two things that get in the way of action—sensitivity and analytical thought, which is, after all, nothing more than thought plus sensitivity. By its very nature, all action is the projection of the personality onto the external world, and since the external world is very largely made up of other human beings, it follows that any such projection of the personality will involve crossing someone else's path and bothering, hurting or trampling on others, depending on how one acts.

An inability to imagine other people's personalities, their pains and joys, is, therefore, essential if one is to act. He who sympathizes is lost. The man of action considers the external world as being made up exclusively of inert matter, either inert in itself, like a stone that one either steps over or kicks to the side of the road, or like a human being who, unable to resist the man of action, might just as well be a stone since he, too, will be stepped over or kicked to one side.

The epitome of the practical man is the strategist, because he combines extreme concentration of action with a sense of self-importance. All life is war, and battle is, therefore, the very synthesis of life. The strategist is a man who plays with life the way a chess player plays with chess pieces. What would happen to the strategist if, with each move made, he thought of the darkness he cast on a thousand homes and the pain he caused in three thousand hearts? What would become of the world if we were human? If man really felt, there would be no civilization. Art serves as an outlet for the sensitivity that action had to leave behind. Art is the Cinderella who stayed at home because that's how it had to be.

Every man of action is essentially positive and optimistic because those who don't feel are happy. You can tell a man of action because he's never in a bad mood. The man who works despite his bad mood is a subsidiary of action; in life, in life as a whole, he might well be a bookkeeper, as in my particular case. What he won't be is a ruler of things or men. Leadership requires insensitivity. Only the happy govern, because to be sad it is necessary to feel.

My boss Vasques made a deal today which ruined a sick man and his family. While making the deal, he completely forgot about the existence of that individual except as a commercial rival. Once the deal was done, his sensitivity flooded back—afterwards, of course, because had it happened before, the deal would never have been done. "I feel really sorry for the chap," he said to me. "He'll be destitute." Then, lighting a cigar, he added: "Well, if he needs anything from me"—meaning some kind of handout—'I won't forget that, thanks to him, I've made a good deal and a few thousand escudos.'

Vasques is not a bandit; he's a man of action. The man who lost the move in this particular game could, in fact, rely on him for help in the future, because Vasques is a generous man.

Vasques is the same as all men of action: captains of industry and commerce, politicians, men of war, religious and social idealists, great poets and artists, beautiful women, spoilt children. The person who feels nothing has the whip hand. The winner is the one who thinks only those thoughts that will bring him victory. The rest, the vague world of humanity in general, amorphous, sensitive, imaginative and fragile, are nothing but the backdrop before which these actors strut until the puppet show is over, the checkered board on which the chess pieces stand until they're put away by the one Great Player, who, deluding himself that he has a partner, never plays against anyone but himself.

376 [26 Jan 1932]

One of my constant preoccupations is trying to understand how it is that other people exist, how it is that there are souls other than mine and consciousnesses not my own, which, because it is a consciousness, seems to me unique. I understand perfectly that the man before me uttering words similar to mine and making the same gestures I make, or could make, is in some way my fellow creature. However, I feel just the same about the people in illustrations I dream up, about the characters I see in novels or the dramatis personae on the stage who speak through the actors representing them.

I suppose no one truly admits the existence of another person. One might concede that the other person is alive and feels and thinks like oneself, but there will always be an anonymous element of difference, a perceptible discrepancy, that one cannot quite put one's finger on. There are figures from times past, fantasy images in books, that seem more real to us than these specimens of indifference-made-flesh who speak to us across the counters of bars, or catch our eye in trams, or brush past us in the empty randomness of the streets. The others are just part of the landscape for us, usually the invisible landscape of a familiar street.

I feel closer ties and more intimate bonds with certain characters in books, with certain images I've seen in engravings, than with many supposedly real people, with that metaphysical absurdity known as "flesh and blood." In fact "flesh and blood" describes them very well: they resemble cuts of meat laid out on the butcher's marble slab, dead creatures bleeding as though still alive, the sirloin steaks and cutlets of Fate.

I'm not ashamed to feel this way because I know it's how everyone feels. The lack of respect between men, the indifference that allows them to kill others without compunction (as murderers do) or without thinking that they are killing (as soldiers do), comes from the fact that no one pays due attention to the apparently abstruse idea that other people have souls too.

On certain days, at certain times, with an awareness wafted to me on some unknown breeze, revealed to me by the opening of some secret door, I am suddenly conscious that the grocer on the corner is a spiritual being, that his assistant at the door, bending down over a sack of potatoes, truly is a soul capable of suffering.

Yesterday, when they told me that the assistant in the tobacconist's had committed suicide, I couldn't believe it. Poor lad, so he existed too! We had all forgotten that, all of us; we who knew him only about as well as those who didn't know him at all. We'll forget him more easily tomorrow. But what is certain is that he had a soul, enough soul to kill himself. Passions? Worries? Of course. But for me, and for the rest of humanity, all that remains is the memory of a foolish smile above a grubby woollen jacket that didn't fit properly at the shoulders. That is all that remains to me of someone who felt deeply enough to kill himself, because, after all, there's no other reason to kill oneself … I remember thinking once, when I was buying some cigarettes from him, that he would probably go prematurely bald. In the event, he didn't have time to go bald. But that's just a memory I have of him. But what other memory is likely to remain of him, if my memory is not in fact of him but of a thought I had?

I have a sudden vision of the corpse, of the coffin they placed him in, of the alien grave to which they must have carried him. And I see that in a way, badly cut jacket and all, the tobacconist's assistant represents all humanity.

The vision lasted only a moment. Today, of course, being merely human, I think only that he died. Nothing more.

No, other people don't exist … It is for me alone that the setting sun holds out its heavy wings of harsh, misty colors. It is for me alone, even though I can't see its waters flowing, that the wide river glitters beneath the sunset. It is for me alone that this open square was built looking out over the river and its turning tide. Was it today that the tobacconist's assistant was buried in a common grave? Today's sunset is not for him. But, even as I'm thinking this, quite against my will I suddenly understand that it also ceased to be for me …

377   [29 Jan 1932]

Once the last heat of summer had relented and given way to a mellower sun, the autumn started—even before it was properly upon us—with a slight, long, undefined sadness, as if the sky had lost the will to smile. It was sometimes pale blue, sometimes almost green, but always tenuous even where the color was at its most intense; there was a kind of sluggishness about the clouds in their different shades of faded purples; now, filling the whole still desolation across which the clouds drifted, there was a feeling of tedium, not torpor.

The start of autumn was signaled by a genuine chill in the not-yet-cold air, by a fading of whatever colors had remained unfaded, by the appearance of a hint of shadow and absence that had not been there before in the tone of landscapes and the blurred aspect of things. Nothing was dying yet, but everything, as if with a smile as yet unsmiled, looked longingly back at life.

Then, at last, the real autumn arrived: the air was cooled by winds; the leaves spoke in dry tones even before they had withered and died; the whole earth took on the color and impalpable form of a treacherous marshland. What had been a last faint smile faded with a weary drooping of eyelids, in gestures of indifference. And so everything that feels, or that we imagine as having feelings, clasped its own farewell close to its breast. The sound of a gust of wind in a hallway floated across our awareness of something else. One longed, in order truly to feel life, to be a patient convalescing from an illness.

But, coming as they did in the midst of this clear autumn, the first winter rains almost disrespectfully washed away these half tints. Amidst the occasional exclamatory bursts of rain, high winds unleashed distracted words of anonymous protest, sad, almost angry sounds of soulless despair, whistling around whatever was motionless, tugging at whatever was fixed and dragging with them anything movable.

And at last, in cold and grayness, autumn ended. It was a wintry autumn that came now, a dust finally become mud, but it brought with it what is good about the winter cold, with the harsh summer over, the spring to come and the autumn finally giving way to winter. And in the sky above, where the dull colors had lost all memory of heat or sadness, everything was set for night and an indefinite period of meditation.

That was how I saw it without recourse to thinking. I write it down today because I remember it. The autumn I have is the autumn I lost.

My head and the whole universe ache. By some spiritual reflex, physical aches and pains, more obvious than moral ones, unleash tragedies they themselves do not contain. They express an impatience with everything, everything, including the whole universe down to the very last star.

I never take communion, I never have. Neither, I suppose, will I ever be able to partake of that bastardized concept according to which we, as souls, are consequences of a material thing called the brain that exists from birth inside another material thing called the cranium. I cannot be a materialist, which is, I believe, what that concept implies, because I cannot establish a clear link—a visual link I mean—between a visible mass of gray or any other colored matter and the "I" which, from behind my eyes, sees the skies and ponders them and imagines other nonexistent skies. But, even though I could never fall into the trap of supposing that one thing is the same as another simply because the two things exist in the same place, like a wall and my shadow falling on it, or of assuming that a relationship between the soul and the brain is any more logical than a relationship between me, on my journey to work, and the vehicle in which I travel, I still believe there is an intimate relationship between what is pure spirit in us and what is body and that this can give rise to disputes between them. These disputes are like those in which the more vulgar of two parties starts pestering the less vulgar one.

My head aches today, an ache originating perhaps in my stomach. But the ache, once suggested by my stomach to my head, will interrupt any meditations going on behind the fact of my having a brain. If someone covers my eyes, he may temporarily prevent me seeing, but he does not blind me. And yet now, because my head aches, I find the present monotonous and absurd spectacle of the world outside me so completely lacking in value or nobility that I can scarcely conceive of it as being the world. My head aches, which means that I am conscious of an offence against me on the part of the material world and because, like all offences, it upsets me, I feel predisposed to being bad-tempered with everyone, including the person nearest me, even though it was not he who offended me.

My one desire is to die, at least temporarily, but this, as I said, is only because I have a headache. In this moment I suddenly think how much more nobly one of the great prose writers would put all this. Phrase by phrase, he would unwrap the anonymous pain of the world; inspired paragraphs would appear before his eyes that would conjure up all earthly human dramas and, out of the pounding of his fevered temples, he would construct a whole metaphysics of misfortune. I, however, lack all stylistic nobility. My head aches because it does. The universe hurts me because my head does. But the universe that really hurts me is not the real one, which exists because it does not know I exist, but my very own universe, which, if I run my fingers through my hair, seems to make me feel that each hair on my head suffers only in order to make me suffer.

379 [c. 5 Feb 1932]

What I feel above all else is weariness and the disquiet that is the twin of weariness when it has no reason to exist other than the fact of existence itself. I feel a deep dread of gestures as yet unmade, an intellectual timidity about words as yet unspoken. Everything seems doomed in advance to insignificance.

The unbearable tedium of all these faces, foolish with intelligence or the lack of it, grotesque to the point of nausea in their happiness or unhappiness, horrific in the mere fact of their existence, a separate tide of living things quite alien to me ...

380 [16 Mar 1932]

Months have gone by since I last wrote anything. My understanding has lain dormant and I have lived as if I were someone else. I've often had a sense of vicarious happiness. I haven't existed, I have been someone else and lived unthinkingly.

Today, suddenly, I returned to what I am or what I dream I am. It was in a moment of great weariness that came upon me after completing some fairly meaningless task. I rested my head on my hands, with my elbows on the high, sloping desk. Then, closing my eyes, I found myself again.

In the remoteness of that false sleep I remembered everything I had been; suddenly, with all the clarity of a real landscape, there rose before me the long wall of the old farm and then, in the midst of that vision, I saw the empty threshing-floor.

I had an immediate sense of the meaninglessness of life. Seeing, feeling, remembering, forgetting were all one, all mixed up with a slight ache in my elbows, the fragmented murmurings from the street below and the faint sounds of steady work going on in the quiet office.

When I rested my hands on the desk again and glanced round with what must have been the terrible weariness of worlds long dead, the first thing my eyes saw was a bluebottle perched on my inkwell (so that was where the vague buzzing extraneous to the other office noises came from!). Anonymous and watchful, I regarded it from the pit of the abyss. Its lustrous green and blue-black tones were oddly repellent, but not ugly. It was a life!

Perhaps there are supreme forces, the gods or devils of the Truth in whose shadows we wander, for whom I am just a lustrous fly resting for a moment before their gaze. A facile observation? A clichéd remark? Unconsidered philosophy? Perhaps, except that I did not just think it: I felt it. It was directly, with my own flesh, and with an obscure sense of horror that I made this laughable comparison. When I compared myself to the fly I was a fly. I felt myself to be a fly when I imagined I felt it. And I felt I had a fly's soul, I went to sleep as a fly, I felt myself trapped in a fly's body. And the most horrific part was that at the same time I was myself. Involuntarily I looked up at the ceiling to check there was no supreme being wielding a ruler to squash me just as I could squash that fly. Fortunately, when I looked again, the fly, noiselessly, it seemed, had disappeared. Quite against its will, the office was once more bereft of all philosophy.

381 [28 Mar 1932]

Hovering over the surface of my weariness is that same golden light you see on water as the setting sun abandons it. I see myself and that imagined lake, and what I see in that lake is myself. I don't know how to explain that image or that symbol or that "I" I imagine myself to be. But I'm sure that I do see, as if I really could see it, a sun sinking behind the hills, casting a dying light on the lake that receives it in the form of dark gold.

One of the dangers of thinking is seeing while you are thinking. Those who think with their reason tend to be distracted. Those who think with their emotions are sleeping. Those who think with their will are dead. I, however, think with my imagination, and everything in me that should be reason or sorrow or impulse is reduced inside me to something distant and indifferent, like that dead lake set among rocks over which hovers the last lingering ray of sun.

Because I stopped, the waters trembled. Because I thought, the sun withdrew. I close my slow eyes full of sleep, and there is nothing inside me but a lacustrine region where the night is beginning to cease to be day in a dark brown pool of waters on whose surface green weeds float.

Because I wrote, I did not speak. My impression is that whatever exists does so in another region beyond the hills, and that there are great journeys to be made if only we had soul enough to take those first steps.

I stopped, like the sun in my landscape. All that is left of what was said or seen is a dark night full of the dead glow of lakes, on a plain with no wild ducks, dead, fluid, damp and sinister.

382 [2 May 1932]

I never sleep: I live and I dream or, rather, I dream both while I live and while I sleep, which is also life. There is no break in my consciousness: I sense what is around me even when I'm not quite asleep or when I don't sleep well. I start to dream as soon as I'm properly asleep. I'm a perpetual unfolding of connected and disconnected images—always disguised as something external—that stand between men and the light if I'm awake, or between ghosts and the visible dark if I'm asleep. I really do not know how to distinguish one from the other, nor would I venture to affirm that I'm not sleeping when I'm awake, or that I'm not on the point of waking when I'm asleep.

Life is like a ball of wool that someone has tangled up. There would be some sense in it were it unraveled and pulled out to its full length, or else properly rolled up. But, as it is, it's a problem no one has bothered to roll into a ball, a muddle with nowhere to go.

I feel now what I will later write down, for I'm already dreaming the phrases I will use; I sense through this night of half-sleeping the landscapes of vague dreams and the noise of the rain outside making them even vaguer. They are guesses made in the void, trembling on the brink of the abyss, and through them vainly trickles the plangent sound of the constant rain outside, the abundant detail of the landscape of the heard. Hope? None. A wind-borne watery grief falls from the invisible sky. I sleep on.

Doubtless the tragedy out of which life was created occurred along the paths of the park. There were two of them and they were beautiful and they wanted to be something else; love waited for them far off in the tedious future and the nostalgia for what would be arrived as the child of the love they had never felt. Thus, beneath the moonlight in the nearby woods—for the light trickled through the trees—they would walk hand in hand, feeling no desires or hopes, across the desert of abandoned paths. They were just like children, precisely because they weren't. From path to path, silhouetted like paper cut-outs among the trees, they strolled that no man's land of a stage. And so, ever closer and more separate, they disappeared beyond the fountains, and the noise of the gentle rain—which has almost stopped—is now the noise of the fountains

411

they moved towards. I am the love that was their love and that's why I can hear them in this sleepless night and why I'm capable of living unhappily.

383 [15 May 1932]

Nothing weighs so heavily on one as other people's affections, not even hate, because hate is more intermittent than affection; being a disagreeable emotion, it tends instinctively to be less frequent among those who feel it. But both hate and love are oppressive; both feelings seek us out, track us down, and won't leave us alone.

My ideal would be to live everything as if in a novel, and to use life as a place in which to rest—to read my emotions, to live my scorn for them. For those with a highly sensitive imagination, the adventures of the protagonist in a novel provide us with quite enough excitement, especially since they are both his and ours. There is no greater adventure than to have loved Lady Macbeth truly and frankly; what can anyone who has known such a love do now but rest and love no one in real life?

I don't know what the point is of this journey I was obliged to make between one night and another, in the company of the entire universe. I know that I can read in order to distract myself. I consider reading to be the simplest way of passing this and any other journey; and now and then, I look up from the book in which I am experiencing genuine emotions and, like a foreigner, see the landscape flying by—fields, towns, men and women, affections and yearnings for things lost—and for me that is merely an episode in my repose, an inert distraction on which to rest my eyes from those too intensely read pages.

What we dream is what we really are, everything else, because of the simple fact that it exists, belongs to the world and to everyone else. If I were actually to fulfill a dream, I would be jealous of it, because it would have betrayed me by allowing itself to be fulfilled. I have fulfilled all my dreams, says the weak man, but that's a lie; the truth is that he merely dreamed prophetically everything that life fulfilled through him. We ourselves fulfill nothing. Life lobs us into the air like a stone, and we fly along, saying as we go: "You see, I'm moving."

Whatever it is, this interlude performed beneath the spotlight of the sun and the sequinned stars, it is as well to know that it is just an interlude; if what lies beyond the theatre doors is life, then we will live; if it is death, then we will die, and the play is irrelevant.

That is why I never feel closer to the truth, more fully involved, than on the rare occasions when I go to the theatre or the circus: I know then that I am finally witnessing a perfect representation of life. And the actors and actresses, the clowns and the magicians, are important, futile things, just as the sun and the moon, love and death, plague, famine and war are important for humanity. Everything is theatre. If I want the truth, I'll carry on reading this novel...

384 [23 May 1932]

I don't know what time is. I don't know what, if any, is the truest way of measuring it. I know that the way the clock measures time is false: it divides time spatially, from the outside. I know that the time kept by the emotions is false too: they divide not time but the sensation of time. The time of dreams is also wrong; in dreams we brush past time, sometimes slowly, sometimes fast, and what we experience is either fast or slow according to some peculiarity in the way it flows, the nature of which I do not understand.

Sometimes I think everything is false and that time is just a frame used to surround anything foreign to itself. In my memories of my past life, time is ordered on absurd planes and levels, so that I am younger in one episode of my life as a solemn fifteen-year-old than in another as a baby sitting surrounded by my toys.

If I think about these things my consciousness grows tangled. I sense an error in it all; I don't know, however, where that error lies. It's as if I were watching some kind of magic trick and, because I recognize it's a trick, I'm aware of being deceived, but I can't work out the technique or mechanics of the deceit.

Then I'm invaded by thoughts which, though absurd, I can't totally reject. I wonder if a man meditating slowly inside a fast-moving car is moving fast or slowly. I wonder if a suicide hurling himself into the sea and someone merely slipping on the esplanade actually fall at the same speed. I wonder if three actions taking place at the same time—my smoking a cigarette, writing this paragraph and thinking these obscure thoughts—are truly synchronous.

One can imagine that of two wheels turning on the same axle there will always be one ahead of the other, even if only by a fraction of a millimeter. A microscope would exaggerate that dislocation to the point of making it unbelievable, impossible were it not real. And why shouldn't the microscope prove truer than our feeble eyesight? Are these just futile thoughts? Of course they are. Are they just the illusions of thought? They are. What is this thing, then, that measures us without measure and kills us even though it does not itself exist? It is at moments like these, when I'm not even sure that time exists, that I experience time like a person, and then I simply feel like going to sleep.

385 [31 May 1932]

It's not in broad fields or large gardens that I first notice the spring arrive. It's in the few pathetic trees growing in a small city square. There the bright green seems like a gift and is as joyful as a good bout of sadness.

I love these solitary squares that are dotted amongst quiet streets and are themselves just as quiet and free of traffic. They are things that wait, useless clearings amidst distant tumults. They are remnants of village life surviving in the heart of the city.

I walk on, go up one of the streets that flows into the square, then walk back down just to see it again. It's different seen from the other side, but the same peace bathes in unexpected nostalgia the side I did not see before.

Everything is useless, and that is how I feel it to be. Everything I've lived through I've forgotten as if it were something I had only vaguely overheard. And of what I will be there is no trace in my memory, as if I had already lived through and forgotten it.

A sunset full of subtle griefs hovers vaguely about me. Everything grows cold, not because it really is colder, but simply because I've walked up a narrow street and can no longer see the square.

386 [7 June 1932]

Amiel said that a landscape is a state of mind, but the phrase is the feebly felicitous one of a feeble dreamer. A landscape is a landscape and therefore cannot be a state of mind. To objectify is to create and no one says of a finished poem that it is a state of thinking about writing a poem. To see is perhaps to dream but if we use the word "see" rather than the word "dream," it's because we distinguish between seeing and dreaming.

Anyway, what's the point of these speculations on the psychology of words? Quite independently of me the grass grows, the rain waters the grass as it grows and the sun turns to gold the whole field of grass that has grown or will grow; the mountains have been there since ancient times and the wind that blows sounds just as it did to Homer (even if he never existed). It would be more correct to say that a state of mind is a landscape; that would have the advantage of containing not the lie of a theory but the truth of a metaphor.

These random words were dictated to me by the great expanse of city I saw lit by the universal light of the sun, from high up on São Pedro de Alcântara. Every time I look out like this on a vast landscape and free myself of the 1 meter 70 and 61 kilos of which I am physically constituted, I smile a great metaphysical smile at those who dream that a dream is just a dream and, with a noble virtue born of understanding, I love the truth of the absolute exterior world.

The Tejo in the background is a blue lake and the hills on the far shore a squat Switzerland. A small boat—a black cargo steamer—leaves the shores of Poço do Bispo for the estuary mouth that I cannot see from here. Until the day when this outward aspect of my self should cease, may the gods preserve in me this clear, sunny notion of external reality, this sense of my own unimportance, this comforting feeling of being small and capable of imagining being happy.

387 [11 June 1932]

Once the heat had passed and the first light spots of rain began to fall heavily enough to make themselves heard, there was a quietness in the air that had been absent from the earlier heat, a new peace into which the rain introduced a breeze all its own. Such was the bright, sheer joy of that soft rain, with no storms or dark skies, that even those who had come out without umbrellas or waterproof clothing, almost everyone in fact, laughed as they hurried, chattering, down the shining street.

In an idle moment I went over to the open window in the office—it had been opened because of the heat and left open when the rain came—and looking out at the scene with my usual mixture of intense and indifferent attentiveness, I saw exactly the scene I had described even before I had seen it. Sure enough, there was joy walking down the street in the guise of two ordinary men, talking and smiling in the fine rain, not hurrying, just strolling briskly through the clean clarity of the darkening day.

However, a surprise was waiting just around the corner: suddenly, a miserable old man, poor but not humble, came making his ill-tempered way through the slackening rain. This man, while clearly without any urgent goal, was possessed at least of a keen impatience. I studied him intently, not with the distracted eye with which one usually looks at things, but with the analytical eye reserved for deciphering symbols. He symbolized nobody; that was why he was in such a hurry. He symbolized those who have never been anybody; that was at the root of his suffering. He did not belong with those who smiled beneath the inconvenient joy of the rain, he belonged to the rain itself—an unconscious being, so unconscious that he could feel reality.

But that isn't what I wanted to say. A mysterious distraction, a crisis of the soul that rendered me incapable of continuing, insinuated itself between my observation of that passerby (whom in fact I immediately lost sight of because I stopped looking at him) and the nexus of these observations. And at the back of my distractedness, I hear without hearing the sound of the post-room boys at the other end of the office where the warehouse begins and, on the table by the window that looks out onto the yard, among the joking voices and the click of scissors, I see without seeing the twine wound twice around the packages wrapped in strong brown paper and fastened with double knots.

One can see only what one has already seen.

388 [14 June 1932]

No one understands anyone else. We are, as the poet said, enisled in the sea of life; between us flows the sea that defines and separates us. However hard one soul struggles to know another soul, he can only judge by what words are spoken—a formless shadow on the floor of his understanding.

I love aphorisms because I have no idea what they mean. I am like the philosopher and occultist Louis-Claude de Saint-Martin: I content myself with what is given to me. I see, and that is quite sufficient. Who can understand anything?

Perhaps because I am so sceptical about what is truly intelligible, I look with equal interest upon a tree and a face, a poster and a smile. (Everything is natural, everything artificial, everything equal.) Everything I see is, for me, the purely visible, be it the vast blue, green-tinged sky of the coming morning, be it the false grimace of pain on the face of someone watching the death of a loved one and aware that he is being watched.

Etchings, illustrations, pages that exist and are turned … My heart is not in them, nor even my attention, which wanders across the surface of things, like a fly on a piece of paper.

Do I even know that I feel, think, exist? Nothing: only an

objective summary of colors, shapes and impressions of which I am the vacillating mirror—up for sale.

389 [23 June 1932]

Life is an experimental journey undertaken involuntarily. It is a journey of the spirit through the material world and, since it is the spirit that travels, it is in the spirit that it is experienced. That is why there exist contemplative souls who have lived more intensely, more widely, more tumultuously than others who have lived their lives purely externally. The end result is what matters. What one felt was what one experienced. One retires to bed as wearily from having dreamed as from having done hard physical labor. One never lives so intensely as when one has been thinking hard.

The person standing apart in the corner of the room dances with all the dancers. He sees everything and, because he sees, he experiences everything. When it comes down to it, it is just another feeling, and seeing or even remembering someone's body is just as good as any actual contact. Thus when I see others dance, I dance too. I agree with the English poet who, describing how he lay far off in the grass watching three mowers mowing, wrote: "A fourth man is mowing, and that fourth am I."

All this, which I speak just as I feel it, has to do with the great weariness, apparently without cause, that came on me suddenly today. I feel not only tired but embittered, and yet the cause of that bitterness is also unknown. I feel such anguish I'm on the verge of tears, tears to be suppressed not cried, tears born of a sickness of the soul, not of any physical ill.

I have lived so much without ever having lived. I have thought so much without ever having thought. I feel weighed down by worlds of unenacted violence, of stillborn adventures. I am sick of what I never had nor will have, weary of gods always just about to exist. I bear on my body the wounds of all the battles I did not fight. My muscles are weary from efforts I never even considered making.

Dull, dumb, empty ... The sky above belongs to a dead, imperfect summer. I look at it as if it were not there. I sleep what I think, I lie down even as I walk, I suffer and feel nothing. My great nostalgia is for nothing at all, is itself nothing, like the sky above, which I do not see and which I gaze at impersonally.

390 [16 July 1932]

Convalescence, especially if the preceding illness affected one's nerves, has a sort of gay sadness about it. There is a touch of autumn in all one's emotions and thoughts, or rather one feels like one of those early spring days when the air and sky seem more like autumn than spring, except, of course, that no leaves fall.

We experience a pleasant tiredness but our sense of well-being also hurts a little. Whilst still in life, we feel somewhat apart from it, as if standing on the verandah of the house of life. We are contemplative, but think no thoughts, we feel, but feel no definite emotion. The will grows quiet, because we have no need of it.

It's then that certain memories, certain hopes, certain vague desires slowly ascend the ramp of our consciousness, like distant travelers seen from a mountain peak. Memories of futile things, hopes for things that never came to pass and about which we no longer care, desires that were neither violent by nature nor in intention and that could never really have wanted to exist.

When the day is right for such feelings, when, like today, even though it is still summer, the blue sky is striped with clouds and the light wind feels cold simply because it isn't warm, then that state of mind grows more noticeable in the way we think, feel or experience these impressions. It isn't that the memories, hopes or desires we had are any clearer, they are simply more present, and, however absurd it may seem, the uncertain sum of their parts weighs a little on one's heart.

There is something distant about me just now. I stand on the verandah of life, but it's not quite of this life. I'm both in the midst of life and observing it from where I stand. It lies before me, descending in ledges and slopes, like a varied landscape, down to the smoke rising from the white houses of the villages in the valley. If I shut my eyes I continue to see it just because I can't see it. If I open my eyes I see no more, because I never really saw anything. Every part of me is a vague nostalgia neither for the past nor for the future: the whole of me is a nostalgia for the anonymous, prolix, unfathomable present.

391   [25 July 1932]

Generally speaking, the classifiers of the world, those men of science whose only knowledge consists in their ability to classify, are ignorant of the fact that what is classifiable is infinite and therefore unclassifiable. But what amazes me most is that they know nothing of the existence of certain unknown classifiable categories, things of the soul and the consciousness that live in the interstices of knowledge.

Perhaps because I think or dream too much I simply cannot distinguish between existent reality and the nonexistent reality of dreams. And so I interleave in my meditations on the sky and earth things that neither gleam in the sun nor are trodden under foot: the fluid marvels of the imagination.

I clothe myself in the gold of imagined sunsets, but what is imagined lives on in the imagination. I gladden myself with imaginary breezes, and the imaginary lives when it is imagined. Various hypotheses furnish me with a soul and since each hypothesis has its own soul, each gives me the soul it possesses.

There is only one problem: reality, and that is insoluble and alive. What do I know about the difference between a tree and a dream? I can touch the tree; I know I have the dream. What does that really mean?

What does it mean? That I, alone in the deserted office, can live and imagine without detriment to my intelligence. My thoughts can continue untroubled by the presence of the abandoned desks and the post-room with its paper and balls of twine. I've left my own high stool and, enjoying in advance a hypothetical promotion,

I lean back in Moreira's curve-armed chair. Perhaps it's the influence of the place anointing me with the balm of abstraction. These very hot days make one sleepy; I sleep without sleeping, for lack of energy. That's why I have these thoughts.

392 [after 4 Aug 1932]

The outside world exists like an actor on a stage: it's there but it's pretending to be something else.

393 [28 Sep 1932]

For some time now—it may be days or months—I haven't really noticed anything; I don't think, therefore I don't exist. I've forgotten who I am; I can't write because I can't be. Under the influence of some oblique drowsiness I have been someone else. The knowledge that I do not remember myself awakens me.

I fainted away a little from my life. I return to myself with no memory of what I have been and the memory of the person I was before suffers from that interruption. I am aware only of a confused notion of some forgotten interlude, of my memory's futile efforts to find the other me. But I cannot retie the knots. If I did live, I've forgotten how to know that I did.

It isn't this first real autumn day—the first cold rather than cool day to clothe the dead summer in a lesser light—whose alien transparency leaves me with a sense of dead ambitions or sham intentions. It isn't the uncertain trace of vain memory contained in this interlude of things lost. It's something more painful than that, it's the tedium of trying to remember what cannot be remembered, despair at what my consciousness mislaid among the algae and reeds of some unknown shore.

Beneath an unequivocally blue sky, a shade lighter than the deepest blue, I recognize that the day is limpid and still. I recognize that the sun, slightly less golden than it was, gilds walls and windows alike with liquid reflections. I recognize that, although there's no wind, nor any breeze to recall or deny the existence of a wind, a brisk coolness nonetheless hovers about the hazy city. I recognize all this, unthinkingly, unwillingly, and feel no desire to sleep, only the memory of that desire, feel no nostalgia, only disquiet.

Sterile and remote, I recover from an illness I never had. Alert after waking, I prepare myself for what I dare not do. What kind of sleep was it that brought me no rest? What kind of caress was it that would not speak to me? How good it would be to take one cold draught of heady spring and be someone else! How good, how much better than life, to be able to imagine being that other person, while far off, in the remembered image, in the absence of even a breath of wind, the reeds bend blue-green to the shore.

Recalling the person I was not, I often imagine myself young again and forget! And were they different, those landscapes that I never saw; were they new but nonexistent, the landscapes I did see? What does it matter? I have spent myself in chance events, in interstices, and now that the cool of the day and the cooling sun are one, the dark reeds by the shore sleep their cold sleep in the sunset I see but do not possess.

394 [28 Sep 1932]

No one has as yet produced an exact definition of tedium, at least not in language comprehensible to someone who has never experienced it. What some people call tedium is nothing more than boredom; others use the word to mean a certain physical malaise; for still others tedium is simply tiredness. Tedium does contain tiredness, malaise and boredom but only in the way water contains the hydrogen and oxygen of which it is composed. It includes them without resembling them.

If some give tedium a restricted, incomplete sense, others lend it an almost transcendental significance, as, for example, when the word "tedium" is used to describe someone's deep sense of spiritual nausea at the randomness and uncertainty of the world. Boredom makes one yawn; physical malaise makes one fidget; tiredness prevents one from moving at all; none of them is tedium. Neither is it that profound sense of the emptiness of things, out of which frustrated aspirations struggle free, a sense of thwarted longing arises and in the soul is sown the seed from which is born the mystic or the saint.

Yes, tedium is boredom with the world, the malaise of living, the weariness of having lived; in truth, tedium is the feeling in one's flesh of the endless emptiness of things. But, more than that, tedium is a boredom with other worlds, whether they exist or not; the malaise of living, even if one were someone else, with a different life, in another world; a weariness not just with yesterday or today but with tomorrow too, with all eternity (if it exists) and with nothingness (if that is what eternity is). It isn't just the emptiness of things and beings that hurts the soul when it is immersed in tedium, it's the emptiness of something else too, the emptiness of the soul experiencing that emptiness and feeling itself to be empty, the emptiness that provokes a sense of self-disgust and repudiation.

Tedium is the physical sensation of chaos and of the fact that chaos is everything. Someone who is bored, uncomfortable or tired feels himself to be imprisoned in a tiny cell. Someone disenchanted with the narrowness of life feels himself to be chained up in a large cell. But someone afflicted by tedium feels himself the prisoner of a futile freedom, in a cell of infinite size. The walls of the cell surrounding the bored, uncomfortable or weary prisoner might crumble and bury him beneath them. The chains may fall from the limbs of the prisoner disenchanted with the narrowness of the world and allow him to flee; or, unable to free himself from them, the chains may hurt him and the experience of that pain may revive in him his appetite for life. But the walls of an infinite cell cannot crumble and bury us, since they do not exist; nor can we claim as proof of our existence the pain caused by handcuffs no one has placed round our wrists.

These are my feelings as I stand before the placid beauty of this immortal but dying evening. I look up at the high, clear sky where vague, pink shapes, like the shadows of clouds, are the impalpable down on the wings of distant life. I look down at the river where the water, shimmering slightly, is of a blue that seems the mirror image of a deeper sky. I look up again at the sky and already, in the invisible air, among the vague colors that unravel without quite disintegrating, there is an icy dull whiteness, as if in all things, at their highest and most incorporeal level, there were some malaise, a tedium in matter itself, a sense of the impossibility of something just being what it is, an imponderable nexus of anxiety and desolation.

But what if there is? What else is there in the high air but the high air, which is nothing? What else is there in the sky but borrowed color? What is there in these tiny scraps, barely clouds, whose presence I already doubt, but a little reflected light scattered by a submissive sun? What is there in all this but myself? Ah, but in that and only that lies tedium. It's the fact that in all this—sky, earth, world—there is never anything but myself!

395 [2 Nov 1932]

Mist or smoke? Was it rising from the earth or falling from the sky? It was impossible to tell: it was more like a contagion of the air than an emanation from the earth or a precipitation from the sky. At times it seemed more like an affliction of the eyes than a reality of nature.

Whatever it was, the whole landscape was pervaded by a murky disquiet, composed of forgetting and attenuated reality. It was as if the silence of the sick sun had mistaken some imperfect body for its own. It was as if something, which could be sensed in everything, was about to happen and for that reason the visible world drew a veil about itself.

It was difficult to make out what it was covering the sky—clouds or mist. It was more like a dull torpor touched here and there by a little color, an odd yellowish gray except where this fragmented into a false pink or blue, but even then you couldn't tell if it was the sky showing through or merely a layer of blue.

Nothing was definite, not even the indefinite. That's why one felt inclined to call the mist "smoke," because it didn't look like mist, or to wonder which it was, mist or smoke, because it was impossible to tell. The very warmth of the air was accomplice to this doubt. It was neither warm, nor cold, nor cool; it seemed to derive its temperature from something other than heat. In fact it seemed that the mist was cold to the eyes but warm to the touch, as if sight and touch were two different ways of feeling the same sense.

There was not the shading-off of edges and sharp angles that lingering mists usually lend to the outlines of trees or to the corners of buildings, nor were they half revealed and half obscured as one would have expected had it been real smoke. It was as if each thing projected all around it a vague diurnal shadow, but without there being any source of light that could produce such a shadow, nor any surface onto which it could be projected and which would account for its visibility.

Not that it really was visible, it was more a suggestion (apparent in equal measure everywhere) of something about to be seen, as if what was about to be revealed hesitated to appear.

And what kind of feeling did it create? The impossibility of there being any, a confusion of heart and mind, a perplexity of feelings, a torpor of awakened existence, a sharpening of some sense in the soul equivalent to that of straining to catch a definitive but vain revelation, always just about to be revealed, like the truth, and, like the truth, the twin of concealment.

I've dismissed the desire to sleep which thoughts bring on, because even the first yawn seemed too much effort. Even not seeing hurts my eyes. And beyond this blank abdication of the whole soul, all that remains of the impossible world is the distant sounds beyond.

Oh, to have another world, full of other things, another soul with which to feel them and other thoughts with which to know that soul! Anything else, even tedium, but not this melding together of soul and world, not the bluish desolation of this all-pervading lack of definition.

We were walking, together and separate, along forest paths that kept abruptly changing direction. Our steps, which were not ours, were united, treading in unison over the crisp softness of the fallen leaves scattered, yellow and faded green, over the rough ground. They were also disunited because we were two different thoughts, with nothing in common except that what-we-were-not was treading in unison over the same heard surface.

It was already the beginning of autumn, and, as well as the leaves we were walking over, we could hear, everywhere we went or had been, the continual fall, to the brusque accompaniment of the wind, of other leaves, or the sounds of leaves. There was no other landscape but the forest, which obscured all others. It was enough, though, as a site and a place for those like us, whose only life was to walk in diverse unison over the dying earth. It was—I believe—the end of a day, of any day, or perhaps of all days, in an autumn that was all autumns, in that real and symbolic forest.

Even we could not have said what houses, duties or loves we had left behind us. At that moment, we were merely travelers walking between what we had forgotten and what we did not know, knights on foot defending some abandoned ideal. However, in this, as in the constant sound of the leaves beneath our feet, and the still-brusque sound of the hesitant wind, lay the reason for our setting off or for our return, because, not knowing the path or the reason for the path, we did not know if we were setting out or coming back. And all around us—only heard, never seen—the sad sound of the falling, ruined leaves was lulling the forest to sleep.

Neither of us took any notice of each other, although neither of us would have carried on alone. Our companionship was a kind of shared sleep. The sound of our steps in unison helped us each to think without the other, whereas our solitary steps would have reminded us of the other's presence. The forest was all false clearings, as if it were itself false or about to come to an end, but neither the falseness nor the forest ended. Our steps in unison continued ever on, and along with the noise of the trampled leaves there was the faint sound of falling leaves, in the forest that had become everything, in that forest that had become the universe.

Who were we? Were we two or two forms of the same person? We did not know nor did we ask. There must have been some kind of sun somewhere, because in the forest it wasn't yet dark night. We must have had some kind of goal too, because we kept walking. A world of some sort must have existed, because the forest existed. We, though, were indifferent to what was or might be, interminable travelers crunching in unison over the dead leaves, anonymous, impossible hearers of falling leaves. Nothing more. A whisper, now shrill, now soft, from that mysterious wind, a murmur, now loud, now quiet, from the trapped leaves, a gap, a doubt, a failed attempt, an illusion that never was—the forest, the two travelers, and me, and I don't know which of them I was, if I was both or neither, and I witnessed, without waiting to see how it ended, the tragedy of nothing ever having been more than the autumn and the forest, and the still-brusque and hesitant wind, and the leaves always fallen or falling. And always, as if there really were a sun and a day out there, I could clearly see, although to no purpose, the murmurous silence of the forest.

397 [c. November 1932]

Despite the clear perfection of the day, the sun-filled air stagnates. It isn't the present tension created by a gathering thunderstorm, the unease of bodies lacking all will, a vague dullness in the otherwise true blue sky. It is the perceptible torpor of the promise of leisure, a feather lightly touching a drowsy cheek. Though it's the height of summer, it feels like spring. The countryside seems tempting even to someone who wouldn't usually enjoy it.

If I were someone else, I think, this would be a happy day, for I would just feel it without thinking about it. Full of anticipated pleasure I would finish my day's work, the work that is monotonously abnormal to me each and every day. I'd take the tram out to

Benfica with a group of friends. We would dine in the open air just as the sun was going down. Our happiness would seem a natural part of the landscape and be recognized as such by everyone who saw us.

Since, however, I am myself, I squeeze a meager enjoyment out of the meager pleasure of imagining myself that other person. Yes, soon he-I, seated beneath a vine trellis or a tree, will eat twice what I can normally eat, drink twice what I dare to drink and laugh twice as much as I could ever imagine laughing. First I was him, now I am me. Yes, for a moment I was someone else: I saw and lived as another that humble, human happiness of existing like a dumb beast in shirtsleeves. What an excellent day to bring me such a dream! Up above it is all blue and sublime like my ephemeral dream of being a hale and hearty traveling salesman off on some after-hours jaunt.

398 [13 Dec 1932]

For as long as I have been thinking and observing—insofar as I am capable—it has become clear to me that men do not know or cannot agree on what is truly important in life or useful as a guide to living it. The most exact science is mathematics, which lives cloistered in its own rules and laws; it is, of course, useful, when applied, to elucidating the other sciences, but it only elucidates what they discover, it doesn't help them to make discoveries. The only certainties in the other sciences are irrelevant to the supreme aims of life. Physics knows the expansion coefficient for iron; it doesn't know the actual mechanics of the composition of the world. And the higher up we go in what we would like to know, the lower down we sink in what we do know. Metaphysics, which should be the supreme guide since it alone concerns itself with the supreme aims of truth and life, is not a scientific theory, but a pile of bricks, out of which, depending on who is doing the bricklaying, spring shapeless houses with no mortar holding them together.

I notice, too, that there is no difference between the lives of animals and men, apart from the manner in which they deceive themselves or the degree to which they are ignorant of what life is. Animals don't know what they do: they are born, they grow up, they live, they die, without ever thinking or reflecting or having any real future. How many men, though, live any differently from animals? We are all sleeping, and the difference lies only in what we dream and in the degree and quality of the dreaming. Perhaps death will wake us up, but there is no answer to that either, apart from faith, for which it is enough to believe, and hope, for which to desire is to have, and charity, for which to give is to receive.

It's raining on this cold, sad winter's day, as if it had been raining monotonously like this since the world's first page was written. It's raining, and my feelings, as if the rain were bowing them down, bend their gaze to the ground, over which flows a water that feeds nothing, washes nothing clean and brings no joy. It's raining, and I suddenly feel the immense oppressive weight of being an animal that doesn't know what it is, dreaming its thoughts and emotions, hunched, as if in a hovel, in a spatial region of being, as contented with a little warmth as it would be with an eternal truth.

399   [30 Dec 1932]

After the last of the rain had fallen from the sky and come to earth—leaving the sky clear and the earth damp and mirror-bright—the world below grew joyful in the cool left by the rain, and the greater clarity of life that returned with the blue of the heavens furnished each soul with its own sky, each heart with a new freshness.

Whether we like it or not, we are slaves to the hour in all its forms and colors, we are the subjects of heaven and earth. The part of us that despises its surroundings and plunges deepest within ourselves does not take the same paths when it rains as when the sky is clear. Simply because it's raining or has stopped raining, obscure transmutations take place, felt only perhaps in the very heart of our most abstract feelings; we feel these transmutations without knowing it because we feel the weather even when we are unaware that we do.

Each of us is more than one person, many people, a proliferation of our one self. That's why the same person who scorns his surroundings is different from the person who is gladdened or made to suffer by them. In the vast colony of our being there are many different kinds of people, all thinking and feeling differently. Today, as I note down these few impressions in a legitimate break brought about by a shortage of work, I am the person carefully transcribing them, the person who is pleased not to have to work just now, the person who looks at the sky even though he can't actually see it from here, the person who is thinking all this, and the person feeling physically at ease and noticing that his hands are still slightly cold. And, like a diverse but compact multitude, this whole world of mine, composed as it is of different people, projects but a single shadow, that of this calm figure writing on Borges's high desk, where I have come to find the blotter he borrowed from me.

400 [1932?]

The heat, like a piece of invisible clothing, makes you want to throw it off.

401 [1932?]

A blade of languid lightning fluttered darkly in the big room. Before the imminent sound of thunder there was a pause, as if for a gulp of air, followed by a deep migratory rumble. The rain moaned, like professional mourners during breaks in the conversation. Indoors, the least sound seemed inordinately loud and restless.

402 [1932?]

Everything unpleasant that happens to us in life—for example, when we appear ridiculous in the eyes of others, behave badly or lapse from virtue—should be considered merely external events without the power to touch the depths of our soul. We should think of them as the toothache or the corns of life, things that give us some discomfort but which, although ours, are outside us, as things that it is up to our organic existence to deal with, things that only our biology need concern itself with.

Once we fully adopt this attitude, which, in a way, is that of the mystics, we are defended not only against the world but also against ourselves, because we have conquered what is other, what is external and contrary to us and therefore our enemy.

That's what Horace meant when he spoke of the just man who remained unmoved even as the world crashed about his ears. The image may be absurd, but the truth of its meaning is indisputable. Even if what we pretend to be—because the real we and the pretend we coexist—even if it collapses around us, we must remain unmoved, not because we are just, but because we are ourselves, and being ourselves means having nothing to do with those external things collapsing about us even if, in falling, they destroy what we are for them.

For the best of us, life should be a dream that eschews all comparisons.

403 [1932?]

In me all affections are superficial, but sincerely so. I've always been an actor, and a good one. Whenever I have loved, I've only pretended to love, even to myself.

404 [1932?]

The morning unfurls itself upon the city, interleaving light and shade (or rather degrees of intensity of light) among the houses. It does not seem to come from the sun but from life itself, it seems to issue forth from the city's walls and roofs (not from them physically but from the simple fact of their being there).

As I feel that, I feel full of hope, at the same time recognizing that hope is a purely literary feeling. Tomorrow, spring and hope are all words connected poetically with one emotion and in the soul with the memory of that emotion. No, if I observe myself as closely as I observe the city, I realize that all I have to hope for is that today, like every other day, will come to an end. The eyes of reason also look at the dawn and I see that the hope I placed in it, if it ever existed, was not mine. It belonged to those men who live for the passing hour and whose way of thinking I, for a moment, unwittingly embodied.

Hope? What have I got to hope for? The only promise the day holds for me is that it will be just another day with a fixed course to run and a conclusion. The light cheers but does not change me for I will leave here as I came—older by a few hours, gladdened by a new feeling but saddened by thought. Whenever something is being born one can as easily concentrate on the fact of its birth as imagine its inevitable death. Now, in the strong, generous sunlight, the city landscape looks like a field of houses—broad, natural and orderly. But, even as I see all this, can I really forget my own existence? Deep down, my consciousness of the city is my consciousness of myself.

I suddenly remember as a child seeing, as I no longer can, day breaking over the city. The sun did not rise for me then, it rose for all of life, because I (still an unconscious being) was life. I saw the morning and I was happy; today I see the morning and I am first happy, then sad. The child in me is still there but has fallen silent. I see as I used to see, but from behind my eyes I see myself seeing, and that one fact darkens the sun, dulls the green of the trees and withers the flowers before they even appear. Yes, once I belonged here; today, however new a landscape might be to me, I return from my first sight of it a foreigner, a guest and a wanderer, a stranger to all I see and hear, grown suddenly old.

I've seen everything before, even what I have never seen and never will see. Even the least significant of future landscapes already flows in my blood and the anguish of knowing that I will have to see again landscapes seen before fills me with anticipatory boredom.

Leaning over the balcony, enjoying the day, looking out at the diverse shapes of the whole city, just one thought fills my soul—the deep-seated will to die, to finish, no more to see light falling on a city, not to think or feel, to leave behind me, like discarded wrapping paper, the course of the sun and all its days, and to peel off the involuntary effort of being, just as one would discard one's heavy clothing at the foot of the great bed.

405 [1932?]

(storm) A dark silence palely overflowing. As well as the occasional cart passing rapidly down the street, a truck nearby booms out its own private thunder—a ridiculous, mechanical echo of what's happening for real in the looming heavens.

Again, without warning, another shaft of magnetic light flickers, blinking, across the sky. The heart takes a sharp in-breath. High above, a glass dome shatters like a cupola breaking into shards. A hard sheet of evil rain attacks the sound of the ground beneath.

(my boss Vasques) His ashen face has taken on a bewildered, false green tinge. With the fraternal feeling that comes from knowing I must look the same, I notice him gasping for air.

406 [1932?]

I was already feeling uneasy. All at once, the silence stopped breathing.

The infinite day suddenly splintered like steel. I crouched down like an animal, my hands useless claws gripping the smooth tabletop. A cruel light had entered every corner and every soul, and a voice from a nearby mountain fell from on high, a shout ripping the silken walls of the abyss. My heart stopped. My throat pounded. The only thing my mind was aware of was an inkblot on a piece of paper.

407 [1932?]

I don't know why but sometimes I feel touched by a premonition of death ... Maybe it's just a vague malaise which, because it does not manifest itself as pain, tends to become spiritualized, or else it's a weariness that calls for a sleep so deep that no amount of sleep could satisfy it; what is certain is that I feel as if at last, after a gradually worsening illness, I had let my feeble hands slip without violence or regret from the bedspread on which they rested.

I wonder then what is this thing we call death. I don't mean the mystery of death, which I cannot penetrate, but the physical sensation of ceasing to live. Humanity is, albeit hesitantly, afraid of death; the average man comes off lightly, for the average man, when sick or old, rarely casts a horrified glance into the abyss that he finds within the void. That is merely a lack of imagination, as it is in someone who imagines death as being like sleep. How can it be if death does not in the least resemble sleep? The essential feature of sleep is that one wakes from it whereas, at least as far as we know, one never wakes from death. If death were like sleep we should have some notion of waking from it. This is not, however, what the average man imagines: he imagines death as a sleep from which one does not wake, which is quite meaningless. What I say is that death is not like sleep, because in sleep one is alive but sleeping; I don't know how anyone can compare death to anything, because one cannot experience death or anything even remotely comparable to it.

When I see a dead person, death seems to me like a departure. The corpse looks like a suit someone has left behind. The person has departed and had no need to take with him the one suit he owned.

408 [1932?]

I wonder how many people have contemplated as it deserves to be contemplated a deserted street with people in it. Even putting it that way makes it seem as if I were trying to say something else, which in fact I am. A deserted street is not one along which no one walks, but a street along which people walk as if it were deserted. It isn't a difficult concept to grasp once one has seen it; after all, to someone whose experience of the equine is restricted to mules, a zebra must seem inconceivable.

Feelings adjust themselves within us to certain degrees and types of comprehension of them. There are ways of understanding that dictate the ways they are to be understood.

It's a suffocation of life in my own self, a desire in every pore of my being to be another person, a brief warning that the end is near.

409

In what feels like my now distant adolescence—and because it feels so remote it seems to me like something I must have read about or a personal story someone once told me—I twice enjoyed the painful humiliation of loving. From my vantage point of today, looking back at that past, which I no longer know whether to describe as remote or recent, I think it was a good thing to have experienced that disappointment so early.

It was nothing really, except what I felt at the time. From an objective point of view, legions of men have been through the same torments. But […]

Thanks to another simultaneous and related experience that touched my sensibility and my intelligence, I absorbed far too early on the idea that the life of the imagination, however morbid this might seem, is the one best suited for temperaments like mine. The fictions of my (later) imagination may weary me, but they do not hurt or humiliate. To impossible lovers the false smile, the fraudulent show of affection, the cunning caress are all equally impossible. They never abandon us or vanish from our life.

The great anxieties felt by our soul are always cosmic cataclysms. When they happen, the sun falters and the stars are troubled. In every feeling soul the day comes when Fate stages an apocalypse of anxiety—causing all the heavens and all the worlds to rain down upon that sense of desolation.

Feeling superior and yet finding that Fate treats us as inferior even to the most lowly of creatures—who can be proud of being a man in that situation?

If, one day, I were given a talent for expression so great that it distilled in me all art, I would write an apotheosis of sleep. I know of no greater pleasure in life than being able to sleep. The extinguishing of life and soul, the complete withdrawal from everything that makes you human, a person, the night empty of all memories and all illusions, having no past and no future, [...]

410 [1932?]

To write is to forget. Literature is the pleasantest way of ignoring life. Music lulls us, the visual arts enliven us, the performing arts (such as dance and drama) entertain us. The first, therefore, removes itself from life in order to make of it a dream; the others, however, do not, some because they use visual and, therefore, vital formulae and others because they live from human life itself.

This is not the case with literature. Literature simulates life. A novel is a history of what never was and a play is a novel without narrative. A poem is the expression of ideas or feelings in a language no one uses, since no one speaks in verse.

411 [1932?]

To live a dispassionate, cultured life beneath the dewfall of ideas, reading, dreaming and thinking about writing, a life slow enough to be always just on the edge of tedium, but considered enough not to slip into it. To live a life removed from emotions and thoughts, enjoying only the thought of emotions and the emotion of thoughts. To stagnate, golden, in the sun like a dark lake surrounded by flowers. To entertain in the shadows that noble individuality of mind that consists in not expecting anything from life. To be in the turning of the worlds like the dust of flowers that an unknown wind lifts through the evening air, and that the torpor of nightfall lets fall randomly, to lie unnoticed among larger things. To be all this with an assured knowledge, neither happy nor sad, grateful to the sun for its brilliance and to the stars for their distance. To be nothing more, to have nothing more, to want nothing more ... The music of the hungry man, the song of the blind man, the relic of the unknown traveler, the footsteps in the desert of the empty camel with nowhere to go ...

412 [23 Mar 1933]

For most people life is a bore that is over before they realize it, a sad business interspersed by a few happy interludes, rather like the anecdotes told by people watching over the dead in order to pass the still night and complete their vigil. I always found it futile to think of life as a vale of tears: it is a vale of tears but one where people rarely cry. Heine said that every great tragedy was followed by a general blowing of noses. As a Jew, he saw all too clearly the universal nature of humanity.

Life would be unbearable if we were truly conscious of it. Fortunately we are not. We live as unconsciously as animals, in just the same futile, useless way, and if we think about our own death, as one supposes animals do not (though one cannot be sure of that), we do so in such an absentminded, distracted and roundabout way that we can barely be said to think about it at all.

Since that is how we live, there is really no justification for our thinking ourselves superior to animals. We differ from them only in purely external details, in the fact of our speaking and writing, in having an abstract intelligence to distract us from our concrete intelligence, and in our ability to imagine the impossible. All these things, however, are just the chance attributes of our organism. Speaking and writing make no difference to our basic instinct to survive, which is quite unconscious. All our abstract intelligence is good for is constructing systems, or semi-systematic ideas, which for animals is a simple matter of lying in the sun. Even our ability to imagine the impossible may not be a unique talent, for I've seen cats staring at the moon and for all I know they may be wishing for it.

The whole world, the whole of life, is a vast system of unconscious minds operating through individual consciousnesses. Just as an electric current passing through two gases creates a liquid, so if you pass life and the world through two consciousnesses—that of our concrete being and that of our abstract being—you create a superior unconscious.

Happy the man, then, who does not think, for he grasps through instinct and his own organic destiny what we only grasp via the most circuitous routes and our inorganic, social destiny. Happy the man most like the brute beasts because he effortlessly is what we all struggle to be; because he knows the way home which we find only through the byways of fiction and after much retracing of steps; because, rooted like a tree, he is part of the landscape and therefore part of its beauty and not, like us, a transient myth, a mannequin wearing the bright costumes of vanity and oblivion.

413 [29 Mar 1933]

I don't know why—I've only just noticed it—but I'm alone in the office. I had already vaguely sensed it. In some part of my consciousness there was a deep sense of relief, a sense of lungs breathing more freely.

This is one of the odder sensations afforded us by chance encounters and absences: that of finding ourselves alone in a house that is normally full of people and noise or in a house that belongs to someone else. We suddenly have a feeling of absolute possession, of an easy, generous mastery, an ample sense—as I said—of relief and peace.

How good to be all alone! To be able to talk out loud to ourselves, to walk about with nobody's eyes on us, to lean back and daydream with no interruptions! Every house becomes a meadow, every room takes on the amplitude of a country villa.

All the sounds one hears seem to come from somewhere else, as if they belonged to a nearby but independent universe. We are, at last, kings. That's what we all aspire to and, who knows, perhaps the more plebeian among us aspire to it more eagerly than those with false gold in their pockets. For a moment we are the pensioners of the universe, existing on our regular incomes with no needs or worries.

Ah, but in the footstep on the stair, the approach of someone unknown, I recognize the person who will interrupt my enjoyable solitude. My undeclared empire is about to be invaded by barbarians. It isn't that I can tell from the footsteps on the stairs who it is, nor that they remind me of the footsteps of one particular person. It is some secret instinct of the soul telling me that, though they are as yet only footsteps, whoever is approaching up the stairs (which I suddenly see before me just because I am thinking about the person ascending them) is coming here. Yes, it's one of the clerks. He stops, I hear the door open, he comes in. I see him properly now. And as he comes in, he says to me: "All alone, Senhor Soares?" And I reply: "Yes, I have been for a while now ..." And then, peeling off his jacket while he eyes his other one, an old one, hanging on the hook, he says: "Terrible bore being here all alone, Senhor Soares ..." "Oh, yes, a terrible bore," I say. He has on his old, threadbare jacket now, and, going over to his desk, he says: "It's enough to make you want to drop off to sleep." "It is indeed," I agree, smiling. Then, reaching out for my forgotten pen, I write my way back into the anonymous health of normal life.

414   [5 Apr 1933]

To consider our greatest anguish an incident of no importance, not just in terms of the life of the universe, but in terms of our own souls, is the beginning of knowledge. To reflect on this while in the midst of that anguish is the whole of knowledge. When we suffer, human pain seems infinite. But not even human pain is infinite, because nothing human is infinite, nor is our pain ever anything more than a pain that we have.

How often, weighed down by a tedium that verges on madness, or an anguish that seems to go beyond all anguish, do I stop and hesitate before I rebel, do I hesitate and stop before making myself a god. The pain of not understanding the mystery of life, the pain of being unloved, the pain of others' injustice to us, the pain of life crushing us, suffocating and imprisoning us, the pain of toothache, of pinching shoes—who can say which pain he finds the worse, let alone which is worse for others, or worse for others in general?

To some people who speak and listen to me I must seem an insensitive soul. However, I am, I think, more sensitive than the vast majority of men. I am, moreover, a sensitive man who knows himself and therefore knows what sensitivity is.

It isn't true that life is painful, or that it's painful to think about life. What is true is that our pain is only as serious and important as we pretend it to be. If we lived naturally, it would pass as quickly as it came, it would fade as quickly as it bloomed. Everything is nothing, and our pain is no exception.

I write this beneath the weight of an oppressive tedium that seems about to burst the bounds of my being or rather seems to need some larger space than my soul to exist in. Everyone and everything oppresses me, chokes and maddens me; I am troubled by a crushing physical sense of other people's lack of comprehension. But I look up at the blue sky, bare my face to the unconsciously cool breeze, then lower my eyelids having seen the sky, and forget my own cheek once I have felt the breeze. I don't feel better, I feel different. Seeing myself frees me from myself. I almost smile, not because I understand myself, but because, having become other, I'm no longer able to understand myself. High up in the sky, like a visible void, hangs one tiny cloud, a pale forgotten fragment of the whole universe.

415 [7 Apr 1933]

Though I walked among them a stranger, no one noticed. I lived among them as a spy and no one, not even I, suspected. Everyone took me for a relative, no one knew I had been switched at birth. Thus I was like yet unlike the others, everyone's brother but never one of the family.

I came from prodigious lands, from landscapes more beautiful than life itself, but I never spoke of those lands, except to myself, and told no one of the landscapes glimpsed in dreams. On wooden floors and on paving stones my steps echoed just like theirs, but, however near my heart seemed to beat, it was always far away, the false lord of a strange, exiled body.

No one recognized me beneath the mask of equality, nor did they once guess that it was a mask, because no one knew masked players existed in this world. No one imagined that there was always another by my side, the real me. They always thought me identical to myself.

Their houses sheltered me, their hands shook mine, they saw me walk down the street as if I were really there; but the person I am was never there in those rooms, the person living in me has no hands to be shaken by others, the person I know myself to be has no streets to walk along nor can anyone see him there, unless those streets are all streets and the person who sees him all people.

We all live such distant and anonymous lives; disguised, we suffer the fate of strangers. To some, however, this distance between another being and ourselves is never revealed; to others it is revealed only every now and then, through horror or pain, lit by a limitless lightning flash; for yet others it is the one painful constant of their daily lives.

Knowing clearly that who we are has nothing to do with us, that what we think or feel is always in translation, that perhaps what we want we never wanted—to know this every moment, to feel all this in every feeling, is this not what it means to be a stranger in one's own soul, an exile from one's own feelings?

But, on this last night of Carnival, the man in the mask whom I had been passively staring at and who was standing on the corner talking to an unmasked man at last held out his hand and, laughing, said goodbye. The man without a mask turned left up the lane at the corner of which they had been standing, and the masked man—in unimaginative domino—walked on ahead, moving between the shadows and the occasional lights, in a definitive farewell that was quite different from what I was thinking about. Only then did I notice that there was something else in the street apart from the street lamps: a diffuse moonlight, hidden and silent, full of nothing, like life ...

416   [29 Aug 1933]

Even the city has its moments of country quiet, especially at midday in high summer, when the country invades this luminous city of Lisbon like a wind. And even here, in Rua dos Douradores, we sleep well.

How good for the soul it is to observe beneath a high quiet sun the silence of these straw-laden carts, these empty crates, these slow passersby, transported here from some village! Watching them from the window of the office, where I'm alone, I too am transformed: I'm in a quiet provincial town, or stagnating in some obscure hamlet and, because I feel other, I'm happy.

I know that I have only to raise my eyes to see before me the sordid skyline of the houses, the unwashed windows of all the offices in the Baixa and the empty windows of the top-floor apartments and, above them, around the garret roofs, the inevitable washing hung out to dry in the sun among flowerpots and plants. I know this but the golden light that falls is so soft, the calm air that wraps about me so empty, that I lack any visual motive to give up my false village, my provincial town where commerce brings rest and quiet.

I know, I know ... It's the time when everyone has lunch or takes a rest or a break. Everything floats blithely by on the surface of life. Even while I lean out over the verandah as if it were a ship's rail, looking out over a new landscape, I too sleep. I let go of all tormenting thoughts as if I really were living in the provinces. And, suddenly, something else arises, wraps about me, takes hold of me: behind the midday scene I see the entire life of that provincial town; I see the immense foolish happiness of domesticity, of life in the fields, of contentment in the midst of banality. I see because I see. But then I see no more and I wake up. I look around, smiling, and before I do anything else, I brush down the elbows of my suit, a dark suit unfortunately, made dusty from leaning on the balustrade of the verandah that no one has bothered to clean, not realizing that one day it would be required, if only for a moment, to be the rail (free from all possible dust) of a ship setting sail on an endless cruise.

417 [8 Sep 1933]

High up in the lonely night an unknown lamp blooms behind a window. Everything else in the city is dark except where feeble rays from the street lamps hesitantly rise and, here and there, resemble the palest of earthly moonlight. In the black of the night the different colors and tones of the houses are barely distinguishable; only vague, one might almost say abstract, differences point up the irregularities of the unruly whole.

I am connected by an invisible thread to the anonymous owner of the lamp. It is not often we are both awake at the same time, and there is no possible reciprocity in this for, since I am standing at my window in the dark, he cannot see me. It's something else, mine alone, something to do with the feeling of isolation, that participates in the night and the silence, and chooses that lamp as something to hold on to because there is nothing else. It seems as if it is only because that lamp is lit that the night is so dark. It seems that it is only because I am awake, dreaming in the blackness, that it is there, alight.

Perhaps everything exists only because something else does. Nothing just is, everything coexists; perhaps that's right. I feel that I wouldn't exist at this hour (or not at least in the exact same way, with my present consciousness of myself, which, because it is consciousness and because it is present, is, at this moment, entirely me) if that lamp were not lit over there, somewhere, a lighthouse marking nothing, erected on the false prestige lent it by its height. I feel this because I feel nothing. I think this because this is all nothing. Nothing, nothing, just part of the night and the silence and of whatever emptiness, negativity and inconstancy I share with them, the space that exists between me and me, a thing mislaid by some god …

418 [19 Sep 1933]

They say tedium is a sickness that afflicts the inert, or only attacks those who have nothing to do. However, this affliction of the soul is subtler than that: it attacks those with a predisposition for it and is less lenient on those who work or pretend to work (which comes to the same thing anyway) than on the truly inert.

There is nothing worse than the contrast between the natural splendor of the inner life, with its own Indies and countries still to be explored, and the sordidness, even when it isn't really sordid, of the everydayness of life. Tedium weighs more heavily when it doesn't have inertia as an excuse. The tedium of the great and the busy is the worst tedium of all.

Tedium is not a sickness brought on by the boredom of having nothing to do, but the worse sickness of feeling that nothing is worth doing. And thus, the more one has to do the worse the tedium.

How often have I looked up from the book in which I'm writing and felt my head quite empty of the whole world. It would be better for me if I were inert, doing nothing, with nothing to do, because that tedium, though real, I could at least enjoy. In my present state there is no respite, no nobility, no comfort in feeling discomfort; there is a terrible dullness in every gesture I make, not a potential weariness in gestures I will never make.

419 [2 Nov 1933]

There are some deep-seated griefs so subtle and pervasive that it is difficult to grasp whether they belong to our soul or to our body, whether they come from a malaise brought on by pondering the futility of life, or whether they are caused rather by an indisposition in some chasm within ourselves—stomach, liver or brain. How often my ordinary consciousness of myself is obscured by the dark sediment stirred up in some stagnant part of me. How often existence wounds me to the point that I feel a nausea so indefinable that I can't tell if it's just tedium or an indication that I'm actually about to be sick! How often …

My soul today is sad to the very marrow of its bones. Everything hurts me—memory, eyes, arms. It's like having rheumatism in every part of my being. The limpid brightness of the day, the great pure blue sky, the steady tide of diffuse light, none of this touches my being. I remain unmoved by the light autumnal breeze that still bears a trace of unforgotten summer and lends color to the air. Nothing means anything to me. I'm sad, but not with a definite or even an indefinite sadness. My sadness is out there, in the street strewn with boxes.

These words do not convey exactly what I feel because doubtless nothing can convey exactly what someone feels. But I'm trying in some way to give an idea of what I feel, a mixture of various aspects of me and the street below, which, because I also see it, belongs to me, is part of me, in some intimate way that defies analysis.

I would like to live different lives in distant lands. I would like to die another person beneath unknown flags. I would like to be acclaimed emperor in another time (a time better simply because it is not today), which appears to me in shimmering colors, among unknown sphinxes. I want anything that makes the person I am seem ridiculous just because it does make what I am seem ridiculous. I want, I want … But there is always the sun when the sun shines and the night when night falls. There is always grief when grief afflicts us and dreams when dreams cradle us. There is always what there is and never what there should be, not because it's better or worse, but because it's other. There is always.

The dustmen are working down below, clearing the street of

boxes of rubbish. Laughing and talking, they put the boxes one by one onto the carts. From high up at my office window I watch them with indolent eyes beneath drooping lids. And something subtle and incomprehensible links what I'm feeling to the boxes I watch being loaded up; some unknown feeling puts all my tedium, anguish, nausea or whatever into a box, lifts it up on the shoulders of a man making loud jokes and places it on a cart that is not here. And the light of day, serene as ever, falls obliquely along the narrow street, onto the place where they're loading up the boxes, not on the boxes themselves, which are in the shade, but on the corner down there where the errand boys are busy randomly doing nothing.

420 [23 Dec 1933]

When considered in the light of our inner serenity, we see all those unfortunate chance events in our life—when we were either ridiculous or despicable or appallingly late—as misfortunes that happened on the journey. In this world, we travelers, whether voluntary or involuntary, between nothing and nothing, or between everything and everything, are mere passengers and should not give too much importance to any setbacks experienced en route, to any bumps and bruises suffered along the way. I console myself with that, whether because it does console me or because there is something genuinely consoling about it, I don't know. But that fictitious consolation does become real if I don't think about it.

And there are so many consolations! There's the clear, high, calm sky, across which the occasional imperfect cloud floats by. There's the light breeze that shakes the thickly leaved branches of the trees if you're in the country, and that sets the clothes flapping when they're hung out to dry at fourth- or fifth-floor windows if you're in the city. There's the heat of hot days and the cool of cool days, and always, in the background, a memory or a nostalgia or a hope, and someone smiling at the window opening onto the void, and our desires knocking at the door of who we are, like the beggars who are the Christ.

421

In the gentlest of voices, he was singing a song from some far-off land. The music made the strange words seem familiar. It sounded like a fado composed for the soul, though it was nothing like a fado really.

Through its veiled words and its human melody, the song spoke of things that exist in every soul and yet are unknown to all of us. He was singing as if in a trance, standing in the street wrapped in a sort of ecstasy, not even aware he had an audience.

The people who had gathered there to listen to him did so with little sign of mockery. The song belonged to us all and sometimes the words spoke to us directly of the oriental secret of some lost race. The noise of the city, if we noticed it at all, went unheard and the cars passed so close to us that one brushed my jacket. But I only felt it, I didn't hear it. There was an intensity in the stranger's singing that nourished the dreamer in us, or the part that cannot dream. For us, though, it was just something to look at in the street and we all noticed the policeman coming slowly round the corner. He came towards us at the same slow pace, then paused for a moment behind the boy selling umbrellas, like someone who has just spotted something. At that point the singer stopped. No one said a word. Then the policeman stepped in.

422

The storm that was threatening the uneasy calm has finally passed over, and three consecutive days of unending heat have brought to the lucid surface of things a tepid but delicious coolness. Much the same thing happens when, in the course of living, the soul, weighed down by life, feels the burden suddenly and inexplicably lift.

I think of us as climates constantly threatened by storms that always break somewhere else.

The empty immensity of things, the great forgetting that fills sky and earth …

423 [1933?]

Fictions of the interlude, covering with color the apathy and idleness of our own disbelief.

424 [31 Mar 1934]

It's been such a long time since I last wrote anything! During those days I lived centuries of hesitant renunciation. I stagnated like a deserted lake in a nonexistent landscape.

During that time, the diverse monotony of days, the ever-varying succession of unvarying hours, in short, life, flowed over me, flowed pleasantly over me. I would have felt its flow no differently had I been asleep. I stagnated like a nonexistent lake in a deserted landscape.

I often fail to recognize myself, a frequent occurrence among those who know themselves. I observe myself in the various disguises in which I live. Of the things that change I retain only what stays the same, of the things one does only what is worthless.

Far off in me, as if I were engaged on an inward journey, I recall the varied monotony of that house in the provinces ... That's where I spent my childhood, but, even if I wanted to, I couldn't say if my life was more or less happy than it is today. The person who lived there was not me, but another: they are different lives, diverse, not comparable. The same monotonies that seem similar from the outside were doubtless different from within. They were not two monotonies but two lives.

But why do I remember? Out of weariness. To remember is restful because it does not involve action. How often, to obtain a deeper sense of repose, do I remember what I never was, and there is no clarity, no nostalgia about my memories of a provincial town where I lived as people do, measuring out each floorboard, moving in and out of the long ago, in vast rooms I never knew.

So completely have I become a fiction of myself that the minute any natural feeling (should I experience such a thing) is born, it becomes at once an imagined feeling—memory becomes dream, dream a forgetting of dreams, self-knowledge a lack of self-reflection.

I have so completely divested myself of my own being that to exist is to clothe myself. Only disguised am I myself. And all around me, as they fade, unknown sunsets wash with gold landscapes I will never see.

425 [5 June 1934]

I grow still at last. Any remaining debris or detritus of disquiet vanishes from my soul as if it had never been. I sit alone and calm. The moment just past was like a moment of religious conversion, except that nothing draws me heavenwards, just as nothing drew me down. I feel free, as if I had ceased to exist but yet retained my consciousness.

Yes, I grow still. With the sweetness of the utterly useless, a great calm penetrates the depths of my being. Pages read, duties performed, the actions and chance events of my life—all this has become for me a vague penumbra, a barely visible halo surrounding some strange and tranquil thing unknown to me. The effort I sometimes put into forgetting my soul; the thought I occasionally put into abandoning all action—both come back to me now in the form of an unsentimental tenderness, a bland, empty compassion.

It's not this slow, sweet day, cloudy and soft. It's not the barely existent breeze, scarcely more insistent than the air I feel on my skin. It isn't the anonymous color of the sky, touched feebly here and there with blue. It isn't that. Because I feel nothing. I simply see unintentionally, unwittingly, the attentive spectator of a nonexistent spectacle. I cannot feel my soul and yet I'm quite calm. Everything in the external world, even those things that move, has grown clear and motionless, and it seems to me as the world must have seemed to Christ when he looked down at the city spread before him and was tempted by Satan. These things are nothing, and I understand why Christ wasn't tempted. They are as nothing and I cannot understand how an old hand like Satan could possibly have imagined they could prove to be a temptation.

Flow lightly, life that does not even feel itself, a silent, supple stream beneath forgotten trees! Flow softly, soul that does not know itself, a murmur hidden from view by great fallen branches! Flow vainly, aimlessly, consciousness conscious of nothing, a vague, distant glimmer through leafy clearings, with no known source or destination. Flow on, flow on and leave me to forget!

Faint breeze of all that never dared to live, dumb breath of all that did not want to feel, vain murmur of all that did not want to think, go slowly, lazily down into the whirlpools that inevitably await you and down the slippery slopes placed there for you, go into the shadows or into the light, brother of the world, go forward into glory or into the abyss, son of Chaos and of Night, always remembering in some corner of your being that the Gods came later, and that the Gods too pass away.

426   [9 June 1934]

With the beginning of summer I grow sad. One would think that the brilliance of summer hours, however harsh, would seem sweet to someone ignorant of his own identity. But that's not the case with me. There is too sharp a contrast between all that exuberant outer life and what I feel and think, without knowing how to feel or think—the perennially unburied corpse of my feelings. I have the impression that, in this formless homeland called the universe, I live beneath a political tyranny which, although it does not oppress me directly, still offends some hidden principle of my soul. And then slowly, secretly, there grows within me the anticipated nostalgia of an impossible exile.

What I most want is to sleep. But the sleep I desire, unlike other varieties, even those induced by sickness, does not include the physical reward of rest. Nor does it help one to forget about life, or even bring with it the promise of dreams, balancing on the tray it carries as it approaches our soul the calm gift of a final abdication. No, this is a sleep that never actually sleeps, it weighs on one's eyelids but never closes them and puckers the corners of unbelieving lips in a gesture one feels to be a combination of repugnance and stupidity. This is the sleep that weighs on one's body during periods of great insomnia of the soul.

Only when night comes do I feel, if not happiness, at least some kind of repose which I experience as contentment by analogy with other states of repose that do bring contentment. Then the drowsiness passes, the confused mental twilight of that state fades and grows clearer, almost lights up. For a moment a hope for other things arises. But such hopes are short-lived, overridden by a sleepless, hopeless tedium, the comfortless waking of one who has not slept. And, a poor soul weary of body, I stare out from the window of my room at the multitudes of stars; at multitudes of stars and nothing, nothingness, but oh so many stars ...

427   [c. 19 June 1934]

When we live constantly in the abstract—whether it be abstractness of thought or of feelings one has thought—it soon comes about that contrary to our own feelings and our own will the things in real life which, according to us, we should feel most deeply turn into phantasms.

However good or genuine a friend I might be to someone, hearing that he is ill or has died leaves me with such a vague, uncertain, dull impression that I'm ashamed to feel it. Only seeing the event itself, finding its landscape laid out before me, would move me. Living so much on one's imagination actually erodes one's ability to imagine, especially one's ability to imagine the real. Living mentally on what is not and cannot be, we are, in the end, unable even to ponder what might really be.

I learned yesterday that an old friend of mine, whom I haven't seen for a long time but whom I always think of with what I take to be nostalgia, has gone into hospital for an operation. The only clear, positive feeling I had was what a bore it would be to have to go and visit him, with the ironic alternative that, if I couldn't be bothered to visit him, I would only regret not having done so.

That's all … After years of wrestling with shadows, I've become one myself, in what I think, feel, am. Then the nostalgia for the normal person I never was enters the very stuff of my being. But that and only that is all I feel. I don't really feel sorry for the friend who's going to be operated on. I don't really feel sorry for all the others who are going to be operated on, all those who suffer and grieve in this world. I just feel sorry that I don't know how to be someone who feels sorry.

And, inevitably, the next moment, driven by some unknown impulse, I'm already thinking about something else. And then, as if in a delirium, the murmur of trees, the sound of water flowing into pools, a nonexistent garden all intermingle with what I didn't manage to feel and what I could not be … I try to feel but I no longer know how. I've become a shadow of myself to whom I've surrendered my whole being. Unlike the character Peter Schlemihl in the German story, it was not my shadow I sold to the Devil, but my very substance.* I suffer because I do not suffer, because I do not know how to suffer. Am I alive or am I only pretending? Am I asleep or awake? A light breeze, cool in the heat of the day, makes me forget everything. My eyelids feel pleasantly heavy … I imagine that this same golden sun is falling on the fields where I am not and where I do not wish to be … A great silence emerges from the bustle of the city. How sweet it is! But how much sweeter, perhaps, if I could really feel it!

428 [21 June 1934]

Once we believe this world to be merely an illusion and a phantasm, we are then free to consider everything that happens to us as

---

* Peter Schlemihl: The eponymous hero of the novel by Adelbert von Chamisso (1781–1838).

a dream, something that only pretended to exist because we were asleep. And then a subtle and profound indifference towards all life's vexations and disasters is born in us. Those who died simply turned a corner and are out of sight; those who suffer pass before our eyes like a nightmare (if we feel), like an unpleasant daydream (if we think). And our own suffering will be nothing more than that nothingness. In this world we all sleep on our left side and hear in our dreams the oppressive beating of our heart.

Nothing more ... A little sun, a light breeze, a few trees framing the distance, the desire to be happy, our pain at feeling the passing of the days, the knowledge that is never quite complete and the truth always just on the point of being revealed ... Nothing more, nothing more ... No, nothing more ...

429 [29 June 1934]

To receive from the mystic state only the undemanding pleasures of that state; to be the ecstatic devotee of no god, the uninitiated mystic or epopt: to spend one's days meditating on a paradise in which one does not believe—all those things please the soul, if the soul knows what it is not to know.

The silent clouds drift by high above me, this body trapped inside a shadow, just as the unknowable truths drift by high above me too, this soul captive in a body ... Everything is drifting by high above ... And everything happens high above as it does down below, with no cloud leaving anything more than rain, no truth leaving anything more than pain ... Yes, everything that is high up passes by high up; everything one might want is far away and passes by far away ... Yes, everything attracts, everything is other and everything passes.

So what if I know that, come rain or shine, body or soul, I too will pass? It doesn't matter a jot, apart from the hope that everything is nothing and, therefore, that nothing is everything.

430 [c. 29 June 1934]

Inaction is our consolation for everything, not acting our one great provider. The ability to imagine is all, as long as it does not lead to action. No one can be king of the world except in dreams. And, if we are honest, each of us wants to be king of the world.

Not to be, but to think, that is the true throne. Not to want, but to desire, that is the crown. Whatever we renounce we preserve intact in our dreams, eternally bathed in the sun that does not exist or the moon that will never exist.

431 [26 July 1934]

A belief in God exists in every healthy mind, but not a belief in a definite God. God is just some supreme, impossible being who rules over everything; whose person, if he has one, no one can define; whose intentions, if he has any, no one can understand. By calling him God, we are saying exactly that, because the word God has no precise meaning, and so we affirm his existence without actually affirming that he does exist. The attributes of infinite, eternal, omnipotent, supremely just or kind that we sometimes attach to him detach themselves as do all unnecessary adjectives when the noun itself suffices. And so we cannot give Him any attributes because he is indefinite and, for that same reason, he is the ultimate noun.

The same certainty and the same vagueness surround the survival of the soul. We all know that we will die; we all feel that we will not. It isn't really a desire or a hope that brings us the shadowy sense that death is a misunderstanding, it is a deep-seated instinct, like the one that makes certain flowers turn towards the sun.

432 [c. 26 July 1934]

The countryside is wherever we are not. There and only there do real shadows and real trees exist.

Life is the hesitation between an exclamation mark and a question mark. After doubt there is a full stop.

The miracle is a sign of God's laziness or, rather, the laziness we attribute to Him by inventing the miracle.

The Gods are the incarnation of what we can never be. The weariness of all hypotheses ...

433   [1934?]

Phrases I will never write and landscapes I will never be able to describe: with what clarity I dictate them to my inertia and describe them in my meditations when, reclining in a chair, I have only the remotest of ties with life. I carve out whole sentences, word-perfect; complete dramas plot themselves in my mind, in every word I sense the verbal and metric movement of great poems; and a great enthusiasm, like an invisible slave, follows behind me in the shadows. But if I move one step away from the chair in which I sit nurturing these almost finished feelings, and make a move towards the table in order to write them down, the words flee, the dramas die, and all that remains of the vital nexus that drew together these rhythmic murmurings is a distant longing, a trace of sunlight on far-off mountains, a wind stirring the leaves on the edge of the desert, a never-to-be-revealed relationship, the pleasures enjoyed by others, the woman whom our intuition tells us would look back, and who never actually existed.

I've undertaken every conceivable project. An inspirational logic lay behind *The Iliad* I composed, and its epodes had an organic coherence that Homer never managed to achieve. The studied perfection of these verses never put into words makes Virgil's precision seem laxity and Milton's strength weakness. The symbolic exactness of every apposite detail of my allegorical satires exceeded anything Swift produced. And the number of Verlaines I have been!

And each time I rise from my chair, where these things have an existence beyond mere dreams, I suffer the double tragedy of knowing them to be worthless but at the same time knowing that indeed they were not entirely dreamed and that some trace of them lingers on in the abstract threshold of my thinking them and their existing.

I was more of a genius in dreams than in life. That is my tragedy. I was the runner who fell just before the finishing line, having led the field all the way until then.

434 [1934?]

The simplest things, the truly simple things that nothing can make anything other than simple, are made complex just by my experiencing them. I feel intimidated sometimes by having to say good morning to someone. My voice dries up, as if to pronounce the words out loud were an act of extraordinary audacity. It's a kind of embarrassment at my own existence—there are no other words for it.

Constant analysis of our feelings creates a new way of feeling that seems artificial to anyone who analyzes only with his intellect rather than with feeling itself.

All my life I have been metaphysically frivolous and playfully earnest. I never did anything seriously, however much I may have wanted to. A mischievous Destiny has made of me its playground.

How I'd like to have emotions made of chintz or silk or brocade! How I'd like to have emotions as easily describable as that, to have emotions that could at least be described!

There rises in my soul a feeling of regret that is God's regret for everything, a dumb, tearful fury at the condemnation of dreams in the very flesh of those who dreamed them ... And I hate without hatred the poets who wrote verses, all the idealists who realized their ideals, all those who got what they wanted.

I wander aimlessly through the quiet streets, I walk until my body is as tired as my soul, until I feel that familiar pain that revels in being felt, a maternal compassion for oneself, set to music, indefinable.

Oh to sleep, finally to sleep! To find some peace! To be an abstract consciousness of one's own quiet breathing, with no world, no stars, no soul—a dead sea of emotion reflecting only an absence of stars!

435 [1934?]

Like Diogenes of Alexander, all I asked of life was that the sun should not be taken away from me. I had desires, but the reason for having them was denied me. As for what I found, it would have been better if I had really found it. The dream [...]

While out walking, I have constructed perfect sentences, which, once I'm home, I forget. I don't know if the ineffable poetry of those sentences belongs entirely to the fact that they were lost or partly to the fact that they were never written down.

I hesitate before doing anything, often without knowing why. How often—like the straight line appropriate to my nature (conceiving this in my head as the ideal straight line)—I deliberately seek out the longest distance between two points. I've never had a talent for the active life. I always bungled the gestures no one else gets wrong; what others were born to do, I always had to struggle not to forget to do. I always want to achieve what others achieved almost casually. Between myself and life there have always been panes of opaque glass, undetectable to me by sight or touch; I never actually lived life according to a plan, I was the daydream of what I wanted to be, my dream began in my will, my goal was always the first fiction of what I never was.

I never knew if my sensibility was too advanced for my intelligence or my intelligence too advanced for my sensibility. I was always too late, for which I don't know, perhaps for both, for one or the other at any rate. Or perhaps it was a third thing that came late.

The dreamers of the past centuries—socialists, altruists, humanitarians of all kinds—make me feel sick to my stomach. They are idealists without ideals. They are thinkers without thoughts. They love the surface of life because of a fatal love of rubbish, which also floats on the surface of the water, and which they think is beautiful, because empty shells float on the surface of the water too.

436 [1934?]

Anyone reading the earlier part of this book will doubtless have formed the opinion that I'm a dreamer. If so, they're wrong. I don't have enough money to be a dreamer.

The great melancholies, the sadnesses filled with tedium, can exist only in an atmosphere of comfort and sober luxury. Thus Poe's Egaeus sits in his ancient ancestral castle, immersed in long hours of morbid meditation, while beyond the door of the great hall ordinary life goes on, invisible majordomos organize the meals and the household chores.

The great dream demands certain social circumstances. One day, captivated by a certain musical plaintiveness in what I had written, I imagined myself to be another Chateaubriand but brought myself up sharply with the realization that I was neither a viscount nor a Breton. On another occasion, when I seemed to notice in my own words a similarity to Rousseau, again it did not take me long to see that I did not have the advantage of being a nobleman or a castellan and, moreover, was neither Swiss nor a vagabond.

But, after all, the universe also exists here in Rua dos Douradores. Even here God ensures the continuing presence of the enigma of life. And that's why, though poor, like the landscape of carts and packing cases, the dreams I manage to extract from among the wheels and planks are what I have and what I'm able to have.

No doubt there are real sunsets elsewhere. But even in this fourth-floor room above the city one can ponder on the infinite. An infinite built over warehouses, it's true, but with stars above it … These are the thoughts that occur to me standing at my high window watching the slow end of evening, feeling the dissatisfaction of the bourgeois I am not and the sadness of the poet I can never be.

I went into the barber's as I usually do, experiencing the pleasure I always get from being able to enter places known to me without suffering the least distress. My sensitivity to all things new is a constant affliction to me; I only feel safe in places I have been in before.

When I sat down in the chair, and the young barber placed a clean, cold linen towel around my neck, it occurred to me to ask after his colleague, a vigorous, older man, who had been ill, but who usually worked at the chair to my right. The question arose spontaneously, simply because the place reminded me of him. As fingers busied themselves tucking in the last bit of towel between my neck and my collar, the voice behind the towel and me answered flatly: "He died yesterday." My irrational good humour died as suddenly as the now eternally absent barber from the chair beside me. My every thought froze. I said nothing.

Nostalgia! I feel it even for someone who meant nothing to me, out of anxiety for the flight of time and a sickness bred of the mystery of life. If one of the faces I pass daily on the streets disappears, I feel sad; yet they meant nothing to me, other than being a symbol of all life.

The dull old man with dirty gaiters I often used to pass at half past nine in the morning. The lame lottery salesman who pestered me without success. The plump, rosy old gentleman with the cigar, who used to stand at the door of the tobacconist's. The pale-cheeked tobacconist himself. What has become of those people who, just because I saw them day after day, became part of my life? Tomorrow I, too, will disappear from Rua da Prata, Rua dos Douradores, Rua dos Fanqueiros. Tomorrow I, too—this feeling and thinking soul, the universe I am to myself—yes, tomorrow I, too, will be someone who no longer walks these streets, someone others will evoke with a vague "I wonder what's become of him?" And everything I do, everything I feel, everything I experience, will be just one less passerby on the daily streets of some city or other.

Freedom is the possibility of isolation. You are only free if you can withdraw from men and feel no need to seek them out for money, or society, or love, or glory, or even curiosity, for none of these things flourish in silence and solitude. If you cannot live alone, then you were born a slave. Though you may be possessed of every superior quality of spirit and soul, you are still nothing more than a noble slave or an intelligent serf, you are not free. But that is not your tragedy, for the tragedy of being born like that is not yours but Destiny's. Woe betide you, though, if the very weight of life itself makes you a slave. Woe betide you if, having been born free and capable of providing for yourself and leading a separate existence, penury forces you into the company of others. That tragedy is yours alone, which you alone must bear.

To be born free is Man's greatest quality; it is what makes the humble hermit superior to kings, superior even to the gods, who are sufficient unto themselves only by virtue of their power but not by virtue of their disdain for it.

Death is a liberation because to die is to need no one else. The poor slave finds himself prised free from all his pleasures, his griefs, from the uninterrupted life he so desired. The king finds himself free of dominions he had no wish to leave. The women who freely offered their love find themselves free of the conquests they so adore. Those who conquered find themselves free of the victories to which their lives predestined them.

Death ennobles and clothes the poor absurd cadaver in unaccustomed finery. There you have a free man, though admittedly it was not a freedom he sought. There you have a man set free from slavery, though he wept to lose his servitude. A king may be laughable as a man and the only splendid thing about him be his title but, by virtue of that title, he is nonetheless a superior being, just as, however monstrous he may seem, the dead man is superior, because death has set him free.

Weary, I close the shutters on my windows, I exclude the world and for a moment I am free. Tomorrow I will return to being a slave; but now, alone, not needing anyone, fearful lest some voice or presence should disturb me, I have my own small freedom, my moment of exaltation.

In the chair in which I sit, I forget the life that so oppresses me. The only pain I feel is that of having once felt pain.

Appendices

to The Book of Disquiet

TWO NOTES

[1929?]

Author's notes for any future editions (and also usable in any Preface)
At a later date, collect together in a separate volume the various poems that have escaped inclusion in the Book of Disquiet; said book should have a title indicating, more or less, that it contains detritus or is some kind of hiatus or something equally off-putting.

That book would, moreover, form part of a definitive collection of dross, a published warehouse of the unpublishable that can remain as a sad example. Rather like the unfinished poems of some lyric poet who died young or the letters of a great writer, except that the material contained in the book would be not just inferior, but different, and that difference would be the reason to publish it, since it would make no sense to publish what should not be published.

[1931?]

The organization of the book should be based on as rigorous a selection as possible of the various existing texts, adapting any older ones that are untrue to the psychology of Bernardo Soares as it is now emerging. Apart from this, there needs to be a general revision of style, but without losing the personal tone or the drifting, disconnected logic that characterizes it.

There may be a case for inserting longer passages, with grandiose titles, like "Funeral March for King Ludwig II of Bavaria" or "Symphony of the Unquiet Night." There's also a case for leaving the "Funeral March" passage as it is or for including it in another book together with all the other longish passages.

FICTIONS OF THE INTERLUDE

[1929?]
Preface to "Fictions of the Interlude"
I insert certain characters into stories or put them in the subtitles
of books, and I sign what they say with my name; others I don't plan
at all, nor do I put my signature to them either except to say that
I created them. The two types of character can be distinguished
as follows: those who are completely different, whose very style is
alien to me, and, if the character so demands, completely contrary
to my style; with the characters I endorse, though, their style is no
different from my own, except in inevitable small details, without
which they would be indistinguishable.

To give an example, let me compare some of those characters.
The assistant bookkeeper Bernardo Soares and the Barão de Teive
are both me and not-me, in that they write in substantially the
same style, with the same grammar, the same use of language: they
write in a style which is, for good or ill, my own. I compare these
two because they are examples of the same phenomenon—an in-
ability to adapt to the reality of life, and for the same motives and
reasons. However, while the Portuguese of the Barão de Teive and
Bernardo Soares are the same, their styles differ, in that the Baron's
Portuguese is more intellectual, devoid of imagery, a little, how
can I put it, stiff and starchy; whereas that of the bourgeois Soares

---

This was the general title Pessoa gave to the collected works of his heteronyms,
which he planned to publish in several separate volumes. In the end, it served
only as the title for five poems published under his own name in 1917.

is fluent, more musical and painterly, quite unarchitectural. The nobleman thinks clearly, writes clearly, and masters his emotions if not his feelings; the bookkeeper masters neither emotions nor feelings, and when he thinks, his thinking is subsidiary to feeling.

On the other hand, while there are notable similarities between Bernardo Soares and Álvaro de Campos, the Portuguese of Álvaro de Campos is looser, his imagery more extravagant, more personal and more spontaneous than that of Soares.

[1929?]
[Fictions of the Interlude]
There are inconsistencies in the way I distinguish these characters, which is something that weighs like a heavy burden on my intellectual powers of discernment. How to distinguish some musicianly composition by Bernardo Soares from a similar composition of my own . . .

There are times when I can do so instantly, with a perfection that astonishes me, and there is nothing immodest about this astonishment, because, since I do not believe we humans possess so much as a fragment of freedom, I am as astonished by what happens in me as I would be at what happens in someone else—both are strangers.

Only a powerful intuition can serve as a compass in the wide wastes of the soul; only with a sense filtered through our intelligence, but which, while based on it, is quite unlike it, can we distinguish the realities of those dream characters one from the other.

[1929?]
Fictions of the Interlude
These disparate personalities, or, rather, inventions of different personalities, fall into two categories or types, which will, if followed closely, be revealed to the reader by their distinctive characteristics. In the first category, the personality will have certain ideas and feelings quite different from mine, just as, in a lower level

of that same category, there will be ideas, set out perhaps in a discourse or argument, that are clearly not mine, or, if they are, I do not recognize them. The Anarchist Banker is an example of that subgroup; the Book of Disquiet and Bernardo Soares, on the other hand, belong to the higher level.

The reader will notice that, even though I'm publishing the Book of Disquiet (if I do publish it) as being written by a certain Bernardo Soares, assistant bookkeeper in the city of Lisbon, I have not included it in these Fictions of the Interlude. That is because, while Bernardo Soares is different from me in his ideas, feelings, ways of seeing and understanding, he is not different from me in the way he expresses those things. I give him a different personality, but expressed through the style that comes naturally to me, which means that there is only the inevitable difference in tone that comes from the particular nature of the emotions being expressed.

Among the authors of Fictions of the Interlude, it is not only their ideas and feelings that distinguish them from mine: the actual technique of composition, the style, is different too. There, each character is not just conceived differently, but created to be a wholly different persona. That's why poetry predominates in Fictions of the Interlude. In prose, it's harder to *other* oneself.

From THE BOOK OF DISQUIET:

"It's as if someone were using my life to beat me with."

"Today, during one of those periods of daydreaming which, though devoid of purpose, still constitute the greater part of the spiritual substance of my life ..."

"Whatever we renounce, we preserve intact."

"Nothing satisfies me, nothing consoles me, everything—whether or not it has ever existed—satiates me. I can be neither nothing nor everything: I'm just the bridge between what I do not have and what I do not want."

"I don't get indignant, because indignation is for the strong; I don't resign myself, because resignation is for the noble; I don't keep silent, because silence is for the great. And I am neither strong nor noble nor great. I suffer and I dream. I complain because I am weak and, because I am an artist, I amuse myself by weaving music about my complaints and arranging my dreams as best befits my idea of beautiful dreams. My only regret is that I am not a child, for that would allow me to believe in my dreams and believe that I am not mad, which would allow me to distance my soul from all those who surround me."

"Life, obvious and unanimous, flows past outside me in the footsteps of the passersby."

"I'm always astonished whenever I finish anything. Astonished and depressed. My desire for perfection should prevent me from ever finishing anything; it should prevent me even from starting."

"Nothing will remain of the person who puts on feelings and gloves."

"Anyone reading the earlier part of this book will doubtless have formed the opinion that I'm a dreamer. If so, they're wrong. I don't have enough money to be a dreamer."